Be Bold

Be Bold

DANIE BOTHA

Published in the United States by Charbellini Press

ISBN-13: 9781999462031 paperback
ISBN-13: 9781999462048
ISBN-10: 1999462031

For Isabella

Table of Contents

Author's Note

During the years 1948 to 1994, the period of state-sanctioned racial segregation in South Africa, many publications, individuals, and organizations were banned.

Although the creation of apartheid (meaning "being apart or separate" in Afrikaans and Dutch) is usually credited to the Afrikaner-dominated government of 1948–1994, it is in part a legacy of the British colonial rule which had introduced pass laws in the Cape Colony and Natal, as early as the 19th-century.

Dr. Hendrik Frensch Verwoerd, prime minister of South Africa from 1958–1966, a professor of philosophy, a journalist, and a politician, is often seen as the "Architect of Apartheid." Born in 1901, much of his relentless push to segregate the races and protect the Afrikaners stemmed from the near annihilation of the Afrikaans-dominated Boers and their families during the Second Anglo-Boer War of 1899–1902.

The ANC (African National Congress) and PAC (Pan Africanist Congress) were declared banned organizations in South

Africa in 1961, following the Sharpeville Massacre and Langa shootings of March 1960.

Dr. Verwoerd was assassinated on 6 September 1966, by Demetrio Tsafendas, after having survived a first attempt on his life in 1960.

In 1994, Mr. Nelson Mandela, from the ANC, became South Africa's first democratically elected prime minister.

One of the many books which were banned was Alan Paton's well-known novel, *Cry the Beloved Country* (1948). If ever there was a phrase to amply describe the country, South Africa, twenty-six years after the apparent end of apartheid, it is still this, *Cry the Beloved Country*.

Be Bold brings homage to the sub-continent and its people.

Be Bold is a work of fiction. Apart from well-known actual people, events, and locales, characters and incidents are the product of the author's imagination. Any resemblance to actual persons, living or dead, is entirely coincidental.

South Africa: 1910–1994

*The most courageous act is still to
think for yourself. Aloud.*

—Coco Chanel

Prologue

The cable car jarred to a halt in midair. Knuckles white, Rianna groaned as the car toppled sideways.

The fog was present before they got in—it now snaked around the car, obliterating the grand view of the tip of Africa. They were swallowed whole by the indomitable mist.

"Something's wrong," she whispered.

Her companion pressed his nose against the glass panels as if to pierce the palpable whiteness. He chuckled. "That's why we've stopped."

"No, Lukas. Somebody made the car stop."

"*Professor* Vermeulen, your imagination . . . ."

Both occupants grasped for a handrail as the car slid another foot along the steep incline and quivered to a stop a second time. The triple overhead cables groaned in protestation as the circular cabin swayed slowly. From where they hung, it was a sheer thirty-meter drop to the mountainside, and almost seven hundred meters down by cable to the lower cable station. The muskiness of the *fynbos* wafted into their round space. Even the mist had a smell.

"See?" She scuttled along the inside of the car facing the mountain, nose flattened against the glass in her attempt to get a glimpse of the docking platform, fifteen meters above them. The fog made it an impossible task. Those absurd high heels didn't help, either.

Just at that moment, a window in the fog appeared. Rianna turned to face Table Bay—forgotten, now, the panorama of jagged cliffs, *fynbos,* and her cherished mountain. "Didn't you think it odd that there were only the *two* of us to board?"

Lukas repositioned his hands. "Why did you make us get on?"

"I panicked. Those two men outside the restaurant—"

"There were many people outside."

"You have to know what to look for. I've grown careless. I thought the Secret Police had stopped following me each time I visit the country." She brushed the bangs from her eyes. "That's why I ran for the cable car—to get away. If we'd taken the trail, one of the footpaths, we'd have lost them by now. But we're not dressed for hiking down the mountain. Not with fancy shoes and Sunday-best."

"Shouldn't there at least be a driver with us—to operate the central console?"

"They're called controllers."

"Where's our cable car controller then?" Lukas's voice climbed.

"I told you. It's a set-up."

Lukas scoffed as he reached for her hand. "I wanted to hike up the mountain in casuals, but you insisted on dressing up for the silly meal."

"Birthdays are special occasions."

"How can anyone pull this off? Not with all the visitors."

Her voice was tired. "They're professionals. They only had to place a 'Maintenance. Please wait for next available car' sign in front of the entrance."

"What about the cableway staff?"

"Bribe them. Threaten them."

"Come on; this isn't Manhattan. We're miles from any ghetto. Not in such a prime tourist attraction spot."

Her mouth pulled into a thin line. "Most tourists don't pay attention. The country's changing. The Rainbow Nation is ten years old, and of the promised pot of gold, there's no sign—only a battered cast iron pan, which is perpetually empty."

Lukas's laugh died when the car gave a vicious jolt. "Hold tight!" He braced himself, legs planted wide, as the car gained momentum down the mountain. Inching toward his companion, Lukas laughed again, but this time it sounded forced. "At least we're going again. You worry too much. We'll be at the bottom in less than three—"

"We're going too fast!" Rianna slipped in between his arms.

They were both breathing fast.

"The brochure said the maximum speed is ten meters per second," Lukas reassured her.

"This is closer to thirty!"

RIANNA could feel her heart hammer in her chest. *This is faster than the time I went down a zipline in high school and almost broke my leg!* They continued plummeting down the incline, ever accelerating. *The bastards. They must be desperate.*

Lukas spun around. "The consoles, Rianna!" He scrambled toward the middle section, unclipped the phone, and pressed several buttons. "Hello? Operator?" He shook his head—the line seemed dead. He tried again. Pressed different buttons. "Hello?" No response. He slammed the phone against the console, then allowed it to slip from his hand.

The phone dangled in midair, swaying in slow motion, in synchronized rhythm with the car. The fog opened up and closed in, allowing them glimpses of the mountainside and the city far beyond, and, for a moment, the sea.

"Bloody mafia."

"No, the Secret Police . . . ." Rianna's nails bit into his arm. "Your cell—use your phone."

"It's 10-111?"

Nodding, Rianna pulled him along, plastering her face once again against the glass. "I don't understand. Where's the other car? It's a counterbalance system: if we go down the other car must come up."

Rianna's jaw dropped, the phone and emergency number forgotten. A window in the mist revealed the fast-upcoming car—packed with tourists—all windmilling their arms. Panic written over their faces. It seemed they all shouted. Rianna threw her hands in the air; they were wrapped, once again, in an alabaster veil.

The cables zinged as they continued their accelerated descent.

Shivering, she turned and threw her arms around Lukas's neck.

The car jerked, shuddered, and groaned to a slower speed as the overhead runners found grip on the cables when the brakes kicked in. The squealing diminished.

"Lukas . . . ." She buried her head in his shoulder.

"Who are those men? Why would they do this?"

"To scare me away." She repositioned her arms. "I've become an embarrassment. Years ago, I did some snooping. I found things I shouldn't have."

The car jumped. Rianna tightened her grip.

He wriggled himself free. "That's decades ago."

"A few years ago, I started digging again—I must have reappeared on their radar. I was hoping to uncover facts about a good friend I had when I was in high school. But it seems even the new government wants to keep certain things under wraps."

"You didn't break any laws?"

Rianna gave a nervous laugh. "Governments don't appreciate curious citizens."

A sudden jerk of the car crushed her against his chest. She groaned with pain. Lukas mumbled an apology and relaxed his hold. He murmured into her hair. "Rianna Vermeulen, you don't do half-measures. We had set out for a civilized brunch-hour appointment, and two hours later it seems we are narrowly escaping with our lives. We have men in suits with sunglasses chasing us."

"It's not funny."

"It's true. At least we can claim to be the first visitors to the Table Mountain National Park who have abseiled down eighteen-ton cables. You've been in the mother city not even a month and already have the South African mafia barking at your heels."

Her voice dropped. "Prepare yourself, Ferreira. More men in suits with sunglasses are waiting for us at the lower station."

One

Try as she might, Rianna found it impossible not to get goosebumps when the shrill steam-whistle sounded. The train, destined for Cape Town, steamed from the Pietersburg station with sixty seconds to spare, at 4:54 a.m.

It was punctual, as always. A sleep-train with a thirty-five-hour scheduled journey-time dared not waste a single minute. Unhurried, the night surrendered to the approaching day, as the star-speckled sky faded away. The conductor's whistle mixed with the chuck of the locomotive as it spewed colour heavenward—mushrooming ever higher—in columns of white, and black, and every colour in between.

Rianna, the lone passenger in the second-class half-compartment, groaned as she pushed the window open. She rubbed her arms—the chill in the early morning air surprised her. She was unaccompanied——this was the Republic, after all, and there was peace in the land. It was deemed safe for a fourteen-year-old girl to travel by rail. The compact space, wood-paneled, housed three sleeping berths in seasoned navy-blue leather. The middle-berth could be folded back to serve as a backrest when the passengers weren't sleeping. She leaned out and inhaled the breeze, cocking her head—a rooster's announcement of daybreak unmistakable, in spite of the engine's loud thrusting at the front.

How she cherished the unfamiliarity of it all—when she leaned back in, holding onto the lower rim of the window, the stuffiness of the old sleeping-bunks embraced her, and leaning out, the wind plucked at her, billowing her hair, bombarding her with sounds and smells and colours. The air, saturated with years of oil and grease spilled onto ties underfoot; the carriage, carrying its own stifling aroma; the aroma of one sleeping city that yielded to yet another as they traveled through the landscape; and always, coiled around the coaches, the coal-flavoured plumes that disappeared into the pale skies above her.

She took another deep breath—the earth outside was damp from the morning's dew.

Oh, she could never tire of the clicking and clacking of the coaches—and there it was again, the engine's soul-piercing whistle. She shivered, then shrieked as the train lurched—clutching the lower rim of the opened window.

Then, with a cry, she fell back into the upholstered bench. Blind for a moment, she squeezed her eyes tight and blinked repetitively—*the darned soot.* And that in spite of her sleeping car being two-thirds of the way to the back, the last one before the third-class section. The wind had carried the tiny particles all the way from the locomotive's smokebox.

However, she refused to close the window, still stubborn and curious, still enjoying the gusts that twirled through her narrow space. Soon enough, they would fry in the summer glare of the Transvaal bushveld.

When she heard the stampede approaching—scores of feet that stomped past her compartment door, only to come to a crunching halt around the corner, right where the little toilet was—Rianna slid across the long bench, away from the window and toward the door. It was impossible not to hear the giggling and snorting outside, but she wanted to hear more. *Children? Girls and boys. They have to be from Messina—there were no children who got on in Pietersburg with me.*

The children had probably received the same instruction—do not enter the third-class section of the train—it was *verboten.*

Why had they all become silent?

Rianna slid the window-cover on her door back three inches and pressed her nose against the pane, to better inspect the commotion in the corridor. She snapped upright when another face—that of a boy—laughed at her from the other side of the glass, not two inches away, his lips touching the little window, his breath fogging it over. In response to her look of surprise, he stuck out his tongue. Rianna slammed the small window-cover shut and leaned against the backrest, listening to the hollering outside.

How dare he? Her breathing came fast, her face glowing.

She unclipped the compartment door and yanked it open, poking her head out. The same boy stood there—a wide grin plastered over his features. He towered over her, but he had a gentle face. *But never mind that.* She hissed at him. "Hey! Didn't your mother teach you *manners?*"

His grin widened as the rest of the children, girls and boys her age, formed a semi-circle behind him. He bowed and made a twirl with his arm. "She did, Your Highness."

"Then leave me alone!" She banged the door shut. More laughter followed before the cries and footfalls receded toward the front of the train.

Ever curious, Rianna slid the door open a second time, prepared to follow the children. Having a compartment all to herself had lost its charm.

But after one step out into the corridor, she clasped her hand to her mouth and stepped back—that boy was there again. He stood at a safe distance—five feet away. Alone. His eyes didn't waver—they laughed at her.

"*What* do you want?"

He didn't move, his thumbs hooked into his belt, head tilted. He rocked on the balls of his feet. "You're not *really* so feisty."

She leaned back against the narrow doorframe, arms across her chest. "How would you know, *Mister?*"

"Your eyes have stopped spitting fire."

She pulled her hand through her unruly hair, and twirled a strand around her fingers. She was aware of the warmth crawling up her neck. *What is it with this boy?* "Why don't you run along with the other children? You'll fall behind—seems you like chasing them."

The tall boy with the gentle face stepped closer, shrugged, and shoved his hands in his pockets. He looked down and kicked an imaginary stone out of the way. When he looked back up, his cheeks had a tinge of vermillion. "I was bored, so I tagged along. I'm tired of babysitting them."

"Isn't it a bit early to run up and down the sleeping cars? Some people are trying to get an extra hour of sleep."

He leaned against the outside corridor window, arms folded, the smirk back in place. "Only the old people. You sound just like our teacher."

"Perhaps it's because I'm more *responsible*?"

He laughed as he put out his hand. "I'm Albert—from Messina. I was right—you *are* a princess."

She sighed as she gave his hand a firm shake, firm enough to make his eyes widen. "I'm *Rianna*. You're wrong about *many* things."

He shrugged again. "Are you coming along to the dining car?"

"It's too early. They won't allow—"

"Oh, *come on*."

Rianna backed into her compartment. "Then give me a moment."

She slipped a thin-strapped leather purse over her head, waving him ahead as she did so. *He will not walk behind me and stare at my bottom. That's what boys do.*

The rhythmic sway of the coaches made them widen their steps. Rianna giggled as she watched him.

He glanced over his shoulder. "*What*?"

"You walk *funny*."

"I was born with crooked knees." He accentuated his sideways stomping, making her snicker louder.

"That's not what I'm talking about. You walk like a *dronkie*."

"I'm no drunk—"

The train lurched, then heaved again. Rianna lost her footing and stumbled forward, crashing into him. She called out, clutched his arm with one hand, and fumbled for the railing with the other.

Albert roared with laughter as he helped her back upright. "Who's the *dronkie* now?"

Straightening her clothing, she avoided his eyes. No mirror was needed to tell her the colour of her face. *The silly machinist. Thank goodness I have on pants and not a dress.* "How far still?" Her voice sounded suddenly small.

She found herself wondering how often he shaved. The soot-coloured stubble on his cheeks matched his hair. Their faces had come this close when she had peeped through her little side window and he had stuck his tongue out at her. But then a glass had separated their faces. He smelled nice—of sun and lime soap.

His eyes followed the rise and fall of her chest.

Rianna's cough made him return his eyes to her face. "Sorry." He swallowed. "Three more cars—the dining car is between the first- and second-class sections."

In the dining car an impassive figure apprehended them—the head-waiter guarding his domain. Even at 5:30 a.m. he was impeccable: starched white shirt, hair *brylcreemed* and parted, moustache lacquered and curled, bowtie straightened, the waistcoat buttoned up, dress pants ironed, and shoes shining in their dark glory.

The man's right brow twitched. If they wouldn't mind, he said, the dining car was not open to the public. Seating for breakfast would commence at 6:45 a.m. He glanced at his wrist, nodding his head.

Rianna rewarded the man with a smile, then leaned closer to read his nameplate: *Mr. K.D. Krige*. The man snapped his head back and cleared his throat, his lips a pencil line. Both eyebrows were twitching now. Rianna scuttled back.

Mr. K.D. Krige cleared his throat a second time—there was no question—it was time to scoot.

Of the other children there was no sign—Mr. Krige must have made them scamper for their compartments already. *Likely under threat of setting their teacher loose on them or at the risk of grave bodily harm—perhaps thrown out the windows.* It seemed trespassers were immediately dealt with. They would have to retreat.

So they headed back, trying to look casual, rolling along with the clicking and clacking of the cars. Neither said a word.

In the next car, safely out of sight of Mr. Krige, Albert paused, his hand on the doorhandle. "Will it be okay if I come and get you at half past six?" His thumb was tucked in his belt again, his right foot kicking at the floor. The smirk was gone—his narrow nose underlined by a soft smile.

Rianna didn't trust her voice. She nodded and disappeared down the hallway—feeling, despite the train's constant rocking, as if she was walking on air.

No CHARGE of running feet this time, just a hesitant knock on her door. It was 6:25 a.m. Albert stood a respectful distance away when she slipped through the sliding door. The half-smile suited him.

Mr. K.D. Krige acknowledged them with an almost undetectable nod and gestured to follow him—he would seat everybody.

Boisterous chattering announced the arrival of Albert's schoolmates—the presence of their teacher notwithstanding. Then Rianna gulped, her eyes nailed to the young woman forming the rear guard. Prim. A vision. A real lady. She would love to look like that one day—chic—comfortable in her body. It was the way the teacher carried herself. Not a day over twenty-five—with fire-engine-red glasses, matching lipstick, clutch-purse, and heels to complete the statement that her figure-hugging polka-dot dress made. She cocked her brow at Rianna, whose face promptly turned the colour of the woman's clutch-purse.

Albert must have struck a deal with his teacher as far as his chaperone-role was concerned, because he ignored the children who were allocated to seats at the adjacent tables by Mr. K.D. Krige.

The children, however, would have none of Albert's cold shouldering. The punishment was immediate. "Bertie has a girlfriend! Bertie has a girlfriend!"

There was a silent exchange between Albert and his teacher—her pencilled eyebrows raised heavenward—him shaking his head. Then the teacher clapped her hands once and murmured, "*Children.*" Like magic, the mocking simmered down to an inaudible hum.

Rianna tilted her head—her eyes brightened—she had increased respect for the elegant female in black and white and red. She gave the children only a grin. *Brats.*

Then she clasped her hands between her knees and gave Albert an innocent stare. "Why did you *lie* to me? You introduced yourself as *Albert* from Messina. And all the time it's *Bertie*—"

Albert's brow furrowed—the smile gone, his voice pained. He sounded decades older than his sixteen years. "My name is *Albert Vosloo*. Please *don't* encourage the children."

Two

Rianna stomped back to her compartment—red-faced and incensed. Her breakfast had been cut short, and she was angry. The teacher had turned out to be a *teef*: a real closet bitch in a fancy dress.

She pushed her window open with so much force that she lost her balance when the train jerked and sent her, grasping at air, arms and legs flailing, halfway through the opening. By the time she stopped moving and found something to grab on to, she was hyperventilating. Now, gasping for breath, crying from pain as well as humiliation, she hauled her upper body back inside the train. Her fingers gingerly felt her side—even her ribs got grazed. She groaned. *I'm lucky it wasn't worse.*

Minutes later she kneeled on the berth, back at the window but careful this time to poke only her head outside. *I refuse to let that woman ruin my life.* The warm Transvaal Highveld wind toyed with her mane. It fanned the red hair around her face, dried the salt streaks across her cheeks. *The entire inside of my arm and leg and ribcage is going to turn purple. I'll even have a lilac nipple. How horrible.*

Miss Nichols, the polka-dot lady, of whom Rianna had thought so highly, had turned unreasonable in such an unexpected fashion. Throughout the meal the teacher had kept her poise, but the moment she noticed Rianna was done she had, without mincing words, made it clear that Rianna should keep to herself. In front of everybody, the teacher had admonished her. She, Rianna, the lone girl who got on in Pietersburg, was an outsider—and a negative influence on the children. See how unruly the children had become, Miss Nichols shouted. She couldn't tolerate such dissent and insubordination. She, Miss Nichols, had no time for those modern parents who thought it wise to send their pubescent daughters into the wide world, unchaperoned.

Pubescent. Unchaperoned. Rianna sighed.

She had rolled her eyes at the polka-dot figure's language. *Good heavens—this was no longer the Victorian nineteenth century.* And Albert had sat there with his mouth shut, eyes downcast—too scared to squeak.

To be fair, Rianna had not uttered a single word either—unless you counted the antics with her eyes. She simply snuck away like a no-good hound. Had she owned a tail—it would have been tucked between her hind legs.

I hate her. Rianna was in the fetal position now. *I hate her gorgeous outfit.* Her breath came faster and faster. Her fingers tingled.

I hate the children from Messina. She struck the navy-blue leather with both fists. *I hate them all!*

Then, eyes closed, she slumped onto her back. It took many minutes for her breathing to slow. Her eyes stung. How she longed to be back in Katete, in Zambia, with Mother, Father, PJ and Casper, and her beloved mango tree. Even the much younger Lukas would be better company to keep than these weird people from the border-town of Messina, next to the crocodile-infested Limpopo River.

SUDDENLY Rianna snapped upright. She rubbed her eyes. Albert must be Miss Nichols's cabana-boy. How could she have been so blind?

She cocked her head—then listened again. The engine chucked and whistled; the coaches clacked along on their jittery two-track trajectory. There it was again—unmistakable—some light tapping, knocking on her door. She swung her legs down, rubbed her eyes once more, unclipped the door, and stuck her nose out. It was Albert. "Go *away*." She raked both hands through her hair—she must look like a scarecrow—that silly wind.

His right foot kicked at the floor. "I want to apologize—Miss Nichols was unreasonable."

"Unreasonable? She's a *bitch*!"

His head snapped upright. "She's not always like this."

"The only thing you need to apologize for is saying *nothing*."

"She's still the teacher—in charge of us. It was not my place . . . ."

Her eyes flashed. "You're bigger and taller—"

"I'm only sixteen. I know, I look older."

"I thought you were *braver*."

"That's *unfair*."

"*Life's* unfair." Rianna withdrew to her compartment and slumped down next to the window, but she did not shut the door. Instead, she patted the wide seat next to her. "Or are you prohibited from ever again speaking to the school girl from Pietersburg, Albert from *Messina*?"

He plopped down on the far end of the berth, away from her. They both stared straight ahead—in absolute silence. Miss Nichols had made it clear that proximity to this girl was unacceptable.

When the train lurched, he pulled his leg under him and faced Rianna. "How far are you going?"

"*Cape Town*—Westerford High."

He snickered.

"It's just a silly *school*."

He pursed his lips and glanced out the window. "I'm only going as far as Stellenbosch."

"That's too bad. And the *tefie*?"

"Don't call her that. Bloemfontein—the children are participating in a choir festival."

"*Choir?* What about you, Bertie?"

"I don't sing."

"You're lying."

Albert shrugged and studied the countryside. "We're close to Pretoria—"

Rianna jumped from the berth and peered out the window. "Will we be allowed to get off?"

"You mean disembark? The stopover is only fifteen minutes."

Fifteen minutes! She groaned. "What time is it?"

"Ten-thirty. The Johannesburg station is bigger—we'll stop for forty-five minutes there."

"I'll *love* that." She stood on tiptoe, reached for a brush from her bag on the top berth, and pulled it through her hair. Then she leaned forward and peeked into the small mirror above the stainless steel hand basin. "There. Are you joining me?"

There was only one possible answer to that. He stood up, stepped out into the hallway, and, with a mock flourish, held the compartment door open for her. His smirk was back in place. "Where to, Your Highness?"

Rianna grabbed his hand and pulled her compartment door closed behind her. "We're going on an expedition." Then she hooked his elbow and pulled in the direction of the back of the train.

They had travelled about three steps before Albert pulled free and grabbed her by the shoulders. "We're not *allowed* into the third-class section."

She shrugged his hands from her shoulders and stepped back, just out of reach. "How brave are you?"

"This has nothing to do with courage—"

"Why can't we go there?"

"It's the *law*!" He reached after her.

She was faster. She sidestepped him and dashed to the end of their car—and then around the bend in the corridor and through the door into the gangway. She gasped as the wind in the gap between the two cars hit her, glanced at her feet and the ties and rails rushing by, visible through the narrow slits in the floor, stepped wide, and crossed over into the third-class coach. Once inside she halted dead in her tracks, which made the pursuing Albert crash into her. He grasped her shoulders as they struggled to regain their balance, stopping just short of crashing to the floor. He mumbled a cuss.

Both were breathing hard.

"You *have* to stop! It's only for non-Whites. You can't—"

"Albert from Messina." She spun around, their noses brushing. "I grew up with non-whites—with black people. How are they different? They were my friends in Zambia. Well, most of them . . . . *What's* the big deal?"

Her eyes were on fire; he stepped back from their intensity. "I didn't make the laws. You'll get us in trouble." Again, he reached for her hand.

"*Forget* it!" She shook her head and bounced away again, heading down the hallway, determined to reach the conductor's car in the back.

Halfway down she stopped and turned, suddenly uncertain. "What *language* do these people speak?"

There was nothing for it. He simply could not leave her on her own. When he was close enough to answer without shouting, he replied, "*Venda* if they're from up north and *Sepedi* if they're from around here. Many of them also speak Afrikaans and English."

"Do you speak? I only know some *Chichewa*."

He shrugged. "A little."

Just then a door to one of the compartments opened, and a women and young child slipped out, closing the sliding door behind them. When they saw the two teenagers they pressed back against the door and waited for them to pass, their eyes cast down. Rianna stole a glance inside the compartment before the woman got the door shut.

"*Ndi matseloni.*" That was Albert!

The woman's face broke into a wide smile as she returned the good morning greeting. "*Ndi matseloni!*"

He nodded and clasped both the mother's and little girl's hands in his. The three conversed in Venda's flowing sentences. Rianna stood back and smiled at the shy child—she pulled faces until the little girl grinned back at her.

When the conversation ended, Rianna and Albert sauntered down the hallway, waving back at the beaming mother and child behind them. Albert called a final goodbye.

Only when they rounded the corner at the very end of the corridor did Rianna turn to her companion. Her eyes were ablaze. "Albert from Messina, you're dead. You speak only a little Venda? And my name is *idiot.*"

"I'm sorry. I grew up on a farm with her people."

Rianna sniffed and accelerated her pace down the corridor of the second car.

"How far do you want to go, Rianna? You've *made* your point—"

"I'm not trying to make a point, Bertie. These laws are silly and unfair—they hurt people." She glanced over her shoulder. "I counted the cars—there are six third-class coaches. I'm only planning on saying 'Hi' to the conductor."

"You'll give him a heart attack."

"I don't care. This is *ludicrous*." Her eyes met his. "Did you see how poorly their compartment was furnished? Drab wooden benches—painted emerald green."

"Emerald is the colour of precious—"

She swung and hit him on his arm; he yelped in surprise. "That's for making fun of their hardship."

He rolled his eyes. "Can we please go back now?"

Her answer was to dart farther down the hallway, closer to her goal.

On their way, they passed several passengers—each looking at them in disbelief. What were the two white children doing there? Rianna remained oblivious to her effect on them, while Albert nodded and waved and greeted them with, "*Ndi matseloni*" and "*Dumela*." Rianna had to keep picking up her pace so Albert couldn't force her to turn back.

As they turned the corner that marked the end of the last third-class coach, almost running by then, they crashed into the tall, unyielding bulk of the conductor himself. The impact sent his cap flying and themselves sprawling across the narrow hallway.

"What the hell?" the man hollered as he scrambled after his hat. His black and white attire was similar to the uniform worn by his counterpart in the dining cart, but for the bow tie. His ample waistcoat was two sizes too small, his face an unhealthy rose—unlike Mr. K.D. Krige's. The conductor must not have had time to shave the past three days.

Maybe Albert wasn't kidding about the heart attack. The man panted as he gestured at them both, stopping just short of dabbing his thick index finger against their chests. "*What's* the meaning of this? Can't you kids read? It says 'Non-Whites'!"

Rianna gulped and breathed fast, her young breasts rising and falling, but stood her ground. "*You're* white," she piped.

The conductor croaked in disbelief.

Rianna looked up and met his eyes squarely. "I wanted to see for myself. I think it's unfair—treating black people like this. Separate in cattle-coaches."

The plump man drew himself up to his full height. He towered above her. But then he stepped closer and bent down, bringing his potato nose inches from Rianna's. His peach-mottled expression had acquired a worrisome plum. "Are you heading to *Cape Town*, Missy?"

Rianna's lower lip quivered. She nodded. Soon her entire body trembled. The man's breath reeked of onions and chewing tobacco. He must not have taken a bath in several days. She had little trouble identifying with Jack, right after he had clambered up the beanstalk to reach the clouds and got busted by the giant.

"So *why* don't you, *after* your arrival in the Cape, go to the prime minister's office and tell him you *disagree*?" He inched closer, spewing it out. "*Huh*?"

Rianna cringed, gave a sob, and clasped her mouth. "I *will*," she stammered.

"Well, I'll be *damned!*" The giant slapped his thigh as he steamrollered closer. On top of the heart attack, a stroke seemed eminent. Or maybe he would start foaming at the mouth.

Albert lurched forward and pulled Rianna, now frozen to the spot, away from the brute. "We did *nothing*—" he began.

The conductor rose to his full six foot five and shouted, "*Out of here!*" His arms windmilled. "I give you punks *three* minutes, then I'll come and check. If you're not tucked safely in your respective compartments, I will ask the ticket-controller to put you off at Pretoria Central." He gave another step in their direction and bellowed, "Or better still, at the next *unmanned rail-crossing!*"

The troll used his stained sleeve to mop the perspiration from his brow. "I have the *authority* to put you off—for breaking the law!" He advanced, reaching for them. "Have I made myself *clear?*"

There was nothing to say, nothing she *could* say. She clutched Albert's hand and catapulted him along with her down the hallway—away—not waiting for permission. She sobbed as she ran.

Three

LAND OF OUR FATHERS. 1965

*I*t took the length of six railway cars for Rianna to come to her senses. She had no memory of how passengers in the non-White section had dodged to get past as the two of them fled the conductor's car. The farther they went, the harder she sprinted—as if possessed. Soon, Albert lagged behind—his calling on her to slow down only spurred her on. Wiping her cheeks, she ran—tears of humiliation, tears of justifiable anger—not of fear, she told herself.

Her self-imposed exile took immediate effect. The moment they reached the apparent safety of the second-class section, she slipped through her door, and then paused with it still open, wheezing, sucking rapid breaths. Albert, halfway down the hallway, stood with hands resting on his knees, also breathing hard. She motioned him to continue to his own compartment. He didn't move. "I can't leave you like this."

"I'm a big girl." She pressed on her chest, willing her breathing slower. "I'm filled with righteous anger."

"I know, that man . . . ." He kicked at a joint in the floor.

"A barbarian. He's such a bully."

"Rianna—"

"*Go*. I'll see you later."

RIANNA refused to respond to Bertie's knock on her door an hour later when they reached Johannesburg. *They can shove the city of gold.* Her door remained locked. She kept to her compartment until they reached Bloemfontein in the Free State—the halfway mark to Cape Town.

She had no plan to die of hunger. Her small pack of rusks was rationed—each one of the eight pieces were divided into four equal parts—small chunks, washed down with lukewarm water from the miniature sink in her compartment.

Having locked herself in from those who could come through the door—the likes of Miss Nichols and the troll in the conductor's car—she turned her attention to the world that rushed past her window. Only when the wind became too invasive, billowing her shirt, threatening to blow her like a kite out the window, did she push it closed. Having had to sacrifice the loss of the wind's touch on her face and neck and arms, along with all the smells and sounds carried from outside, there was some consolation in flattening her nose against the pane—capturing frame upon frame of landscapes, of worlds, that jetted past.

She was a baby the last time they had travelled this route. Every spot now was new—each telephone post, each fence, each farmhouse, each hill and tree and rock. Especially the towns.

The change in the landscape occurred without warning; made her snap to attention. *The goldmines.* She shoved the window open again—the only way to see better was to lean far out and breathe it in. The shaft-towers, black monstrosities, their robust steel frameworks towering stories high, housed elevator shaft wheels the size of motorcars. The geometrical symmetry of the mine dumps reminded her of pictures in the *Encyclopedia Britannica* back home of the pyramids of Giza. These were not triangular, but gigantic nevertheless, rectangular man-made mountains— made up in their entirety of pale white dirt mixed with cadmium yellow—bleached in the relentless African sun.

Sallow soil, scooped from the hidden bowels of the earth.

Pallid earth filled with tons of concealed gold.

Rianna pinched her eyes tight.

Those mountains of earth—she had read—were washed, combed, then washed again and again and again—extracting the precious metal—spitting the less valuable, pasty sand to the surface. And next to the rectangular dumps, also brought to the surface—there must be the bodies of all the less fortunate miners. Men who toiled, dug, and laboured and eventually perished underground. From too much digging and tunneling and placing explosives came some dying—she had also read.

They didn't make it up about there being gold and blood in that earth. Is that why the heaps of earth were so sickly pale—having had not only all the gold but also the blood extracted from it?

Rianna shuddered as she visualized the men crawling underground—in burrows filled with eternal night, tunnels without end, tunnels that could cave in without warning. Networks of tunnels which required supports, rafters, beams, and braces, and fresh air pumped in through wide ducts, all the way down into the dark belly of the earth, for the men to breathe, to live from. Like moles—armed with picks and hard hats—with a single light, glowing bright, casting tall shadows as they chipped away at the gold-speckled rock; only to be paid a pittance to unearth its ensconced treasures, inch by precious inch, ounce by inestimable ounce. Their masters taking the money to build themselves countless mansions and a sprawling city of gold.

An hour later, as they crossed the Vaal river into the Orange Free State, there was a light tap on the door. Rianna peeked through the small hallway window. Bertie. She poked her head out, looking him over from head to toe, before motioning him inside with a curt nod. "You can come in if you promise to be quiet."

Albert from Messina rewarded her with a lazy smile.

The land changed once more—as if they had entered a foreign country. Their puffing metal centipede had turned into a *melk-trein*—the locomotive started making frequent stops for milk pickups. The train tracks continued following the main road, cutting through farmland and fields and flat hills. It seemed every farmer saw it as their patriotic duty to keep a collection of milk cows—to make their humble contribution to the Fatherland.

Bertie lurched to his feet, startling his companion. He tapped on the window, pointed at a homestead closer to the tracks. "My grandfather's neighbour!" Nose flattened against the glass, he waved Rianna closer. "Quickly. The next one . . . the red roof beyond the eucalyptus trees. *There*—that's Grandpa's!"

Rianna brushed shoulders with the boy as she looked out at the fast receding red-roofed house. "When last did you visit them?"

Bertie turned away from the window and his companion and plopped into the far corner.

"*Bertie?*"

"Four years."

"And you *loved* visiting the farm."

Albert from Messina told his new friend how his mother and grandfather had a falling-out some years ago. Both refused to give in.

"What about?"

Bertie shrugged. "Mom confided in Grandpa that we had changed churches—from *Gereformeerde Kerk* to *Hervormde Kerk*." (Reformed Church to a sister denomination.)

"That's silly."

"Grandpa didn't think so."

"Don't you *hate* it when adults act like children?" Rianna's gaze remained unwavering.

Bertie grinned, crossing his legs at the ankles, hands shoved deep in his pockets. "I'm just glad they didn't start a civil war about the church thing."

Rianna tutted as she smiled at him.

Without much warning, the countryside flattened out like an ancient table. Only the occasional ridge and *koppie*—small outcrop—decorated the plains and fields in golds and ochres and limes. The *Karee* and *Kiepersol* made room for a landscape of sweet thorn, eucalyptus, pine and wattle—scattered among acres of maize and corn fields—that stretched far beyond what the eye could see. The homesteads, tucked away, shielded by clusters of pine and eucalyptus.

Rianna laughed as she watched the swallows draped along the phone lines—clothes pegs on a washing line—swaying with the wind.

She yanked the window open, breathing deep, eyes closed. But not for long. The rowdy crows preferred the fence posts and the trees—restless flitting bullies, intimidating their smaller-in-stature feathered brothers.

She faced Bertie. "Crows. Horrible birds."

Bertie scoffed. "Grandpa turned a blind eye when we aimed the air rifles at them."

"That's cruel."

"They're cruel birds."

The rail tracks were too far away to hear the cooing of the wood doves that kept to the homesteads and surrounding wooded areas, away from the smoke-puffing reptile that snaked through the flowing land.

Decorating the farmers' fields now were windmills—the locals called them *windpompe*—tapered steel structures planted adjacent to circular cement dams with drinking troughs for the cattle. Leaning far out, Rianna listened for the zinging of the gigantic wheel atop the windmill platform. The gusts tucked and played with the wide blades—made it spin fast—spewing water through the above-ground discharge pipe, the size of a man's wrist, gushing into the concrete dam. She narrowed her eyes—if the wheel came loose from up there, it would cut across the field, cut through the fence, cut right into their train!

She cringed and shuddered, covered in goosebumps. "Do you hear that, Bertie?"

He joined her at the open window. "The zinging?"

She told him about her *Oupa's* farm where they would pull themselves up onto the narrow circular cement wall, one eye always on the turning *windpomp*, the other on the discharge pipe. A balancing act was required—leaning in only far enough to reach and grasp the ice-cold pipe, kicking wild with the legs to counterbalance, resting on their bellybuttons, then, letting go with the second hand to scoop water—hand to mouth, hand to mouth—slurping the wet coolness from the innards of the earth. Heaven. While all the time, the risk of crashing headfirst into the mire-covered water remaining an exhilarating danger.

Bertie bumped her shoulder. "Did you ever fall in?"

"Once." Rianna shivered as she sat back. "I almost drowned. The water level was too low to reach the top of the wall. *Oupa* pulled me out."

As the *melk-trein* wound through the province, cutting through the occasional hill, a mosaic of cosmos unfolded—painting the drab railway corridors in pastels, pale pinks, and off-whites—an unending tapestry. The long-stemmed flowers wove in the breeze—beaming at the sun—lush, as if planted by hand, fed and watered by an invisible legion of railroad fairies.

It became the established pattern. The engine sounded its shrill whistle—the next moment screeching to a halt in the middle of nowhere. Voices outside. Clatter and clanging. Another whistle, a shuddering chuck, and they were on their way again. Endless times, the children didn't bother to move or to look.

In time, Rianna tired of the unpredictable gusts that twirled her hair into a crow's nest, shoved the window close, and turned her back on the outside world. She told Bertie about Pietersburg and the land beyond the Zambezi, to the north.

For long stretches, after that, they said nothing, enjoying each other's company.

Rianna was the first to close her eyes, her breathing becoming deep and regular.

It took the abrupt shudder of the train coming to a standstill to wake Rianna. It sprawled her across the berth, sent her halfway to the floor. Bertie's snort got drowned out by the commotion outside. Rianna picked herself up and, groaning, wrestled the window down, only to step back and cover her ears.

Loud clanging and shrill voices rushed at them. A sharp curve in the tracks had brought the conductor's car in close proximity to their second-class section. Bertie pushed past her to get a better view. "All that racket for *nothing*. A thorn tree and a silly old truck."

"No Bertie. It's a special milk-stop." In spite of the tepid air, Rianna breathed deep—inhaled the earth and veld and cosmos. Such grateful flowers. She sniffed again, raised her head—the aroma of fresh milk wafted across. The clanging sounded again. Milk cans.

"They're all the same." Bertie scuttled back to his corner.

"Shame on you. You'll let life pass you by."

The other passengers had followed her example—they all dangled out their respective windows—gawking at the ruckus.

Commotion at the conductor's car made Rianna squint her eyes—a modest ramp to the side of the tracks served as platform and housed six silver milk cans, all placed in symmetrical fashion, close the edge. An unassuming man with a broad-rimmed hat, pulled low over his eyes, stood next to the truck, under the acacia—waiting. Man, hat, and vehicle seemed of equal age. Of the original dove-blue pickup, only a faded grey with rusty edges had remained. The man in the hat raised a solid hand in acknowledgment as the grotesque bulk of the conductor appeared on the steps of the railway car.

An unintelligible conversation followed as the troll eased a sliding door open on the side of the conductor's coach. His dinner-plate–sized hands had little trouble grabbing hold of a milk can, each housing ten gallons, in each hand and hoisting them, as if empty, into the interior. Three quick trips and he was done. The giant surprised her when he bounced with ease into the car and clattered around inside, securing the milk containers. Moments later he reappeared and paused in the door opening, facing her way.

Rianna squirmed. It seemed the conductor's eyes burned into her—she returned the glare. Then the man jumped down, slammed the door shut, clipped the latch in place, gave the farmer a slip of paper with a half-salute, and clambered back up the steps at the rear end of his car.

"Weird man." Bertie, having sensed her discomfort, had joined her at the window.

"He gives me the creeps."

A whistle sounded, then another, the train chucked, and they were on their way once more.

They steamed through the remainder of the *platteland*, passing the likes of Parys, Kroonstad, and Welkom, skimming the town of Virginia, then on toward Theunissen and Brandfort, before finally heading for Bloemfontein, the halfway mark on the journey to Cape Town.

Approaching Bloemfontein, the skies lost its infinite blue. Above the horizon, thinned-out cotton wool clouds developed streaks of grey—the pinks and reds and yellows faded fast—becoming watercolour washes, soon drained of colour.

Head resting on folded arms, Rianna eyed the fiery ball as it cringed lower. She sighed—a sunset like none other before it and none other to follow. *What a blessing to share this with somebody.* At that moment her stomach churned. She glanced sideways at Bertie who laughed. He also heard her stomach complaining.

"Why don't we go and say hi to Mr. Krige?" Rianna reached up on tiptoes to fumble in her bag on the overhead berth for her brush.

Two quick steps and Bertie stood ready at the door.

Rianna freed the brush from her entangled hair. "I'm really hungry . . . . But I don't know. What about Miss Nichols?"

"Forget about her." Bertie stepped outside. "She and the children will be gone after supper—they're getting off in Bloemfontein."

Rianna gave him a grateful smile as she trailed him to the dining car.

Mr. Krige was at his post—flawless and formal. Rianna rewarded him with a wide smile when she noticed the corners of his mouth soften. He only pretended to be made of marble. A single nod and he led the way. Of Miss Nichols there was no sign.

Rianna shivered at the thought of Miss Nichols—she had to force herself not to grab Bertie's hand.

They were allowed only in the first half of the dining car—the second-class section. Short dividing curtains stretched from the ceiling to the back of bench-seats on each side, and a third curtain spanned the walkway, barring snoopy eyes from feasting on the first-class guests. Rianna leaned forward on her elbows, imploring Albert to do likewise. "Why can't we sit over *there*?" She kept her voice down, pointing with her fork at the greener pastures beyond the curtains.

"They pay more."

"It's *discrimination*."

"It's called an economic reality."

"*What*?"

Albert gave a humourless laugh. "My dad's a business man. That's what he always says: 'You get what you pay for.'"

"It's unfair." Rianna shook the starched napkin out as if to free it of invisible impurities, placed it on her lap, and ironed out each wrinkle with wild strokes.

Mr. Krige's discreet cough made her snap upright and give him a silly grin. Her face burned. He placed her meal in front of her. She mumbled a thank-you.

"What's unfair?" The server leaned an inch closer—his eyes gentle.

Rianna crumpled the white napkin into a ball. She motioned in the direction of the first-class section. "Them and us."

Mr. Krige placed Albert's order in front of him, still facing Rianna. "The rich?"

Rianna rolled the large napkin in her hands, squeezing with all her might. She nodded. Both Albert and Mr. Krige laughed.

Her dark pupils spat fire. "They're wealthy because they participate in sleazy business deals."

A muscle twitched in Mr. Krige's face. "I believe it's possible to be wealthy *and* honest."

"Impossible!" Rianna insisted.

"You might be surprised, young lady." Their prim and proper server gave her an encouraging smile and moved away to wait on another table.

Albert leaned back, not touching his meal. His smirk had returned. "Are you a communist?"

Rianna gasped, then sighed and hunched her shoulders. She gave a timid smile, her eyes moist. "You're using all kinds of clever words. I still get confused with communism and socialism and capitalism. Communism, I know, is the bad one . . . . We never went to bed hungry—but there never was any extra money." She poked at her food with her fork. "My parents are missionaries." She swallowed. "I don't know what came over me . . . being so ungrateful . . . even our second-class coach is an abundance of luxury."

Albert leaned across, the smirk gone. He swallowed. "I'm sorry—I've been silly."

Rianna drew a hand over her eyes. She pointed at the curtains behind her companion. "I guess, separating the rich from the less affluent with a curtain is less unfair than separating—" and she gestured behind her, "us from them—from the black people with signs and laws and wooden benches . . . ."

Albert raised his shoulders. "It's called separate development, according to my dad. They're over *there*—and we're over *here*. It makes perfect sense. Each one has his allotted spot, his place in society, his place in the world."

"No, Bertie . . . don't sugarcoat it. It's unfair. They're people like us. It *hurts* them."

RIANNA and Albert remained seated in the dining car after finishing their meal—the fact that Mr. Krige didn't throw them out immediately was as good as a written invitation to stay. Soon they would be in Bloemfontein.

It was Albert's antics with his eyes that made Rianna snap out of her reverie. *Look next to you*, his eyes pleaded. She had allowed the swaying coaches to soothe her, her eyes half-closed, shivering with goosebumps at the train's weary whistle as they slowed down and steamed into the station. Only when he kicked her shin under the table did it register—they were no longer alone—somebody stood next to her—a woman.

Rianna gulped as she noticed the pointy black shoes. The polka-dot outfit had been replaced by a soft mauve two-piece, which clung to the trim figure. The lady had the finest bosom—with a fearless cleavage. All the accessories were raven black.

"How far are you travelling, *child*? Cape Town?" The woman's nostrils flared, like a racing mare.

Rianna crumpled the napkin behind her back as she scrambled to her feet. She backed into the narrow walkway between the tables. The teacher's pursed lips were not lost on her. She would not be looked down upon. She pulled her shoulders back. "I have a name—it's *Rianna*." Her chest heaved. She swallowed several times, maintaining eye contact. "Yes, Miss Nichols—I'm going to the end of the line—to Cape Town."

The older woman stepped closer—her rose-petal perfume snaking around them, heavy, asphyxiating. "*Good*. Albert and you will be travelling together as far as Stellenbosch. But I warn you—don't even *think* of flirting with him." She inched so close, Rianna could see the golden specs in her irises. "Do you understand?"

And then, without warning Ms. Nichols straightened and turned, her bosom brushing Rianna's shoulder.

RIANNA gasped as she staggered back, blinking several times, then remained rooted. *The bitch.* "Why do you hate me? You don't know me—"

"Oh, I don't hate you, child." The woman's delicate nose flared and pulled up as if smelling a dead rodent. "But I know the likes of you. You spell *trouble*."

Rianna clutched both fists until her fingers went numb. The napkin had dropped to the floor.

The teacher's nose pinched in disgust. To Albert she directed, "Remember what I told you about her." Then her voice softened, turning into a purr. "Come, Albert . . . . *Come* say goodbye to me." Then Miss Nichols spun around, gave Rianna a final glare, and marched from the car. At the exit she paused, watching over her shoulder until Bertie jumped from his seat and went to her.

Four

*A*lbert Vosloo got off the train in Stellenbosch, at 1:11 p.m. the next afternoon.

The train was eleven minutes behind schedule, and the personnel scurried about—hurrying to help passengers disembark and embark. They were instructed to push hard, though without being rude. Time was of the essence—their name was on the line—the South African Railways prided itself in running a punctual enterprise.

Mr. Krige, always the exception, dismissed his colleagues' consternation—he went to the trouble of greeting Albert with a formal handshake, mumbling under his breath, "We're not uncivilized barbarians—there's always time to say goodbye to guests, you know."

Rianna, on Albert's insistence, accompanied him off the train and onto the platform.

She took his offered hand and squeezed hard. "Goodbye, Bertie. It was nice having you as a friend for a day and a half."

He counter-squeezed. "I liked it a lot. But remember, my name is *Albert*—"

He received only a grin. "*Sorry*, Bertie . . . ." She stood on tip toes, pecked him on each cheek, then scurried back up the first step of the train car. She leaned forward, holding onto the railing. "Miss Nichols—she's so beautiful, and yet was *so* unreasonable. Why did she call you to go and say goodbye to her?"

He shrugged. "They all got off there . . . ."

"*So?*"

He looked away. The troll called from the back of the train, waved his flag and blew his whistle.

"Has she ever kissed you . . . on the *mouth?*"

"Don't be silly."

"I saw how she looked at you."

His answer was a smirk.

The second whistle sounded. The train chucked.

"She's *not* your friend . . . she'll only hurt—"

"*Goodbye*, Rianna."

Rianna yelped and scuttled up the steps as the train lurched. She called out, "Goodbye, Bertie!" yanked open the door and jumped inside, then closed it behind her. She spun around and waved through the small window, pressing her nose against the pane, but of Bertie there was no longer any sign. He stood on the platform, tens of feet behind her now, as the train whistled and steamed from the station like a snake slithering along a shining silver track without an end or a beginning.

THREE hours later a taxi dropped Rianna off in front of the main buildings of Westerford High School in Cape Town. She still marveled at how Father and Mother had managed to scrape together her tuition and boarding fees; the onus was on her not to waste a penny and to make them proud. She craned her neck and stepped away from her single piece of luggage—the expansive school buildings and grounds forgotten—because towering behind the tree line, to her left and to her right, stretched the mountain. She sucked in her breath.

Nobody had told her, and no encyclopedia, not even the one in the Pietersburg public library, could do justice do the majestic mount, now standing three thousand feet tall in front of her—its foothills not three city blocks away. *Oh my goodness.*

She would later learn this was the southeastern outcrop of Table Mountain—Devil's Peak's rear end.

Will I ever grow tired of this mountain? Stepping away from her trunk, now abandoned in the middle of the empty parking lot, she watched as the turquoise mountain clouded over—from the north—as if a gigantic wool blanket had just been pulled over it. She suppressed a grin. *It's like Mother said—Van Hunks and the devil is at it again—having a smoking contest.*

"You'll get used to it."

Rianna spun around. She shielded her eyes against the western glare. Two girls, older than her, in burgundy blazers, grey skirts, short white socks, and black shoes, stood next to her trunk, arms folded across their bosoms. Rianna stole another glance at the mountain, then faced the girls. "*Never.*"

The spokesperson of the duo, the taller one, her sand-blonde hair braided, uncrossed her arms. She reminded Rianna of a bamboo growing wild. "I'll give you six months—max. You'll grow sick of the mountain. All the stupid fog. The endless rain." Her brows arched. "You're an *entire week* late." She tapped Rianna's luggage with her shoe. "This yours?"

Rianna scuttled closer. "Yes . . . it's mine. We made arrangements with the school, with Mr. Benson . . . ." She swallowed when she noticed the tall girl cross her arms again. "They are *aware* that I would only arrive this afternoon—"

The quiet one of the two stepped forward and twirled around Rianna, mimicking a ballerina. "Oh, so you're one of those: a student with *privileges.*" Then she repeated with an affected voice, as she traipsed around the newcomer, "'We have made *special arrangements* with *Mr. Benson.*' I'm such an exceptional student, I can come whenever it suits *me.*" She stopped in her tracks and jutted her face closer to Rianna's, who cried out and scuttled back.

The girl's piercing eyes relaxed as she laughed and put out a hand. "Welcome to Westerford High, Miss Rianna Vermeulen." She tapped her own chest. "I'm Bianca Brown." Then she let go of Rianna's hand and pointed at her tall friend. "She goes by Clare . . . Clare Collins."

Bianca held out her hand. "One more thing." She gave Rianna a look-over as she made the fourteen-year-old do a 360-degree turn, clicking with her tongue. "You'll have to do. At least you can stick to your guns—you'll need to here." She chuckled and winked, lowering her voice. "Clare *hates* mountains . . . it's called *acrophobia*—this fear of heights thing."

"I *heard* that." Clare brushed the other girl out of the way and grabbed the one end of Rianna's trunk. "Care to take your end?"

Rianna adjusted her shoulder bag and grasped the opposite handle, but dropped it immediately. She stepped back and studied the trees. Her discovery made her gasp.

"What's it *now*?" Clare murmured. "You still can't get over the stupid mountain?"

"The trees—where are your *mango* trees?" It was a mere whisper.

"So you don't like our Cape holly, yellowwood, stinkwood, fir trees, giant figs—"

Rianna shook her head as she grasped her end of the trunk. "No, I had just—"

Clare grinned. "Welcome to the Cape. This is not the tropics." She leaned in, raised her end of the chest, then cussed as she hastily repositioned her grip. "What's inside? Half a dozen anvils?"

Rianna laughed as she held tight and lifted, ready to follow. But Clare seemed to expect an answer to her question, so she added in a mumble, "Books." She groaned as they went up the first set of stairs. Her eyes danced between her two companions. "The school is . . . the school has *boys* as well?"

Clare hollered at her friend. "Partner, we have a problem. This young lady has been on the school grounds not fifteen minutes. She's done the unthinkable—fallen in love with the stupid mountain. She doesn't like our trees. I doubt that she's even thirteen, and already she's asking after the boys." She gave Rianna the look. "Wait till Miss Clark hears about *this*."

"That's not what I meant," Rianna groaned. She sighed as she switched hands." How far do we have to go? These books of mine are damn heavy. I was thinking to ask some of the boys to help us carry my trunk—"

"You'll make Miss Clark faint. You also cussed. She hates that as well. Three strikes. She discourages fraternizing with the boys. As Mr. Benson's second-in-command, she's one to keep an eye open for. She never got married." Bianca lowered her voice, glanced around. "She hates men. Boys are men-in-training as far as she is concerned and are anyway not allowed in the girl's dorms." She bounced along in silence for a second or two and then chirped, "We're over halfway."

"Okay, but where *is* everybody?"

"It's Saturday afternoon, Missy. The hostel dwellers are out for the weekend," Clare offered, "and those who stayed in went to watch the rugby."

"Don't you guys like rugby?"

"Someone had to participate in the 'welcoming party' for this lass from Pietersburg." Bianca pouted her lips. "The special student who's a week late."

"I-I-It's awfully nice of you guys . . . ."

"Yeah, yeah . . . you're welcome, but Miss Clark didn't leave us much choice," Clare muttered.

"Can we at least take a rest?" Rianna pleaded as she lowered her side of the trunk, wiping the perspiration from her forehead.

Clare put her end down and immediately grabbed Bianca by the sleeve, pulling her toward the trunk. "Your turn."

"I have a bad back," Bianca muttered as she steered away.

"Oh, *please*, drama queen." Clare pushed her friend out of the way and picked up her end. "Mr. Read would be interested to know *how* you injured your back. He won't excuse you from gym class."

Her friend refused to answer and walked ahead, nose in the air.

"What about servants?" Rianna asked as she picked up her end. "Can't they at least help us?"

"Servants?" Clare laughed. "Where do you come from? A castle? You'll find out—this is not a hotel. Another one of Miss Clark's arrangements—they are called domestic workers—they are not our *servants*." She shrugged. "Those that we do have are off till tomorrow."

Rianna cleared her throat. "In Zambia each household had a *cooky*, a houseboy, and a *bwalo boy*."

Bianca whistled and bowed. "Oh-la-la! We have royalty in our midst."

Rianna groaned and rolled her eyes. "That's not true. Even the poorest missionary in the Mission field had Chichewa people who helped them in their households. It created jobs for the locals. It stimulated the economy . . . ."

"Three servants per family. Stimulate the economy." Bianca wheezed from indignation as she spun toward Rianna, who moaned as she carried the trunk, following Clare. "My dear child, seems you are going to keep the teachers of Westerford High on their toes—which is not a bad thing in and of itself. But, do you want a revolution in the country? Three servants?" She shook her head. "Be grateful if you get *one* someday."

"Settle down, everyone. Bianca Brown, why don't you be a sweetheart and hold the door?"

The two girls turned into the bedroom with the trunk, while the third one who held the door open stuck her tongue out at Clare. She and Rianna lowered the trunk next to one of two single beds, the one closest to the window.

RIANNA dropped her shoulder bag on the bed, oblivious of the other girls as she pulled the curtains apart. "The *mountain*," she sighed, and sat down on the bed, inhaling the vista. The next moment she shrieked and performed a victory dance. When she stopped and faced the older girls, her face turned crimson. "I'm sorry . . . . But I'll be able to see the mountain every morning when I wake up, and every evening when—"

Clare groaned. "Spare me, Missy from Zambia. I told you . . . six months and you'll be cured."

Rianna laughed as she lurched forward and gave each girl a quick hug, a peck on the cheek and a thank-you. Both older girls squealed.

Clare was the first to clear her throat, straighten her blazer and skirt, and resume the role of student council leader. In a formal voice, she recited to the newcomer how the rest of the weekend would play out. She told Rianna when she would meet the staff and teachers, and when the other students. If she wanted to unpack a bit and rest, the two of them would come and get her in an hour's time for supper in the dining hall. By that time the rugby fans would be back as well.

As the two seniors turned to leave, Rianna called out, "Excuse me, ladies. Bianca . . . you said a white family should be grateful if they got *one* servant to help with household duties one day . . . ?"

"I never said *white*, but they'll have to. The country is changing—"

"I don't understand. If there are so many black people in South Africa—surely there couldn't be a shortage of servants, of workers—"

Both Clare and Bianca burst out laughing.

Clare raised her hands. "Enough questions, Rianna Vermeulen. Unpack!" She ushered Bianca toward the door, then paused. "You'll find the Republic quite different from Zambia. The people are different too—their aspirations included. They not only speak different languages. There's a vast unhappiness here. It's peaceful, on the surface. Nothing has been the same . . . for years now . . . not since the Sharpeville killings and the Langa uprising in 1960." She narrowed her eyes, sizing Rianna up. "On top of that, every non-White person now has to carry a passbook."

Rianna's hands grew quiet on her trunk's lock. "Won't *I* have to get a passbook when I turn sixteen?"

Clare shook her head. "You have *much* to learn. See you in an hour."

Five

"I cannot give my permission for a project on such a topic."
Mrs. Knox adjusted her glasses, her lips a bitter line. She crossed her arms as she rose from her desk.

"But you said we could decide *ourselves* about an appropriate topic." Rianna fidgeted next to the teacher's desk. "Provided it was about individuals who made a social and political impact in the world, during the last hundred and fifty—"

"I know what I said."

"So I can do it?" Rianna bounced around the table toward the older woman, who knocked her chair backward in her haste to sidestep the girl who seemed intent on hugging her.

"No, you can't!" Rianna froze. Mrs. Knox's slim frame, clad in black, stood like an aspen in winter, stripped of its leaves and its softness.

"But what's *wrong* with 'The hidden motives behind the assassinations of J.F. Kennedy and Mahatma Gandhi—'"

"*Everything.*" Mrs. Knox had Rianna by the arm and marched her back to her school desk and made her sit. "For starters, it's not a topic for standard six students."

Rianna jumped back up, mouth open to speak, but Mrs. Knox pushed her back down, raising her index finger. "Second, those are morbid topics—"

"I'll *make* it interesting."

"Choose a *different* topic, child." Mrs. Knox spun around and retreated to the sanctuary of her desk. She busied herself with the horn-rimmed bifocals—it was difficult getting used to the elusive focus point.

Rianna's hand shot up. "Pardon me, Mrs. Knox, but if I add a third section about the shooting of Archduke Franz Ferdinand and his spouse in 1914, it will definitely—"

"No, no, *no.*" Mrs. Knox groaned, dropping her head in her arms before straightening up. Her arms rose like an umpire counting out a floored boxer. "No more! *Silence,* Vermeulen!"

She turned to her blackboard, stood on tiptoe, and wrote in large unhurried cursive letters—as high as she could manage. She was determined to fill every square inch of its surface. Doing so always helped her relax. "1836—*Die Groot Trek.*" The Great Move. The class forgotten, she continued writing.

Dusting the powder from her hands, she finally faced the class. "Get out your notebooks and take notes." Her eyes bore down at Rianna, challenging her to say another word.

The fourteen-year-old shrugged her shoulders and dug into her satchel for her pen and her history notebook.

When the bell rang and children scraped their chairs back to leave, Mrs. Knox called out above the din, "Vermeulen, at my desk."

Brenda Knox remained seated at her desk and waited until the last student had left the room and had closed the door, before she indicated a desk in the front for Rianna to sit down at. Then she wrote for several more minutes, ignoring the girl. When she walked around her desk, her eyes drilled into her student.

"*Why* do you defy me?"

"But, *Mrs. Knox* . . . ."

Brenda Knox stepped closer—her perfume snuggled like a Roman cloak around Rianna, making her sneeze. Mrs. Knox scrunched her nose. "I cannot allow it—you making a fool of me in class. How do you know about Franz Ferdinand? That's only in the standard nine syllabus—"

Rianna jumped to her feet. "I *love* history."

Brenda Knox groaned. She shook her head. In all her years as history teacher.

"Does that mean I can do my topic, Mrs. Knox?"

"Absolutely not! Sit *down*." The teacher did an about turn and paced in front of the blackboard. "Why can't you choose one of the Groot Trek leaders, such as Louis Trichardt or Hendrik Potgieter, or even Jan Cilliers?"

It was Rianna's turn to groan. "But Mrs. Knox . . . *everyone* is writing about them."

"What's wrong with that?"

"I am intrigued by more recent world history . . . the nineteenth century is so long ago. Please, Mrs. Knox. Allow me. I won't let you down—"

Mrs. Knox slammed both her hands on her desk, "Don't you *get it*, child? I said *no!*"

Rianna zoned out as her teacher's voice droned on and on, explaining how she expected the students to do their research, but on appropriate topics if you please. She watched her teacher from underneath half-lowered lids—she dared not roll her eyes. Teacher was being unreasonable. How does one convince the doing-everything-by-the-book-and-stick-to the-syllabus lady?

At long last the teacher became silent. She had stopped her pacing and stood in front of the window now, gazing outside. It was unclear whether she breathed. It seemed she had forgotten about Rianna.

"*Come,*" Mrs. Knox hissed as she made for the door. "You're set in your ways. There's only *one* place for children like you."

Rianna stood rooted. Her chest heaved. Crimson crept up her neck. She shuddered, blinking, as if that would free her. This has never happened before—her seeing the images during broad daylight. The nightmares always attacked at night—when she was alone in bed—long after lights-out time. She whimpered. The man's maniacal laugh, the ropes biting into her wrists. It was darker than night in the back of the truck.

A cough at the door made Rianna's eyes snap open. Mrs. Knox held the door, motioning with her head. "Don't try my patience, Missy."

IT WAS the end of the school day, and the cleaning staff scurried through the deserted building with brooms and carts as the grim-faced history teacher marched her student to the administrative block. "*Wait* here," she instructed Rianna. They had woven their way past the surprised secretary in the front office.

The teacher's glowing face reappeared from behind the principal's door, motioning Rianna closer. Rianna squeezed through the door like a convict on death row—then slumped into the indicated chair and mumbled a greeting at the silver-haired man. Mr. Benson stood in front of the floor-to-ceiling window, impassive, in a three-piece suit. He nodded in Rianna's direction.

Mrs. Knox turned state prosecutor. The winter aspen appeared to have been struck by lightning—it spewed fire.

Time ceased in Mr. Benson's office.

The only indication that the principal hadn't fallen asleep was that he tilted his head from time to time as the teacher stated her case. Only when the prosecutor ran out of steam did the judge turn toward the accused.

"How plead you, Miss Vermeulen?" His face was turned away from the teacher, making it possible for the fourteen-year-old to see him rolling his eyes, twitching his brows.

"Sir?" Rianna's eyes darted from principal to teacher.

"You heard Mr. Benson's question!"

His easy smile encouraged Rianna—his face was still turned away from Mrs. Knox.

"I didn't mean to be disrespectful, sir. It's just that I love history so much. Especially international and the early twentieth-century period . . . ."

When Mr. Benson turned to Mrs. Knox with knotted brows, Rianna continued. "And *all* the other kids are already doing the different aspects of the *Groot Trek,* sir."

The educator straightened his lanky frame, his eyes fixed, first on the accused, then on the accuser. He pulled a face. "How many words for the essay, Mrs. Knox?"

"Fifteen hundred, sir."

Mr. Benson clasped his hands behind his back and paced in front of the wide window. No one said a word. When the pacing stopped, the man rubbed his chin and addressed the accused.

"Why don't we make it three thousand?"

He turned his head toward Mrs. Knox. "As punishment for her insubordination, but we allow her to stick to her *original* topic." He coughed into his fist. "I've always been intrigued by the circumstances surrounding the events in Dallas in 1963. Perhaps this young lady—"

Mrs. Knox snapped to her feet. "But, *sir!*"

"*Thank you*, Mrs. Knox. I believe it'll be punishment enough to double the word count, don't you agree?"

He maintained eye contact with the teacher until she nodded in agreement.

"Good." Mr. Benson turned back to Rianna. "Do *not* disappoint me, Miss Vermeulen. You may go."

He gestured for the teacher to remain behind as Rianna slipped through the door, avoiding her teacher's eyes. She had to be quick—adults often changed their minds.

Rianna bolted from the school's offices—her shoulder bag bobbing, thrown far back as she flew around the corners, arms flailing. She yelled when she rounded the corner into the main hallway too fast, slipped on the polished linoleum, and ended up scrambling on all fours. But she hardly cared. Her eagerness to reach the connecting hallway with the hostel was overwhelming—there she'd be safe.

An off-key whistle behind her made her stop in her tracks.

"Hey, *Rianna*. Wait up!" Jess Taylor, her roommate, bounced closer and grabbed her hand, pulling her along.

"What are *you* still doing here?" Rianna panted, trying to catch her breath as she ran alongside her friend.

Jess pouted her lips. "I had to see that you're okay. That's what friends do. See . . . you're *ghastly* pale."

Rianna pulled free. "I'm *fine*."

Jess Taylor narrowed her eyes. How could she tell her friend about the sleep-talking, the nightmares? Perhaps she should discuss it with Miss Clark. Many a night she had been woken by her roommate's thrashing in her bed across the room, mumbling, sometimes shouting weird names and talking of strange places—like a soul squirming in pain.

Of course she was worried. Rianna needed help.

"I had to make sure the witch didn't get you banished to *Robben Island*."

Rianna laughed, then glanced around and whispered, "Mr. Benson was *so* cool. My punishment is to double the word count—*three thousand*."

"*That's it?*"

"That's it—with the original topic of my choice."

"She must *hate* you now."

"But it was Mr. *Benson*—"

"You've made an enemy in Mrs. Knox."

Rianna shrugged as she hooked arms with Jessica Taylor and climbed the stairs to their room. "I wasn't disrespectful *at all*—"

"Nothing to do with respect. You *thought* outside the syllabus. *Her* syllabus. How dare you?"

Six

Rianna's essay, titled "Possible Motives Behind the Assassinations of J.F. Kennedy, Mahatma Gandhi and Archduke Franz Ferdinand," ran 3010 words. A typed copy was made available to Mr. Benson in the front office.

Jessica Taylor's insight into the psyche of their history teacher proved to be prophetic. Rianna, under the close scrutiny of her friend, opted for an indefinite ceasefire. For the remainder of the year she refrained from speaking her mind—that is, in the history class of Mrs. Knox. She completed each and every assignment and essay as per the standard six syllabus guidelines—nothing more and nothing less, and always on time.

RIANNA groaned as she rolled on her stomach. "*Why* are you up?" She stared at the figure in front of the window, then moaned. "It's

Sunday morning—have *mercy*. We don't need to be ready until nine." She blinked several times, rubbed her eyes, and pulled the pillow over her head. "It's still *dark* out."

"I couldn't sleep." Jessica ran her hands down the diaphanous inner curtains, then pulled the heavy drapes apart, eliciting an even louder protest from her roommate. "Look . . . the east is lighting up." She cocked her head, a grin spreading over her face. "You can even see your beloved mountain—"

"Aghhh . . . . *Stuff* the mountain for once."

Jess shrugged. "You had that *dream* again."

Rianna rolled on her back and propped the pillow behind her head. She yawned. "*Everybody* dreams."

Jess turned away from the window. "Not as much as you do."

"How do you *know* I was dreaming?"

Jess plopped down on the foot of her friend's bed, swung her legs up, rested her chin in her hands, and peered at her friend with gentle eyes. "Because you *talk*"—then added in staccato—"at night in your bed when *you're not awake*."

Rianna was not known for being a pushover. "What did I say, Miss Know-it-all?" The dreams were her secret. Her private cross—hers alone.

"Who is *Mapopa*?"

Rianna sucked in her breath. In spite of her still being in bed, a blanket wrapped around her shoulders, shiver after shiver shook her body. She clenched her teeth, saying nothing.

"*Rianna?*"

"I'm *fine*." Rianna pushed Jessica's hand away.

"Before last night you only mumbled and thrashed about in your sleep . . . I could never make out the words."

Jessica returned to the window and pressed her nose against the pane, drinking in the vista, waiting on her friend. Each morning they were rewarded with this spectacle: the mountain exposed in all its naked glory as the sun inched from far behind the ocean.

Rianna cleared her throat. "*Mapopa* . . . . He was a young man in Zambia who meant me harm—"

"You also called out to *Lukas* and *Anthony*—"

"I said . . . all that?"

"You were upset with this Mapopa fellow—Lukas and Anthony you sounded more concerned about—especially Anthony."

Rianna let out a muffled cry and pulled her knees to her chin, clasping her legs. She watched Jessica through downcast eyes. "I'm so *ashamed*."

Her head dropped between her knees as silent sobs shook her shoulders.

Jessica Taylor slipped to the head of the bed and pulled Rianna tight against her side, stroking her disordered mane. She allowed her friend to cry—until the tears stopped and she went quiet.

The two girls, arms locked around one another, huddled in silence, rocking from side to side—as if their embrace could ward off all the horrors.

Only when the first golden bands inched into the room and onto her bed did Rianna sit back, relax her clasp on her friend, and invite her to step aboard. She took Jessica to the land of the Luangwa valley—took her along on the inside of the Chevrolet truck, which had reeked of flour, gasoline, and unwashed bodies, when her hands were bound behind her back. It was July 1964.

It was minutes before nine by the time the two roommates of Westerford High, on the foothills of Table Mountain, reached the outskirts of Paishuko Village in eastern Zambia, where three shots had been fired in close succession, months before.

It was Jessica's turn to gasp. "Shouldn't you tell Miss Clark at least? She'll know what to—"

Rianna wiped a hand across her eyes like a withered grandmother. "What can *she* do?" Her voice purged of its fire. "What's done, is done—"

"But the nightmares—"

"*Dreams.*"

Jessica grasped her friend's hands. "Call them what you wish—it's getting worse, Ree."

Rianna pulled her hands free, casting her eyes.

"Mr. Benson?"

"Why do you want me to tell? They're *adults*."

"Doctors and therapists are adults too. *They* can help. One of them may understand . . . ."

"They'll say it was all *my* fault."

"Good heavens, Ree, you were kidnapped. Mapopa *assaulted* you! You suffer from delayed shock. The dreams are getting worse. They not only interfere with *your* sleep; they're affecting mine. This situation is affecting both our well-beings. You need a psychologist—"

"How do you know all this?"

"You're not the only one who reads a lot. And my uncle is a doctor."

"We don't have a school psychologist."

"What about Mrs. Knox?"

Rianna choked. "Then I'd rather die." She sniffled loudly. "Perhaps . . . I can tell Mr. Read."

"He's a *bodybuilder.* He's a man." Jessica started pulling day clothes on.

"He's a gym teacher who *reads.*" Rianna blushed a second time. "I trust him."

"Oh-la-laa . . . ." Jessica dramatized, hands held wide as if reading a newspaper. "Gym teacher breaks yet another schoolgirl's heart." She bent down and slipped her shoes on. "We'd better hurry—it's five past."

Rianna plopped flat on her back. "Can't we skip Sunday chapel this once?"

"Not if you're staying in over the weekend. Miss Clark will notice."

"She's a witch."

Jessica dragged her friend upright. "She's a lonely spinster who's married to her job."

Rianna groaned. "Like a Mother Superior."

"Be careful—she has ears—she'll make you go to confessional."

RIANNA did not discuss her distressing dreams with her teachers, her friend's concerns notwithstanding. Jess was sworn to silence.

Not a living soul could know.

"It will get better, I promise," became Rianna's refrain.

Herself a mere child, Jessica Taylor conceded. Rianna was right: they—doctors, psychologists, and psychiatrists—may blame her for what had happened.

What would happen, Rianna had argued, if the adults decided she was insane?

"There's nothing wrong with me, Jess. What if those smart doctors decide I'm mad? Unstable even? It's only dreams."

"Nightmares," Jess insisted.

"They may declare me mad—make me end up in *Tara*."

"Tara?"

"I read about it in the library—it's a fancy mental hospital near Johannesburg. Do you want me to end up in a mental hospital, Jess?"

Her friend moaned, shaking her head. "I want your dreams to *stop*."

"Jess, are you saying there's something wrong with me?"

Another groan, another shake of the head, another firm embrace as one friend succumbed to the relentless pressure of the other—agreeing to secrecy in the name of loyalty and camaraderie.

Seven

THE LOVELY MR. READ. JUNE 1965

*M*r. Rupert Read's popularity was no flight of fiction or fad. When Rianna first heard the other students whispering and swooning about the gym teacher, she had only smirked. She was above rolling her eyes. *Ridiculous.*

"He's so cool," many whispered.

"Nonsense, he's *sexy.*"

"Oh, he's into bodybuilding."

The rumours abounded. Soon, it was difficult to discern fact from fiction.

"That's nothing—he was at the Olympics—gymnastics. Nineteen-sixty in Rome."

"Really?"

Indeed.

Without exception, both boys and girls, standards six through ten, were of a similar opinion—their gym teacher walked with titans—a man of legend. Half of the girls had a crush on him, while the boys tried to emulate him—soon pushing and nagging the principal to fund a "weight room" for the school.

By the end of 1965, Westerford High opened its "state of the art" weight room. It boasted two benches, protective rubber mats, a rack with bars and free weights, and—against an entire wall—floor-to-ceiling mirrors. A new sanctuary for dreamers and hopeful body sculptors.

Whether Mr. Read was aware of his celebrity status, especially his effect on the girls, always remained a mystery to Rianna—he never let on. Neither could she fathom when he did his own intense workouts. To remain chiseled as he was required fierce discipline and hard work—yet whenever she ran into him, his nose was always buried in a book. He seemed the eternal bookworm, not an image-obsessed bodybuilder.

JESSICA Taylor became one of the early sufferers of gym-teacher infatuation.

"*What* are you doing?" Rianna whispered into the dark interior, listening to her roommate's panting. It was long after lights-out.

"Push-ups."

Rianna groaned as she turned her bed lamp on, squinting her eyes. "*Really*, Jess Taylor?"

"Eleven . . . twelve . . . ."

"We do have gym class tomorrow."

The panting increased, mixed with wheezes. "Fifteen . . . . He has to notice me. Sixteen . . . ."

"Who? That Martin boy in standard eight?"

"Twenty-one . . . ." A snort and a cough followed. "No, silly. Twenty-three . . . . Rupert Read!"

"*Mister* Read?"

A thud followed when her roommate collapsed on her bed-side mat. "Twenty-five. Of course *Mr. Read.*"

"You're out of your—"

A shoe thudded against the wall behind Rianna.

"I *hate* you, Rianna Vermeulen. I don't have your gorgeous breasts. I have nothing but two sunny-side-ups that he'll hardly notice. So I have to work on my biceps and triceps and abs. Do you have *no* compassion for my wounded soul?"

It did not help when Rianna snickered in her pillow. From the other bed she only received a suppressed sob.

"Don't you think he's a bit old for you?"

A second shoe crashed into the wall above her head. "He's only *thirty-one.*"

"He's seventeen years your senior—"

Another sob followed. "I still *hate* you."

Rianna turned the light out. "Haven't you noticed the looks James Martin gives you?"

Silence from the other bed. Then a deep sigh. "James Martin isn't into push-ups."

"Push-ups can be *taught.*"

An even deeper sighed shuddered through the room. "No wonder Mrs. Knox dislikes you."

"Good night, Jess."

"'Good night, dream-crusher."

WHAT RIANNA loved most about Mr. Read wasn't his Greek-god physique—a glorious bonus—it was that he was instrumental in the founding of the running and hiking clubs at the school. Joining the two clubs saved her life—prevented her from spiraling into an unfathomable pit of self-pity and despair once her altercation with Mrs. Knox became common knowledge. Rianna was able to distance herself from accusing eyes—other students thinking her some aberration. How dared she venture outside the prescribed syllabus? Just because she was born in the African bush didn't grant her the right to stand out. And how could any normal teenager love history? About the nightmares the children couldn't know—Jess was sworn to secrecy at least once a week.

When Rianna went for a run, she had to explain herself to nobody. She only had to show up and place one foot in front of the other. Mr. Read had three requirements—wear appropriate running attire (which needn't be fancy), be on time, and put your heart into your activity. It didn't matter whether she ran hard, far, or fast—or not at all—she was the master of her ship, according to Mr. Read. For a considerable time, she didn't care about winning. She craved only the freedom the running brought. The escape. A legitimate way of getting off the grounds. Over the ensuing years, though, she began to crave the highs that intense exercise brought. The exhilaration. The burn. The glow. Especially afterwards, when she felt invincible.

JESS TAYLOR joined the running group the day she got word about its existence. She didn't care for hiking. The mere thought of carrying a backpack, clambering up and down mountains and footpaths, was so *primitive*. Since her youthful chest lagged behind in its budding process, and her biceps and triceps remained modest in size, in spite of being able to perform fifty proper push-ups without rest by the middle of the year—Jess soon found her calling in running. Mr. Read would have no option but to notice her then, in spite of her lack of upper-body contours.

Mr. Read, like everyone else, noticed Jess's enthusiasm—her obsession—she always finished in a comfortable time, ahead of everyone, including her roommate and the other team members. However, he remained indifferent. His rules were crystal clear—each student received the same respectful treatment—there were no favourites.

In the beginning, most of the students, the redhead included, couldn't care less about their running times—so taken were they with the routes, with the scenery, which included not only the *fynbos* and the mountains but the chiseled, toned, and tanned contours of their gym instructor—having their own demigod celebrity close at hand.

The route depended on the time at their disposal, and the weather—Mr. Read had shorter and longer routes for the students to run. The run to the Kirstenbosch Botanical Gardens, to the west of the mountain foothills, soon became their staple run, a comfortable six-mile run there and back—with little gradient—the ideal run for a lazy day. The students who pleaded for "a shorter run, please, sir," soon had ample time for regret. Mr. Read found the perfect solution—a quick two-mile dash, he called it— to the Rhodes Memorial. But to get there, they had to run uphill.

November was the only dry month—when it didn't drizzle every single day. June was the worst—moist and miserable—the almost-monsoon month. Mr. Read's intention became clear enough: to toughen them up—he loved boot-camping his students. But he had limits—there was no wicked bone in his body.

MANY A day, Rianna wished she could take her umbrella with her on the run, if not for the fear of becoming the laughing stock of the running club. It was no shame to be wet, but it was no great honour or joy either. *One day—one day I will run with my umbrella, and no one will dare say a word.*

What endeared Rupert Read to the students most was that he always ran with them. He wasn't only talk. He was not the general-sitting-at-home-giving-orders kind of leader. The students seldom complained—they were allowed to *look* at him. Drool behind his back. Dream alongside him. He apparently often remarked to Mr. Benson, "I have to keep an eye on those younger ones, sir."

Rianna never tired of the view from the Rhodes Memorial. The runners were given five precious minutes to appreciate the view from the steps before heading back. To the left and to the right, as far as the eyes could roam, stretched the outskirts of the city and the entire Cape Flats, into infinity, where the blues of the sky and the mountains bled into each other. And toward the north, and the south—the Hottentots Holland Mountains beckoned with their secretive turquoise shadows.

By the fourth month Mr. Read stepped up the challenge—he came up with a third run, the perfect distance for a Saturday morning—a seven-and-a-half-mile run one way to the *Kloof*

Corner, to the lower cable car station. They would run along the foothills of Devil's Peak, past the University of Cape Town, round the butt-end of Table Mountain, and approach the mountain from the front, from Table Bay's side. The gradient was considerable—the reward equally grand.

With this run they were granted half an hour to enjoy the view and catch their breath, before heading back—weather depending. If it dribbled and the weather was horrible, the break was only long enough to catch their breaths and fill up on water. Rianna cherished those drawn-out minutes of rest of apparent solitude. Her fellow runners knew she preferred to sit to the side, apart— drinking in the view of Table Bay and the world beyond, but on her own. Her mango tree and the river, north of the Zambezi, belonged to the past—watching the bay helped to ease that pain.

THIS HABIT of Rianna's of sitting on her own during rest-times never ceased to irk Jessica. She struggled to accept the fact that her roommate would tolerate her only on the condition of shutting-up and sitting on one spot for the entire half-hour like a marble statue. One day, unable to help herself, Jessica plopped down an arm's length from Rianna, daring her friend to respond. Rianna's back went rigid as she turned away. "Why are you so bloody arrogant?"

Rianna winced. "It's not intentional." She peered into the distant north. "Is it too much to ask—to be allowed these precious few minutes, once a week, to drink with my eyes as much as I can?"

"You're such a drama queen."

Rianna shrugged as she faced her friend. "It's balm for my soul. I still miss Katete—the river and the bush and my people."

"*My people*. When will we be good enough, Miss African princess?" Jessica lurched to her feet, glaring at her roommate, "If you could have your way, you'd rip out all the centuries-old oak trees and shove mango trees in their place, wouldn't you?"

"Jess, you're twisting my words."

"*Hah*. I knew it!" Jessica hollered as she stomped down the steps and joined Mr. Read and the rest of the children, preparing for the return run.

Rianna suppressed a sob. Below her, for a thousand yards, stretched the veld-covered mountainside, speckled with *fynbos*, dotted with colour, before the neighbourhoods with houses and tree-lined streets took over. The streets zig-zagged lazily down toward Table Bay, then ran into narrow roads that lined the wharf, skirting the endless comings and goings of ships and boats and people.

To their far left, the outcrop of Signal Hill framed the view, the wide hollow of the bay underlining the fading horizon. To their right, to the northwest, Bloubergstrand was hidden in the infinite mist-covered distance. And beyond it there lay a coastline that ran north another five hundred miles until it reached the Orange River, on the outskirts of the Namib Desert. Even on a clear day, which was a rare occasion, the human eye seldom could see that far.

Never would Rianna leave, run down the mountain, and not feel uplifted—breathing the mountain air, the veld, the sugar bush—her soul soaring—ready to face another week in an unpredictable world.

She sighed. Shame on Jessica. Her friend must have started her period that morning—that would explain her unexpected bitchiness. She ambled over to the group of runners.

To THAT third route, Mr. Read added a fourth: a nine-mile run from the school to Camps Bay. This one was the toughest, but also the loveliest. They would not stop at Kloof Corner but would instead head on toward the neck, down through the valley between Signal Hill and Lion's Head, off the plateau of Table Mountain, before dropping down to a different sea—the Indian Ocean, and head down toward Clifton and Camps Bay, not far from Sea Point, marking the junction with the Atlantic—the southernmost point of Africa.

The following Saturday morning, Rianna choked on her breath during her run, not from exhaustion but in surprise to find Mr. Read waiting on them as they reached the neck, the moment the bay came in sight and they could see the other ocean. Jess, as always, was one step ahead of her. What superpowers had made the teacher get there ahead of them? It was impossible not to notice his glistening physique, accentuated by his scant running clothes.

"*Come on* Vermeulen, you're slacking."

"Sir?" Rianna panted as they passed him.

He joined them running. "You heard me. Show me you can reach the beach ahead of Taylor."

"She's *faster* than me, sir."

Jessica laughed as she immediately pushed harder—she loved showing everyone she *was* the best.

Rianna grimaced as she remained one step behind. They were all breathing hard.

Rupert Read laughed out loud. "I disagree, Vermeulen. Jessica's only more determined. Why don't you channel the energy from your nightmares into your running? Then you'll kick dust—"

Rianna shrieked as she took off, flying ahead of her roommate and teacher, yelling over her shoulder. "How *could* you, Jess?"

Jessica stretched her strides, calling after her friend. "Let me explain, Ree!"

The redhead only sprinted faster. "Traitor. I *hate* you!"

Mr. Read stretched to keep up. "What was that about?"

Jessica's breaths came in gasps, "You're not supposed to know, sir . . . no one was supposed to know . . . about her freakish dreams—"

"They're not freakish, Jessica Taylor. You swore you wouldn't tell!"

Both girls were crying now as they ran, faster and faster downhill. The gym teacher did his best to keep up with the crying girls who careened downhill while he struggled for words.

"You know the nightmares visit *every* night . . . ."

"*Traitor!*"

"I was desperate!"

"I *hate* you!" The redhead gave another scream as she increased the distance between them. *I'll show Mr. Read I can run. The bastard—channel my energy—how dare he.*

RIANNA arrived a comfortable ten seconds ahead of her roommate and gym teacher at the parking lot at the beach—their endpoint.

She jumped the low log-and-chain fence and then stood with hands resting on her knees, leaning forward, panting, facing the ocean. *Thank you, Lord. I will never tire of these gifts. First the mountain, and the running, and now the bay.*

She squinted against the morning glare, blinding on the water. The melancholic screeching of a handful of seagulls swept over her as the birds dove, like air acrobats in formation, skimming the surf—calling, dipping, then sweeping lower, only to shoot up the next, up and up—ever squawking.

A shadow made Rianna spin around.

"I'm *sorry*, Ree."

"You *promised*—"

"I had no right, I know." Jessica's modest bosom heaved as she caught her breath. "And yet . . . I had to tell *somebody*. I thought you said Mr. Read . . . ."

Rianna plopped down in the sand, shielded her eyes with one hand as she glared at her friend. "Why didn't you rather tell Miss Clark? Why him?" Rianna nudged her head. "I will now die of shame . . . what does he think of me?"

"That you're brave."

"Bullshit." Rianna wiped the tears from her eyes. "Did you tell him Mapopa cut my bra straps with a hunting knife?" Her voice broke. "Then kissed me while I was roped to those trees . . . and, had his hand down my—"

"Please stop." Jessica sniffled loud, raised her hands as if in defense. She shook her head. "I didn't tell him that part."

Rianna shrugged.

Jessica cleared her throat. "He'll be able to *help* us."

"Us?"

"Okay—*you*."

"So now I need *help*?"

"Ree . . . ." Jessica reached and touched Rianna's warm arm. "But he knows people who can help . . . ."

As if electrocuted, Rianna's arm snapped away, and she clambered to her feet, first shaking the sand from her clothing, then brushing it from her legs and shoes. She shivered uncontrollably.

Mr. Read called from the parking lot.

"I don't need *his* help, or *yours*." Rianna glared at her friend, gave a sob as she crossed the low fence. "And I *trusted* you."

"Rianna . . . ."

"Don't *speak* to me."

Eight

The essence of friendship and the basics of hiking. September 1965

Miss Clark refused to grant Rianna her request—change roommates with immediate effect. She had insisted Rianna tell her what the dreams and nightmares and yelling session during the run to Camps Bay was all about. Without interrupting she listened until the redhead went quiet.

"Kiss and make up."

"But it's unforgivable, Miss. Jessica broke my trust—" Rianna choked out as she jumped from her chair in the vice-principal's office.

Miss Clark waved her arms. "*Sit down.*" She cocked her head. "You surprise me, Vermeulen. You're not perfect, you know. If it wasn't for your few good points we'd have thrown you out a long time ago." She shrugged. "Sent you back even." She turned, her gaze fixed outside, beyond the windowpane. A reluctant smile framed her face. "I never thought you'd be an ungrateful friend, though."

Rianna perched on the tip of her stool. "Miss, I'm *not*. But this is not what friends—"

"You're mistaken." Miss Clark rose from behind her desk, leaned forward, demanding the fifteen-year-old to meet her eyes. "You're a smart one, but you still have to learn about life. Jessica Taylor cares greatly about you." She stood back up. "Enough talking." She walked around the desk and steered the redhead toward the door, her voice soft. "There's no shame in what happened to you, Rianna . . . ." She squeezed her arm. "We'll find you the necessary . . . support."

When Rianna glanced at her in alarm, she added with a smile. "It's okay . . . your secret is safe with us. I know someone who does counselling."

"But I don't *need*—"

"I'm four times your age and I still don't always realize what's good for me. We'll find you help. Never mind Mrs. Simmons in the front office—I'll get in touch with you myself." She opened the door. "Now *go*." As Rianna rounded the corner, she called after her, "Be *nice* to your roommate, or I'll have your hide."

UNDER guidance and at the insistence of Miss Clark, Rianna saw a psychologist once a week for the following three months. Then the talk-sessions (or psychotherapy as Rianna soon discovered it was called) slowed down to bi-monthly, and by the end of her first year at Westerford High they took place once a month.

Maintenance therapy, Miss Clark loved to call it. It continued for two full years before she allowed Rianna to slowly phase it out. The strained relationship between Rianna and Jessica healed as 1965 rolled to a close. Like the break in a weight-bearing long bone, however, it required time to heal. Painstakingly slowly it recovered.

Rianna remained reluctant to admit—perhaps Miss Clark was not a witch after all—perhaps she knew a thing or two or three about life. A remarkable feat for a spinster.

In its early years, the hiking club had fewer members than the running club—a great surprise to Rianna. She could not fathom the students' distaste for carrying a pack on their backs. Such a small price to pay for the liberation it brought. She craved it. She had fallen in love with walking while still in the African bush. Here, in the Cape Town area, they had so much more—the bush was different, scarcer and less wild, although being under an endless sky and being outside was a similar reward. And here they had two enormous pluses—the mountains and the oceans. In her hiking boots, she was able to step places no airplane could go, or any vehicle, not even the sturdiest of Land Rovers.

If the running had opened up vistas, the hiking took it a hundred steps further. Standing on a ridge, a neck, an outcrop, a vantage rock—looking out over the vast land or ocean—remained a blessing each time. It became healing for the wounded. Those moments, those hours outdoors, was when time blurred. There, time ceased to exist, the experience became hallowed, as if inside a church—in nature's vast cathedral. And, when paying close attention, one could drink it all in, listen to the silent choirs singing the beauty of creation.

Rianna could find no words in English, Afrikaans, or Chichewa to express what she experienced. Language is finite, she learned.

Soon she gave up trying to explain to her roommate (who merely rolled her eyes) why she loved hiking, or backpacking as she called it. She pitied the students, Jess included, who knew not what they forfeited. *The loss is theirs*, she murmured, as she planted her walking stick securely and scaled higher. And yet the longing for Katete and her mango tree remained—it was where Father and Mother, PJ and Casper were. That was still home.

As with the running club, Mr. Read started the students first on day walks—training-wheel walks he called them. When the students complained, Rianna included, he assured them that the overnight walks, the week-long walks, would follow. Once they were ready. Once he was satisfied they understood the basics—grasped the principles—then they would be advanced to the next level. He made them scale the width and breadth of Table Mountain National Park, sticking to the lower foothills. If it accomplished only one thing, it instilled in them respect for the mountains. Respect for nature. Respect and knowledge—but not fear.

He cultivated in them a love for the outdoors. Made them understand the delicate balance between enjoying nature in a responsible manner, without being a killjoy or becoming obsessive. They learned basic first aid. Next, he taught them about survival. About caring for your buddies. He taught them how to read a topographical map. Why it was important to keep an eye on the time of the day, the skies, and the sun (even the moon and the stars for that matter). They learned the names of many of the trees, the shrubs, and the flowers. (But only some of the Latin names—Rupert Read was an outdoors enthusiast, not a botanist.)

Mr. Read loved to compare the mountain to a circus tiger—beautiful to behold, majestic even, something one could get used to when tamed, considering it to be a pet—only to get the fright of your life one day when the tiger roars, bares its fangs, and jumps you, attempting to sever your head from your shoulders. Only then do you discover the true nature of the beast. As painful as it may be—a tamed tiger was at heart always a wild animal, a brute, impossible to predict. Years later Rianna would recall his mantra: *never* underestimate your opponent.

It became second nature on any hike to always carry a small bag with a filled water bottle, a light-weight wind and rain jacket, a skinny hat, a small flashlight, fire-making tools, basic first aid, a plastic whistle, and emergency rations—all taking up little space. When on and around Table Mountain Mr. Read was relentless about *five* things. Always know the time (he made them wear a watch), always know the twenty-four-hour weather report (it was heresy to give the sky a mere glance before heading out); always tell someone where you are heading and when to expect you back; never be found without your basic equipment; and lastly, walk with a buddy if at all possible.

The Transkei Coast hike required special preparation. Mr. Read, true to form, did not disappoint. That particular coastline spreads over one hundred sixty miles, of which they would do a sixty-mile stretch over five days, from Port St. Johns south to Coffee Bay. He would see to it that the youngsters were ready. Consideration was even given by the Westerford School Board to make this an annual event—the Transkei hike. The hope was that it would metamorphose into an outreach opportunity for the school, become a combined project of the Xhosa language course and the athletics program, immersing the students in learning about nature, fitness, and their fellow countrymen. The hiking club members would become guinea pigs.

First, they had to graduate on the mountain foothills. Next, beach walks were added. Mr. Read had them walk from Camps Bay around Sea Point, clamber across the rocks like crabs, sprayed by the surf, and then hike across many flat beaches, until they reached Bloubergstrand on the West Coast.

It was time for Miss Gloria Whitehead to enter the hiking picture—the day the Wild Coast hike was officially added to the itinerary. She was Westerford High's Xhosa teacher. The hiking club members gave a collective gasp when Miss Whitehead was introduced as their latest hiking buddy. Their disbelief had ample grounds. Even Rianna questioned Mr. Read's sanity. The language teacher weighed in at a hundred and two pounds—with clothes and hiking boots. It was unclear how her body weight became common knowledge, but the fact remained she only filled a size four shoe and had to shop in the extra-petite section. How would she ever manage to carry a twelve-gallon backpack, never mind carry it for five consecutive days across river mouths, scale rocks, cross vast beaches, and overcome sea-currents? The woman was barely the size of a twelve-year-old.

Bianca Brown posed the burning question everyone feared to ask about the appropriateness of Miss Whitehead joining their ranks.

Rupert Read only laughed and warned them, "She'll kick your collective butts."

The boys snorted, the girls rolled their eyes.

Gloria Whitehead wasn't only slight, but she was also a quiet, unassuming creature—not unlike a field mouse. There was little glorious about her. She didn't even wear makeup, for goodness' sake. She smelled nice though—of cinnamon and Japanese cherry blossoms. But a five-day hiking trail, carrying her own gear?

The students were dead wrong. During a day hike up the mountain, Miss Whitehead reached the upper cable station a step behind Mr. Read—both of them an entire minute ahead of the front runners among the student hikers. James Martin, a standard eight student known for his loose mouth, shot from the hip as soon as the students caught up to the two teachers, comfortably seated outside the cafeteria. "Shame on you, Miss Whitehead," he huffed. "I thought we had agreed not to use the cable car to reach the top." He gulped from his water bottle. "*Speak* to her, Mr. Read."

The other young hikers shouted and cheered as they caught their breaths, dancing around the Xhosa-language teacher, who had turned crimson. She took her time before responding. "With your blessing, Rupert, I would like to take the cable car down, *with* James, and then hike back up *immediately*. Alongside him." She cocked her head toward the school boy and grinned. "Are you up for it, James? Then we can test your theory that I'm a fake?"

It was Rianna who took the lead and chanted, "Challenge! Challenge!"

The chanting students surrounded James Martin, who now looked concerned.

"James?" Mr. Read asked.

"But it will take *two* hours, sir." Everyone laughed.

Gloria Whitehead was ready. "Not if you hike with me—it will only take us an *hour.*"

Rianna shouted louder. "Challenge! Challenge!"

James Martin turned red as he lowered his head, mumbling an apology, fidgeting with his water bottle.

"What was that, James?" Rupert Read insisted.

"Sorry, Miss Whitehead." James Martin straightened up. "I'll definitely take you up on the invitation *next* time. Then I'll come better prepared and have my *monitoring team* and observers set up along the entire route." He made a half-bow and withdrew to an open table farther away under loud applause.

By DECEMBER students who belonged to both the running and hiking club had an established routine—early Saturday morning was for running to Camps Bay and Sunday morning, after church, was for hiking up the mountain and back down. Taking the cable car cost money—even a one-way ticket was excessive.

Mr. Read and Miss Whitehead took turns accompanying them on the Sunday hikes. As always, his philosophy remained: safety first. Being surprised by impenetrable fog in the middle of the day was not uncommon. The unpredictability of Table Mountain's mist, the young people would soon learn, was like that of a man scorned—when its fury was unleashed—devastation was sudden, often certain, and not uncommonly severe.

Nine

A STURDY WALKING STICK

Rianna, much to the chagrin of her fellow hikers, insisted on hiking with a walking stick—at all times. "I'll be as good as *naked* without my walking stick," was her defense, when pressed.

James Martin, a short step behind her, elbowed his friend, Andries Steenkamp. "I'm not sure how much hiking we'll get done the day you don't wear clothes, Vermeulen." He ogled her trim bottom.

She spun around and challenged the two snickering boys, her stick held as a sword. "Watch your tongue, Martin," she hissed.

But just as Martin opened his mouth to retort, Miss Whitehead called out to her from the front of the line of hikers.

"Coming, Miss!"

Columns of mist had crawled around the summit and plateau since midday. "Rianna!" the teacher called again, this time from higher up.

They had reached the halfway mark up the mountain and fingers of mist now twirled around their shins and ankles, making them creatures who walked on stumps, as if plodding on feet growing from their knees. Rianna paused so that the boys were forced to catch up with her; while she waited for them, she waved at Miss Whitehead. Then she pointed at the fog. "*This* is why I carry a rod, James. It keeps me safe—when conditions change."

He smirked as he jumped from rock to rock. "It's because you're scared you might run into a wild cat."

Rianna bared her teeth and lurched at him. One hand was suddenly a claw and the stick a spear. She growled. "I at least have a *spear* to defend myself against a Cape lion or leopard."

Andries Steenkamp laughed as he sidestepped her attack. "All the bigger cats have been driven from these mountains . . . you'll be lucky if you set eyes on a little *rooikat.*"

"*Little* red cat? They're big enough to hurt you." But her spear became a walking stick once again, since by this time they had caught up with Miss Whitehead who, agile as a mountain gazelle, had remained ahead of the group throughout their ascent.

"Okay guys, head count." The fog surrounded them in dense columns now. They could be five feet apart and yet invisible.

James Martin threw his head back and howled as Miss Whitehead called the names. "Martin? Adams? Brown . . . ."

James gave another howl, which resulted in a quick jab from Rianna.

"What was that for?" he hissed.

"You're making fun of her."

"So?"

"Pick on someone your own size."

"Martin! You've got your whistle?"

"No, Miss. I'll howl." He choked laughing. "Andries and I will follow Rianna's walking stick—it will be a shining beacon—" Another poke in the ribs cut him short.

"Find your own bloody staff," Rianna barked.

"Martin, this is serious. *Pay attention*," Miss Whitehead commanded. "Remember, stay closer together." She spun around and waved. "Bianca, you form the rear guard, please!"

Banks of fog moved in and made their leader disappear from sight. "That's so neat," James sighed as he tried to capture handfuls of white twirling fog.

"Yeah, until you lose your way, or don't see a steep cliff coming up," Rianna murmured.

"You're no fun, Vermeulen. You're always such a Miss-goody-good-spoilsport-lass," Martin mumbled. "Go ahead."

"Suit yourself." Rianna took her position behind two standard-nine girls, Lilly Milner and Patricia Partridge. Once all the other hikers were ahead of her, the group continued their ascent. At regular intervals Miss Whitehead would blow her whistle or call and listen for Bianca's response from the rear. Every so often James Martin gave a confirmatory howl.

For a moment the fog cleared, and the upper cable station appeared three hundred feet above them, only to be swallowed by even more impenetrable whiteness. "Almost there, guys!" Miss Whitehead called out.

Voices and hard breathing became disembodied sounds, as hikers inched up the mountain. The aroma of *fynbos*, rotten leaves, moss, and moist earth wrapped tightly around them. One by one the hikers appeared and disappeared in the whiteness as they scaled higher.

BLOODCURDLING screams froze the team in their tracks. A growl, a hiss, a crash, shrieks, more cries, then silence.

Then everybody yelled simultaneously.

Gloria Whitehead's whistle sounded. Again and again. "*Martin? Steenkamp?*"

"*Oh shit!* Damn . . . Miss *Whitehead* . . . guys!" It was James Martin crying out from the left of the trail, far below. His voice had lost its bravado. "*Dries!* Where *are* you buddy?" Oh, *God*, it hurts!" Again, Martin's agonized voice pierced the whiteness.

"*Martin!*"

"Over *here,* Miss."

They came upon James Martin as the fog opened and closed—he crawled toward them from among fractured protea and sugar bushes, some twenty feet lower down.

"Where's Steenkamp?"

"On the ridge below where I was. He slipped further down," James panted. He brushed something from his eyes. "Oh, God. I hope he's okay. Didn't you guys see that cat . . . it must have been a cougar." His eyes darted from person to person as he pantomimed a creature the size of a lion. He was whimpering. His arms and legs were covered with bleeding scratches—several of which had puckered his flesh.

Miss Whitehead pointed at the wounds. "Cat . . . or the bushes?"

"Bushes, Ma'am."

"*Isiphukuphuku*," she mumbled under her breath. *Idiot.*

"You howled so loud, we thought the growling was you!" Rianna whispered.

James shook his head and pointed at the abyss beyond the bushes he had crawled from. "I thought the bloody lynxes sleep during the day."

Miss Whitehead, followed by Bianca, gingerly made her way to the edge of the shrubbery and rock face and peered down. "*Steenkamp?*"

"Down here, Miss!"

She had brought rope with her, of course, so she abseiled down to Andries Steenkamp. Bianca acted as her anchor. Andries had suffered a broken arm as well as deep, blood-streaked scratches on his torso and all four limbs, and his clothes were in tatters.

It took the eleven-person party an entire hour to cover the last two hundred feet to the upper cable station. There, Andries's arm was placed in a makeshift splint. No one objected to taking the cable car down the mountain instead of hiking.

For years following the incident on Table Mountain, James Martin continued to insist that it was a stray mountain lion and not a forty-pound tufted-ear red cat that had spooked him and Andries Steenkamp. Nothing less than a mountain lion had forced them to lose their footing and slip down the *krans*.

Ten

The Wild Coast. March 1966

*J*ames Martin agreed to come along on the Wild Coast hike only once Mr. Read had joined his voice to Miss Whitehall's and convinced him there were no mountain lions, red cats, or lynxes along the route. What they failed to point out, though, was that the hikers had to cross several river mouths—all potentially shark-infested. Ignorance is not without its hidden blessings.

What he didn't tell his teachers was that he had agreed only once he was certain that Rianna had signed up too.

Andries Steenkamp's fractured arm was healed, and he was deemed fit for the coastal hike, since no mountains with sheer cliffs appeared on the relevant topographical map.

At sunrise, the group of ten hikers headed out in two vehicles toward Port St. Johns, the starting point. The fast-developing storm and the darkening clouds had robbed the day of its light, turning it almost into darkness, in spite of its being only midday. The drivers, unfazed, pushed the noses of the vehicles down the winding roads, the wind whipping branches and leaves and sand across their windshields.

After dropping off the students in Port St. Johns, threatening them with death if they misbehaved while they waited for the teachers to join them, Mr. Read followed Miss White in his pickup to Coffee Bay. The hiking route was a straight line. Leaving his truck behind, the two teachers returned to Port St. Johns in Miss White's vehicle. Once they had completed the hike, they could just squeeze everybody into the back of Mr. Read's truck before heading back to the starting point to pick up the second vehicle.

Within minutes after being dropped off by the teachers, the young people had staked their claim in a corner of the local Wimpy bar, grateful to escape the foul weather. However, excitement about their upcoming adventure, combined with raging hormones, soon turned them into an unruly mob. Reprimands from both Henry and Bianca, two standard ten students, had scant effect—the youths' exuberance knew no bounds. They grew even louder.

Silence fell over the group only when the unsmiling figure of the restaurant manager loomed over them—the lady had to clear her throat three times. "Excuse me!"

"Ma'am?" Bianca unfolded herself from the booth.

No one breathed.

Outside it had become inhospitable—the heavens bullet-grey with winds whipping the rain in salvos against the wide windows. Those inside cringed each time the rain and sand and tree branches pelted the glass panes. Lightning crisscrossed the sky, each thunderbolt snapping like a gunshot at close range. How much more could the building endure? It was only mid-afternoon and of the daylight little remained.

"You guys should leave." She pointed her substantial thumb at the entrance.

"But, ma'am. The weather—"

The woman crossed her arms over her ample bosom, legs planted wide in practical flat-sole shoes, face impassive She adjusted her fire-engine-red apron. A nervous tick twitched her head as she cleared her throat. "You kids should have given more thought to the weather before you decided to turn this place on its head."

"Ma'am, I'm *really* sorry—" Bianca was ready with her award-winning smile.

"You should leave. My servers are complaining—you're scaring away customers."

Bianca deepened her smile. "I am so sorry you feel that way, Ma'am, but there are no other customers. Only that elderly couple."

Rianna scrambled to her feet, joining Bianca. "It must be the weather, don't you think, Ma—?" Lightning flashed and snapped outside, showering the gloomy interior with brilliant light, its proximity making them all jump and hide behind their arms. At one particularly vivid streak the manager staggered backward and made the sign of the cross, then offered the young people a feeble smile.

Tucking several auburn curls under her cap, she bit her lower lip as her gaze shifted between Bianca and Rianna. "Certainly, the weather plays a role, but I'm talking about *potential* customers. It affects our bottom line—our tips."

Rianna stepped forward and touched, first Bianca's, and then the woman's arm. "I *love* your hair, Ma'am. It's a shame you have to tuck it under your working-cap." When the thin line of the manager's mouth softened, Rianna continued, "Why don't I tell my friends to each order another milkshake as restitution for their horrible behaviour? They're not used to being trapped in this kind of weather, especially not in such a fine establishment. We'll each leave a proper tip. *Please* let us stay . . . ."

Gesturing first at the windows, beyond where the storm still raged, Rianna brushed the woman's arm a second time. "We're *really* sorry, and I absolutely adore your hair."

The woman patted her ponytail through her paper cap as she returned Rianna's smile. "You're such a sweetheart . . . I'll let them add extra ice cream to your shakes." She twirled her ponytail. "Perhaps you kids should stay until your teachers return. I don't want them to think I'm a nasty old witch with a heart of stone. Business *is* a bit slow at the moment." As she took her leave she glanced outside. "Bloody rain."

Mr. Read, with three boys, and Miss Whitehead, with five girls, spent the night in two adjacent motel rooms. The plan was to hit the trail by the time the sun skimmed the horizon. Rianna prayed all night for the skies to clear. Addicted to hiking as she was, she had her standards—rain during the hike was acceptable, but *starting* out wet was always a bad omen, if not a joy-dampener. It set the tone for the entire journey. Starting out dry was crucial.

Her prayers were answered. They bade Port St. Johns farewell as a coy sun poked its head above the Indian Ocean—painting the horizon, first in soft reds and pinks, then in yellows and soon blinding golds and whites, as they crossed the first mile-wide ivory beach. It was easier to stick to the high-water mark where the sand was still damp and firm. The soft dry sand would make walking twelve miles a day with a pack too exhausting, and wading through the surf, unless in bare feet, would be foolish—money for good hiking boots was scarce.

Rianna mourned the fact that there was no need for her rain jacket or small collapsible umbrella, which she had tucked (in secret) in the bottom of her twelve-gallon backpack.

A handful of gulls screeched in joy as they dove in formation and skimmed the foaming surf.

Plodding ahead with Sarah Smit, a fellow standard seven student, Rianna dragged her walking stick behind her, making twirls and lines around broken shells, seaweed, and the occasional jellyfish.

The hikers followed the general direction of the footprints of James Martin and his bosom pal, Andries Steenkamp, who had opted to explore ahead. The only requirement Mr. Read had for them was to wait for the group when they reached the first river mouth, and remain in visual contact.

Following Sarah, Rianna, and her walking stick, came Bianca, Lilly, and Patricia—all in standard ten. Henry Cross, always deep in thought, walked on his own.

And thirty feet behind him, at the very back, walked Gloria Whitehead and Rupert Read, debating one contentious topic after the other, loud enough for those ahead of them to overhear. They made quite a pair: she, petite at a hundred pounds in her fire-engine red hiking socks, boots, and eight-gallon backpack, opinionated to a fault; and he, with his two hundred pounds of chiseled physique, carrying his sixteen-gallon pack as if it were a helium balloon, listening with a bemused grin.

They had been going steady for three hours, the one wide-open beach flowing into the next, in the same loose and unstitched fashion, when Mr. Read waved and called to Bianca and Rianna. "Get Martin and Steenkamp to wait for us!"

Bianca waved and hollered at the boys, who kept going strong. Her voice didn't carry far enough.

Rianna waited for a nod from Bianca before taking several brisk paces toward the boys. She cupped her mouth with both hands. "*Mar-tin!*" Another deep breath and she yelled, again at the top of her lungs, "*Steen-kamp!*" The whistle in her side-pocket entirely forgotten, she followed this up by waving her walking stick with a red bandanna tied to the tip, like a signaler on a schooner.

Martin and Steenkamp turned and waved back.

Gloria Whitehead caught up to them. "Vermeulen! Where did you learn that?"

As the others gathered closer, laughing, the redhead shrugged. "Survival in the African bush, Miss? I often had to call my younger brothers to return home when they were out playing with their friends. The Mission station was big."

"You're a keeper. We need someone with a loudhailer. But don't you guys have whistles?"

Rianna nodded, rose creeping up her neck. "Martin needed a good scolding, Miss."

Once Martin and Steenkamp were within hearing distance, Rupert Read raised his voice. "I thought I said maintain *visual contact*?"

"Sir?" James Martin made finger-binoculars in front of his eyes. "Nothing wrong with *my* eyes, sir. I could see the colour of Miss Whitehead's socks, walking with you at the back."

Mr. Read chuckled. "Okay smart guy—visual contact from *my* side." He held his thumb and index finger three inches apart. "I want you guys to stay a *little* closer." He turned and pointed at Rianna, "So I don't need to use my megaphone."

James tapped his friend's deltoid. "You owe me a buck. I told you it was the *klipspringer* who had the big mouth."

Only to flee for his life when Rianna advanced with her outstretched stick. "Who's got the big mouth?"

James grabbed the tip of her stick and whispered, "Big *and* beautiful."

Rianna grabbed his backpack and yanked hard. She turned to Mr. Read. "He needs to be *punished, Meneer*!"

"*Klipspringer. Oreotragus oreotragus*," James muttered under his breath.

"I'll drown you in the first river mouth," she hissed.

"Settle down everyone." Mr. Read raised his arms. "Martin, where are the tide tables I gave you? We have a river to cross."

"Sir?"

"Didn't I tell you about the importance of the tides?"

"You did, sir, but—"

"You gave a copy to *me*." It was the shy Henry Cross who stepped forward. Mr. Read took the tables from the straight-faced Henry while everyone cheered.

Rianna poked the stunned Martin with her stick in the side. "Close your mouth. Who's the *klipspringer* now? Don't forget about the sharks when we cross the river mouth."

Along the route, inland, farther away on the hills, hidden at times by trees and the sweeping land itself, were the scattered thatched-roofed mud houses of the Xhosa people. The outside circular walls were decorated with intricate and colourful designs. Once or twice a day, the hikers had to veer off the pearl-white beaches and scramble over rocks and move deeper inland, closer to the virgin green hills, bringing them close enough to greet the locals. Miss Whitehead did the greetings in Xhosa and the group did the waving.

As they again made their way down the footpath back toward the ocean, away from the small kraal with huts that they had just passed by, Rianna turned to Mr. Read. "What do those people think when they see us walking with our backpacks, sir?"

"That we're adventurous and *brave?*"

"Or that we're idiots?"

He chuckled.

"Do you think they also enjoy the beauty, sir?" Rianna's arm swept across the hills and the beach and the ocean.

"Why would they not?"

"Because they're poor . . . the only thing they may think about is what they're going to feed the kids tonight . . . never mind the spectacular view."

Mr. Read gave her an odd look and shook his head, then ran ahead once they reached the beach and scooped a handful of sand, letting it rain through his fingers. He shrugged as he waited on her, shielding his eyes. "I would come down to the beach *every day* if I lived up there—empty stomach or not." He paused, then grinned wide. "First thing I'd do is learn to fish."

Rianna turned back at the huts and its occupants, higher up on the green hills. How could they not love their grand view of the restless ocean? She laughed out loud before running through the shallows, making a handful of gulls take flight.

The hikers had to learn the three essentials of river-mouth crossings. Don't cross when the tide is going out, unless you're a long-distance swimmer and knew people in Australia. It's always boots off—you cross in bare feet. And a black garbage bag has multiple functions, even with a backpack and hiking boots inside. With a little air trapped and a tight knot, it makes for a marvelous flotation device.

Mr. Read loved to add a fourth essential—always cross with your buddies—one never knew. Currents and water-creatures have the tendency to surprise human beings.

THREE-QUARTERS of the way across the first five-hunderd-foot-wide river-mouth crossing, Rianna shouted, "*James*! *Watch out*!" James was too far away and paid her little attention.

Everybody clung to their floating black bags and kicked and swam, touching bottom from time to time, up to their necks in the water. It was close to one o'clock, and the midday sun forced them to squint against the blinding silver of the water. Of the previous day's rain there was little sign, and the now cloudless skies stretched wide across—white metallic blue.

Unsatisfied with the lack of response, Rianna shouted again, her second cry louder and more bloodcurdling than her first. "*James!* A *dorsal fin!*" She pointed toward the ocean, directly into the blinding sun, and splashed vigorously, as if trying to get away, trying to walk on water even.

They could all hear James's panting as he propelled him and his bag forward, toward the shore, in the general direction Rianna had followed, choking as he swallowed water. He shouted in panic, "*Andries!* Faster, mate! Rianna's seen a fin!" Andries required no such encouragement; he soon was two lengths ahead of his friend.

The moment Martin and Steenkamp ran out onto the opposite shore, panting and coughing, dragging their packs with them, yards ahead of the others, they dropped their bags and spun around, remembering their buddies who were still in the apparently shark-infested waters. James waded back to his waist, all the while screaming, "*Meneer, meneer*, this way!"

Mr. Read was the farthest back and waded unhurriedly across. "Relax, Martin. The shark has left. You must have scared it away, I think."

James remained in the shallows and continued calling out to the others. He was breathing hard while helping each team member ashore, not believing Mr. Read's assurance. *Rianna saw a dorsal fin, didn't she?*

Once everyone was safe on dry land, the incredulous look on all the faces finally hit home. James spun toward Rianna. "*Where* did you see the fin, Vermeulen?"

Rianna stepped closer to Mr. Read and shrugged. "I'm not exactly sure, James." She took another step and stood behind the gym teacher. "I can't see red socks from five hundred feet away like you . . . perhaps it was only the sun on the water . . . ."

James groaned as he rushed at her, arms spread wide.

Rianna shrieked and ducked behind Mr. Read.

"*Martin.*" Mr. Read grabbed the incensed youth by the upper arm.

"I'll *kill* her!" Martin's chest heaved as he fought for control. "A dorsal fin. It wasn't funny, sir."

Rianna poked her head from behind the safety of Mr. Read's torso. "Martin . . . *Oreotragus, oreotragus.*"

James spun around with clenched fists, mumbling, "You're going to pay . . . ."

Mr. Read, remembering his role, cleared his throat, struggling to hide his grin. He faced Rianna. "You owe him an *apology.*"

Arms tucked behind her back, Rianna murmured, "I'm sorry I mistook a piece of driftwood for a Great White, James."

James pursed his lips, "Apology accepted." His eyes rested on her chest for a moment as it rose and fell, straining under the wet fabric, before he stepped closer, meeting her eyes, whispering, "You're going to *pay, Missy.* I'll kiss that beautiful *big mouth* of yours before this hike is over."

When Rianna's breath caught, James laughed and plodded away.

Eleven

MANGROVE SWAMPS AND CRUSTACEANS. MARCH 1966

"Why do we have to cross right *here*?" Rianna pointed at the odd-looking trees lining the shoreline of yet another river mouth. The abundance of air roots amid mud and astringent, murky waters completed the textbook picture of a swamp. Nose scrunched, she waved her fellow hikers to a halt.

"The river is at it shallowest here—only waist-deep," Mr. Read assured her.

"It's *gross*."

Mr. Read laughed. "It's not a big deal. If you insist, there *is* a hang-bridge four and a half miles inland, but it's not worth the trouble. These are only air roots. They feel funny between your toes at first, that's all. And the crabs are harmless."

"*Crabs?*" Lilly Milner and Patricia Partridge shrieked in unison with the redhead.

"Come on people . . . they're little. Tiny crustaceans . . . ."

Miss Whitehead joined the female rebellion and tried her best to get her colleague to change his mind. Why not briskly walk the nine miles if it would help the girls, and everybody for that matter, to not get freaked out?

"You don't walk nine miles unnecessarily. Or *quickly*. Not with a backpack. And not in this unpredictable weather." Mr. Read stared them down.

"Can we at least make it democratic, *meneer*?" Rianna asked.

No one had moved—transfixed they stood. *Crustaceans*. Reluctance written across all the faces, except for those of Rupert Read and Henry Cross.

Rianna waved her arms. "Show of hands, who says *hang-bridge*?"

The hands shot up.

Mr. Read gave a mock gasp and held his hand toward Henry. "The tide tables, please." Gloria Whitehead slapped his upper arm, which only made him study the tables more intently. "Let's try and be *scientific*."

The girls cried in unison, "Shame on you *meneer*. You've already *memorized* the tables. You're an *autocratic* lead—"

"No, he's an *idonki*," Miss Whitehead mumbled.

Mr. Read laughed as he sidestepped the reaching hands and returned the tide tables to Henry. "Let's be realistic. There's little danger involved in crossing here. It's our squeamishness against four hours of unnecessary walking." He glanced at the blank faces. "I thought I'd toughened you guys up over the past year?"

He received only half-smiles and shrugs.

"Sorry, guys, then I use my veto powers." He pulled out a black plastic bag and stuffed his backpack inside. Boots went around his neck. "We're crossing *here*."

When the group remained motionless, Rupert spun toward his colleague. "*Gloria, please.*"

She shrugged and pursed her lips.

"*Guys*—it's about safety. If we do the hang-bridge, we'll be screwed with the tides at the next river. And it's a wide one—close to half a mile. We have to respect the tides." He raised his bag. "We cross the rivers when and where they are safest." With that he stepped into the water with his bag. "Martin, Steenkamp, give the girls a hand."

That was enough for Rianna. "We're not invalids." She shoved James away with her walking stick and entered the marsh. "Don't *touch* me, Martin!" But in her haste to get away, she bumped into Mr. Read, knocking him sideways, headfirst into the water and mud. "So sorry, *meneer!*"

Unperturbed, the teacher bounced back and steadied them both, holding unto her bag until she had regained her balance. There he remained at the ready, waiting for the rest of the group to wade deeper.

Scores of seagulls cried and darted and dipped above the breakers, far out—white restless specks. Unstitched bands of clouds streaked across the pale expanse above the hikers. "Rianna, *look*." He spread his arms as wide as the beach and the skies.

"*Meneer?*" Her face had turned crimson. She turned away.

He sighed. "Forget about the crabs and the mud . . . that's fleeting. Enjoy this moment . . . this is one of the most, if not *the most*, beautiful coastlines in the world."

At that he waded further into the shallow mud, hugging his bag, then turned to look at her. "Don't allow the crustaceans of the world to rob you of the splendour that surrounds you."

Rianna shrugged and trudged on. It was impossible not to gasp at the horror her toes felt and sent desperate messages about to her brain. Firm ground was found at a depth of twelve inches—mid-calf in the mud—each time they ventured another step forward.

To claim it didn't feel horrendous to walk barefoot, feeling the soft air roots crushed underfoot, listening to and feeling the sucking of the chocolate-coloured mud, which pulled like quicksand mixed with glue, sinking twelve inches down with *each* step—would be a horrible lie.

And as it soon turned out, gender had nothing to do with how well one could tolerate it. Not when every fiber, every morsel in one's body cried, "Go faster! For heaven's sake, get out!"

To see hundreds upon hundreds of quarter-inch crabs crawling from their dimpled hiding places—tiny breathing holes in the undisturbed surface—before giant human feet came crashing down; and then to feel the brittle crustaceans crawling underfoot as they scrambled to safety—the unfortunates crushed and driven into the sticky, slurping mud—required herculean willpower. To the untrained and undisciplined mind, the fifty-foot distance became fifty miles.

Rianna, Sarah, Lilly, and Patricia competed with who could squeal the loudest as they stomped through the shallow marsh. Their *No, no, no no's* and *Oh gosh, oh gosh, oh gosh*! ricocheted across the river, the beaches, the hills, and the ocean. Rianna, somehow gaining momentum, soon led the determined slog. The girls' cries were not much louder than the boys'.

"*Pasop, meneer!*" she shouted as she barged toward the open water to her right, away from the air roots, the skinny trees, the crabs, the sucking mud, and endless horror, heading toward Miss Whitehead and Bianca. Those two had been wiser and had followed the boys, walking further upstream in order to cross where the river was shallower and less wide. With her pack she had become a projectile on auto-pilot that torpedoed past him, plummeting headfirst into the water, drenching him in the tidal wave.

"*Vermeulen!*"

"Sorry, *meneer*, for a second time," she wailed as she struggled to catch her breath. Miss Whitehead and Bianca had paused to appreciate the water-acrobatics.

In the end, they all survived the mangrove swamp—all ten minutes of it.

By the time the entire group reached the opposite shore the laughing and horsing around had returned. It was James Martin who dragged his floating bag closer to Rianna as they clambered onto dry land. He nudged her shoulder. "You've forsaken your sentry-duty, Vermeulen."

"*What's* it with you?"

"No dorsal fin sighting today?"

"Leave me alone."

"Not even a sand shark?"

"Why do you keep bugging me? Did you wish to give us a repeat performance of yesterday? You put the apostle Peter to shame—walking much further on water than he ever did at the Sea of Galilea."

James scoffed as he swung his pack onto his back. "No need to become nasty, Missy."

"Okay, I'm sorry. Perhaps sharks hate the mangrove swamps just as much as we do."

He remained next to her as they followed the group toward a sheet of rocks to put their boots back on. "You seem mighty friendly and touchy-touchy with Mr. Read."

"Are you out of your mind?"

"We're not blind."

"Those were accidents . . . ."

"Careful. Miss Whitehead will kick your ass. Don't touch her man."

"You bastard."

"Don't say I haven't warned you," James said, and he sauntered over to where Andries sat.

As THE group reassembled and stretched out across the next unspoiled beach, Gloria beckoned Rupert to fall in with her at the back, as before. They completed the entire length of the first beach in silence before she turned to him. "*What* are you up to?"

He laughed and scooped up a banded tulip shell and brushed it free of sand. "Still mad about us crossing through the mangrove?"

She met his gaze, her lips pencil straight. "What's with the girl?"

"Girl?" He chortled. "*What* are you talking about? There are *five* here besides you—"

"Don't play dumb, Read—the *redhead*. Rianna."

"*Nothing*. You know how she is—always pushing things." He shrugged. "I try and keep up with all their antics."

"You're flirting with her."

He snorted and spun the shell far out into the surf.

"You're not denying it."

He slowed his pace and faced Gloria, touching her arm, which she yanked away. He laughed again. "She's only a child."

"Bullshit. She's a young *woman*. Beautiful. And smart. She knows what she's doing."

"Don't be silly. She's in standard *seven*."

"Exactly." Gloria cleared her throat. "Don't insult the children's intelligence and eyesight, or mine. *Remember,* she's in standard *seven*, for heaven's sake!"

She gave a shrill laugh and called at Bianca and Lilly to wait on her. When she caught up to the girls, she turned and shouted back at him, "*Idonki.*"

Twelve

The naturalists

The wind picked up along the beach as the skies turned to ash. Soon the gusts were toying with them as if they were beach umbrellas. The clouds deepened to Prussian blue—and it wasn't midday yet. Little protection, if any, was to be had on the unprotected coastline. The ivory sand pelted the hikers' legs, their bodies, forcing them to walk bent crooked against the insolent wind; like weeping willows twisted with age. Soon after the wind came the rain—an hour's walk away from the next river mouth. The heavens emptied. In mere minutes they were drenched to the skin—a rain jacket was of little use. Miss Whitehead and Bianca, who had moved up to the front, started singing silly songs, holding hands and laughing at their miserable state. Even the quiet Henry Cross joined in, although off-key. At the back droned the deep baritone of Rupert Read—apparently content with his banishment to the rear.

Rianna pulled her flimsy *lap hoedjie* firmer over her head—at least the hat kept the stubborn rain from her eyes. She kept pace with Sarah, prayed again for sun, and wondered about the shift in interaction she had noticed between their two teachers and what had caused it. Until they had come on the hike, Miss Whitehead had never bothered with lipstick. The last day now, she had more makeup on than Miss Nichols with the polka-dot dress had on the train.

The wind ceased its onslaught first. Rianna plucked her soaked hat from her head and squeezed it dry the moment the rain joined the wind in a ceasefire. Then, arms wide, face turned heaven-wards, she began to run, pack bouncing on her back. "There's blue sky, people!"

"Blue sky the size of a penny," Sarah muttered, so Rianna turned, grabbed her hand, and pulled her along. The two ran together until they caught up to Miss Whitehead and Bianca.

"Is that the next river mouth, Miss Whitehead?" Rianna pointed with her stick in the distance.

"Looks like it."

"I'm positive we'll have sun beating down on us by the time of our crossing," Rianna called.

"How do you *do* this?" Sarah protested. "We've been hiking six hours, two of them through a bloody coastal storm, and you're . . . all bubbly?"

Rianna stared at her friend, then shook her wet mane, not comprehending. "Isn't it amazing how everything just clears and opens up—just when you're on the brink of giving up all hope?"

Sarah only groaned and sighed as her friend let go of her hand and propelled herself ahead. Behind them, James Martin and Andries Steenkamp dragged their miserable selves along the wet beach, both uncommonly quiet.

Rianna's excited chatter wouldn't quiet down.

"What's wrong with you, Vermeulen?" James grumbled.

"I'm so happy," she gushed.

"Because you're used to nothing. A patch of blue sky. My ass . . . ."

"Suit yourself, sourpuss," Rianna cried, as she increased her lead.

From the back Mr. Read hollered. "*Steenkamp! Martin!* Get her to slow down."

"You *heard* him, Vermeulen." James was quick on her heels, and grabbed her arm—glad for permission to interfere. "*Meneer* says, 'Slow down.'"

She yanked her arm free and pushed him off balance. "I told you not to *touch me*."

"Jeez. What is it with you?"

She stared a warning at him. Sarah by then had joined them.

Martin shrugged, "It's okay if it's *that time* of the month for you—"

Rianna shrieked and pushed him with both hands, so hard that he lost his balance and fell.

"*Vermeulen!*" It was Mr. Read.

Rianna turned to face her teacher. "*Martin* owes me an apology, sir." Then she spun around and took Sarah's hand, ignoring the men. "Let's get away from these jerks."

Shaking his head, Mr. Read bit back his response.

Once they reached the river it was clear that they had company. On the opposite shore, four people were heading their way—already in the water, calling.

"What are they saying, Rianna?"

"It's too far to understand, *Meneer*." Calmer now, she slipped her wet boots and socks off and shoved them into a black bag.

"*Listen*," he commanded. "Those people are shouting at us . . . waving and pointing, too. Can you figure out what they're trying to say?"

"Sounds like German . . . something about a strong current?" Rianna speculated.

Mr. Read stepped closer. "Okay guys, in that case—we'll wade much deeper inland and then allow the current to push us out toward the spot on the opposite shore that we aim for. And stay closer to one another."

Miss Whitehead chimed in. "That's the *theory*, kids."

Mr. Read forced a laughed as he tied the black bag around his pack, shaking his head. Eyes on her teachers, Rianna's brow furrowed. She looked for help at Sarah, who only shrugged her shoulders.

"*Those* people must have swimming costumes on." Rianna was the first of their group in the water.

Sarah was close on her heels. "They're smart—keeping their hiking clothes dry."

Halfway through the river, the current's pull became dangerously strong. Mr. Read reiterated the instruction to remain closer to one another and steer farther inland, then allow the current to push them toward the opposite shore.

Sarah, now wading next to Rianna, whispered, "Two of the other group are women."

"Oh dear, the one at the front doesn't have *any* clothes on . . .," Rianna murmured back.

The water was surprisingly clear, in spite of the heavy rains just hours earlier.

As the two groups approached one another it became clear to the hikers that their rescuers had shed their clothes. Putting on swimming attire in the inclement weather must not have crossed their minds.

The woman, a tall brunette, her hair caught in a ponytail, laughed as she held onto the rope anchored by her two remaining partners on the beach—oblivious to the effect their nudity had on the group.

"*Guten Tag*!" the man at the front greeted.

Rianna managed a feeble "Hi" and Sarah only nodded, not risking speaking.

The man chuckled and continued in broken English, as he gripped the approaching students' outstretched hands and steered them and passed them on to his lady friend, equally trim and fit. The rope was tied to their waists. He was leaner than Mr. Read, but similarly chiseled.

It was impossible not to hear the gasps and giggles and whistles as the group of ten was assisted to the opposite shore. The students went first while Miss Whitehead, lips in a prim line, her face drained of colour, steered toward Mr. Read for an urgent consultation in the middle of the river.

He only snickered.

"It's not funny, Rupert. *Do* something!"

"There's nothing I can do."

"What will Miss Clark or Mr. Benson say?"

"They won't know unless you tell them."

"What about the students?"

"Do you want me to close their eyes?"

"Do *something*."

"Why are you so embarrassed? These are beautiful people . . . part of God's perfect creation . . . like this incredible coastline we've been walking. They are comfortable with their bodies. It's no shame. And their clothes, like ours, must be wet."

James and Andries allowed the young woman to lead them to the safety of the shore. They watched, enraptured like all the others, as the naked woman waded from the waters. Their eyes never left her chest—her unrestrained breasts, two firm peaks, rising and falling as she walked, unconcerned, gracious, like a gazelle. Even more astounding was her shaven, hairless pubis.

Rianna stood, for a moment uncertain, when the first rescuer, the man, pulled her from the raging river. She had never seen a man entirely without clothes. The naked man's speech was strange to her untrained ears as she eyed him—water dripping from every part of his body. She was reminded of Michelangelo's David. Her rescuer seemed taller. She swallowed as her eyes traveled over his trim torso. Her gaze dropped and rested on his groin, his manhood—asleep and mysterious—less than an arm's length away. She shuddered. His laugh made her snap her eyes back to his face. She glowed, praying the beach would swallow her whole as he tapped his forehead in a mock-salute, unapologetic, before stepping back into the swift stream to help her remaining friends.

Rianna closed her eyes—her world was twirling out of control.

Behind her Mr. Read pulled Miss Whitehead onto the shore and kissed her. "Remember what you've said: 'They're not children.' I agree." He laughed as he kissed her protests away. "Today our students grew up. They had an unscheduled biology lesson—perhaps more—a *life* lesson."

Thirteen

HISTORY PROJECTS AND THE READING OF BANNED BOOKS. APRIL 1966

Mrs. Knox lived for her history projects. It was no secret: her students wrote essays. She had garnered a name for herself in educational circles in the city—her students' work was exemplary.

At a young age Brenda Knox had fallen in love with everything *Groot Trek*—The Great Trek—the movement of pioneers in the mid-eighteen-thirties, inland, away from the interfering and oppressive rule of the British. She never could unearth enough facts about those ensuing decades. What better use of students was there than to get them to do the research while she earned the accolades? History to her was celebration and acknowledgment of the endeavours of one's ancestors—dwelling in the far-off past helped her escape the realities of her own bleak life.

For the second year now, by contrast, her student Rianna Vermeulen was discovering an increasing passion for twentieth-century history. There was no greater satisfaction (other than running and hiking) than immersing herself in contemporary world history. Soon, she referred to her preference as "current international history." To her, history was about what happened yesterday and the days prior to that and about how we could make life better if we could learn from it. She found little challenge in learning about ox-wagons and assegais and front-loaders.

However, Mrs. Knox dismissed her student's preferences as preposterous, part of political science and not the study of history for middle high school—as per the syllabus. Whenever Rianna tried to bring up twentieth-century history she bestowed her rebellious student with an I-dare-you-to-challenge-me-and-we'll-walk-to-the-principal-and-this-time-you'll-draw-the-shorter-end-of-the-stick look. This made Rianna hunch forward in history class, her lips pulled into an anguished line.

Ms. Clark, the vice-principal, had been correct that Rianna still had much to learn about life—especially about people. Jess Taylor often had to remind her friend: Don't mess with the lady dragon—she's seeking her next victim. But it seemed to Jess that Rianna's promise to keep her opinions to herself when in history class was wearing thinner by the day. Rianna had not told Jessica yet—she had a new secret.

Four Saturdays ago she had bused down to the city center, past the old Van Riebeeck Castle, and had become a card-carrying member of the Central Library. She had snuck away immediately following their usual morning jog. Her excitement knew no bounds. Each book she devoured taught her something new—introduced her to worlds unknown. She had also learned about the practice of banning. She learned about banned books, banned organizations, and banned people. She also discovered that the official term for what the government did was exercise censorship—decide what was good for its people to know and to read.

At first, she read about organizations like the Communist party, the African National Council (ANC), and the Pan Africanist Congress (PAC) who were all banned by the South African government, along with certain individuals and several publications and books. She was blissfully ignorant of the reasons why. Those groups and people must all have evil motives then, she decided.

Yet before long, as she read and learned more, she found it odd that the ban was so wide and deep, that even books about nonviolent protests, especially in the outside world, in places like India and America, were included in the ban and deemed undesirable. *Why would our government want people to remain ignorant? What if those books could help the two sides understand each other better, instead of resorting to fear and hatred—wanting only to fight and hurt and harm one another?*

What made all the difference was her chance encounter with the part-time librarian's assistant, Hugo Marais. Saturday after Saturday she delved around, looking for new material to read—anything, really, that wasn't fiction or a local newspaper. Her research was haphazard until she ran into the scrawny Marais boy, who took an interest in her hunger for the printed word. Hugo was a free spirit, an eclectic soul, obsessed with obtaining more knowledge and desperate to share his love of knowledge (often questionably obtained) with an equally famished mind.

When Rianna finally did confide in her roommate, she met with chastisement. "That's why I could *never* find you after our runs," Jessica complained. "Why didn't you ask me to come along?"

"You've never liked libraries. Or books."

"But I'm your *friend*."

"C'mon Jess . . . you wouldn't have liked it. I was digging around in the archives—old books, spiderwebs, moth balls—"

"They *allowed* you?"

Rianna chuckled. "I met this boy. He's a part-timer. A librarian's assistant. A student at UCT."

Jess whistled. "That's why I wasn't welcome . . . a new *boyfriend*."

Rianna shook her head, perhaps a few times too many.

"Then why are you blushing?"

"Wait till you see him . . . ." Rianna made a contorted figure.

"You're not a loyal friend. Does he really look like Quasimodo from the Cathedral of Notre Dame?"

Rianna turned scarlet. "It's not that . . . he's sweet, but *different* . . . almost gaunt. He doesn't eat at all, it seems. And he doesn't get much sun. He only drinks Coke—and reads rare books."

Jessica Taylor gave her friend a piercing look. "What's the deal with your fancy library card and the secret friend?"

Rianna sighed. "Nothing. Our school library is grand—but what I found in the city library is . . . so much more. There's just no comparison."

Jessica blew kisses at her friend.

"Make fun of me as much as you like. I now have access to almost any book in the world."

"*So?*" Jessica preferred listening to music on the radio when she didn't run or had pressing school assignments. Why anyone would read more than what the teachers meted out was beyond her.

"I have access to international newspapers and difficult-to-obtain books."

Her friend snickered. "*Lady Chatterley's Lover?*"

"Jess! I'm reading about political stuff and social issues, not about racy sex."

Jessica closed her eyes. "It's a love story . . . ."

"It's raunchy."

"Are you talking about *banned* books?"

"I'm selective."

"How would *you* know? You're barely fifteen."

"I'm not stupid. I want to learn about our history. The politics of our country. About separate development and what it's doing to people—to the black people, to us. Here, and in other parts of the world."

"That's not history. Mrs. Knox calls it political science."

"She's stuck in the distant past. She doesn't apply the history she teaches. She makes us memorize and repeat hundreds of facts like parrots. Even with our research papers we are only allowed to regurgitate what we read. We gain little insight from it; we don't learn about what we can do better, or different."

"You're arrogant, Missy Vermeulen. You're only in standard seven. You'll learn all about that when you're in standard ten. And anyway, history *is* about the distant past."

Rianna clenched her fists and spun toward the window. She bit her lip. Jess didn't understand.

Van Hunks and the devil were pulling their cloud blanket over her beloved mountain. Clare Collins, the student leader from last year, had been wrong. Each month, Rianna had fallen only deeper in love with the mountain.

Once her fists relaxed, Rianna turned back. "The other day, I found this book by an American civil rights leader."

Jessica snapped upright. Even she had heard about the black Baptist minister giving all those speeches. "The Negro preacher?"

Rianna nodded. "Yes. Dr. Martin Luther King Jr."

Jessica smiled. And James Martin and his clique claimed she was this big ignoramus because she didn't sleep with a library book under her pillow or read every morning paper.

Without another word Rianna extracted the borrowed book from behind her overflowing bookshelf—taking care not to dislodge the others.

"You *hid* it?"

"Neither you nor Mrs. Knox would give your blessing."

"It's not important what we think. Isn't it *banned*?"

"Why would it be?" Rianna avoided eye contact.

"Because the preacher incites civil disobedience."

"But not violence."

"That's not the point. *He's Black.*"

"It's wrong to ban his books."

"You're a child, like me. Do you know better than the prime minister?"

Rianna shrugged. "It's still wrong to ban it."

Jessica shook her head. "His books are *definitely* banned."

"How do you know all this? Are you a closet reader?"

"I keep my ears open. My uncle on my father's side is a police-man—in the Secret Service. He's told Dad bits and pieces—and I've eavesdropped on them. The Baptist preacher's name has come up." She held out her hand.

Rianna pulled the book into her bosom. "Rather not. I had to promise the librarian—"

"The *librarian* wouldn't have given it to you."

"Okay. Hugo Marais let me have it."

"You can go to jail."

Rianna laughed nervously. "I'm under age."

"Your friend can go to jail."

Rianna shook her head. "He's being careful."

Jessica plopped down on Rianna's bed. "Do you realize how many people, having been 'careful,' are in prison?"

"Can't we just forget about the book?" Rianna placed her cheek against the window pane to soak up the remains of the day's heat.

"You won't forget about it . . . so, come sit." Jess held her hand a second time.

"You have to promise. You can *never* tell."

"I promise," Jessica murmured. "What's it called?"

"Careful—it's seriously *borrowed*."

Jessica turner the cover. "*Stride Toward Freedom: The Montgomery Story.*" She whistled. "Mrs. Knox will get a stroke and Mr. Benson a heart attack."

"They don't need to know."

"You'll be glad to know Mrs. Knox has progressed from the Great Trek leaders of 1836 to the formation of the Boer Republics."

Rianna groaned.

"Dr. King . . . why are you so obsessed with *Black people*?"

"Jess. He's a remarkable leader. He happens to be a *Negro* man. I've been reading lots. I've experienced the turmoil in Northern Rhodesia and now I see what is happening here, in South Africa. I grew up with black people there. I have black friends. They are people like us—some with light in their hearts and some with darkness. And I see what our laws do to the people here."

"It keeps order in our society. We're so different from them—"

"No Jess—it's not *us* and *them*. Our laws hurt."

"You have to get rid of this book."

"I'll hide it."

"*Impossible*." Jessica grasped her friend's arm until she squealed. Her eyes brimmed. "I'm scared. Promise me you'll take it back."

"Jess—"

"Ree. There are laws. Take it *back*." Jessica Taylor's slipped off her friend's bed, her face ashen.

Rianna followed and gave her a quick hug, then stroked her arm with unexpected tenderness. "Hush now. I'm halfway done reading it. I'll finish it tonight and take it back tomorrow. I *promise*."

JESSICA Taylor's predictions concerning Mrs. Knox remained on target. The next morning Mrs. Knox gave them their new assignment: *Discuss the factors that played a role in the signing of the Sand River Convention on 17 January 1852, between Great Britain and the Boers of the South African Republic.*

Rianna's shoulders slumped. Mrs. Knox's eyes remained on her like an eagle that had cornered a field mouse.

So Rianna opted for a different tactic to the previous year. She was convinced Mrs. Knox would listen to her arguments this time. While she waited for class to end, she stifled two yawns. She had finished the book about the bus boycott of 1955 the previous night—well, at four that morning. She raced to the front as the last of her classmates ambled out the door. Her stomach twitched. She waited in silence as the teacher continued writing.

Mrs. Knox dropped her pen. "Vermeulen?"

"Mrs. Knox, I've given your assignment serious thought."

Brenda Knox's pained expression softened—she allowed her narrow lips to turn upwards. For a moment it seemed as if a wave of guilt flushed over her. Consistent discipline always bore fruit. This rebellious girl was finally coming home. "I'm glad to hear that, child."

Rianna cringed. Mrs. Know refused to call her by her name. She rolled on the balls of her feet as she had seen Bertie Vosloo do on the train. "While my classmates will write about the Sand River Convention, I've recently stumbled upon a fascinating piece of relevant history."

Mrs. Knox leaned back in her chair, joy seeping from her face.

Rianna gulped. "It took place a hundred and three years after the Convention . . . across the Atlantic—the 1955 Montgomery bus boycott. I was considering calling the piece, 'Are There Lessons to Be Learned from the Sand River Convention and the Montgomery Bus Boycott—'"

Mrs. Knox shot from her chair as if electrocuted, making her chair crash against the wall.

"Montgomery happened eleven years ago. How do you know about that?"

"I often go to the Central Library where I read—"

"Ughh!" The teacher slammed her desk and leaned across, so close that Rianna could smell her angry breath. "Why can't you be a normal standard seven student? I was so wrong. For I moment I thought . . . I hoped. You're . . . incorrigible."

Rianna backed away until she bumped into the first row of school desks.

Mrs. Knox already stood waiting at the door. "*Come*. You know where we're going."

This time the front office secretary had left for the day when they passed through. Mr. Benson's tall figure wilted when he noticed Rianna. When Rianna saw Mr. Benson, however, she stifled a giggle and turned away from both the principal and teacher. She blinked several times. The rumour was true. Mr. Benson had had, according to Bianca Brown, a mid-life crisis. He had abandoned his three-piece tailored suits for safari suits with cravats. He had apparently also taken a mistress.

It was impossible to pay any attention to what Mrs. Knox was accusing her of. Rianna studied Mr. Benson. She tried to picture the kind of woman who would find a middle-aged man with a receding hairline, a protruding midline, in a kiwi-green safari suit, with a flamboyant aquamarine cravat hiding his chest hair, attractive. *The poor, poor man.*

"*Vermeulen!*"

Rianna jumped. Mrs. Knox had delivered her charge. *Probably high treason.* Rianna turned toward Mr. Benson. "Sir?"

The man seemed exhausted. Lost. He didn't pace as he always did. He didn't even stand when they had entered—he had remained seated behind his desk—where he sat now. Listless.

"*Why* do we have to go through this *again*, Miss Vermeulen?" He shoved his glasses up his nose. Squinted at her. The silver goatee made him look seventy instead of fifty.

"Sir, I've done extensive reading." She glanced at Brenda Knox. "On top of what Mrs. Knox expects us to know. With the present political tension in the country, I thought it would be appropriate to apply lessons from the Montgomery boycott to—"

"*Enough.*"

Rianna froze. She had never heard him speak like this.

For the first time since their arrival, Mr. Benson stood, cleared his throat, repositioned his cravat and stepped toward the window. It was clear he longed to be outside. Perhaps with his new lady friend.

He spun around and reached his desk with three quick steps and plopped down on the corner, closest to her. Rianna squirmed in her chair.

He leaned forward, resting his hands on his knees. He was the first man that Old Spice had ever smelled good on. The only thing about him that was good. "*Extensive* reading? Hmm?"

"Yes, sir."

Mrs. Knox had jumped from her seat and now paced behind Rianna. A lioness, ready for the kill. "As I've pointed out to you, Mr. Benson. Such a degree of repetitive insubordination is unacceptable. It's sufficient grounds for expulsion. Her behaviour in class makes teaching intolerable, if not—"

"But, *Meneer!*" Rianna raised her hand.

Mrs. Knox's breathing came fast. The woman's cheeks were blotched.

"*Expulsion?*" Rianna was no longer sitting. Her eyes darted from principal to teacher. "Sir, you can ask any of my classmates. I've behaved in class since we last had this discussion—since last year." She wiped over her eyes. "I don't speak out of turn in her class anymore. Ever. She only gave us the assignment today. I went to her desk after all the students had left the room. I never said a word."

Mr. Benson's raised his hands to silence her. He cocked his head at Brenda Knox.

"Did you give them the assignment today, Mrs. Knox?"

The teacher nodded with visible reluctance.

"Did Miss Vermeulen say *anything* to you in class after you assigned the essay topic?"

The history teacher shook her head.

Mr. Benson fiddled with his cravat and cleared his throat. "Not expulsion, Mrs. Knox, but a first warning."

"*Sir!*" Rianna staggered and grasped her chair's backside.

Mr. Benson had moved to behind his desk—arms now folded across his chest, resting on his soft belly. "This is a school after all, Miss Vermeulen. We have rules. Consider this your first warning."

Brenda Knox exhaled loud. Fifteen love. She pursed her lips for Rianna to see.

Mr. Benson faced the teacher. "Why don't we do *this*, Mrs. Knox? Miss Vermeulen will do your project about the Sand River Convention *as well as* her additional essay on the lessons we can learn from the Montgomery boycott?"

Brenda Knox's lips curled up—her eyes remained cold.

Rianna bounced up and down while she waited for him to finish. "But, sir. Did you even see the wording? Our assignment's title alone is thirty words long. *Discuss the factors that played a role in the signing of the Sand River Convention on 17 January 1852, between Great Britain and the Boers of the South African Republic.* Thirty, sir!"

"Miss Vermeulen! Here's your solution: *The Sand River Convention.* Four words."

"But—"

"*Enough*, Vermeulen. Get out!"

As Rianna stomped from the office, he called after her. "I want a copy of both essays on my desk in two weeks' time."

Fourteen

Part-time employment in the Table Mountain Café. June 1966

"Life isn't fair."

Hendrik Willems stared open-mouthed at Rianna from behind stacks of soiled dishes. He rolled his eyes when she repeated her lament, unloading her tray. He had grown used to the spirited girl's recitals about how cruel the world seemed to be—especially toward fifteen-year-old girls. She had found part-time employment in the Table Mountain Café, where his mother was the assistant manager. Rianna would soon enough tell him what was gnawing at her soul.

He chided himself for not confiding in his mother about Rianna's real age. Then again—she looked sixteen. Eighteen even. She was bilingual. She was a knockout. The customers loved her—she was good for business. It wasn't a difficult decision. Perhaps he gave his mother too little credit.

He preferred the dishes to cooking and waiting on tables—it gave him time to think, while at the same time he could be close enough to keep an eye on his mother. She was more brittle than usual—it was hard on her with Sarah, his sister, in the process of escaping the confines of the Coloured community—she was on a quest to be reclassified as "White."

Sarah had befriended an Afrikaner man in the offices of the minister of Bantu Affairs. She had passed the pencil test. Her hair was much straighter and more flowing than Hendrik's. Her skin was also a shade creamier. He dared not ask his mother whether he and his sister shared the same father. Mother wouldn't hesitate to smack him, petite as she was.

Rianna wiped her hands on her apron, then clasped the tray to her chest before balancing it against her hip. She urged Hendrik to meet her eyes. "I *need* to speak to you," she whispered, amidst the clanging of dishes and pots and pans, while he scraped leftovers into the garbage can.

He cocked his brows, hands paused in midair, but she had already spun around and pushed through the kitchen door, which now swung back and forth. He was content to inhale the whirlwind of her departure—cinnamon, warm apple, and young girl.

RIANNA always chose the table farthest away from the restaurant for her short outside breaks—next to the stone fence, a perfect lookout. Hendrik chuckled—perhaps it was smarter to always sit this far, away from the scrutiny of the public eye, including that of the white boss. With the unending bustle of international tourists, it was easier to "mix" with her, more difficult for the race police to tell an infringement was taking place.

She faced the ocean, her back to the café. The wind plucked at her red mane, now tied into an unruly ponytail. She turned with a wide grin when she heard him approach on the uneven stone paving.

"Life just isn't fair," she repeated as she rose and faced him, her lips pursed. Her chest rose as she inhaled the subtle whiff coming off the mountain *fynbos*.

"You were born white as snow—you know little about *unfair*. But let's hear, what horrible blow has your privileged life *now* been dealt, Miss Vermeulen?"

She plopped down after a furtive glance in the direction of the restaurant. The adjacent tables were empty. She clasped his hand. "You know how I feel about these ridiculous laws." She sighed. "Miss Clark, our vice-principal, threatened to prevent me from coming—from *working* here."

Hendrik smiled as he freed his hand. He was no fool. It was not wise to be seen holding hands—not in public. Even sitting too close to her was taking a risk. Not with a White girl—tanned as she was, not if she didn't have dark frizzy hair.

He scraped his chair a safer distance away and faced his friend. In spite of being two years her senior, many days he felt overwhelmingly inadequate and ill-equipped to jump on board her latest quest to establish social justice in a cocked-up world. He loved reading and was studying hard for his matriculation examination in four months' time, but the way she found the extra time to do all her secret reading, always coming up with such incredible, outlandish information, obviously acquired through illegal sources, what with all her running and hiking, never ceased to astound him.

They would soon have to return to the kitchen—he had been unable to get away on time for his break. The park superintendent was in the building today, and it wouldn't be a good thing to leave Mother too long on her own with the man—a brusque and burly creature.

He inhaled deeply, clenching his fists as he rose, willing himself not to kiss those rouge lips, parted as Rianna unconsciously licked first the upper lip, then the lower. She now bit the lower one. A gazelle prancing across the savannah—gracious, undaunted, always alluring. He tore his eyes away. She must be blissfully unaware of her effect on people—on men, on him, in particular. *Dear Lord, why did you create such gorgeous people? Why must she be White?* He sucked another breath and shoved his chair in. "What's the principal's complaint? You're only here for four hours on Saturdays and the same on Sunday afternoons?"

Rianna rattled her chair in her haste to reach for his hand as he started walking back. "Why are you in such a hurry? Miss Clark claims I'm too young to work here."

"Are you?"

Her breath caught. "You didn't tell your *mother?*"

Hendrik shook his head. "When will you be old enough, according to your vice-principal?"

"She says eighteen."

Hendrik shrugged his shoulders.

"Perhaps if I ask your mother to write me a letter stating she can't manage the café without my help on weekends . . . ."

Hendrik laughed as he held the door. He leaned closer and whispered, "I hereby certify that this precocious fifteen-year-old is indeed older than her chronological age as stated on her birth—"

Rianna jabbed him in the ribs as she slipped through the door. She murmured, "*Idonki.*"

WHEN THEIR shifts were done, they each took a spot, close to the front of the cable car docking platform but standing apart. The moment the wide door slid open, they slipped in ahead of the other travelers. Only then did he acknowledge her with a grin. The two stood shoulder to shoulder with throngs of tourists—all bursting with excitement to get off the mountain and return to their hotels, able to mark as completed another item on their sightseeing to-do-list.

She fumed as they became separated inside the cableway car. *He did it deliberately—the coloured boy can be so stubborn.*

Hendrik stood apart now, taking pains to allow more passengers to squeeze in ahead of him, surround him, push him away from her. She willed him to feel the fire of her glare drilling into him. The only response was a shrug as he slung his bag over his shoulder, turned his back on her, and grasped the vertical railing.

The doors hissed closed and the car started down the incline, zinging along the overhead cables. Rianna's knuckles blanched as she adjusted her hands. She sighed and followed her friend's example, turned her back, and stared out the window. *Let him be a donkey then.*

She sighed again, this time with contentment—the view was always grand. The azure of the ocean, far beyond the city, fused into the shimmering horizon—blue had turned blinding-white. More than an hour and a half of daylight was still theirs. As long as she found herself inside the gates of Westerford High by the time the first street lamps turned on, she was on safe ground with the school.

Safe ground. She closed her eyes, exhaling slowly, remembering. She had found similar solace every time she scaled her mango tree in Katete and looked out over the river, along the Luangwa valley; that view had also always appeased her colliding emotions and longings. *Dare I still call it home? Lord, be with Father and Mother and PJ and little Casper in the land beyond the Zambezi.*

Rianna inched toward the sliding doors as the car docked in at the lower station. Hendrik was right behind her, but she dashed for her bicycle, chained to a cast iron fence, without looking back. The peace she had just felt, drinking in her mountain, evaporated as she recalled Hendrik ignoring her in the cable car. She crunched down to insert the key.

"Are you mad at me?" He stepped closer.

She turned her face to look at him then, but the pools in her eyes were still spitting lava. "Don't *talk* to me," she hissed. And then she slipped the chain and lock into her shoulder bag. He waited for her to turn the bicycle around and walk it alongside them. This time she made certain to keep the iron horse between them.

She often walked with him the two steep miles to his mother's house on Cambridge Street, before cycling back to the school hostel. If there was sufficient daylight they would wander farther down to the wharf and watch the ships and fishing boats. They were both keenly aware of the risk they took in doing so.

Only when they reached the first residential street would she glance at him. "You accuse the government of applying unjust laws, and then you play high and mighty yourself—applying your own kind of apartheid."

"The laws *are* unjust."

"Okay, but why did you, once again, refuse to stand next to me inside the car, riding down the mountain? As if we're strangers."

He remained silent and strode ahead.

In response, she jumped in the saddle and began to pedal slowly beside him. "Speak the word if you want me to leave. If I embarrass you. I thought we were *friends*." Then her bike screeched to a halt. She stepped down, legs planted wide. It was impossible to avoid her glare.

He glared back. "Why are you so *insensitive*?"

"Insensitive?" Rianna groaned. She spun the bicycle halfway around, changed her mind, spun back again, and jabbed a finger at him. "*You*, Hendrik Willems, are *too* sensitive for your own health. You need a thicker skin—not a whiter one. You can't change your colour—neither can I—but you may learn to change its thickness. And you are embarrassed to be seen with me. I *get* it." She spun the bike in the opposite direction and mounted again and called over her shoulder, "So long, Willems!"

Hendrik was too fast for her—he played on his school's second rugby team. He spun around and a second later stood in front of her, holding her handlebar, their faces inches apart. Rianna let out a muffled cry as she tried to free the handlebars.

He held firm. "I'm sorry, but you know the risks of being seen together. Why will I *ever* stop being your friend?"

"Because you're mad at me for not being *brown* enough," she whispered.

He shook his head. "You can change your mind and your beliefs, not your skin." Hendrik straightened his arm, held his bronze limb high up for her to see, turned it this way and that to catch the afternoon sun, before grasping the handlebar again. "How *thick* do you think one's skin must grow?"

Her cheeks were blotched as she took several deep breaths to bring her unsettled heart under control. Through clenched teeth she instructed, "*Let go of my bicycle, Hendrik Willems. I didn't make the hurtful laws. I'm trying to help. You don't want to make a scene here in the street. Not with the cops patrolling the neighbourhoods.*"

He snapped back, throwing glances in all directions. Seeing nothing out of the ordinary, he bent, scooped a rock the size of a chicken egg, and rolled it in his hands.

Rianna stepped to one side of the bicycle, turned it around a third time, and fell in beside him. "Will you then tell me how sorry you are for behaving like a bloody donkey?"

He chuckled. His eyes never left her face. "Walk with me to the docks."

When she didn't move, he added. "*Please*. Then I'll tell you."

THEY PASSED Van Riebeeck's castle.

The remainder of the way to the pier they completed in silence. The squawking of scavenging seagulls blended with car horns, dockworkers calling, and laden cranes whirring overhead. Only when a ship's horn blared next to them, piercing her reverie, did Rianna jump and glance at her companion. "*What?*"

"Missy, not only are you insensitive, you're ignoring me. I've been calling your name since we came through the boom gate back *there*."

Rianna bit her lower lip. "Sorry. I've been daydreaming." She pushed her bicycle a little faster. "Let's go sit on our usual spot—then we'll be out of the workers' way and their scrutiny." She rested her bike against an empty shipping container, dashed across the narrow passage, and before Hendrik could give her a hand, scrambled up the side of the wide concrete wall. He sighed as he joined her on their vantage point.

Only when a gull screeched above them did he face her. "Out with it, Vermeulen. You don't daydream—you make plans. Concoct grand schemes of how you will create a fair and just society."

She nudged him in the ribs. "What's wrong with *that?*"

He laughed, facing the harbour. When he turned back his lips were a tight line. "You're dreaming up a utopia. Meantime, back here on earth, it's finally happening. It's raining shit in District Six. The authorities are throwing us out of our house—perhaps as early as next year."

Rianna got hold of his hand and pressed his fingers to her lips. "As in *evicted?*"

"As in forceful removal. They'll probably give Mom a few miserable pennies before bulldozing our house. Four months ago, on February 11th, District Six was declared a *slum*. Big surprise. It has to be demolished and turned into a Whites-only area."

Rianna took his other hand as well and kissed the remaining fingers. "But some of your neighbours are already White. What's the big deal?"

"The ministry of Interior Affairs thinks it's a big deal. The Groups Area Act says we have to leave."

"But *why?*"

"The government claims interracial interaction breeds conflict."

"That explains why you make me *so mad*, Mr. Willems."

Hendrik pulled his hands free, giving her a feeble smile. "Be serious."

She bit her lower lip as she followed the flight of a gull.

"Don't *do* that."

"Do what?" Her head slanted.

"Bite your lip." He reached for her hand.

"Why?"

"It-it becomes impossible to think clearly . . . the urge to kiss you becomes *overwhelming*."

Rianna raised her brow. "I didn't know you liked me in that way, Hendrik Willems. Not when you act as if I'm a stranger. Never let the minister of Interior Affairs hear you utter those words." She leaned across and gave him a peck on the lips, then jumped to her feet and pulled him along. "Another closet admirer." She clicked her tongue. "I'm underage." Before he could open his mouth, she gave him a firmer kiss on the lips and slid down to the walkway below.

"I'm not asking for your hand—" When Rianna snorted, he was fast to add, "I *like* you. I like you a lot. I enjoy your company. Why can't I be friends with people of my choice? It's so simple."

Rianna leaned forward as she pushed her bicycle up the incline toward the boom gate at the top of the narrow road. She bit her lip. "It will *never* be simple, my friend."

AT THE very moment Rianna cycled up Mount Road to turn through the gates at Westerford High, the first street lamps flickered to life. She grimaced and pedaled harder—it was all Hendrik Willems's fault; he had so many stories today, and he made her walk down to the wharf. All because he had such a thin skin. Visits to the vice-principal's office should be restricted to birthdays and year-end celebrations—it was better to leave well enough alone. Rianna doubted whether Miss Clark ever liked a young man when she was fifteen.

Fifteen

DEATH OF A PRIME MINISTER. 6 SEPTEMBER 1966

*I*t didn't rain that first Tuesday in September. The Southwestern held its breath—not a breeze to rustle the leaves.

Mr. Read stood to the side, in all his chiseled glory—he wasn't even breathing hard or sweating from the run. The remainder of the running group caught their collective breaths on the lower steps to the Rhodes Memorial. They had left for their run as soon as school was out. Rianna and Jessica, as had become their habit, stood apart, on opposite ends of the wide stairs of the Memorial, and they were looking out over the Cape Flats when the church bells started tolling.

Even from up where they were, on the foothills of Devil's Peak, it was clear something had happened in the mother city. From across the entire metropolis the tolling soon washed over them—from the harbour, from around the mountain, from the flats in front of them, from beyond the plains—wave after wave rolled in. Car horns joined the tolling bell-song.

As if on cue, although haphazard, scattered across the city, swarms of birds took to the skies, blocking out the sun at times, disturbed by the unexpected cacophony. It reminded Rianna of what the skies must have looked like in the days of Noah, once the ark had stranded on the mountain following the flood, when all the animals were set free. They watched as flocks of turtle-doves and rock pigeons, sparrows, fiscals, Cape bulbuls and olive thrushes took flight from tree-lined streets and gardens.

Jessica mused. "The bells—it's not Sunday yet."

"Someone must have died," Rianna offered.

"People die every day and they don't ring the bells."

"Somebody *important*." Rianna snapped her hand like an umpire. "Listen . . . they've added the city hall's carillon." Above the incessant ringing of church bells and the din of horns now came the distinct melody from the bay's side.

"It's Carol of the Bells!" Rianna and Jess called in unison as Mr. Read waved for them to join the rest of the team. It was time to head back.

"*Meneer*, do you hear that?"

He shrugged in answer as they took off. The girls squealed when a rasp of guinea fowl scuttled into the long grass as the running group thumped down the hill.

Mr. Read waved again and circled his hand. "Let's go find out."

*T*he runners reached the school just as the bell tower struck the three o'clock hour. Without pause, the city bells continued to boom.

Every radio station was broadcasting the news—Dr. Hendrik Verwoerd, sixth prime minister of South Africa, had been killed at 2:14 that afternoon.

Stabbed to death.

Already flags were lowered to half-mast. The car horns died down, but the tolling persisted. The carillon was played on the quarter of every hour. At Westerford High, students and teachers huddled around radios. Many gathered in small groups in the dining hall. Speechless, frozen in disbelief, nailed to the spot, they leaned closer—thirsty for news. Many brushed tears from their eyes—girls *and* boys, and many an adult—as they listened to the radio broadcaster. "The whole population of South Africa has been shocked to the depth of its soul by the tragedy that unfolded in the House of Assembly this afternoon. On behalf of all South Africans, I have to state our tremendous sense of loss. We are overwhelmed by grief on this tragic day. Indeed, a cedar of Lebanon has fallen."

Rianna cried out and freed her hands from Jess who had her fingers in a death-grip. Jessica sniffled as she wiped her eyes. "Sorry, Ree," she mumbled.

"I didn't know you cared for the man," Rianna whispered, where they sat huddled together with the other students in the dining hall, who had formed semi-circles around a handful of radios.

"He was my prime minister too you know."

"You're *English*. He was a *Boer*."

Jessica shrugged, jabbed Rianna in the ribs, and hunched forward, placing her index finger on her closed lips. She wanted to hear every word.

Miss Clark sat in front, an open seat between her and Miss Whitehead, who was an inch closer than she should be to Mr. Read. The gym teacher listened with his chin supported in his hands, elbows resting on the table, eyes fixed on the ceiling. Miss Clark's eyes were closed; she shook her head from side to side, as if in solidarity with each sentence the news anchor uttered.

It was clear Mr. Read remained oblivious to the antics of Gloria Whitehead, who now clutched both her hands around his bulging upper arm. Her eyes flew open when she felt Rianna's resting on her, and then narrowed into a glare. Since the Wild Coast hike, the Xhosa-language teacher had remained cool and aloof, almost indifferent.

Rianna shrugged, hunched forward like Jessica, and closed her eyes. *Miss Whitehead can be such a tefie. If she's jealous of the running-group girls, why doesn't she join us on the runs? It's so childish. I wouldn't dare look at Rupert Read as a potential boyfriend. I'm only fifteen. The silly woman.* She turned back to face Jessica who immediately took that as permission to grab hold of her hands again.

According to the reporter, the parliamentary bells were still sounding when every attendant took their places. Dr. Verwoerd had just sat down when a uniformed parliamentary messenger stepped closer, and Verwoerd had held out his hand, expecting a letter. The next moment the messenger fell forward, lurching onto Verwoerd. At first it seemed he was hitting the PM with his fist. Only when they saw the blood did it register that the man was stabbing the PM in the chest and neck. A concealed dagger was apparently used in the attack.

By the time the assailant was dragged off the prime minister, the latter was already heavily wounded. Some members of Parliament who were also doctors immediately gave assistance and started with life support. Within minutes, Dr. Verwoerd was rushed off to Groote Schuur, but he was declared dead on arrival. The assailant, who worked as a parliamentary messenger, was identified as one Demetrio Tsafendas, a man of Greek descent.

SOON ENOUGH, the official explanation from the office of the minister of Justice was released: the assassination was the work of a lone operator, a troubled man suffering from mental illness, and the deed was therefore not politically motivated. He was classified as White, being from European heritage—his dark complexion and frizzy hair notwithstanding—so apartheid could not have had any bearing in all of this. It was deemed highly unlikely to have been the motive for the attack.

The nation sighed with relief—the work of a madman. Thank God. Politics had nothing to do with the killing. Apartheid was safe. To an asylum then with the killer, the nation cried. But whichever version was correct—the Architect of Apartheid was dead.

Those who had paid closer attention, however, were prompted to ask questions. Hard questions. Irritating even. But their queries remained unanswered over the ensuing days and weeks and months and, eventually, years. The prime minister's office doggedly stuck to their script—the killing was the work of a single deranged man.

And yet, if the assailant had been known to suffer from a mental illness, the most pressing question then became, why was he employed in the House of Assembly and placed in a work situation where he had access to the prime minister? Or, if his was a new illness, why was he not properly diagnosed, effectively medicated, and prevented perhaps from working in Parliament at all? And lastly, what happened to the security measures in Parliament that fateful Tuesday afternoon? How could a man, sane or otherwise, have carried a concealed dagger and it not be detected? Why was he able to get that intimately close, and allowed to do what he did to the prime minister, with everyone only looking on?

The world held its breath. In South Africa the news was met with responses that ranged from shocked silence, tears, and disbelief, to cautious relief, elation, and even bold optimism.

Rianna, surprised by the public display of emotion from her English-raised roommate (and others like her), who had shed genuine tears for a man they had never met in person, realized there was much in the world she had yet to fathom.

To all, friend and foe, it was evident—a man of consequence had passed away. A man of stature, a brilliant politician, an eloquent orator, an imposing statesman was no more. He was no less a man just because he was also the enforcer of laws that had divided and hurt millions of fellow countrymen—men, women, and children whose skins happened to be darker than his—black and brown and other colours in between.

The essence of his political vision for South Africa was that every person who wasn't Caucasian, snow-white like himself, had to be segregated. Under his watch the laws were enforced. New laws were added. Laws based upon the colour of one's hide and the language one learned as a child.

The peculiar thing was this—and in the ensuing years, Rianna gave much thought to this truth—of the latter two realities, no human being had any control. Not since the beginning of time, not until the end of mankind, will any human have any say in who their birth parents are, and therefore what will be the colour of their skin; in who will raise them from birth, and therefore what will be the first language they learn as an infant, or where they will be born and raised. No baby, no child, had a choice in the matter.

And yet, we humans, throughout the ages, act as if we do have a say—as if we deserve to be blamed for our skin, parents, and tongue—as if those things determine our value. *What barren philosophy.*

As Rianna pulled Jess against her, in front of the radio, soothing her shaking body, stroking her arms, she found herself back on the swaying coach, on the train from Pietersburg, steaming toward Cape Town. Across from her stood the burly conductor. And next to her, Bertie—Albert from Messina, trembling, shocked like her into silence. Too scared to move as the intimidating brute, foaming at the mouth, hollered at her to visit the prime minister's office once she reached Cape Town and inform the man she disagreed with his "Whites only" policy of separate development.

She shuddered. *Now I'll never get the chance to talk to the prime minister, and ask him why Hendrik Willems and his family have to leave their home in District Six. Why Hendrik's sister could start the process to turn into a White person because the pencil slipped out of her beautiful waving auburn hair. Perhaps she had a White Daddy. Now I won't be able to tell the prime minister that I am honoured to call Hendrik my friend and enjoy holding his hand and kissing him. Not only did Dr. Verwoerd make my friendship against the law, he declared it a sin!*

And she had also hoped to ask Dr. Verwoerd (if there remained time during the interview), why she, Rianna Vermeulen, born in Northern Rhodesia, white but an African nevertheless, wasn't required to carry a passbook.

From under half-closed lids she glanced around the room, surprised by how wrong she had been. Just because people spoke English didn't mean they couldn't or wouldn't have sympathy with the Afrikaner nation.

Six o'clock came and went. Nobody stirred. Hunger pangs were ignored. Ears remained pressed to the radios. They listened to the reverberations, the shockwaves, the shaking of the earth, at the felling of the once tall cedar. The vice-principal kept a cool head and sent a message to the kitchen to hold supper till at least 7 p.m.

Toward the end of the very late dinner, Miss Clark got to her feet. She snapped her fingers to get everyone's attention. "We're all shocked and surprised and saddened by this afternoon's events." She cleared her throat, glanced at her wrist and scanned the room. "But life goes on. I would love to have remained here, listening.

We all wish to know more. However, we have to get you off to bed. Following dinner, you'll have to listen to news broadcasts in your rooms, if you so wish. I'm sorry, boys and girls, but homework still needs to be done. Lights-out and silence will be at 11:30 p.m., instead of the usual 10:00 p.m."

Sighs and murmurs rose from across the room until Miss Clark cleared her throat a second time.

At the moment Rianna and Jessica pushed their chairs back from the dinner table, James Martin—trailed by his ever-present shadow, Andries Steenkamp—popped up behind the girls' chairs, like *meerkats* on lookout. The teachers by then had all left the dining hall. "Hello, ladies," James crooned.

Rianna scuttled sideways. "*Bastards*," she hissed, groping for a chair backrest to regain her balance.

"Settle down, Vermeulen. Hi, Jess." James made a small wave with his hand, ignoring the annoyance written across the redhead's face.

"What do you want, Martin?" The red-faced Rianna moved the chair between herself and James.

He chuckled and stood his ground. "Andries and I wanted to make certain you guys are okay." He shrugged. "You know . . . today's events. Dr. Verwoerd . . . perhaps offer our services as student counselors."

Rianna raised the chair a few inches off the ground and took a step back. "Student *what?*"

Martin stood his ground. "I'm not messing with you. I've done counsellor-training. If either you or Jess wants to talk, needs a willing ear . . . ." He glanced at Jessica's red, puffy eyes. "Perhaps a shoulder to cry on?"

Jessica gave a sob, spun around and bolted from the dining hall.

Rianna shoved the chair against Martin, banging him in the shins. "How *could* you?" She turned from the surprised boy and raced after her friend. "*Counselor?* You're an arrogant *fool!*"

FOR THE REMAINDER of the week, until Rianna went to work in the cable station café on Saturday, the newspapers and news broadcasts embroidered on speculations about the motivations of the prime minister's assailant—the man who had a Greek for a father and a Mozambican for a mother. Rianna took great pains to avoid the two standard-nine boys, Martin and Steenkamp.

She couldn't wait to speak to Hendrik about what had happened. About how this would impact him and his mother and Sarah and her friend in the department of Bantu Affairs and their house on Cambridge Street in District Six. *Will Hendrik gloat? Shrug his shoulders? Wipe a tear? Perhaps jump with joy? Will he be different toward me?*

Sixteen

The company of friends.
10 September 1966

By the time Rianna fastened her work-apron early Saturday afternoon on Table Mountain, Dr. Hendrik Verwoerd had been laid to rest in the Hero's Acre in Pretoria. His state funeral was attended by tens of thousands of people earlier that day—most of whom were of European descent. Hendrik Willems was silent behind his dishes—turned into himself. Rianna carried her own thoughts.

She was still seething. James Martin had, this time without his sidekick, apprehended her inside the gate to Westerford High as she had pedaled hard to get to her afternoon shift. She dared not be late. Martin, invisible until she was alongside him, had stepped from the shadows of the Wisteria that covered the entire wooden fence leading to the gate.

She had shrieked when he grabbed hold of her bicycle. They stopped short of crashing to the tarmac.

"You, bloody *ass*!" she managed the instant her balance was restored, trying to yank her handlebar free. She was breathing fast—the heady smell of the clusters of mauve flowers choked her—on hot days its sweetness was overbearing.

"Slow down, Missy."

Her eyes drilled through him as she yanked the bar a second time—her mouth tight.

"Where are you going in such a hurry?" Martin repositioned his grip on the bars, brushing her fingers in the process. "Why wouldn't you let me *kiss* you?"

"Don't touch me," she hissed as she pulled on the handle-bars—but Martin had it in an iron grip. "*Kiss* you? Forget it. You'll make me late for work." She jerked the handlebar free with unexpected force and shoved the taunting boy away, but not before she inhaled his clean young-man scent. He must have had a shower when he noticed her at the bicycle shed from their room upstairs and then ran here to set up the ambush—his hair was all wet and tousled. His angular jaw made him quite attractive, according to Jessica, but he gave Rianna the creeps. She jumped in the saddle. "I'm not your Missy or a girl you can kiss. Stop stalking me!"

"You must be off to see your *Coloured* boyfriend," James Martin called after her as she pedaled away.

Rianna slammed the brakes, braced herself as she skidded to a stop and glared over her shoulder. "*What* are you talking about?" Her cheeks burned, her chest heaved. She felt lightheaded.

"I'm not blind, Vermeulen. You forget I also love the mountain—I'm often at the upper station. Dr. Verwoerd may have been buried this morning, but the laws of the land still stand."

Rianna gasped as she righted her bicycle. "He's *not* my boyfriend. His mother is the assistant manager at the cableway café—" She jumped back in the saddle, ready to take off. She glanced at her wrist. Hendrik's mother would kill her if she was late.

"What you're doing is illegal, Vermeulen."

"I am old enough to work there!" she hollered as she took off, disappearing through the open gate.

"You're guilty of *two* misdemeanours, Missy. Lying about your age and fraternizing across the colour line."

"You're such a bully!"

"The first one's going to bite you in the behind and the second one may make you end up in *prison*."

Rianna pedaled harder and yelled, "*Bastard!*"

When she approached the stop sign at the corner, outside the grounds, the breeze carried his final words across the fences. "That's what they'll call your babies if you become too friendly with *Hendrik Willems*."

Saturday morning at the hostel was mail day—if there were any letters. The only letters she ever received were from her parents, four times a year. Then this morning, there were two— one from Katete in Zambia and the second from Stellenbosch, from Bertie. Even after all this time he had remembered where she went to school. Albert Vosloo was inviting her to attend his choir competition the following Sunday morning—they were performing at the music department of the University of Cape Town. Following the performance, he also wished to go on a short hike on the mountain.

He had lied to her—about not singing. She was convinced, more than ever, that he had also lied about him and Miss Nichols.

She wondered about the tall boy who loved to tilt his head, shove his hands deep in his pockets, and kick at imaginary pebbles. Perhaps he had grown up. Perhaps Miss Nichols had grown tired of him not growing up fast enough. *How long can a woman wait for a boy to become a man?* For a moment Rianna hoped Bertie didn't grow up too fast.

⁂

*R*ianna gasped when Hendrik allowed a plate to explode into pieces on the tile floor at his feet. Her tray swayed and almost fell—she fought for balance. This has never happened before—him dropping a plate.

The scullery was around the corner from the kitchen, but a silence fell over the entire establishment. Every guest, every server, every kitchen employee, the manager included, paused. Held their breaths. Hendrik sensed the vacuum, the hesitation, and hollered, "*I'm okay!*" Everyone gave a nervous chuckle.

Rianna remained frozen to the spot, facing him, the tray white-knuckled in her hands.

Hendrik met her eyes. "*What?*"

"Are you sure you're okay?"

"Why would I not be?" he spat. "Leave me the hell alone!" He attacked the next plate with his scraper, kicking the broken pieces away with his foot. Rianna gave a sob and escaped through the inside swing doors to go wait on her tables.

Later, toward the end of her shift, when she paused on the outskirts of Hendrik's domain a second time, his hands went quiet and he glanced at her.

When he remained silent she stepped closer. "Hendrik?"

The grim line of his lips softened. "Ree, I'm sorry . . . ."

She threw a glance over her shoulder toward the kitchen and stepped into the scullery. She brushed his upper arm before backing off. "Will you wait for me when we're done?"

His nod was imperceptible but the smile reached his eyes.

Later, she stood to the side, yet close enough to get into the cable car ahead of the throng of tourists. Hendrik joined her, but kept a respectable distance. You could never be too certain about who was paying close attention. It was as if the Southwestern had carried James Martin's voice across the mountain: "Dr. Verwoerd may have been buried this morning, but the laws of the land still stand." Perhaps Hendrik Willems had also heard the words carried by the wind.

This time neither spoke a word until they passed under the boom gate at the wharf. Rianna had pushed her bicycle without so much as glancing at him, remaining a bicycle length behind him, just in case. Who knew how paranoid the law enforcers had become the past five days? She dared not speak. She'd wait. She sensed Hendrik's struggle. First the dinner plate. Then him yelling at her. Both firsts.

Their prime minister murdered with a knife. The entire country still reeling from the unthinkable deed. Unfathomable. Also a first.

District Six soon to be bulldozed—yet another first.

It was as if the seagulls' cries were more forlorn that Saturday afternoon—did the birds sense the mood in the land? They must have noticed the half-mast flags, their tiny ears still ringing from the tolling of each and every city bell, in commemoration of the state funeral earlier that day.

"Old place?" Rianna asked as she leaned her bicycle behind the shipping container. Hendrik nodded and helped her clamber up the battered concrete barrier wall. It was impossible there for passersby, six feet below them on dock level, to notice the Coloured boy and White girl, perched side by side atop the barrier wall, facing the water, well above where curious eyes would think to look.

A FRESHLY loaded freighter sounded its horns as it pushed away from the quay, unhurried, churning the dark water of the harbour as it slowly turned its prow toward the harbour mouth. Its crew scattered behind the railings high above them, some even waving down at the duo.

Hendrik returned the wave. "One of these days will see *me* standing up there, like those guys, waving at the poor country rats staying behind." He gave a shrill laugh.

Rianna shielded her eyes against the afternoon sun. She shivered. "You never told me you dreamed of sailing the seas?"

Hendrik shrugged. "I guess just to get *away*."

"What will it solve?"

"It'll be a grand adventure."

"And when the adventure is over, when you return—who will be waiting on you? Who will you be? Who will you have become? Will your problems be solved?"

Hendrik sighed and fell silent, resting his chin on his knees, watching two gulls screeching it out as they tucked at opposite ends of a piece of debris that had fallen overboard. "He never intended to become a politician," Hendrik murmured.

"*Who?*"

"Dr. Verwoerd. He was born in the Netherlands, grew up in South Africa and in Rhodesia and planned on becoming a *dominee.*"

"A preacher?"

Hendrik leaned back against the concrete wall. "Following standard ten, he completed his BA and applied to continue his studies in theology. But the school, the university, dragged their feet with his application because they insisted on a letter of reference from his pastor in Brandfort, where he had only lived for a short while."

Rianna cocked her brows. "How do you know this? Did you meet the man before he was—"

Hendrik shook his head. "You're not the only one reading outside the teachers' curriculum, remember?"

Rianna laughed, jabbed him in the ribs. "So what did he *do?*"

"Verwoerd said, 'Stuff you,' to the School of Theology and went on and studied psychology and philosophy, travelled to Germany for further studies, and got himself a PhD."

"And the rest of the story we know?" Rianna asked.

Her companion nodded again, before falling into a deep silence, his eyes on the cargo ship that had shrunk to a morsel on the horizon.

"Why did you drop the plate this morning?"

"It was wet."

She rested her head on her knees, facing him. "You've never dropped one before." She reached out and brushed his arm. Hendrik Willems shrugged his shoulders.

"Were you glad . . . when you heard the news on Tuesday?"

He shook his head. "How could I be? He was a man like me . . . he was a father, a grandfather . . . I never knew my dad."

"But he enforced horrible laws . . . ."

"I cannot hate him. I think he did it because of the fear the Afrikaner has of disappearing from the land. They're outnumbered. I think it stems from their horrible experiences with the British during the Anglo-Boer wars—from the atrocities committed against them. They have a legitimate fear."

Rianna took his hands. "But now they do the same? What will happen? Won't this be the *end* of apartheid?"

Hendrik laughed. "If only."

"Why did you drop the plate then?"

Hendrik sighed. "I'm upset. I'm scared about the future. With Verwoerd we at least knew what he was up to. Who will take over now? They are going to throw us out of the house I grew up in— one of these days—they will bulldoze it flat. I'm worried about Mother. What will this do to her? She refuses to talk about any of this. Not even about Sarah and her white friend."

Rianna squeezed his hand, beaming. "You also have a *white* friend."

"But mine doesn't work in the department of Bantu Affairs. Mine can't pull any strings . . . ."

Rianna slapped his shoulder. "I can run fast and hike up mountains and speak up about racial injustice and atrocities committed by so-called civilized governments." She leaned closer and gave him a peck on the cheek. "And I will *remain* your friend."

Hendrik leaned closer, lifted her hand, and kissed her fingertips. "What will we be if not true and loyal friends?"

She smiled up at him. "I have to go."

Hendrik leaned closer, took her face in his hands and planted a kiss on her parted lips. For an entire second the world paused. Their eyes locked as their lips found each other. Then he jumped to his feet and pulled her along, before helping her slip down toward the walkway. Rianna walked her bicycle, struggling to bring her pounding heart under control. Neither said a word. Her cheeks glowed. Her first proper kiss.

Once they reached the boom gate at the top of the wharf entrance, Rianna turned to her companion. "Do you know a James Martin?"

She could hear him suck in his breath.

"Hendrik?"

He avoided her eyes.

"He threatened me this morning over being friends with you."

She stopped until he faced her.

"What did he say?"

"You're my *boyfriend*."

Hendrik's eyes laughed at her. "Am I?"

The crimson intensified up Rianna's neck and cheeks as she tapped him hard on his arm. "You're mocking me."

Hendrik's eyes became unreadable. "He confronted me at the cafeteria last Saturday, before you arrived."

"Why didn't you *tell*?"

"There was nothing to tell. I'm not scared of a spoiled white boy." They resumed walking in silence.

Just before Hendrik turned off to his mother's house, Rianna whispered as she mounted her bicycle, "I'm scared of what the likes of James Martin can do to us, Hendrik."

Hendrik met her eyes. "Martin's not your friend. You will now learn who your *true* friends are."

"Be careful, Hendrik."

"Goodbye, my brave friend."

Seventeen

ALBERT FROM MESSINA. LIES AND
MORE LIES. SEPTEMBER 1966

*R*ianna did not recognize the young man in the crisp blazer and bowtie who approached her in the music auditorium's foyer.

"Hello, Rianna." He towered over her.

"Bertie?" She hesitated only for a second, then squealed and hugged him close, only to step back, crimson. She studied him from head to toe. His latest growth spurt had been impressive. Even his face had changed.

"You've *grown*." She had to tilt her head to read his face.

"You sound like my *mother*."

"You're a *man* now," she whispered.

He chuckled, lowered his gaze, and kicked at a mark on the tiled floor. When their eyes met again, he sighed, aware of the heat that crept up his neck. "Thanks for coming."

"You were my friend for a day and a half. You still are."

Albert turned toward a side door. "It's time for me to go to the back—join the others." He gestured toward the auditorium. "It's almost time for you to find your seat."

Rianna cocked a brow. "Why did you lie to me about the singing when we were on the train?"

"Technically it wasn't a lie. I didn't participate in the choir festival in Bloemfontein."

"Fibber."

"I was embarrassed."

"It's an incredible feat to sing."

"I didn't know how you'd respond if you knew. I was afraid you'd think it was a girly thing to do."

"Fibber times two."

Bertie held up his palms. "That was *then*. I'm taller, but I've also grown up some." He laughed as he stepped away. "Please wait for me afterwards." Waving, he stopped, then raced back. "I almost forgot. Will you still join me on the hike up the mountain? You said you would when you wrote."

"Have you checked the weather?"

"The weather prophets predicted a clear afternoon—no fog, no rain. *Please*, Rianna?" He called over his shoulder. "I have something special to show you."

Just as well that she had asked Maria Willems, Hendrik's mother, to be excused from work at the mountain café that afternoon.

<hr />

The standing ovation lasted an entire five minutes. It was impossible not to notice Bertie in the back row, towering above his fellow baritones. The choir had excelled—beyond expectations. Rianna rubbed her arms—all goosebumps—she was so proud of her friend from Messina. It was hard to single out which song she loved best. The choir's voices had flowed so effortlessly from the likes of "The Skye Boat Song" until their moving close with "Ave Maria."

She allowed the throng of pushing and shoving people, all blabbering, to sweep her from the auditorium into the foyer. Pushing back, she steered sideways as if toward shore, closer to one of several exits, then turned around once out of the maelstrom, and waited for Bertie.

The audience was in no hurry to leave—their excited voices rose and fell—everyone waiting to get a closer glimpse of the individual choir members as they emerged.

Suddenly Rianna snapped to attention—she dared not breath. Across the foyer from her stood the polka-dot lady, Miss Nichols. Rianna skulked deeper into the shadows, grateful for the arched doorways at the exits. *What is she doing here?*

Silence fell over those waiting in the foyer, but only for a moment, then the crowded parted like the Red Sea to welcome the choir members. The chatter became deafening. Rianna noticed Bertie craning his neck but she remained in the deep shadows. He couldn't see her in her hiding place. When his eyes found those of Miss Nichols, they beamed at each other, and then he pushed his way through the crowd to reach his teacher.

Rianna took a rescue breath. Miss Nichols, dressed in a body-caressing and low-cut black gown, had stepped closer to Bertie, close enough to touch his arm, close enough for their hips to brush, and whispered in his ear. He immediately straightened up and laughed. Miss Nichol then leaned forward, her cleavage on display, and squeezed the boy's arm for several seconds. Bertie pulled away, glanced around the foyer a second time, turned back to Miss Nichols, said something that made her laugh, and then walked over to where he and Rianna had met earlier that morning. Rianna tore away from her hideout and sauntered over.

"Where did you hide?"

"I had to escape the stampede."

Bertie chuckled. "What did you think?"

"*Incredible.* I am proud of you, Albert from Mesina."

Bertie bowed his head, mumbled, "Thank you," and kicked at a floor tile. He pulled out of his embarrassment and took her hand. His glanced with appreciation at her knee-length dress. "Did you bring your bag with your hiking clothes?"

Rianna pulled her hand free. *What if the tefie sees me?* She was in no mood for a repeat humiliation in public by that woman. "I sometimes follow instructions. Let me get my backpack from the coat check."

He smiled. "I'll meet you here in five minutes—my stuff's at the back in the dressing room."

"Isn't SHE coming along?" Rianna tilted her head in the direction of where Miss Nichols was standing, now surrounded by several other choir members. They both had their backpacks in hand, still dressed in their Sunday-best.

"Who?" Bertie's brow furrowed.

"The *tefie*."

"*Please* don't call her that."

Rianna spun around and darted for the exit. Bertie strode after her and caught the heavy glass door as she shoved it open.

"Ms. Nichols is ten years your senior. You *look* like a man but are still a boy—that makes her a *tefie.*"

"Only nine. I'm almost *eighteen*, Rianna."

"Okay. Then she's a *sugar momma.*"

"Don't be *ridiculous.*"

"You told me on the train there was nothing going on between the two of you."

"We're good friends."

"I observed inappropriate touching between a half-naked female teacher and her virile male student—in public—not minutes ago."

"You have a lively imagination, Miss Vermeulen."

"Don't insult me. There's a *spark* when she looks at you."

Bertie snickered. "*Jealous?*"

Rianna tightened the grip on her bag and walking stick, and ambled ahead, nose in the air. He only caught up with her at the bus stop. Neither of them said a word until the bus that would take them to the lower cable station arrived.

"What's it with you and this shepherd's staff?"

"Laugh as much as you like, Mister. It has saved my life on more than one occasion." Rianna brandished the rod like a sword. "*En garde!*"

"*Touché!*" Bertie cried, as he fell back with arms raised in mock surrender.

When the bus hissed to a standstill, Rianna clambered up the four steps ahead of him. At the sight of the redhead and her companion, both dressed in their finest, each carrying a voluminous backpack, the bus driver rolled his eyes. Bertie shrugged with indifference.

Thirty minutes later, they were both dressed for hiking, their concert clothing safely tucked away in the public lockers inside the lower cable station building. When Rianna joined her companion, the baritone was almost unrecognizable in his hiking clothes. She soon stopped in her tracks when he headed outside for the nearest footpath instead of the cable car. "Why aren't we taking the car to the top?" she implored.

Bertie laughed. "We *need* to hike. It's the only way to show you what I've discovered a week ago."

Rianna studied him. "You seem cozy and familiar with this place." She pulled her backpack straps tighter. "But you live in Stellenbosch. How often do you come here? Do you have a car?"

Bertie only chuckled and accelerated his pace.

"How often, Bertie?"

Albert pulled up his shoulders. "I don't know. I don't keep track." He turned and led the way up the trail.

An hour later, Albert, who had remained a step ahead of her, stopped at a large boulder to the side of the marked trail. He stepped off the path and gestured for her to follow him behind the boulder.

Instead, Rianna paused and chugged from her water bottle. "Where are you heading, Vosloo?" She wiped the excess water from her mouth with the back of her hand. "What's your story, Bertie?" She didn't move, waiting for an answer, one hand on her hip, the other holding her walking stick.

Finally, Albert stopped and turned back to face her. "Come on, Rianna. We're almost there." She didn't move. He tried teasing. "Or do you need a rest?"

Still she remained on the same spot. "Don't mess with me, Bertie. You know I'm fit. I'm impressed—seems you're even fitter. But that's not the point. We've left the trail. *Why?*"

"Is it illegal to follow one's own path up the mountain, Miss Vermeulen? Scared you'll get lost?"

"It's irresponsible. It causes ground erosion. We call it hikers' code." She shifted her weight from one leg to the other and waited.

Albert retraced his steps and grabbed her hand on the walking stick. "Are you *coming?*"

"Stop it." She yanked free and then glanced at the skies, where a fleece of clouds raced overhead. "I don't have time for your games. You're not honest with me—about many things. I know the mountain but I'm going back." With that she swung around and headed back.

"Rianna, wait!" Bertie caught up within a few strides and reached for her arm a second time. He looked her in the face. "I'm sorry. I should have been more upfront with you. I didn't want to spoil the surprise. I found a lair." He lowered his voice. "It's a little over two hundred feet from here."

"Lair?"

"Yes, the living quarters of the *Caracal caracal*—a female Persian lynx with three young kittens."

"The *rooikat?*"

Albert nodded. Her grin widened. His excitement grew as he reached for her hand once again; this time, the intrigued fifteen-year-old allowed him to lead her forward. "How did you find them?" She hastened to keep up with him as he strode along the narrow path.

He smiled over his shoulder. "Did my homework."

"You're a blatant liar, Albert from Messina."

"Why?"

"You don't simply 'find' the *rooikat*—they're secretive nocturnal animals."

Bertie laughed briefly but then placed his index finger in front of his lips, "Shhuut . . . we're close." A moment later he crouched down, lowered his small backpack to the ground, and dug into it. Within moments he had made himself comfortable in a nearby fallen tree and was adjusting the focus on a pair of binoculars he had trained on a spot thirty yards away. Then he nodded slightly, lowered the field glasses and handed them to Rianna. "Follow the line of my arm. Where you see the sugar bush growing from the gap between those two rocks, immediately to its left, there's an opening in the ground—Yes, three feet lower down . . . the lair. I think that burrow originally belonged to a porcupine family."

Rianna grabbed the binoculars. Her grip on them tightened as she studied the mouth of the lair. She sighed with pleasure. This surprise came a close third to running and hiking.

Bertie tapped his friend's arm. "And you thought I could only sing baritone and make eyes at my school teacher."

At that, Rianna gave him a shove hard enough to make him lose his balance. She snickered when he toppled from the fallen tree trunk. "Show-off."

He just grinned and got back onto his perch, then took the glasses from her. "I want you to see her *babies*."

After half an hour of taking turns observing the lair entrance, Rianna turned to her friend from Messina, who attended school in Stellenbosch. "How many hours did it take you to track them down?" She gestured at the lair. "Don't lie."

Albert shrugged. "Perhaps forty? It took us four nights, sleeping on the mountain, to finally track down a *rooikat* that was expecting. We found her two days before she gave birth."

"*Us*? Who's the *we*?"

He smiled as if embarrassed. "My dad knows the director of the Table Mountain National Park. He allowed me to shadow one of his park wardens. It took us four weekends, sleeping the Friday night on different spots on this side of mountain, to eventually spot not only her but her birthing room."

"Why go to all the trouble with—"

Albert snapped to attention, his knuckles turned white on the binoculars. He whispered, "Quick—there's the mother with one of her babies."

She took the binoculars from Bertie but dropped them in her excitement, cussed at her clumsiness, and scooped them out of the dry long grass. "Sorry, Bertie," she murmured, as she wiped the lenses clean on her stomach. Seconds later she choked from inhaling her own spit. "Oh my goodness, Bertie! The mom plus *two* of the little ones now." Her rapid breathing slowed as she kept the binoculars trained on the red cat family. *Wait until I tell Hendrik and Jessica—they won't believe me.*

When Albert touched Rianna's shoulder to request the binoculars, she handed them to him and then brushed his upper arm.

"Albert, this is so special. Thank you for sharing it with me. It's *unbelievable*." She leaned forward and kissed him smack on the cheek.

Unperturbed, Bertie mumbled, "My pleasure," and kept the glasses zoomed on the frolicking cats. Without moving a muscle, he added, "Now I only have to decide where to place the trapping cages."

"The *what*?"

"Traps—special cages." He clicked with his tongue. "You thought this was for sightseeing only? I have a plan. We're catching them. I only need the mom, then the babies will follow her."

Rianna lurched to her feet and knocked her friend from his seat a second time—this time with intent and with considerable force. Running and hiking toughens a body. The binoculars flew into the yellow grass. She glared at him. "You're not only a liar and a fornicator, but a poacher as well!" She swallowed hard. "I thought you were my *friend*."

"Calm down, *jou, helkat*!" Bertie scrambled to his feet, scowled at Rianna as he brushed grass and leaves from his clothes and scrounged around on all fours for the field glasses. "Thanks to *you*, the cats have now disappeared back into their lair!"

"It may just save their lives." Rianna also wiped herself clean and stomped away. Bertie found the binoculars and caught up with her. "*Fornicator* is a strong word, coming from a fifteen-year-old."

She spun around, eyes spitting. "I'm almost sixteen. You want euphemisms? Do you prefer *mistress* or *lover*?"

"You're jealous." He smirked. "I told you, we're *friends*."

"Friends with intimate privileges?" Face glowing, Rianna marched back to the trail. "Does the park manager know about your plans to trap the cats?"

Albert scoffed. "He won't be any the wiser. There's enough of the cats on the mountain. We did a count. These four won't be missed."

"You couldn't settle for just one. It had to be a gravid female."

"I told you. We have plans."

"Then we've established the fact—you *are* a poacher."

"You're ignorant, Vermeulen. My dad and I are no poachers. Dad contributes over five thousand Rand each year to this park. He's big into conservation. We're not killing the animals. I'd rather call what we're planning on doing, selective wildlife preservation. And, for your edification, the rooikat *can* be domesticated. That's what we're planning on doing. Tame them. Breed them."

Rianna darted toward the original trail. "*Ignorant*. You're so bloody *arrogant*. Because your dad is rich, you believe you may break every social norm, including nature conservation laws. You believe you can *buy* people."

Bertie snickered. "Money has the ability to fix many inconsistencies and insecurities in life."

"Pity it can't fix a lack of morals or ethics."

"You're self-righteous. Don't judge me, Missy. One day . . . one day, I'll show you what a domesticated *rooikat* looks like."

"Hah! You're no Egyptian prince or pharaoh."

Bertie laughed out loud. "Who knows? I'm planning on going one step further—train the cats to hunt."

It was Rianna who laughed now. "These cats are small animals—even the males are less than forty pounds. Help you hunt what—birds and field rats?"

Bertie hollered after her as the distance between them increased, "You'll sing a different tune when you see what two of those creatures can do when well trained. I bet you they will be effective watchdogs. Intimidating and *dangerous*."

"Most certainly, *O Rameses*!"

Eighteen

Bells toll only for VIPs—a second funeral. November 1966

The last time Rianna had laid eyes on Lukas Ferreira was in July 1964, in Zambia—in the Paishuko district, when she was thirteen and he ten. She was then hunched forward with a blanket around her shoulders, shivering uncontrollably in the front of the old Chevrolet truck following their kidnapping ordeal. Lukas had walked up to the door, desperate to console her, thinking he could provide comfort by speaking to her. She wasn't ready to talk to anybody then—she had driven him away with venom dripping from her words.

The youth that now stood waiting on her at the front door of Westerford High, next to the lanky frame of Rev. Louis Ferreira, reminded Rianna of her childhood friend. It had to be him. He too must have recalled her jabbing words from inside the truck, making him hesitant, yet brave enough to meet her brooding expression. She forced a smile.

"*Rianna*. What a surprise!" It was the older Ferreira who broke the spell.

Rianna suppressed her first response to curtsy. Respect for one's elders had been drilled into them from her mother's knee. "Hello, Uncle Louis. Hello, Lukas." She greeted both with a handshake, then stepped back a safe distance. The hugging part could be added later. Neither her mother nor Lukas's was present to insist on the customary hug-and-kiss formality.

She felt a blush rise to her cheeks and scolded herself. It was juvenile—Lukas was a childhood friend from long ago, and his father she knew from a distance. Lukas was a child, his voice not even broken she was certain, while she was fending off attention from seventeen-year-old boys—from almost-men. *What do I talk about with them? Lukas has swallowed his tongue and his father is a dominee*. Her gaze shifted from preacher father to son. They seemed waiting for a response. Then she remembered. She took a step forward, using the courtesy title she had been brought up with. "About the *telegram,* Uncle Louis?"

The reverend nodded.

She had received it the previous evening—there was to be a funeral in the Ferreira family, someone close enough to justify travelling three and a half days by road. She had grown used to the practice in the West Cape of inviting people only to birth-day parties and weddings. Not to funerals—that was reserved for the intimate family circle. The practice among the Mission field workers seemed to be one of wider inclusion.

Her crimson intensified. Her chest rose and fell. *Shame on you, Rianna Vermeulen. His grandmother passed away less than a week ago.*

Not only that; he had finished standard five at the Mission school in Zambia, and was to start high school in the south, in the new year, much as she had done more than two years ago.

She smiled, extending her hand a second time. "My condolences on the passing of your wife's mother, Uncle Louis." Rianna shook first the missionary's hand, then that of his son. "Sorry, Lukas." His slender hand returned her firm grip; he swallowed several times, holding her gaze, not saying a word. Rianna sighed, and, without giving it another thought, tugged the quiet boy closer for a thorough hug. He smelled of soap and a tolerable level of boy sweat. The hurt in his eyes unsettled her. Could the agony from the loss of a grandmother he hadn't seen in three years be that vast? Or was he still haunted, like herself, by Mapopa's actions—when Lukas had to witness his childhood friend, Anthony, bleed himself pale on the outskirts of Paishuko Village from a gunshot wound?

Louis Ferreira wiped his exhausted eyes. His head throbbed. He had done most of the driving—close to two thousand miles. Last time he had seen Phillip and Anna Vermeulen's thirteen-year-old, she was a precocious teenager—facing them now as a young woman—who was at an apparent loss for words. He cleared his throat. "Maria, Lukas's mother, inquired whether you would accompany us to the funeral tomorrow? It's at three in the afternoon." He held her dark gaze. Rianna gave a curt nod.

"The funeral is in Stellenbosch—we'll pick you up if you could be ready by two?"

Rianna found her voice. "Thank you, Uncle Louis. I'll meet you here then, at the door—tomorrow at two."

RIANNA drifted away from the extended Ferreira family, once they reached the gravesite. She had expected a bland recital in church by the *dominee*—but the preacher had singled her out, she was certain, the redhead from Westerford High. He had shared the deeply personal and colourful life lived by Lukas's grandmother— a vibrant and remarkable woman. Most unsettling. Rianna scuttled to the side—she needed time to think over what had been said.

If there was one thing Mother had taught her, it was to not impose. None of the other faces assembled, except for Lukas and his parents, now next to the gaping hole, looked familiar. She regretted not having asked permission to bring Jessica along. Rianna closed her eyes and listened. Deep breathing always seemed to calm her. The scent of the pines and firs mixed with that of the freshly trimmed lawn, narrow green strips between the rows and rows of headstones.

Through lowered eyes she imagined the powdery aroma of mallet and chisel as it worked its way into the intricate engraving of each marble headstone that surrounded them. She eyed the mound of earth, huddled dark next to the casket—you could smell the planet's innards. The diggers must have barely finished in time that morning. Uncle Louis probably already had a talk with the foreman of the gravediggers about not preparing further in advance—a freshly dug grave needed time to "settle." What if they didn't finish in time? Unthinkable. Louis Ferreira knew about graves and burials and proper timing.

Their section of the cemetery was flanked on all sides by youthful fir trees to which the masked weavers, sunbirds, and Cape bunting had taken, chattering along, paying scant attention to the solemn proceedings led by the Dutch Reformed *dominee*. Save for the birds, a hesitant silence draped itself across the foot-hills—the bell towers in town were silent. Bells were tolled for people of importance only.

As the casket lowered into the damp earth, those gathered, all clad in black, broke out in singing, *Kom tree ons dan bemoed-igt voort.* (Let us then proceed, encouraged.) Rianna mouthed the well-known words, her eyes following the flight path of an orange-breasted sunbird that darted from tree to tree before tak-ing flight to the ancient oaks that lined the narrow path leading up to the cemetery entrance.

Surrounding them, as far as the eye could see, were moun-tains. Behind them, lulled in somber aquamarine, towered Mount Drakenstein, and to the southeast, the Jonkershoek Mountains. Papegaai berg, a mere hill, was now bathed in the golden after-noon sun—it sloped away, rolling to the west.

Rianna's eyes came to rest on Lukas's mother, Maria Ferreira, where she stood next to her husband, shoulders pulled back, grasping her youngest, her two daughters', hands. Light tremors shook the woman's shoulders—the only part of her that moved. When the song finished, she turned to face the azure of Mount Drakenstein behind them. Only then did her shoulders slump as if giving in to the burden, forcing Louis Ferreira to step closer and catch her fragile frame.

Rianna pictured her own mother and shuddered. *How would I make peace with laying Mother to rest in these rolling foothills, enclosed by these sapphire ridges and secretive valleys? And those majestic oaks. Perhaps I should stipulate it in my will, to be put to rest here—one day. They don't have mango trees in the Cape. Perhaps a fir or an oak will not be such a horrible tree to lie under.*

It was only after they had reached the vehicle, long after the last song had carried beyond the rectangular rows of trees and the embracing mountains, that Lukas turned to Rianna. "When can I go up the mountain with you?"

Rianna blinked in surprise. She had been wrong—Lukas's voice had the timbre of his father—hesitant, but already strong. And deep. She smiled. "Tomorrow afternoon? It's our last week of school—we'll be done earlier, by noon."

Lukas couldn't hide his joy. "I'd like that."

Nineteen

LUKAS FERREIRA. NOVEMBER 1966

Lukas, surrounded by his parents and siblings, paced in the shade of the lower cable station, close to the ticket office. Louis Ferreira glanced at his wrist as Rianna pedaled up the road, breathing hard. She jumped off at a run and skidded to a stop, making the Ferreiras scuttle out of her way. She was five minutes late, despite her eager pedaling. School hadn't let out till 12:15.

Once she caught her breath she apologized, "I'm so sorry, Uncle Louis, Auntie Maria!" Then she wiped her brow, her face glowing, and chained her bicycle to the cast iron fence. "Hello Lukas," she said, still breathing fast, and to his siblings, "Hello Wouter. Suzanne. Celia." She waved at each one and grinned.

Lukas coughed, hands in his pockets. Wouter shrugged, and the two girls giggled in acknowledgment. Celia, almost four, darted over and grasped Rianna's hand, leaning against the fifteen-year-old, glancing at her parents. Rianna smiled and scooped the girl into her arms. She would not let a twelve-year-old's irritation rub off on her. She had pedaled as hard as she could.

Louis Ferreira cleared his throat, his lips a thin line. He didn't suffer latecomers gladly. It seemed he had second thoughts about allowing his teenage son to accompany this free-spirited redhead. "We're sticking to the original plan, Rianna? Lukas and you will hike up the mountain to the upper station where you'll meet us, while we take the cable car?"

Rianna put Celia down and faced father and son, still breathing a little fast and hard. "That's right, Uncle Louis. You'll even have time to complete a section of the paved walking path at the top." She noticed Lukas's new backpack. "It'll take us at least an hour. We'll join you afterwards."

Wouter, Lukas's eight-year-old brother, grumbled how unfair it was that he wasn't allowed to accompany the hiking duo. His father's knotted brow silenced him, making him seek the consoling arms of his mother.

Rianna reached for Lukas's pack. "You got the basic items I suggested you put in?"

"I did." His lips pursed as he turned away, keeping his bag out of her reach.

"Water. Rain-gear. A whistle?"

"*Affirmative*, corporal." This time Lukas's lips turned upwards. His parents laughed.

"Seems you guys are settled then?" Louis Ferreira gave his son's shoulder a squeeze and Maria pulled him closer for a quick hug.

The two hikers waved as they stepped away from the family and hurried up the stairs when Louis Ferreira called after them. "*Rianna!*" The Reverend caught up with them and asked under his breath. "I have to clarify. You're using a map? You told me you know the mountain?" The missionary stared at the upper station behind which a bank of clouds had gathered.

This time the crimson in her cheeks was not from cycling fast. She sighed, meeting the missionary's penetrating glance. "Uncle Louis, I've been up and down this mountain more than fifty times, on foot, in all kinds of weather. Yes, I know the *berg*. I respect its unpredictability. That's why I insisted that Lukas pack those essential items. But I don't need a map."

Lukas whispered through clenched teeth, "*Dad*. Stop treating us like babies."

Louis Ferreira laughed apologetically and he stepped back, palms raised. He waved them on. "Enjoy the climb."

THE REDHEAD faced her companion as soon as they were alone on the foot path. "You're hard on your *Pa*."

Lukas said nothing and ambled on.

"You think the emergency items I made you put in your bag are ridiculous?"

"I didn't say that."

"Then tell me what's wrong?" Rianna cocked her brows.

Lukas shrugged. "Nothing." He chewed his lip as he kept up the brisk pace.

When they rested, he faced her. "Perhaps *everything*. I'm not going back to Zambia. I'm done with school there. But it's the only place I *know*, Rianna. I'll have to make the jump from the twenty-five-student Mission school to a huge city high school. I'm scared. You know about Anthony. And now I've just lost my grandmother." He swallowed loud as he wiped over his eyes. "What doesn't help is when Dad treats me like I'm five." His voice broke.

Rianna soothed. "It's hard, the schools thing. You'll do okay. Seems to me, not many things make your hair stand on end."

Lukas smiled embarrassed. "Is it true you've been up the mountain fifty times?"

"I won't lie to your father." She pulled a face and accelerated her pace, calling over her shoulder. "We're taking a detour. I want to show you something neat."

Lukas fell in behind her. "Why did we leave the footpath?" He inhaled deep. The whiff of the proteas, sugar bush, and heathers was still new to him.

"Patience, my young friend, patience."

"*Yes*, Miss Rianna."

Rianna glanced back and stuck out her tongue. Lukas tittered and shrugged his shoulders.

They hiked in silence until Rianna raised her hand in warning. She spoke in a whispered tone. "It's a *rooikat* with three young ones. Careful where you step—we don't want to warn them."

She crouched lower and moved forward, Lukas following her example. Without warning she stopped, making Lukas bump into her. "Sorry," he mumbled, his face glowing.

Rianna whispered close to his ear. "I just realized. I didn't bring a pair of binoculars and the cats may be gone by now.

Taken. We'll have to get closer to see properly." She gestured for him to keep his head down.

Twenty feet farther she paused once more, going down on one knee.

"Who would have taken them?" Lukas kneeled next to her in the tall grass.

"Bad people." She sighed. "Someone I've met who planned on trapping them with cages. He believes he can domesticate them."

Rianna went down on all fours and made her way toward the *rooikat* lair. Her backward glances were unnecessary—her companion followed suit, on hands and knees.

She waited. "We're going to leopard-crawl the rest of the way. We have to get closer still. I want you to see them. Not a *word*."

Lukas rolled his eyes as he went down on his stomach. They continued a further twenty feet until Rianna gestured him closer, right up to her side.

He inched closer until their shoulders touched. Rianna had a finger on her lips, then pointed at the upright trunk of the sugar bush growing above the lair's opening. They were not twenty-five feet away.

They waited.

They barely breathed.

LUKAS shuddered. Her upper arm touched his, along its entire length, setting it on fire. He had goosebumps over his entire body. Lukas's face glowed from the climbing and unaccustomed crawling, but more so from her immediacy. The sun had warmed the *berg* with its rocks and *fynbos* vegetation. Lukas breathed the steaming earth so close to his nose, but he also inhaled the warmth of his companion. It was impossible not to notice the mysterious valley between her jutting breasts, rising and falling, where she lay on her stomach, supported on her elbows. The vibrant and beckoning lowland, two hand-widths away, was inundated with freckles.

She jabbed him in the ribs. "*What* are you looking at?" Lukas's face turned crimson as he shook his head. She leaned even closer. "You're too young for this. You're not only peeping down my shirt, you're *sniffing* me."

Lukas swallowed and met her eyes, unapologetic. "You smell nice. Your breath's like almonds."

Rianna grimaced as her cheeks turned rose. "You're silly. I'm all sweaty now."

She bumped his shoulder again and placed a finger on his lips, before pointing at the rocks. There was movement in the opening of the *rooikat's* living quarters. One of the kittens appeared, followed by a sibling, seconds later.

Lukas beamed at her, eyes wide in gratitude for letting him experience this small wonder on the mountainside.

The moment was cut short, unfortunately. Rianna grabbed and pinched her nose, brows furrowed, shaking her head in desperation. She turned red, then gave up and sneezed with an explosive bang. With anxious hisses the *rooikat* kittens disappeared into the burrow. Rianna dropped her head in her arms and groaned, then snapped to a seated position and brushed herself clean. "Sorry. The show's over. They won't come out for a while. Stupid sneeze. It was the crawling so close to the grass that did it. Hay fever. *Sorry*, Lukas."

Lukas sat up, his eyes fixed on his friend. He shook his head. "I've seen many animals in the bush, in Zambia, but this was grand. *Rooikat* kittens. Nice. *Thank you*, Rianna." As his voice trailed off his eyes were drawn to her chest once again. Rianna followed his gaze and crossed her arms.

Lukas met her eyes. "Please don't. They're . . . *beautiful*."

She jumped to her feet and brushed her legs clean with vicious strokes. "*Lukas Ferreira*. That's inappropriate. Keep your eyes away from my chest. You're a young boy. Your mom and dad will demand my hide—"

Lukas scowled as he adjusted the front of his pants. "You're just like my dad. Treat me like I'm five."

"But you're *twelve* years old."

"Thirteen in a month's time."

"Lukas, *enough*." Rianna glanced up the mountain. Fog snaked in white tongues down the cliffs, making the upper station appear and disappear.

The boy shuddered. "You're wrong. I've thought of you every day since you left. For the past eight hundred and fifty-two days. From that day in Paishuko when I saw what I saw. I like you . . . I *love* you, Rianna."

The fifteen-year-old gave a shrill laugh. "*Love*. Stop talking nonsense." She pointed at the twirling mist. "See that, Lukas? The weather has changed. The fog is not our friend. We have to hurry. I'm not turning back. We're closer to the top. *Come*." She raced ahead, glancing behind her to make certain he followed and then ahead of them to work out a route where they could avoid the thickest fog. It was clear that she missed her sturdy walking stick, if only to calm her nerves. She seemed unsettled.

"If I'm such a little boy, then why did you blush and cover your breasts with your arms?"

"I didn't . . . please *stop*, Lukas."

"Our bodies don't lie."

She snorted loud. "We're not animals."

"I'm not five. My voice has broken. I shave my chin. I have body hair."

"Exactly—you're growing up, becoming a man."

"I made your body respond. *Deny* it."

She flinched. "Lukas—"

Lukas whistled. "I get it. You prefer *men*. Do you have a boyfriend?"

"I have a friend, yes . . . ."

"Boyfriend?"

"Friend."

"His name?"

"Lukas, please. His name is Hendrik."

"Has he kissed you?"

"*Stop* the questions. We have to hurry. Look—"

She took his hand and pulled him along with her. Mist touched, lapped around their legs. For fleeting seconds, the upper station became visible before being swallowed by giant white tongues, the size of blue whales.

"So, you don't like me?"

"Lukas, you're my friend."

"I want to be more than your friend."

Rianna accelerated the pace. Both of them were breathing hard. She eyed him. "Perhaps *one* day."

"Just because you have beautiful breasts you think you're a grown woman." His voice broke. "Suddenly you're too *grand* for me."

Rianna couldn't hide her grin. "I'm not a little girl anymore."

"I don't like the way you've changed."

Crimson crept up her neck. "None of us are the same people we were in Zambia, Lukas."

"You act as if what had happened, what we had experienced there, together, was *nothing*."

"I never said that."

"*Sure.* You've forgotten about *me*, about *Anthony*."

Rianna sucked in her breath. Her eyes brimmed as she faced her youth friend, shaking her head. "You're terribly wrong, Lukas." She gave a loud sob as she let go of his hand, spun around and disappeared around a boulder and a protea bush. A bank of fog rolled in and swallowed the fifteen-year-old and the entire section of the mountain. But Rianna stomped higher up the narrow path, too upset to bother further with her guest. She couldn't see Lukas behind her. She couldn't care less. Tears made her crash into the underbrush. This only egged her on. She bolted farther, keeping to the faint path. Higher. Faster. She knew that part of the mountain like her hostel room. *Silly boy. What an obnoxious child.*

Only when she missed a step and crashed to her knees did she pause and, then, wince with remorse. *Lukas! You've never been up the mountain. Where is the annoying boy?* By now she could only see as far as her hand ahead of her; beyond that existed a twirling ghost world, shrouded in white. "*Lukas?*" She retraced her steps and raised her voice.

The mountain was silent. For a moment she thought she heard the whirring of a cable car pass over head. It was impossible to be certain. She shouted his name again. Slanted her head and listened. Nothing but the wind, rustling the *fynbos*. She breathed the heady smell of the heathers and sugar bush. Did she hear rocks rolling to her left? She spun around and called. White impenetrable silence answered her.

The whistle. Rianna scrambled in her backpack, hands shaking. When she pulled the whistle free from the side-pouch it slipped and dropped to the ground. She snapped it back up, wiped it clean on her shorts and blew long and hard. No answer but her ears ringing. She jumped when a lone Hadeda sounded its forlorn call, mere yards away. The shrill *ha-dee-dah, ha-dee-dah* ringing in her ears made it impossible to shake the sense of pending doom. Her voice hoarse, she shouted *Lukas* again. It was no use.

Now crying, she turned back up the mountain. What was a person to do? Reach the upper station and get help. Then come back for him. *Lukas, why did you upset me so? Why don't you use your whistle? I promised your dad. And what about your mother? What will Mr. Read say? And Miss Clark? Oh, dear God.* She shivered as she scaled higher, alternating sniffling, calling her friend's name, and sounding her whistle.

A STONE wall loomed above her in the haze—she had reached the top. Panting and wiping her eyes dry, Rianna clambered over the low wall, resting for a second, waiting on the nebulas to lift, to orientate herself. *Praise the Lord.* She was at the back of the little restaurant building. She prayed Hendrik Willems and his mother were on duty and that the Ferreiras were not inside, in the restaurant, as she hurried closer. She'd slip in through the kitchen door at the back. Hendrik would know what to do.

Hendrik was in the scullery, his back turned to her, speaking to James Martin when she barged in. Speaking was an improper word, it seemed, when a loud "You *bastard*!" sounded and the Martin boy shoved Willems against the sink. The dishes clattered.

Rianna's bloodcurdling, "*Stop it, you idiots!*" froze the quarrelling young men. She had Hendrik by the arm and pushed James away. Her breathing came in halting gasps. "I need your help, Hendrik!" Her glance shifted to the trouble maker. "Yours too, James."

James Martin sneered, "Suddenly I'm good enough to be of service to Her Majesty."

Rianna shook her head, grasping both Hendrik and James by the hand, pulling them along. "We've got to find your mother, Hendrik. We need a search party. I hiked up the mountain with a younger boy, Lukas. Friends from Zambia. Then the fog overtook us. We got separated. He was supposed to carry a whistle—" Rianna's voice broke and she sniffed loud, wiping her nose, her eyes overflowing.

The commotion brought Maria Willems to the kitchen. Crimson red, Rianna relayed how she had searched for the twelve-year-old visitor from Zambia, without success. She dropped her voice and told them about his entire family, parents and three siblings, waiting on the two hikers—probably in the restaurant. Rianna gave a dry sob and bolted into Maria Willems's open arms. Rianna whispered against the manager's gentle shoulder, "I'm too scared to go look. They *must* be inside, worried sick. His dad's going to kill me, *Tant Maria*."

"*Ag nee wat, niggie, hy sal nie*," the Coloured woman soothed, holding her close.

A SEARCH party consisting of two groups descended the mountain fifteen minutes later. It was difficult to tell exactly what Reverend Louis Ferreira was thinking when they broke the news to him about his missing son. It was not the first time his son had gone missing. Were it only the two of them, Rianna and the missionary, things may have turned out differently. He may have lost his self-control. His thunderous complexion confirmed that, if left to his own devices, a homicide could not have been excluded. The red-head, once again, was involved in a life-and-death scenario with his son. Maria Willems wasted little time in alerting the upper station.

Louis Ferreira insisted on being included in the effort. He joined James Martin and two of the personnel from the upper cable station. Hendrik Willems and Rianna made part of the second group. Both Martin and Hendrik had experience with rock climbing, and each carried lengths of rope around their shoulders with no little pride.

Lukas Ferreira was found, thirty minutes later, unharmed, but visibly shaken, four hundred feet below the upper cable station. Not far from the place where Rianna and his paths had separated in the fog.

It was Rianna and Hendrik's group who had stumbled upon the youth. Her tears flowing, now with joy, Rianna grasped the boy and hugged him, dancing around with him, clutched him to her chest. Only his loud protestation made her release her blushing friend.

But then joy made room for anger. She couldn't help herself. "Lukas Ferreira, you lied to me. I asked, in your father's presence, whether you had packed a whistle. Why didn't you?"

Lukas mumbled under his breath as he produced the orange whistle from his pocket.

"Why didn't you *use* it!" Rianna cried out. "I *called* you. I *whistled*. I searched like a mad person, close to hysterical. I wept. I was terrified. People die, falling down these cliffs because of the fog. And you remained *quiet*?" The heat in her eyes was replaced by an unfathomable hurt.

"I was mad at you," the youth mumbled.

Reverend Louis Ferreira called her outside, alone, once they had all safely returned to the upper station. His eyes were dark, his words staccato-like. "Rianna Vermeulen, there's a reason cartographers exist. '*I don't need a map,*' you said." He snorted. "You'll agree with me; you're a dangerous influence on my son. This is the second time. I love my boy. The third time may be fatal. You will undertake to never see him again. You will have no contact with him, whatsoever. *Never.*"

There was nothing she could say. Rianna only sucked her breath, shivering. She wanted to tell him about Lukas's refusal to use his emergency whistle, but the look in the reverend's eyes made her bite her tongue. The distraught father stepped closer. So close, she could smell the mint on his breath. "If you give me *any* reason for suspicion, I will not hesitate to inform your parents and lodge a formal complaint with your school principal. Do you *understand*?" he barked.

Rianna cringed and scuttled away, mumbling, "One doesn't need a map of the mountain, Uncle Louis. One only needs a defogger. And using the silly whistle also helps."

Twenty

GIRLFRIENDS AND BOYFRIENDS. JUNE 1967

The desire to obtain and read censored material, books in particular, had become an obsession with Rianna. Banned books, erotic in nature, she had little interest in. They were not worth the trouble or the risk. Her thirst to obtain first-hand knowledge of philosophy, psychology, political science, and social justice issues, however, was insatiable. She pestered her friend Hugo Marais at the Central Library without end. She wanted more. She needed more. Mrs. Knox's syllabus fell seriously short of satisfying the cravings of an inquiring mind.

Soon, Dr. Martin Luther King Jr. took the number one spot on Rianna's list of favourite banned authors. She reread *Stride toward Freedom: The Montgomery Story*. What endeared him to her was the day she learned about him receiving the 1964 Nobel Peace Prize, in recognition of his relentless push to rectify racial injustice by means of nonviolent resistance. She became a loyal follower.

Rianna also learned about the Sharpeville killings and the Langa shootings in March 1960 in South Africa, from archived newspaper clippings, for the most part, from London. She learned about the banning of both the ANC and PAC the following year, 1961. It became easier to confront Hugo with the more difficult questions. "Why is there no black man in South Africa willing to do what Dr. King is doing in America?"

"The leaders of both organizations were forced into exile." Hugo squinted at his eager disciple, pushing his finger-smudged glasses higher up his nose.

"They've all fled the country?"

A nod confirmed it. "The National Party acted with swift precision. They banned the organizations and imprisoned all the ringleaders they could lay their hands on, following Sharpeville. Those who didn't flee, your other hopeful candidates, were imprisoned on Robben Island—locked away."

Rianna glanced at her timid friend. "Why did the black people in South Africa then choose the path of violence and bloodshed? They're not practicing what Dr. King is preaching." She swallowed. "Or what Mr. Gandhi did, for that matter."

Hugo shrugged. "The situation in America is different. Here, in South Africa, the whites are outnumbered, probably one to ten. In the nineteen-fifties the ANC supported nonviolent resistance. They pushed for civil disobedience; they organized strikes, launched stay-at-home actions. To kill was not on the agenda. Not in the beginning."

Rianna's voice became hushed. "Sharpeville changed that?"

Her friend motioned with his head. "I believe the police opened fire that day on unarmed civilians who were fleeing. Sixty-seven died on the spot, but hundreds were injured; most shot in the back. They were *running away* that day in Vereniging, in Sharpeville. Few things could ever be the same in the land following the shooting—for Blacks or Whites."

UPON HER return from the city's Central Library, Rianna found her roommate, planted in the middle of Rianna's bed, *The Montgomery Story* in her lap.

Rianna gasped as she reached for the book. "*Where* did you get that?"

"Your hiding places are unimaginative." Rianna squealed and grasped once more for the book. Her friend yanked it away. "You *promised* to return it." Jessica pursed her lips, rose to her feet on top of the bed, and held the evidence high above her head. The two girls were of equal height.

"But I *did* take it back," Rianna cried. "The next morning." Rianna, weeping, reached in vain for the book.

Jessica scrambled off the bed, keeping the book out of reach.

Rianna's shoulders drooped. "I borrowed it a second time. I'm taking notes this time."

"You're breaking the law. A second time."

"I'm hoping to prevent further bloodshed in South Africa."

"You're arrogant and *infinitely* naïve, Rianna Vermeulen!"

Rianna plopped down on her bed. "You're wrong. I want to take my notes to the political prisoners on Robben Island. Let them read it. Help them understand how it is possible for nonviolent resistance to be effective when it is organized on a national level."

"It's too late for that. You think the Black leaders haven't thought of that? Or tried that?"

Rianna bit her lip. "One of their leaders, Albert Lithuli, keeps pushing for non-violence."

Jessica sighed as she returned the book. "He must be in the minority—he's not winning that battle. How can you blame them when their nonviolent actions were met with such brutal violence by the state? By the police?"

Rianna glowed and leaned closer to hug her friend. "Then you'll help me get permission to speak to the black leaders in prison?" She squeezed hard. "*Please?*"

"No, *silly!*" Jessica plucked the book from her unsuspecting friend's hand. This time, she hid it behind her back. Her frown turned into a sneer. "You're out of your league. You're in standard *eight*. These things don't concern you. You have no right. It's for *adults*. For politicians."

Rianna reached with both hands. "But . . . your uncle in the Secret Police should be able to—"

"Hah!" Jessica's shove was unexpected. Rianna stumbled backward, tripped over the small throw on the floor and landed on her bottom. She cried in surprise. Jessica snapped, "You're a *fool,* Vermeulen. I'm going to show the book to James Martin."

"Not *James!* You dare not show it to anybody!" Rianna sobbed as she wrestled her friend to the floor.

The running had served the Taylor girl well; she was strong. Both girls grunted and moaned and breathed hard as they rolled on the floor and struggled for possession of the book.

"Let *go!* You'll tear it, Jess!"

"You have to come to your senses."

"I'll take it back then. I promise," panted Rianna.

"Too late. If not James Martin, then Mrs. Knox. Choose."

Rianna grunted, shoved her friend aside and rolled away, the book safely in her arms. Her momentum made her crash into her bed's metal foot end with a thud. She cried out, rubbing her head as she peered at Jessica through her disheveled mop. "You seem awfully friendly with the Martin boy."

"His name is James."

"You bawled your eyes out last year when he and Andries mocked us in the dining hall."

"I didn't know him well enough then."

"Okay, you pick your friends. What I don't understand is your anger about the book. Why this sudden animosity? We're *friends*."

Jessica scowled but said nothing.

Rianna staggered to her feet. She wiped her eyes, sniffing loud. "What have I done to you?"

Jessica straightened her clothing, pushing her fingers through her hair. "This is bigger than us. Bigger than friendship. It's no longer about you and me. It's a question of what you are doing to the *country*. You think I'm that ignorant? There's a reason the books are banned. It's to stop people like you getting all kinds of ridiculous ideas. I can't look on and do nothing. Dr. Verwoerd didn't die in vain. He had a Ph.D in psychology and philosophy. He was a learned man. He knew what he was doing. Your actions are placing all the work he's done in jeopardy. I'll put a stop to this."

Rianna paled but held the book secure, yanked her closet open, pulled her backpack out, and slipped the banned book inside with shaking hands. Her lips trembled as she stuffed a knitted jersey and clean underwear on top of the book. "Why do you think they tried to kill Dr. Verwoerd at the cattle show in 1960, and failed? Because the people *loved* him and his policies?"

"He wasn't destined to die then. Two bullets to the head and he survived."

"It was a certain sign. The prime minister didn't heed the warning, he didn't heed the writing on the wall," Rianna insisted.

Jessica yelled, "How *dare* you?"

Rianna shrugged. "Killing is wrong, but it couldn't go on like this. The people had enough. They were successful last year. And this time with a simple knife—a dagger. I doubt whether Tsafendas was driven by madness alone—he must have had a good reason. He had legitimate grievances. I'm certain these things are all somehow connected."

Jessica roared, "Conspiracies? You're *conceited.* Tsafendas was a White man. He had no reason—the laws didn't apply to him."

"He *looked* non-white—what with his dark complexion and fuzzy hair."

Jess hooted, then bowed. "Ladies and gentlemen, allow me to introduce Professor Rianna Vermeulen, world-renowned *expert* in political science . . . ."

Rianna flinched, giving her friend a sorrowful glance. "Verwoerd's laws are unjust and hurting the black people. Well, everybody who's non-European. You forget, nobody gets to pick their skin colour, Jess. How can your skin colour determine your worth?"

As Rianna slipped from their dorm room, Jessica shouted after her, "I refuse to be ashamed of being White. Your curiosity and skewed loyalties will catch up with you, *kaffer-boetie!*" ("n*ggerlover").

———⊰≈≈⊱———

*M*aria Willems peered at the stooped figure on her front porch, the caller bathed in the meager light of the street lamp. She had to remind Hendrik to replace the bulb on the *stoep*. It was too dark out. She was grateful for the safety the door-chain gave her. She shuddered. Law-abiding citizens were all at home this time of the night and not prowling around. She peeped through the slit.

"*Antie* Maria?"

"*Rianna?*"

Her visitor spoke in hushed tones as she stepped closer. "My I come in, please?"

Movement behind Maria made her jump as she tried to unlatch the door. "*Wie's dit, Ma?*" Hendrik asked his mother, peering past her through the widening gap.

"*Jou girlfriend,*" Maria answered as she let go of the latch.

Mother and son hauled the shivering girl into the *voorhuis* and slammed the door shut, slipped the door-chain back in place, and turned the key.

"Rianna, *what's* the meaning of this?" Hendrik implored, holding the shaking girl at arms' length, his eyes drilling into her.

Rianna's glance shifted from mother to son, her teeth chattering. "I had nowhere to go. Hugo Marais . . . my friend from the library wasn't home. I can't stay at Westerford." She eyed Maria

Willems. "I've placed my bicycle behind the coal cupboard out-side. No one will see it from the street."

As if it was a regular thing to do on a weekday night, the sixteen-year-old trudged to the kitchen, where she pulled her jersey from her bag, slipped it on and plopped down into one of the chairs, resting her arms on the Formica table. Her pleading eyes returned to her host.

"Don't look at me like that, child." Glances exchanged between mother and son. Hendrik shrugged at his mother as he pulled out a chair for himself. Maria Willems busied herself with the kettle to order her thoughts.

Hendrik reached for his friend's hand, forcing her to meet his eyes. His frown softened as he noticed the fear and uncertainty in her eyes. "What's wrong with Westerford High tonight? What has Hugo Marais got to do with you being here?"

Rianna shuddered and extracted the condemning evidence from her bag and placed it on the table. Maria Willems's sharp intake of breath was the only sign that she had heard about the pastor from the Ebenezer Baptist Church in Atlanta. Montgomery was not a foreign word in the house on Cambridge Street, it seemed.

"You *promised* me you were done with banned books, Rianna!" Hendrik scolded. His hands balled into fists.

"*Rooibos* tea, Rianna?" Maria tried to defuse the tension in the narrow room.

"*Ja, dankie, Antie.*" Rianna whispered, avoiding Hendrik's glare.

"Hendrik?"

"Thanks, Mom," he mumbled through clenched teeth.

Rianna stroked the spine of the book and righted her shoulders. "I did return the book. I'm rereading it. This time I'm taking detailed notes. I'm almost done, then I'll type them up and return it. I want to pay a visit to the political prisoners on Robben Island. None of them have read the book, since it's banned. I'm convinced, now more than ever, that once they hear what Dr. King has to say, they'll immediately change their—"

"Rianna, *stop it*!"

Rianna cowered as she clasped the book to her chest, her eyes brimming. She blinked several times and wiped her eyes, naked hurt in her face as she watched her friend Hendrik scold her, similar to how Jessica had scolded her. Her glance shifted to Maria Willems. *Perhaps.*

"Hendrik, be gentle." Maria's hand rested on her son's shoulder. She squeezed hard until he winced.

"But Mom, she's not *thinking*. We'll *all* go to prison." Maria Willems placed the cups with tea, milk, and sugar on the table and pulled out a chair for herself. Glancing over the rim, Rianna held the cup to her lips, then took a careful sip from the scalding drink. For her hostess she offered a grateful smile, but her lip trembled when she faced her friend. She righted her shoulders. "*No one* is going to prison."

"What make you so certain?"

Then she told them about her conversation with her roommate, Jessica. About her friend's threat to report Rianna to an older student and their history teacher, if not the authorities. She told them about the contents of the book. About how the Negro preacher from Montgomery voiced his belief that mankind hated one another because of fear. How fear was born of mistrust and suspicion. Born from the lack of knowledge of one another; from a lack of comprehension and insight, due to a lack of proper communication. And the latter wasn't possible without fellowship and community. And that wasn't possible due to the fact that the population was separated in South Africa.

Hendrik rolled his eyes at her. She shuddered and continued. South Africa's problems could be fixed. But racial strife, to be fixed, needs education, willpower, and legislation. If they ever hoped to achieve unity among between the different ethnic groups and between Whites and Blacks . . . .

"You make it sound so easy," Maria murmured as she poured herself a second cup. "It will take much more than willpower."

"Antie Maria?"

"You must have noticed, Rianna. We're not Black—we're *brown*." Hendrik sneered as he placed his arm next to hers on the table, contrasting their skin tones. "But it's as bad as Black, if not worse. For some, sure, being light brown is a way out of the quagmire. Ask my sister Sarah, who is one step away, one document away, from becoming a White person." He grimaced. "Her boyfriend in the department of Bantu Affairs is *this* close to sealing the deal. You have *no* idea."

"I don't have all the answers, and I didn't mean to be disrespectful, Antie." Rianna leaned forward and touched her host's arm. "May I stay here tonight?" Maria Willems drew in her breath. "I can't go back tonight—not to Westerford and Jessica Taylor. Not as long as I have this book." Her furtive glance darted from mother to son and back.

Hendrik pried the book from Rianna's fingers and winked at the coal stove behind him. "There's a solution to your problem, Miss Vermeulen." He chuckled. "It will be nothing new. Books have been burned since the dawn of time, since the first written and printed books came into the hands of common citizens like us."

Rianna let out a tortured groan as she pried the book from Hendrik's hands. She struggled to her feet, face glowing. Clasping the book to her breast, her eyes flashed at her friend. *How could you*, it cried. She turned to her host. "Can I stay here, Antie Maria? *Please?*" Her host scratched her head. "I don't need any food. Only a roof. I'll be fine in the sitting room. A thin blanket will do."

And so Rianna stayed the night in the modest house of Maria Willems in District Six. The narrow couch made for fitful sleeping, despite the thin throw. The immaculately clean but threadbare curtains failed to prevent the yellow glow of the streetlamps from seeping into the room.

BY THE time the first rooster announced the breaking day, the redhead was already pedaling hard up the first of several hills, head slanted, the book safe in her backpack, eyes luminescent, savouring the breeze wafting from the wharf, which, that early in the morning, smelled more of sea than fish.

Twenty-One

A THIRD HISTORY PROJECT—THE
BOER WARS. SEPTEMBER 1967

*M*rs. Knox's back was turned to the class as she stood on tiptoes to write on the blackboard, as was her habit. The moment she stepped back and dusted her hands, Rianna groaned. She read, craning her neck, *The First Anglo-Boer War of 1881: why it was also called the First Freedom War.*

"Is there a *problem,* Miss Vermeulen?"

Rianna shook her head, a wide grin framing her face. "Will it be in order if we expand on the topic and link it to the Second Anglo-Boer War of 1899?" Rianna's hopeful eyes rested on her history teacher. She crossed her fingers, out of view.

A low grumble rolled through the class, and annoyed eyes burned into Rianna. At this her shoulders sagged and smile faltered.

"How will you accomplish that within the limit of three thousand words?"

"But, Teacher! That's *unfair!*" Multiple voices sounded across the room. "The length is always fifteen hundred words."

Mrs. Knox leaned against her desk at the front, arms crossed, lips pursed. "You'll have to thank Miss Vermeulen for the adjustment of your essay length." She gave the class a thin smile as she raised a slim finger. "However, I will accommodate the rest of the class. Three thousand words on my original topic. Vermeulen, you will stick to the new topic you have volunteered."

It seemed, for the time being, the history teacher had her doubts about the ability of the principal, Mr. Benson, to resolve her years-long feud with the defiant and inquisitive redhead. It would be a better use of her time if she took matters in her own hands. Nothing had been normal in the front office, not since the man had started wearing those absurd safari suits and cravats.

Jessica Taylor slid lower in her desk and hissed at Rianna, "*Traitor.*"

Rianna raised her hand and got to her feet, rose creeping up her cheeks. "Mrs. Knox, please don't punish the class because of my inquisitiveness. I can hand in the assignment within two weeks. Allow the class to stick to the original fifteen hundred words, and grant them the usual four weeks. *Please.*"

"Any *other* recommendations?" The teacher threw her willowy arms in the air. "*Sit down*, Vermeulen."

Mrs. Knox paced at the front, then spun around and marched to the window, peering outside, her nose brushing the glass, hands clasped behind her back; the class forgotten. A sudden gust blasted the window with fine sand, making her take a step back. Spring was late. It was almost as dry as in the Karoo. Winter lingered, reluctant to let go of its grip on the land. Inside her history classroom, that was the only season the children were familiar with—winter. How could it be any other way? History was a serious matter. She was not teaching the children silly love stories. The mountain towered in the distance, in azure-grey, impassive and unmovable. At least one thing was certain and unchanged.

When Mrs. Knox turned back, her face pulled as if in pain as she locked eyed with her challenger. "Vermeulen, *five* thousand words for you—*you* have two weeks." She forced a smile, facing the other children. "Class, two thousand words—four weeks. End of discussion." Returning to the black board, chalk in hand, she said over her shoulder. "Open your books at page ninety-seven: The Anglo-Zulu War of 1879."

Rianna tried to be the first to slip out when the bell rang, but she was not fast enough for Jessica's tongue, carrying after her. "Nice try to take the fall for us, Vermeulen. *Inquisitiveness*. Hah! You're still guilty of treason." Her classmates roared and drum-rolled their support on their respective desks, compelling Mrs. Knox to call them to order.

———

*T*wo weeks later, Mrs. Knox handed Rianna her marked history project. "Vermeulen, I want you to stay behind." Rianna's face warped in distress as she waited for her classmates to vacate the room. "You only gave me a C-minus, teacher!"

Mrs. Knox's eyes were cold. "You exceeded the word count by three hundred words."

"It was seven thousand before I trimmed it, ma'am. Once I started reading on the Second Boer War, there was no stopping. I was reminded of an article that had appeared last year following Dr. Verwoerd's assassination. The writer claimed that Dr. Verwoerd's drive to implement all those discriminatory apartheid laws stemmed from his legitimate fear that the Afrikaner nation would be wiped from the surface of the land, as the British Empire attempted to do with the Second Boer—"

"*Enough!*" The teacher's lips curled into a thin line. "You have to learn to stick to your topic."

"But I did, Mrs. Knox. There was so much material. There is a clear line that runs through all these conflicts."

"I didn't like the way you portrayed the Boers as superior to the British. You have to be more impartial. Give the proper historical facts."

"But that's what I did. The Boers got the better of the British. I researched it in our school library, then paid a visit to the Central Library as well. The number of books *they* carry on the topic is *astounding*."

Mrs. Knox groaned and glanced at the mountain as if for help.

Rianna took a deep breath and continued. "Our textbook makes the British sound like heroes. But the reasons the British Crown started both the First and Second Boer Wars were based on skewed assumptions and blatant greed. They placed illegal taxes on the burghers during the late eighteen-seventies, and a man, a certain Piet Bezuidenhout, refused to pay the taxes. When they confiscated his wagon and tried to auction it off, the Boers protested, organized themselves and took the wagon back. Shot were fired and the First War broke out. The Boers outsmarted the British, and within three months the war was over."

"No need to be smug about their accomplishments. A good historian avoids bias, remember? I still don't see where Dr. Verwoerd comes into that picture," protested Mrs. Knox.

"It's not bias, it's fact! In 1899, under the pretext of the Boers denying new immigrants rights and proper representation, the British built a case for war. But the true reason was to lay claim to the rich gold fields discovered in the Free State and the Transvaal during the eighteen-eighties. The British were unable to break the resistance by the Boers, who once again made a monkey of them. However, that changed when the British resorted to drastic new tactics. They started with concentration camps, in which they placed women and children of the Boers who were all away on military service. The British soldiers then systematically burned down the Boers' farms. How come we never talk about those details in history class?"

"There's a syllabus to follow. Another thing: the Afrikaner *genocide* that you referred to? Isn't that rich?"

"Teacher, what *else* can you call it? Seventy-five thousand lives were lost during the Second Boer War, of which twenty-two thousand were British soldiers. Seven thousand were Boer fighters. The rest—*all civilians*, perished in the camps." Rianna rubbed her arms, covered in goosebumps.

Mrs. Knox let out a shuddering sigh.

Rianna frowned and continued. "I believe it was the first time, as far as I have been able to find in my reading, in modern military history, that concentration camps were used during a war. Thought out by the British. Close to twenty-eight thousand Boer civilians (most of them women and children) died in these camps. The British placed the black Africans, the Boer allies, in their own separate concentration camps, where up to twenty thousand of the Blacks died." Rianna shivered. "All that *horror* for control and ownership of the goldmines. For empire."

Mrs. Knox tsk-tsked as she rose and returned to the window. Her back was turned on her pupil as she drank in the mountain. For a moment, the tension drained from her shoulders. "You think I don't know that history, Vermeulen? How naïve *are* you? But I'll make an exception. I'm in a charitable mood. I'll give you a B-plus." She caught sight of Rianna's relieved grin and raised a bony finger. "There's always a 'but.' A price to be paid. You just mentioned Demetrio Tsafendas, Verwoerd's assassin, in the same breath as the First and Second Wars. That's an impressive flight of imagination and free interpretation of historical events applied there, don't you think? *Missy?*"

"Mrs. Knox?"

"You'll write a *new* piece." She faced her student, arms crossed. "My interest is piqued. This doesn't often happen. Five thousand words on Tsafendas and Verwoerd—give me the latest. You have eight weeks."

Rianna jumped to her feet. "Oh, *thank you*, Mrs. Knox!"

The teacher held up her palms, again glancing at the dark mountain. "Don't thank me, child. I'm *not* your friend. Just do the work." She turned her back on the redhead. "Now get out."

Twenty-Two

THE ASSASSIN. IS MADNESS SOMETIMES A
CRY OF THE POWERLESS? FEBRUARY 1968

Brenda Knox, history teacher of Westerford High, fell ill with pneumonia in mid-November, 1967. It soon worsened to double pneumonia. By the time she was discharged from hospital, the schools had closed for the December holidays. Forgotten was Rianna's extra-curricular political essay.

Mrs. Knox's willowy frame was ill-suited for unintentional weight loss. On the ward, breathing oxygen, she lost track of the days. Alone at night, the thought of retiring presented itself. One particular fretful night, she even pondered her mortality. She found it quite disconcerting. The next morning, Mr. Knox was summoned and instructed to have her will updated. It was unwise to tempt fate, she explained to her spouse. Not until January did she get her breath back.

Mr. Benson, grateful to have his stalwart teacher back, tucked his brand-new cravat in place. "Mrs. Knox, Brenda . . . *welcome back*. You had us all worried. Are you certain you don't need more sick leave? This year will be demanding: you're taking on every one of the standard six to ten classes." He eyed her fragile frame. "And you'll have to deal with the troublesome person of Miss Rianna Vermeulen."

"What utter nonsense, Mr. Benson." Brenda Knox unfolded herself. The man was wasting her time. He also had ridiculous taste in appropriate professional attire. Even a standard three student could tell that. She pinched her nose. "I'm sufficiently recovered, thank you, sir. Leave the child to me. I've learned how to handle her."

THE DANCE between teacher and student had become a well-rehearsed affair—perfected over the years. On the teacher's first day back, Rianna stayed behind in class, waiting on her smirking classmates to leave the room. Mrs. Knox, remaining seated, placed the marked essay on the corner of her desk.

Theirs were a choreographed pas de deux. A silent number, requiring no music. "You had fourteen weeks, and this was the best you could come up with? Let's start with the title."

"The title zooms in on the key issue, teacher."

"In which way does '*Tsafendas the Killer: Madman or Aggrieved Citizen?*' do justice to what happened on 6 September 1966?"

Rianna swallowed. "Mrs. Knox, we know what happened that afternoon in Parliament, in the House of Assembly. I didn't downplay his hideous crime, I attempted to uncover the *why* behind it."

Mrs. Knox righted herself. "You're arrogant and conceited. Your final conclusion is that Tsafendas was a chronic schizophrenic, known to suffer from mental illness, but that his decision to kill the prime minister was based on years of living a socially marginalized life, due to his mixed-blood heritage. That he felt himself to be a social outcast because of the discriminatory laws."

"It's *true*. Demetrio Tsafendas's father was a Greek from Egypt who became involved with a Mozambican woman. It's right there in my essay—"

"Vermeulen, your argument falls flat. He was classified as *White* in South Africa. The passbook laws didn't apply to him."

"Perhaps so, teacher, but he was extremely dark-skinned, even for a Greek. And he had fuzzy hair. He was bullied at school—taunted as if he was of mixed blood. His dad moved around a lot, and he ended up in different schools. The children poked fun at him. They called him '*Blackie.*' He hated it, as a child, but it seems the stigma clung to him his entire adult life."

"How would *you* know? I have on record what the then-Justice minister said, after the murder, last year. 'The act was that of a *sole unbalanced individual*, and was not politically motivated.'" She pressed her fingers together, to stress her point. "Meaning, the murderer was a madman.'"

"But teacher, Tsafendas was out of the country for two decades where he learned to speak eight languages. Upon his return to South Africa in 1965, he found work as translator in the immorality acts trials of Portuguese and Greek seamen. According to newspaper articles published in London, these trials only deepened his own unease concerning his racial categorization. Due to his darker complexion he had little difficulty befriending women across the colour line. It is quite possible for him to have felt more comfortable with those classified as non-White than with legally White people."

"Total hogwash! You're guessing now!"

Rianna shook her head. "Those journalists interviewed people who had known Tsafendas for years, people he trusted and talked to about his feelings. From this we learn that Tsafendas was increasingly agitated with Dr. Verword's Immorality Act, which made sexual relations across the colour line illegal. Clearly the Immorality Act was one of the biggest factors in his decision to assault the prime minister."

"Unsubstantiated rumour. It's all gossip and speculation."

Rianna shrugged. "Teacher, I explained my findings in the essay. Nowhere do I claim to have all the answers. I think we'll never know for certain. After all, I'm only in standard nine, but I'm pretty sure about one thing: given the complicated relationship that South Africa enjoyed with other nations, and given the anti-apartheid movement that had gained momentum since 1960 following Sharpeville and the banning of the ANC and the PAC, it was crucial for the minister of Justice to say what he said.

"The message to the outside world had to be clear: that Tsafendas acted as a 'lone killer,' a man troubled by mental imbalance, which made him do the unthinkable. That it was not the product of a disgruntled citizen by his full wits, so unhappy and burdened by the restrictive and discriminatory laws that he saw no other option, no other way out than to kill the prime minister."

Mrs. Knox marched to the window and lost herself in the ivory blanket being pulled over the impassive mountain, towering above them. Her bony shoulders slumped. When she turned back, her eyes had lost its fire. "Where did you find those particulars about Tsafendas's injuries? His fractured nose and jaw on the day of the assassination? Did you list *all* your references?"

"Mrs. Knox?" Rianna lowered her eyes.

"Don't play coy with me, child."

Rianna hugged herself, glancing out the window for a moment. "Police records, Ma'am. Just like I said in my footnotes." Her voice was a whisper now. "There was a struggle in Parliament as those present dragged the assailant off the prime minister. I told you, I visited the Central Library. I have a friend there who reads a lot. He helped me."

Mrs. Knox halted six inches away from her student, making the redhead draw her breath and strain to get away. "Do you have access to restricted material, child?"

"*Teacher?*"

Rianna breathed the overwhelming sweet smell of the older woman's perfume. Her breathing came fast. Mrs. Knox's knotted finger dabbed at her. "Be warned, child. Be extremely careful what you dabble with in your quest to uncover facts. We live in uncertain times. Don't tinker with banned publications, with prohibited material. There are reasons for that. You are not above the law. No one is."

Rianna slumped. "But so many of the rules are unjust . . . . I'm after the *truth*."

"Bah, child! Your job is not to seek truth but to learn your history lessons."

The history teacher had turned away to watch the disappearance of the azure mountain in the twirling fog, swallowed now by giant tongues that spilled like white lava down the slopes. "Your piece wasn't bad. I gave you an A-minus. That will be *all*." She spun around, facing her student. "Enough of politics. You think you're special and gifted. You're not. You *will* stick to my syllabus." She pushed out her modest bosom. "Time that you learn again about proper history. Start thinking about the 1879 British-Zulu War." Her hand snapped toward the door. "I've had enough of you. Get out."

Twenty-Three

THREATS AND VIOLENCE. JUNE 1968

*E*arly on a Wednesday morning, Miss Clark, the vice-principal, had Rianna summoned to her office. Mr. Benson was on stress leave. Rumour had it he suffered from severe depression, perhaps a nervous breakdown. The students whispered that his mistress had broken up with him, once his wife got wind of the affair. Some said he was thrown out of the house and had to move to a motel.

Rianna shook Miss Clark's proffered hand at her office door, holding onto the slender fingers, desperate for a message of good news in her eyes; she only received a tap on her shoulder to enter. Upon entering, her breathing faltered. Seated was a police officer, who rose as she entered, as well as her friend, Jessica Taylor. The latter's face was an impassive mask. Colour drained from Rianna's face when she recognized the slim volume on the vice-principal's desk.

The redhead's glance darted between Miss Clark, the police-man, and Jessica. Her eyes pleaded with Jessica— *Why? Why? Why?* Jess Taylor answered with a smug sneer, leaned back in her chair and pushed out her chest with its padded brassiere. Her eyes challenged, *Don't say I didn't warn you.* Miss Clark had granted permission for the two girls to move to two single rooms, on Jessica's insistence, weeks earlier.

The vice-principal introduced Captain Duvenhage from the security branch of the police and made Rianna take a seat to his left, away from Jessica. Miss Clark scooped the book in question and turned its cover to face Rianna.

Rianna read the title as if for the first time, *Cry the Beloved Country*, by Alan Paton. He was second on her list of favourite banned authors, following Dr. King. Her breath caught when she realized that Paton may move up to her number one spot as live banned author, since the unfortunate events in Memphis in April, a few months earlier.

"Miss Vermeulen, I'm *speaking* to you." Miss Clark's unexpect-edly sharp tone forced Rianna back to the awkward business at hand. The vice-principal raised the book higher. "My hand was forced in the matter." Her glance flitted between her three guests. She looked at the redhead as if pleading. "Miss *Taylor*," and she tilted her head at the other student, "had gone directly to the police with the book, which she claimed was found in your room."

The policeman had joined Miss Clark in front of her desk, took the book and pointed it at Rianna. "Is this your book?"

"*No*, sir." Rianna, unable to remain seated, scrambled to her feet, met the man's direct gaze but was helpless to prevent the crimson from creeping up her neck.

"Your friend claims it's from your room."

Rianna swallowed several times. "May I see it?" She reached for the book and flipped to the back. She found the penciled scribblings of her library friend, Hugo Marais—her secret supplier. Unmistakable. It was the book she had borrowed from him, from the Central Library's confidential stash. She shook her head.

"What does *that* mean, Miss Vermeulen?"

"The book does *not* belong to me, sir."

"That's an outright *lie*, sir!" Jessica Taylor cried, unable to remain seated.

The officer took a snorting breath as he patted his thigh with his cap, knotting his brow as his glance shifted between the two students. "Miss Vermeulen, don't play games with me. This is a serious matter. Was this book found in your room?"

Rianna shrugged. "How did she get the book, sir? My room was locked."

Captain Duvenhage's voice rose. "Then this *is* your book!"

Rianna pulled her shoulders back, her lips thinning. "Sir, the book does not belong to me. I borrowed it. Yes, it was in my room. But I have to report a break and entry, sir. A *theft*."

Miss Clark gasped, Jessica choked, and the officer cleared his throat, slapping his thigh with more force.

"Do you realize the implications of having this book in your possession, Miss Vermeulen?"

"No, sir. But I do know that it's banned."

"*Exactly*! People receive heavy fines for possession of these. They go to prison."

"Have you *read* the book, sir?" Rianna piped.

The officer's shoulders snapped to attention and he coughed behind his hand. He stuttered, "N-n-no . . . Miss. The book is banned. We're not here to discuss my reading habits."

"Have you *ever* been to Ixopo in Zululand, sir?" Rianna asked, despite her glowing cheeks. "It's true about those rolling hills that Paton describes so eloquently. You can picture it. If the rains don't stay away, those foothills are indeed grass-covered, lush, and captivating, beyond description. Breathtakingly beautiful."

Miss Clark inhaled audibly, clasping her hands together.

A muscle in the officer's face twitched. He had a flat stomach, and his shoulders (as broad as Mr. Read's, the gym teacher) seemed to grow.

"Sir, if I *may*," Rianna braved on. "It's the heartbreaking story of a father, this Reverend Khumalo, traveling to Johannesburg by train to search for his lost adult son."

"Miss Vermeulen, the book is banned . . . ."

"Have you never asked *why*, sir? Paton doesn't incite violence or bloodshed in the book. To the contrary. He weaves an incredible story about the love of a father, the love of a man, of how Black and White could reconcile and reach out again, in spite of hurts, in spite of even murder. When given the chance. When taking the chance. Through his simple but profound story he shows how forgiveness of serious wrongs is possible—"

"Rianna, *please*." Miss Clark stepped closer, reaching out for her student's arm.

"You're sketching a fairytale world, Miss Vermeulen." The officer chuckled, as if amused. It was clear he had not expected to travel down this path of thought with the opinionated young lady. This was not scripted.

"Not a fairytale, sir. Reality. If we don't, if all of us, from both sides, don't reach out, we'll see more of what happened to Dr. Verwoerd. The people are troubled. They are unhappy beyond—"

"*Enough,* Miss Vermeulen!" Captain Duvenhage snapped to attention, towering above Rianna. Of the smile there was no sign. "Do you want me to take you down to the station? Do you wish to sleep in the police cells tonight? I *can* arrest you."

"*No*, sir."

"What is the name of the person who provided you with the book?"

"I am not at liberty to tell you, sir."

"Do you want me to go to the Central Library and arrest the entire staff?"

Rianna shook her head, averting her eyes. Miss Clark whimpered under her breath. Jessica Taylor snickered, her arms crossed.

"I can *make* you tell me."

Rianna met his gaze directly. "You're willing to torture me, sir?"

The officer's glance jumped from the forward schoolgirl to Miss Clark. His face glowed. *Damn it.* He didn't like the look of concern, bordering on distrust, that he now noticed in the vice-principal's eyes. Perhaps it was time to defuse the situation. It may be wiser to stay out of quicksand territory. It was advantage to the redhead. He could win the fight another day, without making a scene. He had to keep public opinion in mind. Impressions mattered. The commandant, his superior, was aware of his desperate desire for promotion. "No, Miss, I don't participate in such practices. I am not here to hurt." He returned the novel to the vice-principal's desk.

Rianna stepped closer to Miss Clark, as if for protection. The vicinity of the older woman made her brave again. She breathed the spinster's gentle nectarine scent. "Then there is still the matter of a theft, sir. I understand that the book is banned. I respect that. But a theft is no lesser crime. Mr. Tsafendas *stole* Dr. Verwoerd's life. And my book—"

Captain Duvenhage coughed and choked as he tried to hide his pleasant surprise behind his formidable hand. He turned his back on them for a brief moment. When he faced them, his face was unreadable. "You have an unorthodox way of stating your case, Miss Vermeulen."

Rianna swallowed several times. Her smile was strained. "Sir, Mr. Tsafendas believed he had a good reason for falling on the prime minister's chest with the knife. Whichever way one looks at it, it was wrong. A theft of a life occurred. A murder took place." She faced her ex-roommate. "My room was locked. The book was stolen from my room, sir. Jessica Taylor believed she had a good reason for going to such lengths. If I had committed a crime by having this banned book in my possession, then no less a crime was committed in obtaining the evidence, sir."

The officer sniffed. "The court may have a different view of the matter I'm afraid, Miss."

He clicked his heels together and faced the redhead's accuser. "How did you gain access to Miss Vermeulen's room?"

"*Sir?*"

The slap of the captain's cap against his thigh cracked like a gunshot. The sneer on Jessica's face was replaced by a trembling lower lip. "Sir, I made one of the cleaning ladies unlock it for me."

Captain Duvenhage gave a curt nod in Jessica's direction, spun around, took the book from the desk again, and addressed the still pallid vice-principal. "If you don't mind me taking the book, Miss Clark?"

He gave a friendlier nod in Rianna's direction. "As evidence." He stuck out his hand, took the slim hand of Miss Clark and shook it with gentle care. "My business is concluded here."

He faced the shivering Jessica Taylor. "It may behoove you in future not to enter people's rooms without permission."

Then he faced the redhead. "This is a formal warning, Miss Vermeulen. I will not take the matter further, if you promise that this is the last of this nonsense. Don't force our hand. You are not above the laws of the land." He stepped closer and barked, "Is that *understood?*"

Rianna wheezed out a sob as she nodded. "Yes, sir," she whimpered as she reached for Miss Clark's arm.

Three strides took the captain to the door where he touched his temple, holding Miss Clark's gaze. "I'll let myself out. *Good day*, ladies."

The news anchor had not completed his first sentence of the nine o'clock radio news when the window of the *voorkamer* of Maria Willems on Cambridge Street exploded. The inhabitants, sitting in the back, in the kitchen, the usual evening visiting spot, scrambled to their feet, faces blanched—even those of the two Coloured people.

In her haste to find out what had happened, Rianna bumped into Hendrik, knocking them both to the linoleum. He had been sitting next to her, across from his mother.

"*Shit, Ma! Wat was dit?*" Hendrik scrambled to his feet, grasped the big kitchen knife, and stormed down the short hall-way toward the living room. He halted inside the door opening, making his mother and Rianna crash into his back.

The entire sitting room was littered with glass fragments. The aged curtains were ripped from the curtain rod. Of the large window pane, only shards glared at them from the frame, like the teeth of a vicious killer shark, mouth agape. On the floor, where it had come to a rest against the leg of the seasoned couch, lay a brick: a nine-by-three-by-four-inch baked-clay object. A crude rope appeared to be wrapped around the brick, keeping a piece of paper in place.

Step by careful step, Hendrik crunched into the room, hesi-tant, as if the object of destruction may still jump at him. He stepped across the shards of glass that were covering the floor and carpet, then brushed the brick clean with the tip of the knife he was carrying and picked it up.

"What's the rope for, Hendrik?" Maria panted.

Hendrik cussed under his breath as he waved them back into the kitchen. He carried the brick in after them and placed it on the table, then spun around and rummaged in a drawer. "Mom, where's the flashlight? Somebody did this. Perhaps . . . ." Then, flashlight and knife in hand, he yanked the kitchen door open and slipped outside.

Maria Willems called after her son to be careful, but he was already gone.

The two women stood around the table, staring at the brick with naked horror. None of them moved. They hardly breathed.

Rianna's lip trembled. Her hand pointed at the dreaded brick. "*Antie*? Is that because of me? Because I'm friends with Hendrik?"

The mother and girlfriend jumped when Hendrik barged in through the back door. His breathing came fast. "There's *nothing*. Nobody. The *cowards*." His hands shook as he cut the rope from the brick, pulled the paper free, and smoothed it out on the Formica table. He leaned closer, his lips trembling.

"What does it say, Hendrik?" Maria reached for the torn paper, but her son jerked it from her grasp, rereading the message. His free hand brushed his eyes, and then he handed it to his mother.

Maria Willems sucked her breath as she read, first soft, then out loud. *Coloured boy, be warned. If you so much as touch or kiss the White girl, the redhead (R.V.), a brick, similar to this one, will be used to smash, not the window, but your head to pulp. PS 1. This is not a joke. PS 2. It is called the Immorality Act of 1957. PS 3. This is your first and only warning.*

Twenty-Four

The house on Cambridge Street did not receive another visit from Rianna until late November. The cryptic note attached to the brick was bold and forceful enough, and delivered in such a fashion as to make taking it to heart a formality.

She now only saw Hendrik for the four hours on Saturday and Sunday afternoons when she worked in the Table Mountain Café. Hendrik had progressed to assistant manager, although his place of refuge remained the scullery, where he could do his thinking undisturbed, tucked away behind skyscrapers of dishes. The two friends went to great pains not to be seen together, not even in passing, opting to even ride the cable car on separate runs. This required clever planning. It was impossible to tell where the government's Immorality Act police were stationed, or overzealous members of the public—like Jessica Taylor. It required even greater wisdom to know whom to trust.

The winter rains, late that year, had replenished the berg's *fynbos*. As the vegetation surged back to life, so did the birds and smaller animals—they returned in droves and flourished. The Table Mountain National Park was transformed, once again, into a tourist's paradise, a sought-after destination. The steep and broken rock cliffs burst with shades of green. Lush heathers, sugar bush, and proteas dotted the slopes—scenting the mountain—speckled it in generous bouts of wild pinks, moss pinks, coppers, reds, and pomegranate.

There was much to celebrate: Hendrik had written his last paper that morning, completing his second year of economics at the University of Cape Town. He was working five days a week now in the mountain café to make ends meet and pay for his tuition. His mother's salary only went so far. Rianna however, had one exam left the following week, in her favourite subject: history with Mrs. Knox. The paper would conclude her standard nine year.

During their fifteen-minute break that Saturday, Hendrik broke their current routine. For months he had created the impression of not knowing Rianna, but today he marched over to her outside table and joined her there. They sat close to the stone wall, reveling in the breeze that swooped up the cliffs and raced across the plateau.

"Mother took the train at daybreak, to *Worchester*. For a funeral."

Rianna dared not touch his hand in public and whispered her sympathy.

Hendrik shrugged. "*Antie Griet* was close to Mom's heart. *Antie* became Mom's second mother after she lost her own in high school. However, *I* hardly knew her."

"That's why you're so cocky today. The boss is away. You must miss the scullery. No place to hide when you have to stand on the bridge and keep the ship on course."

Hendrik crowed. "Go ahead. Joke. You think I'm slacking back there. I do all my important thinking. It's *hard* work."

Rianna balanced her chair on its hind legs, eyeing her friend. "*What* do you think so deep about? *Why don't people finish what's on their plates? Why do I have to let all this good food go to waste?*"

He leaned forward, so close she could see the ochre specks on his irises. "*No.* I think about life. About my studies. About Mom. And Sarah, who's going to finally be reclassified by the end of the month. She'll get engaged to her white boyfriend the day she receives the certificate." He pulled a face. "And I think about *you.* About *us.*"

Crimson crept up Rianna's neck. She could feel her heart jump. "*Us?*" She choked back tears as she studied his face. "How I wish I could too. There will never be an *us*, Hendrik. Unless we leave the country. You can't *wait* for me. I have another year. You're surrounded by sophisticated grown-up ladies at university. I'm a freckled, opinionated, standard-nine girl. I'm only seventeen." She shuddered. "It seems you also forget I'm the wrong colour."

Hendrik scraped his chair as he rose, his eyes never leaving her. "We have to get back." His eyes burned into her. It was a struggle not to touch her. If only an arm. "I've made friends at UCT—male and female; but the girls pale compared to you. They're *shallow.* Ambitionless. There's nothing they're passionate about. Nothing of importance. All they do is attend the minimum number of classes, scrape through their exams, do drugs, have sex as often as possible, and float aimlessly from day to day. Oh, and they do their hair and paint their nails. You're lovely—*with* your freckles. You don't even need makeup. You are able to think for yourself. I'm not interested in *hippies*. You force me to think. You always challenge me. But you're wrong, I am reminded every single day of your skin colour—and mine. As if I had chosen it inside my mother's belly long ago."

They walked back to the café in silence. He held the back door for her to go ahead. "I wish we could celebrate my exams. Even if it's only the two of us." Once inside, he steered her toward the scullery. "Mom won't be back until Sunday night." He got lost peering into her dark pupils, his jaw twitching as he balled his fists. "Why don't you come over?"

"*Hendrik?*" Her chest rose and fell as she reached for his hand. This was a *different* Hendrik Willems. *Never mind the prying eyes.* His mouth opened to answer when the chef called from the kitchen, demanding his attention. Rianna sighed, retracted her hand, slipped her apron in place, and pushed through the swing doors to wait on her tables.

---

*R*ianna took the cable car down, only after ensuring Hendrik had gone ahead. It was too dangerous. They had been so careless. They had spent too many minutes in close proximity outside the café that afternoon. Who knows who was paying attention? She pushed her bicycle down the steep road, giving herself time to reflect, to roll Hendrik's words around in her head. Mull on it. *He was thinking about "us." What does that even mean? We'll have to move across the border to South West Africa or Botswana.*

No, that could never work. She had to increase the physical distance between herself and the Willems boy. *Distance.* They needed distance. Who was she fooling? The Willems *man.* He was no longer a boy. He was nineteen, a year younger than most of his university friends. But he was a man no less. She had noticed an intensity in him today—it was new. Intriguing. Unsettling.

She mounted her bicycle when she reached the first houses. Hendrik was nowhere in sight. That was better. She wasn't ready to return to Westerford. The wharf. She'd pedal down to the harbour. Life at school had lost some of its luster as the conflict with Jessica dragged on. She missed the older Bianca, who was now studying in Stellenbosch. Mr. Read seemed more and more withdrawn as his relationship with Miss Whitehead developed.

Rianna leaned her bicycle against the battered shipping container and scaled the concrete barrier with swift strides, finding a seat out of view from people at dock level. Head on her knees, arms clasped around her legs, she immersed herself in the goings-on of the harbour. She loved it. In spite of the fetid aroma of fish and diesel and oil. Her nose wrinkled. She followed the murderous dive of a screeching gull that swooped down on an unsuspecting bird that had dared to steal his piece of flotsam.

Dockworker's banter and calling gradually ceased as the yards closed down for the day. Her glance drifted to her wrist. *Hendrik, what will become of us? How can it be illegal to be your friend?*

When the sky above the bay broke out in fiery hues, she slipped down the graffitied wall. She would have to pedal hard if she hoped to reach Westerford by nightfall. But when she reached Church Street, Rianna decided to change course and head for Cambridge Street. By the time she pushed her bicycle in behind Antie Maria's outdoors coal cupboard, dusk had settled on the city. Yet Rianna had turned her bicycle's headlamp off long before she had turned into the property, praying the iron gate wouldn't give her away. When it squeaked her heart stopped. She froze, glanced up and down the street, forgot to breathe. The streetlamps' meagre glow competed with that of the *stoep light* at the front door.

The street remained silent. She climbed the steps, steeled herself to knock on the kitchen door. She rapped once and she stepped back into the dusk, outside the listless halo of the naked bulb above the pink door. She held her breath. *Will he be mad?* After a moment she darted up the four cement steps and knocked a second time; louder this time. Again she took refuge in the semi-darkness. Again she waited. The blood whooshed in her ears. Her breathing came fast. *He isn't here, Rianna Vermeulen.* She jumped when a dog barked, three houses down. *Shit, someone must have seen me. He's not here. He's not here. Go home, Vermeulen. Go home.* She sighed and turned to collect her bicycle when the door creaked opened.

"*Rianna?*"

She scurried up the stairs and allowed Hendrik to pull her inside and lock the door.

"*Stay here*," he instructed, as he dashed from room to room. She could hear him cuss as he darkened the rooms one by one, pushing light switches, drawing curtains, closing doors. When he had finished, he raced back to where she stood, trembling against the kitchen door where he had left her. He grasped her hands. "*What* are you doing here?"

"Hendrik. I—"

Rianna cringed as his grip tightened, her face glowing. "Has *anyone* seen you?"

She shook her head. Her lip trembled. "Hendrik, I'm *cold*." She shivered as she slipped her back pack off and rubbed her arms. *Hold me*, her eyes pleaded.

But Hendrik backed off, keeping his distance. He filled the kettle and put it on the back plate. Only then did he give her a quick half-hearted hug, after which he mumbled "I'll find you a blanket" and left the kitchen once again.

On his return he wrapped the blanket around her shoulders, avoiding her eyes, then pulled out a chair in which she plopped down, still shivering uncontrollably. She watched him out of the corner of her eye. "I'm sorry. I should leave."

"Please don't." Hendrik spun a second chair around and sat down. Their knees brushed. He grasped her hands. Their eyes locked.

She noticed an artery pulsing on his temple. She felt lost. His eyes had changed, somehow. Never had they appeared so dark, so intense. *Oh God, this was a mistake.*

Then Hendrik brought both her trembling hands to his lips. His words made her hold her breath. "I was hoping you would follow your impulse and do something . . . wild. Like coming here. Do this." He kissed each finger in turn, each palm, each knuckle, his eyes not letting go of hers.

Rianna shuddered.

"Thank you." He placed her palm against his cheek. "This afternoon on the mountain—it has just been too hard the past five months. Not visiting with you. Not talking. Not even a fleeting kiss. I could barely study. My sleep has been erratic. Look at me, I've lost weight. I *had* to talk to you. To hell with the race police." He sighed. "And now you're *here*."

"I'm afraid, Hendrik," she whispered.

"The Immorality Act police. I know. So am I."

"Not just that. Government spies, maybe. I don't know. Jessica and James and Andries. I'm afraid about how far they are willing to go this time. Not for what they'll do to me but to you. I fear for *you*."

Hendrik smiled tenderly. "Then why did you come?"

"I couldn't get myself to pedal back to the boarding school after work today. I went all the way down and sat at the wharf, thinking about what we had talked about. I wasn't planning on it, but when I reached Church Street on my way back to Westerford, my handlebars and front wheel followed their own mind. It felt like I was sent here. I couldn't *not* come."

They both jumped when the kettle whistled and he pulled it off the heat. "Tea's fine? *Rooibos?*"

She nodded, beaming, and pulled the blanket tighter. Their fingers touched when he handed her the mug. The static electricity made her yelp and jump, spilling tea on the floor. "I'm sorry, Hendrik," she giggled.

He scowled but leaned forward and kissed her parted lips, then bent down and wiped the spill with a table napkin.

Rianna rested her elbows on the table, steaming mug in both hands, eyeing him over the rim. It would be easy to get used to such moments. How she wished she could grasp this one like she grasped the mug, hold on to it. Make it last. Hendrik pulled a face and shrugged. They sipped in comfortable silence.

"Please tell me." Hendrik's brow furrowed. He tapped his head. "What's going on inside that fascinating head of yours?"

She fiddled with her fingers. "How can I believe you about the UCT girls? They're two to three years my senior. I can't compete with them." She placed her empty cup on the table.

"You don't have to. You're more mature than people ten years your senior. They're empty-headed."

"You want to tell me there isn't one good *Coloured* girl your mom will be happy for you to bring home?"

He shrugged again. "I have friends among them, but none are girlfriend material. Mother knows how I feel about you."

"How do you *feel* about me, Hendrik Willems?"

He coughed, his voice hoarse. "I told you this afternoon. I can't stop thinking about you. I can't sleep. And when I do, I dream about you." He took her hands and kissed her fingers, then pulled her closer across the corner of the table and kissed her lips.

His mouth was urgent. Her lips parted, tasting his mouth, tasting the *rooibos* he had drunk, tasting him. She was aware of her body glowing. An unfamiliar warmth had settled in her stomach, then crept lower. A yearning. Foreign. Unsettling. She shuddered and pulled away.

"What does that even *mean*, Hendrik?"

He swallowed. "It means," he licked his lips, "I'm in *love* with you."

Twenty-Five

The lovers. November 1968

"You're silly. *Kiss* me." Rianna closed her eyes when their lips met.

Hendrik pulled her to her feet. "*Come*. These kitchen chairs are hard and were never intended for kissing. You can bring the blanket along." He led her to a modest sitting room, down a short hallway, to the side of the house. It used to be the spare bedroom, but his mother had converted it when Sarah's boyfriend came visiting—too frequently to Maria's liking. She had argued, it was better to have her daughter under her own roof than have her gallivanting goodness knows where.

Hendrik held Rianna's hand until she plopped down next to him on the three-seater sofa. She perched forward, her back a broomstick, hands clasped between her knees. She straightened her legs and crossed them at the ankles, letting her breath out in a cautious hiss.

Dear Lord, what will Antie Maria say of me sitting here with her son?

A faded Persian rug covered part of the floor—pristine and clean but dated. Perhaps as far back as Van der Stel's time in the Cape during the late nineteenth century. A single yellowwood *riempie* chair, circa the same time, glistening of wood oil, stood next to a three-legged coffee table, the only other furniture in the narrow room. A faded calendar picture of Table Mountain and Table Bay, as seen from Bloubergstrand, adorned one wall. The framed picture seemed shamefully inadequate for the splendid rug.

Rianna shivered and pulled the blanket around her shoulders. When Hendrik rose to turn out the ceiling light and turn on the coffee table lamp, Rianna, unable to control her curiosity, kneeled down and stroked the carpet, running her fingers through the frayed fringes and turning the corner back. Her nose scrunched.

Hendrik joined her and patted the carpet. "Counting the knots per inch? Oh . . . it's *genuine* enough. Mother says it came into the family a while before the Second Boer War."

Rianna laughed with embarrassment. "It's lovely . . . like *velvet*. Your mother must be pampering it."

Hendrik sat down in front of her, in a semi-Lotus position, their knees touching. He reached for her and lowered his hand to her neck, then rolled a strand of curls between his fingers. "Mom does. The rug is of the same velvet as your hair. *That* was the thing I noticed when I met you. Your *mop* of hair."

"You're a poor liar, Hendrik Willems. You couldn't keep your eyes off my chest."

"Can you blame me?"

Rianna slapped his knee and took his hands. Rose crept up her neck. "Tell me again what it means when you think of me?"

Hendrik rose to his knees and slipped his hand behind her neck. Their noses touched. Rianna stopped breathing.

He inhaled her warmth. "I'll say it again: I am in love with you."

Her lips brushed his. "I'm scared, Hendrik." She took his face in her hands and kissed his nose, then his lips; as if filled with an unnamed thirst. "And yet, this . . . this makes me *happy.*"

She stretched out on her side, supporting her head with her hand, eyes trained on him. She rolled her curls between her fingers. "Perhaps I can dye my hair. Then it'll be dark like yours."

"It still won't be frizzy enough."

"It'll at least be black."

"What about your freckles? Coloured people don't have freckles."

"I'll lie in the sun all day. Flunk school and tan."

"You can't have tan lines. You'll have to try Sandy Bay where the nudists go." He laughed. "Then I'll have to stand guard to protect you from other guys' inappropriate attention. But you'll only get *more* freckles."

Rianna groaned. "I'm doomed. The department of Bantu Affairs will never accept my reclassification." She wiggled closer and placed her arm next to his, comparing the two limbs. "Milk and cacao. How can *this* be a *crime?*"

"It's to keep the races pure."

"*Pure?* Even the air we breathe is impure. How can it be a sin?"

"They're quick to quote the scriptures, cite the laws."

"But Coloured people are a mix of the early European settlers and the Cape Malayan people—from two hundred years ago. You and I had no part in this. Perhaps what our *ancestors* did was immoral."

"It's the law of the land *now*," Hendrik said.

"Laws that claim *you* are more primitive because your skin is darker than mine. It's plain wrong. In the end it will destroy us."

"We're suitable to be servants. Slaves. Property of the Whites."

Rianna snapped into a sitting position. "I know. I'll become even more vocal. We have to change the laws. It has to be about our inherent dignity, about our worth as human beings in God's eyes."

"*Hah!* God has forsaken us. We're his lost children. Dr. Verwoerd, and now Mr. John Vorster, and the entire clique of Afrikaner Nationalists, claim to be God-fearing Calvinists."

Rianna made him lie down, head on her lap, facing her. She held his chin, brushed his jaw. "Don't say that, Hendrik. *He* has a plan for our lives."

Hendrik shook his head. "God has forgotten about us. We're the in-between race. No one wants us—not the Whites, nor the Blacks. I think God too. He must be disappointed with how we turned out in the end—our colour, and especially our hair. And we talk funny too."

Rianna pulled a face, bent down and kissed his protesting lips, silenced him with gentle nibbles. "At least they don't call you a *kaffir* or a *bantu*."

His fierce eyes drilled into hers. "You think it's any better to be called 'boy' or '*hotnot*'?"

She kissed his protest silent. "Stop *saying* that."

"You want to be friends with a *hotnot*?"

"Don't demean yourself. I think Dr. King once said, 'Don't call me *boy*. I am *a man*.'" She cradled his head and peppered him with more kisses. "You're a *man*, Hendrik Willems. A man like Dr. Christiaan Barnard. A man like Mr. John Vorster. You have *worth*." She was unaware how her rising and falling chest brushed his chin. She locked in on his chestnut eyes. Her face glowed. Blood whooshed in her head. She trailed his lips with an index finger. The flutter in her stomach had barely settled, when it crept lower. Everything pulsed and tingled.

She leaned closer and whispered in his ear. "In two months' time I'll be eighteen, but I already know what I want. I want to be with you. Spend my life with you. I *love* you, Hendrik Willems."

He groaned as he took hold of her shoulders and rolled her in one swift movement across him, onto the Persian carpet, flat on her back. Then he scooped the loose cushion from the wooden *riempie* chair and placed it under her head.

She bit her lower lip.

"Don't *do* that."

Her gaze intensified. "How can our feelings for one another be *wrong*? Be a *sin*?"

She was unable to slow down her breathing. She noticed with alarm how her nipples strained through the fine fabric of her shirt, in spite of her brassiere. She prayed Hendrik wouldn't notice. Her blush intensified.

Hendrik was blessed with normal eyesight and peered at her bosom, mesmerized. "You can't deny it, Missy Vermeulen. They're *beautiful.*" He reached out and brushed the side of her chest.

Rianna's breath caught.

He leaned in and kissed her open mouth. "About that *first* day—what I noticed was the glow in your eyes. There was a *fire*, fueled by this indomitable spirit inside you." He traced her brows with his fingertips, slipped it down to her nose, then her lips, tracing the outskirts. "The fire has only grown stronger."

"*Hendrik.*" The way she said it made him pause. It embodied all the yearning and longing and hope and dreams and fears of a young woman, tied together in the single utterance of his name. She said it again. *Hendrik.* It was as if he heard his name for the first time. Spoken in a strange tongue. This was a foreign land he found himself. Unchartered. Untrodden.

He rolled the sound around in his mind. It was bitter-sweet. Lovely even. The redhead was calling him. Beckoning *him*. His hand followed, of its own volition, the contours of her body. Time ceased.

Rianna whimpered. She strained forward to meet him. His hands became those of a musician, leaning into a harpsichord, touching the keys to pluck sweet melodies from the strings. His fingers soon found their own rhythm. Her lips parted as his hands traced the outlines of her breasts. Her hands flew to her chest, struggling to undo the top button of her shirt.

Hendrik placed her hands at her sides, smiling at her. "No. Don't rush." With the back of a hand he traced her hair down to her chin, down her neck, skimmed her chest, paused at her navel, brushed past her knees, and traveled to her feet. Then, changing position and hands, Hendrik shifted and leaned closer. "Close your eyes." His right hand started its journey up her right hand side.

This time his hand closed over her breast, as if measuring it, as if acknowledging its loveliness. Rianna cried out. Her eyes snapped open. "Did I hurt you?" She mouthed *no* and her eyes fluttered closed once more.

Hendrik undid the first button of her shirt and repeated the feather-light tracings of her body. The second button from the top came undone. Then the third. The fourth.

There were five buttons.

Hendrik pulled her shirt free and folded it away in front. Her firm globes, each the size of his closed fist, jutted forward, elated, concealed now only by her diaphanous brassiere.

Rianna's blush deepened, as did her breathing. She pinched her eyes shut.

Hendrik sighed as he stepped wide, sat astride her thighs, resting on his heels. His kisses started afresh from the crown of her head, traveled down her eyebrows, across her eyes, down her neck, hesitating at her collarbones, before venturing to the sloping valley. He hesitated.

Her eyes fluttered open. Rianna got hold of his T-shirt and yanked. "It's unfair. You sit gawking at me—I want to see you too." Hendrik pulled his shirt over his head. Rianna rested her palms on his chest muscles. "Hendrik," she whispered, "why do people make us feel guilty about this?"

He shrugged as he slipped her arms out of her shirt's sleeves. "The church teaches we should wait until we're married."

"But I want to marry you! It's just Dr. Verwoerd and Mr. Vorster's laws that *prevent* us from getting married—forever." She pressed her lips together. "I love you, Hendrik Willems." She straightened her arms and pushed against his chest to move him further back for a better look. "What do you think our children will look like? Redheaded with faded bronze skin?"

"*Children?*" Hendrik stammered. "I-I-I don't want you to get pregnant."

"No, *silly!*" Rianna roared. "*One* day." She nudged his head between her breasts, stroking his hair.

Hendrik's hands slipped behind her back and struggled with the clip. He clicked with his tongue as the clips refused to give. Rianna grinned, beet red, as she leaned forward on one elbow and unclipped it. She dropped back but left the brassiere in place.

Her eyes searched his. "Hendrik, I've never before . . . . What are we doing?"

"It's okay if we stop." He pulled his hands free and leaned back. "Perhaps we *should* stop. I should let you go home. Before you get into trouble. Before all the *skorrie-morries* prowl around in the city."

"*No*. It will make no difference now. I'm late as it is." Rianna grasped his neck and pulled him toward her. "I want this. I've known you for more than three years. I got to know the man you've become. I am so proud of you. I got to know your mom. I trust you. I know what I want, what I need. I have dreams. Dreams for us. *Kiss* me." His kisses became more urgent. She inhaled his warm body. He was a mix of Lux soap and shaving cream and clean man sweat. Rianna sighed when his hands pulled the bra out from between them. She savoured the foreign sensation of his warm chest on her bare breasts. *Dear Lord, thank you for blessing me with this man.*

"Kiss my *breasts*, Hendrik."

"Are you certain?" She guided his mouth toward her chest.

His fingers soon drifted to the front and struggled with the button of her shorts. "Don't stop kissing," she instructed. Their breathing came faster. Their bodies swayed in new-found synchrony, quivering in its joyful discovery. Her hands met his and guided him to unbutton her shorts and helped him push them down her legs.

When his mouth closed over the opposite mound she tugged at his belt buckle. He rolled onto his side, away from her, in his haste to peel the pants down his legs.

For a moment he paused, on his knees, peering down at her, lying on her back. Her hands flew to her chest to cover herself but he stopped her.

"Let me look. *Please*." He inhaled deep, glancing at her from head to toes. Then bent down and touched her lips with his. "You are the most beautiful creature, Missy Vermeulen. I lack the words to tell you what I feel." He inhaled her scent. "Apple blossoms . . . and nectarines." His lips brushed her flesh some more. "I can't marry you, not in this country, not now. It's illegal. But I'll ask you anyway. Rianna Vermeulen, will you *marry* me?"

She lurched forward, eyes wet, embracing him. "I *will*. I *will* marry you, Hendrik. I *love* you!"

He became still. "To marry we'll have to move to Gaborone, in Botswana. No. No, it's too dry there. There's only the heat and the sand. I'll die if I can't see the ocean. Then Walvis Bay in South West Africa."

She laughed through her tears. "Why don't we do it end of next year, when I finish matric?"

"It certainly is possible."

"But what will you do in South West?"

"I'll have my degree. I can teach at a college. Or start by working at the bank."

"And I can go study at their teachers' college and find a part-time job and help make ends meet." She cried out and performed a surprise roll, which ended with him on his back and her sitting astride his hips. She smirked, leaned forward, and kissed his nose.

"Close your eyes." Her lips trailed down to his chest. When his hands travelled up her sides to clasp her breasts, she took hold of his hands and placed them at his sides. "Patience, *please,* Mr. Willems."

"You're *torturing* me."

"'Don't rush,' was what you told me."

Rianna suddenly squealed, raising her pelvis off his hips. "What's happening? It jumped at me." Pupils wide, her eyes darted between his now-amused eyes and the jutting prominence in his underpants.

"Is that your . . . ?" Her crimson intensified.

"That's the effect you have on me."

Rianna shuffled down to his knees, remaining astride his legs. "May I . . . can I?"

Hendrik hesitated, then extracted his legs and peeled his underwear off.

Rianna sucked in her breath when she kneeled down again astride his knees. "It looks so . . . self-assured?" she whispered in awe as she reached out a hesitant hand.

Hendrik pushed himself up on his elbows, his eyes fixed on his friend's face. "You may touch it."

Rianna, crimson, touched him and let out a squeal before retracting her hand, looking at him in alarm. Hendrik laughed.

"You didn't tell me you were Jewish, Hendrik?"

"That was Mother's doing, when I was five."

Rianna's blushing face turned mottled. "It's all curved. It looks almost angry. How can it ever fit . . . ?"

Hendrik shrugged, pulled her down beside him. "Don't worry. Your body is also fearfully and wonderfully made—on the inside as well. When you're aroused and ready, it will make room." He leaned over her and yanked the blanket from the sofa and pulled it halfway over her. He cupped her worried face and kissed her frowns away, relentless, until she relaxed and clasped her arms around his neck.

"How do you know all this?"

He laughed as if embarrassed.

"Have you ever before . . . ?"

"Had *sex?*" He nodded. "Only once. When I was seventeen. A friend of my sister Sarah." He pulled up his shoulders.

"Was it good?"

He blushed. "It was strange."

"Does your mother know?"

Hendrik shook his head.

"Were you in love with her? This woman?"

"No. She was older. She seduced me. Come," and he kissed her questioning mouth into silence, mumbling in her neck. "I believe you still have one piece of clothing to remove."

Rianna tittered, embarrassed, then fumbled under the blanket and pushed her underwear down her legs, kicked it free, and pulled the blanket higher. She shivered uncontrollably. Hendrik pulled her closer, stroking her back until she relaxed.

He turned on his side, facing her. "May I?"

When she gave a curt nod, he peeled the blanket away to reveal her limbs and torso. Inch by inch, the subdued glow from the coffee table lamp revealed her to him. The light caressed her skin. He whistled under his breath. Then he moved to her feet and kneeled, facing her, as she now lay on her back. His arms fell to his sides as he drank in her unclothed figure. Her chest rose and fell under his close scrutiny. Her face glowed. For many moments he forgot to breathe. "What a precious gift you are. God's perfect handiwork."

Hendrik leaned forward and kissed her. He started with her toes. His hands were never still, they roamed in wide circles. Rianna cried out in surprise when he touched her secret folds. Hendrik paused. She was weeping, in silence, her shoulders shaking. "Why are you crying?"

She wiped her eyes, sniffling loud. "You're so *gentle*. As I've always hoped and dreamed it would be." She shuddered. "For a moment . . . I stood outside Paishuko Village with that brute—"

"*Mapopa?*"

She nodded and shivered. She had told him the previous year.

He wrapped her in his arms. "Hush now . . . you're safe. I won't hurt you."

Then he cupped her face, kissing her wet eyes, her running nose, her wet mouth, lapping the salty wetness. "It's okay. I can stop."

"No, please *don't*." She sniffed loud, wiping her nose. "It's just all so new. It's strangely wonderful. Please don't stop."

His hands resumed their steady playing on the harpsichord of her hills and valleys, edging her along. Much later, she muttered, "I'm *ready*, Hendrik."

"I didn't lie to you. Your body has prepared itself."

She shuddered. "*Come.* Please."

"Are you *sure*?"

"If the laws of the land didn't prevent us, I would have first married you, Hendrik Willems. I'm old enough. I have never been so certain of anything in my life. In my heart I have married you. *Yes.* Yes, I want you. Tonight. Make *love* to me."

Hendrik scrambled to the side to retrieve his pants. "Let me just slip a sheath on."

She looked on as Hendrik moved closer on his knees. Their eyes rejoiced and linked hands. She egged him on. She shuddered in synchrony with him, in anticipation. He seemed so certain of himself and yet so vulnerable. *Dear Lord, he's so beautiful. Thank you for the Table Mountain Café. Thank you for letting me meet him there. I love this bronze man.* With great patience, he stroked her some more. "Will it hurt?"

"At first. There's no rush."

"*Kiss* me, Hendrik."

He kissed her as he pressed against her. Her hips heaved to receive him. She clamped her nails in his back, making him cry out. She moaned in his neck, not letting go. "I *love* you, Hendrik Willems."

Hendrik caught his breath, shuddering, cradling her as they melted together. He took great care, as if afraid she would break.

Hendrik didn't lie. It hurt considerably at the start. Her breath caught several times. That changed. They became two waves of the ocean. With each low tide it felt a little better when he pulled back. With each high tide she became one with the surf and the swell and the squeaking gulls as she called his name.

Theirs became a pas de deux—two waves that rolled over an open beach—breaking and backwashing. Tireless. Timeless. In step, in measured synchrony they moved.

Rianna soared. *"Hendrik,"* she cried.

"Hendrik."

*"*I love you, Missy Vermeulen.*"*

The two lovebirds on the Persian rug did not hear when the kitchen door was kicked in. They had lost track of time. It was a quarter to midnight. Only when the spare sitting room door was shoved open did Hendrik raise his head. It was too late. Rianna recalled it was during the thirty-eighth wave that carried her and Hendrik, crashing to the beach, when all hell broke loose.

They were kicked, hit, and yanked apart. Their attackers' faces were distorted, unrecognizable. A cut-off women's stocking pulled on as a balaclava does that to one's appearance. Before

Rianna blacked out she was certain she heard James Martin's voice, above that of Jessica Taylor's. Perhaps there was a third voice. "We warned you, *Coloured* boy. You didn't listen! A man of colour having sexual relations with a *White* girl!"

Then the woman's voice, "And with R.V. of all people!"

The third voice chimed in, "We'll have to make an *example* of you, boy!"

Twenty-Six

THE HATERS

Rianna and Hendrik were blindfolded, once their hands were bound behind their backs. Of that Rianna had little recollection.

"Andries, you're an *idiot*. Why did you hit her that hard?"

"I didn't mean to. *Hey*. No names! Remember?"

"Shit man, she's unconscious." The first man tsk-tsked.

"Andries, get some water in the kitchen to revive her." It was the young woman's voice. "*No*. Look for some ice. In the little freezer box."

"I'm not a baboon."

"Some days I wonder. Get the ice. *Now!*"

"She's beautiful," said Andries's partner.

"The place reeks of their rutting. She's *naked*. Cover her with the blanket." The woman's voice had an edge to it. "I said *cover* her!"

"Okay, okay."

"Breasts too."

"Can I touch them?"

A slap sounded, followed by a cuss. "You've been lusting after her since you laid eyes on her. Haven't you, James?"

"No names, Jess." A deep sigh followed. "With good reason. She has the body of a goddess. Those breasts."

Another slap followed, then a shrill laugh. "Asshole. Too many freckles. Boobs are not everything. You're as clueless as your friend."

Hendrik mumbled something.

"Uh-oh."

The woman must have shoved something into his mouth, because the mumbling stopped.

"We can't alert the neighbours."

The voice belonging to Andries returned. "There's no ice. Here's some water."

"Useless bastard."

"Watch your tongue, Jess."

"No names!"

"Okay, okay. I keep forgetting."

The first man's voice sounded concerned. "Shit, Jess. You've almost killed the Coloured boy." Then came the soft but unmistakable sound of someone kneeling on the floor, a body rolling over. "At least he has a heartbeat. That's a lot of blood he's got on his temple. He's supposed to be *awake* when we do the operation on him."

"Stop whining. Why didn't *you* hit him then?"

"*I* had to hold him down, remember? It helped that they were on the floor already." The first man snickered then. "He was so busy, it slowed him down at least. Otherwise, I don't know. Look at his bulk. He's solid."

She clicked with her tongue. "That's why I hit him so hard. I think I struck him twice. Feel all those muscles." She whistled. There were more sounds of movement, bodies shifting. "How *considerate*. He even wore a sheath."

"Andries, throw me the boy's T-shirt! *Quick!*"

The young woman snorted. "Too late. He's bigger than either of you. Perhaps we should play with him."

"And you say I can't remain focused. You're the one who can't get enough of *mine*," the second man snorted.

The young woman gave a shrill laugh.

When the water hit her face Rianna coughed and choked.

"Imbecile!" The young woman's voice reverberated through the cramped room.

A thud sounded, followed by the unmistakable sound of Andries cussing. The woman piped, "First you crack her skull, now you're trying to drown her." Another slap sounded. "She's supposed to watch. Do I *really* have to do everything?"

"Andries," came the first voice, "let's go home. Let's leave Jess to sort out the mess on her own. We deserve some respect. She'll have a lot to explain. *Come.*"

"Hey! I'm sorry, guys. Okay? I'm stressed. I've never done this."

"It's obvious. *Come*, Andries. Jess is on her own."

"James, I said I'm sorry. *Please.*"

A loud kiss followed. Then a second kiss. And a giggle.

THE VOICE belonging to Andries warned, "Guys, not so loud. It's past midnight. We don't want the entire District Six on our backsides. You have to shush!"

"Where's the *Klipdrift*, James?" the woman whispered and giggled once more. "I can't do this straight. I need some iron in my veins."

"It's in the car," the first man muttered. "Andries, go get it please." He tossed him the keys.

"Gmph." Andries muttered. "You think you can boss me around since you have a car, James. And *you're* the one who failed your matric."

James laughed. "I have the car and the girl. You're the one who flunked your first year at UCT. Come on, Dries. Be a pal."

"He did say please," Jess purred.

"Yeah, you two are ganging up on me, as always."

"But you would also like to collect your reward afterwards, don't you now, Andries?" She gave him a kiss and squeezed his arm. "Run along, please, sweetheart."

"*Whatever*. I remain the fifth wheel."

"On your way back through the kitchen, get us some glasses— real big ones."

"JESS, YOU *can't* have more than a glass. Even half a glass is lots. It'll kick you off your horse. Then you'll be useless to the mission. Unable to do the job."

"Mission? I'm the one who has to do all the thinking, the planning, the doing. I even did all the reading in the library. You were too lazy."

"I was busy."

"Hogwash. You're floating through your repeat year on memory. Perhaps you were too scared to hit him?"

"That's *bullshit!*"

"Whatever. I was the one who studied the surgical textbook. I know what there's to know about the scrotum and its contents. I'll do the cutting. Although it should have been you. You guys were useless *before* we started drinking." The young woman hiccupped loud. "I *love* this stuff." She poured herself another glass. Another hiccup followed.

"Jess, that's *enough!*"

"Cheers!" She clinked her glass. "Your mistake was to forget the Coke. *Brandy and Coke.*" A loud hiccup followed. "When we're done, this Coloured boy won't make more babies. *Ever.* Hurray for the Immorality Act!"

She emptied her glass, slammed it on the floor and burped.

"James, dear . . . be a darling. Where's the knife?" The young women's voice had a slow drawl to it.

"In the backpack." Andries fumbled with the straps. "You're certain you're up to it? You're a bit drunk."

"Andries, and you're a bit slow. Hand me . . . the knife. Or shall I say, *scalpel, please?*"

The young woman staggered toward the door and turned the ceiling light on, blinking against the sudden brightness.

"Ag, no man, Jess. Our eyes!" the first man protested.

She hiccupped. "I need to see what I'm doing." She released a loud burp into the room, sighed in relief. "James, can you recall what we told my uncle?"

"Which one?"

Another hiccup. "Idiot. The Secret Police one. The one who gave us this address."

"You're worried he didn't believe your story?"

"Maybe."

"You think he'll come and check up on us?"

She shrugged. "*Never.*"

She plopped down on the sofa. "Are you boys going help me or what?"

"Where do you want him?"

"Pull him into this corner. Least we can do is not mess his mom's Persian rug. It looks pretty fancy. The book said it's a vascular part of the body—the groin area."

She winked at Andries. "Fetch us a towel from the bathroom, will you, honey?" Andries grumbled and wandered off.

"Help me move the sofa," she mumbled in James's direction.

Grunting and shoving followed. Jessica caught her breath, glancing at their captive. "He's *beautiful*. A perfect specimen. Such a shame." She traced his torso and hiccupped loud.

"Now get Rianna onto the *riempie* chair. She'll have a better view from there. I need her to watch. That's important."

"Cut it out, Jess," James moaned. "Help me with the girl."

"You're so helpless. That's why I wanted you to join the running club. But no. Stuff this gag in her mouth. The neighbours, remember? *Careful!* Not too deep—she still needs to breathe. Tie her arms to the armrests."

"Yes, boss." Andries sneered.

Jessica gave a bitter laugh and tucked the ropes on the girl's arms, then plopped down once more on the sofa. She drew a hand across her eyes. For a moment she didn't move, as if having second thoughts.

"You're thinking we should quit this mad scheme?" James whispered, reaching for her hand.

She yanked her hand away. "*No!* Don't be an idiot!"

"I was just trying to read your mind."

"Don't even try." Jessica cussed, lurched to her feet, crossed the short distance and whacked James against the temple. "James, *cover* her chest."

"*Careful,* Jess. You don't own me."

"How *dare* you? I asked you to cover her chest. I'm not blind. You fondled her breast."

"I pulled up the blanket as you asked me. I accidentally brushed her nipple. Sorry, okay?" He swallowed. "She's gorgeous. I had to know what a full breast feels like."

Another thwack sounded, then a muffled cry. "Sorry, Jess."

"And I'm sorry I had to hit you."

SOMEONE was gently slapping her on the cheeks. "Open your eyes, Rianna, darling," came Jess's voice. "*It's show time.*" Rianna's eyes fluttered open, then closed again, as her head rolled to the side.

Jessica Taylor yanked the gag from her former roommate's mouth, wiped her captive's lips clean. "Only one way to solve that." She took the other girl's face in her hands and kissed her on the mouth, forcing her lips apart in a passionate kiss until the unconscious girl's eyes quivered open in alarm, crying out in protest.

"Jess, are you out of your mind?" James grabbed her by the arm and pulled her away from their captive.

Jessica laughed shrill. "Desperate measures, friends."

"You *kissed* a girl!"

"So? I was getting her attention."

"You're disgusting." James muttered through clenched teeth.

Jessica shrugged as she faced Rianna. "Glad you could join us, Miss Vermeulen."

Rianna strained against the ropes, her eyes flashing. "You-you-you're . . . a devil woman . . . Jessica Taylor!"

Jessica leaned forward and slapped Rianna across the face, snapping her head backward. "You brought this on yourself, Missy. I pleaded with you for more than two years. Two *fucking* years! First the banned books. Then this boy. James warned you as well. Then we warned you once more, months ago—with the brick through the window and the note. But what did you do? You are not above the land's laws. Why did you have to pick *him*? You could have had any White boy."

"I-I-I love him."

"You're pathetic, Rianna Vermeulen. '*I love him*.'" The young woman paced in front of her captive. "Was he any good?"

"You're . . . *despicable*."

Jessica spun around and whacked Rianna through the face with the back of her hand—harder this time, drawing blood. Her captive whimpered.

"Answer my *question*. Did he satisfy you?"

Rianna stifled a sob. "Yes . . . he was gentle and—"

"*Bah!* Boring. I like them rough!"

"You *devil*. What did you do to Hendrik? Why is he lying so still? *Hendrik? Hendrik!*"

Jessica slapped her captive again and shoved the gag back in her mouth. "Shut your mouth." She yanked the redhead backward by the hair. "I want you to watch. I'm going to cut your boy-friend—no, sorry, your lover boy. The plan is to make an eunuch of him—prevent him from propagating his already mixed race. Make an example of him." She hiccupped and shrieked. "In the process, teach you a lesson too. What did you think your children will look like with him as a father?"

Rianna lurched to her feet, still bound to the chair, screaming past the gag when Jessica stepped toward Hendrik with the knife. "No, you can't! You, monster!" She lurched toward the corner where Hendrik lay.

Jessica responded with a vicious kick to the redhead's bound figure. The kick sent Rianna crashing against the plastered brick wall. Her head struck against it. Next, she plucked the bound girl upright and placed her against the far wall, then slapped her face repeatedly, leaving red wheals.

The woman spun toward her companions. "Boys, pay close attention. The time for games is over. Hold the man's legs. He's strong. He will kick you to kingdom come if you don't hold on tight."

Hendrik Willems eyes opened in horror when Jessica's knife sliced through his scrotum. He hollered past his gag as Rianna's muffled screams filled the room. Hendrik's vicious kicks caught both James and Andries, as well as Jessica, by surprise. The knife slipped into his inner thigh and cut a second time—this time much deeper. As the textbook pointed out—it is a vascular area of the human body. Everybody yelled and shrieked. There was blood everywhere. Chaos reigned.

Outside, sirens wailed closer as strobe lights broke intermit-tently through the thin curtains. Jessica lay in a crumpled heap, still dazed from the force of her impact with the wall. James and Andries scrambled to their feet. It sounded like multiple vehicles had roared to a standstill in the street outside.

As her captors fled the room, Rianna crawled closer, still bound to the *riempie* chair, naked, crashing to the floor next to her bleeding friend. Clasped in her hand was the blanket. She fell forward onto Hendrik, weeping, pressing the blanket into his gushing thigh wound.

The three home invaders sped through the shattered kitchen door, cussing and clawing each other.

"Jess, what the hell? Your uncle—"

"He would never split us."

"Shit, Jess!"

"You two are the useless bastards!"

"Traitor!"

They crashed down the four steps to where half a dozen dark figures, clad in midnight-black attack-gear, their automatic rifles trained on the kitchen door, awaited them. Seconds later, the six policemen were joined by six more men in riot gear, who had darted from the front and sides of the house.

---

*B*y the time Hendrik reached the hospital he had lost more than three pints of blood. But Jessica Taylor's consideration had paid off—the eighty-year-old Persian rug was saved.

Hendrik Willems fared less well. He underwent emergency surgery and received a massive blood transfusion, but developed sepsis six days later. When he went into lung failure his life hung in the balance. Throughout his ordeal Rianna stayed at his bed-side every minute she could. Hendrik's mother and sister kept vigil with her. Rianna's eyes were permanently swollen. She didn't sleep or eat. *Rooibos* tea became her sustenance of choice.

---

*M*r. James Martin, Mr. Andries Steenkamp, and Miss Jessica Taylor appeared in the Cape Town Magistrate's court five days following the incident in the house on Cambridge Street in District Six. They were kept in the police cells until their appearance, without the option of bail. Jessica couldn't understand why her uncle, the one serving in the Secret Police, didn't show his face, no matter how many times she asked for him. The uncle's absence had forced her to make a scene at the police cells. She was certain he would be able to solve her and her friends' dilemma. The entire incident rested on a misunderstanding—an innocent prank the three of them had played on her ex-roommate and her boyfriend that had gone awry, she insisted. Youthful indiscretion. Her parents couldn't shed light on the mystery either.

Twenty-Seven

BETRAYAL HAS CONSEQUENCES, AS DOES
BREAKING THE LAW. DECEMBER 1968

The nurse-in-charge filled the doorway to the high care room, arms folded across her ample bosom.

"*Excuse* me please," Rianna piped, trying to slip past to where Hendrik Willems lay.

The formidable figure didn't budge. "No visitors except next of kin. He has been placed under quarantine."

"But I've been at his side this *entire* week—" Rianna blinked back tears, staring at the unfamiliar pink face. She had never noticed the particular nurse on the ward.

"I *know* that." The nurse looked down her nose at the unkempt young lady. "I'm Nurse Edwards. I'm in charge now. I've been informed you've refused to leave when asked by staff—"

"He's so *ill.*" Rianna sobbed. "He's my friend. I only held his hand. *Please* let me in." She tried once more to push past.

The nurse stood her ground. "Miss Vermeulen, do you want me to call security?"

Rianna cringed, "No . . . I didn't mean . . . ."

"Mr. Willems is in organ failure. Those were my instructions: no unnecessary visitors."

"My presence is not unnecessary. My visits are *vital* to his health!"

The nurse's lips curled down. "I didn't realize you're a physician or a trained nurse." Her lips curled down. "Are you *blood* related? *Married* to the patient?" She seemed to enjoy the situation. She leaned closer and hissed, "From what I understand you've been quite friendly with our patient—*across* the colour line. That's how he ended up in hospital, I believe."

Rianna sucked in her breath. It had not been her imagination. Since the first day of Hendrik's admission to the hospital, Maria Willem's attitude had cooled toward her. *She thinks I took advantage of her absence by going to her house. She believes I have led her son astray.* When Maria Willems visited the hospital, she would keep her distance, at most give Rianna a half-hearted hug, then move to the opposite side of Hendrik's bed. Now she realized what that look in Maria Willems's eyes was—it was blame.

THE NURSE's eyes drilled into her. "Wake up, Miss. What's with this hippie lifestyle of yours? Where's your pride? You're a redhead with a glaringly fair skin peppered with freckles. You're both beautiful people, but he's a *Coloured* boy. He will always be Coloured. A *hotnot*. It's called the Immorality Act. It's there for a *reason*." She towered over Rianna. "*Go*, or I'll call security."

Rianna scuttled away, "He's not a *boy*. He's a *man*."

"You're the one who's in the know," the nurse snickered. "But don't forget, a *Coloured* man. And you're a *White girl*."

"I'm almost eighteen. I'm at Westerford High . . . ."

The nurse waved her on. "I thought so. A *privileged brat*. School girl. We know where to find you."

---

*R*ianna threw herself on the mercy of the vice-principal, Miss Clark. She deemed it unwise to bother Mr. Benson with her delicate request. In spite of his having abandoned his habit of wearing the ridiculous safari suits, returning to his respectable three-piece suits and ties, much to everyone's relief, Rianna was not convinced yet of his emotional health. Perhaps it was too soon after the disastrous love affair for the troubled man to be of sound mind. Miss Clark would be a safer wager.

Like Esther of old, the redhead went unsummoned to King Ahasuerus's chamber. Even if it was at the risk of losing her head. She had to see Hendrik. She had nothing to lose. Not since Hendrik's mother had literally turned her back on Rianna whenever she arrived at the unit, walking in the opposite direction. It was as if the Coloured woman was afraid to even speak to her. Something else must have happened. Surely the vice-principal would intervene. Surely the vice-principal would arbitrate on her behalf and negotiate hospital visiting rights. Wouldn't she?

Rianna was wrong.

Not that Miss Clark didn't personally drive to the hospital and speak to the nurse-in-charge. Even to the matron, as well as the superintendent. All to no avail. The hospital authorities were adamant—no visits from anyone but immediate family. The negotiations lasted two entire days.

Rianna continued to stand outside the high care unit to ask. Whenever she insisted upon a daily update on her friend's condition, she always received the same, standardized response: *Mr. Willems's condition remains critical.*

On the third day of his quarantine, Rianna was met by the charge nurse in person, this time in the wide hallway, at the entrance to the unit. The charge nurse seldom bothered to speak to Rianna—she always sent one of her junior nurses. But this time, Nurse Edward's demeanour was a bit less chilly than usual. She reached out a hand to Rianna, although she avoided eye contact. "I'm sorry, Miss Vermeulen. I have bad news. Mr. Willems is no longer with us."

"Where have you taken him?" Rianna's voice rose. "Will I be able to visit him?"

The nurse coughed, "I'm afraid not. He has *passed.*" Only then did she dare look the redhead in the eyes.

Rianna cried out when she read the truth. "He's . . . *dead?*"

Nurse Edwards touched Rianna's arm for a moment, then nodded. "My condolences."

Rianna whimpered, swayed, and slumped to her knees. The nurse grasped the sobbing girl's arms and called for help. Together, the staff half-carried the pale visitor to the waiting room. They sat her down and made her drink sweetened tea, which the charge nurse instructed one of the younger nurses to fetch.

Once Rianna was steadier on her legs, Nurse Edwards took the trembling girl through to the hospital room Hendrik had once occupied. Rianna wiped over her eyes and blinked at the sterile space. The room was empty, the bed freshly made. Of Hendrik, there was no sign. It was as if he had never lain in the room—not even a dent disturbed the mattress.

Rianna plopped into the chair she had sat in for six days, clasping Hendrik's hand. She pressed on her chest, breathing fast. She closed her eyes. Only when the nurse cleared her throat did Rianna glare at her. "Can I see him?"

The nurse returned the glare, saying nothing.

Rianna choked out the words. "His *body*." The nurse shook her head. "At least let me see his remains," Rianna cried, searching the nurse's face, reaching out an arm. "Allow me to say *goodbye*."

Nurse Edwards's lips were a thin line as she clutched Rianna by the arm, steering her toward the exit, gesturing for a junior nurse to accompany their visitor. "I'm afraid that's not possible."

Rianna halted. "He must be down in the mortuary. I'll go there."

"I told you—Mr. Willems was under quarantine. His body was immediately taken away." She cleared her throat. "He's not in this hospital's morgue. All of this was done for infection control. We can't afford the risk—"

"That's *bullshit!*" Rianna lurched to her feet, sniffing defiantly.

"Miss Vermeulen, how dare you? You're not a pathologist or a microbiologist! The body has been removed by the authorities. It will be burned—"

Rianna teetered. "*Burned?*"

"I'm sorry, I misspoke. He'll be cremated."

Rianna yanked her arm free. "Why don't I believe you? I need to see his body!" She clasped her hand over her mouth, retching. "*Please.*" Rianna slumped over a garbage can in the hallway and heaved, doubled over. Nurse Edwards pressed the panic button. Rianna's stomach was empty—only bile-streaked spit came out. She wiped her mouth with the back of her hand and tried to swallow the vomit-taste away. She leaned against the wall, panting.

Two male orderlies appeared. Nurse Edwards instructed them to accompany the distraught lady to the front entrance of the hospital. They were to stay with her until they had ensured that she had left the facility. As they escorted the redhead down the hallway, the charge nurse called after her, "If we see you here again, I will call the police!"

---

*R*ianna instructed the taxi to drop her off at the house on Cambridge Street.

Since the first day of Hendrik's admission to the hospital, Maria Willems had little to say to the fair-skinned freckled-face girl who used to be her right hand in the Table Mountain Café.

Rianna had also met Hendrik's sister, Sarah, at the hospital. Sarah followed her mother's example in treating Rianna as if she had the plague—to be avoided at all cost.

Rianna had to repeat her knock on the front door. When the door swung open, Sarah's slim figure slipped into the doorway, arms crossed, face unsmiling. "What do you want?"

"I am so sorry about Hendrik."

Sarah shrugged. "Whatever. Is that all?"

Sobs shook Rianna's shoulders. "Don't you understand. I loved him."

"You're such a drama queen. You *knew* it was against the law. And yet, you still—"

"That's *fresh*. How is your situation any different?"

"We're talking about *Hendrik*."

Rianna sniffled loud, wiping over her eyes. "Hypocrite. May I see his . . . your mother?"

"She didn't take the news well. She's in bed."

"Sarah . . . *please*."

A burly man appeared behind Sarah in the door opening. He eyed Rianna as he pushed his glasses higher on his ample nose. His blond hair, brylcreemed flat to his head, stood in sharp contrast to Sarah's well-kept dark bob. It was a pale arm and an even paler plump hand that touched Sarah's shoulder, making her face him. He squeezed her shoulder.

For a moment Sarah's broomstick shoulders softened. "Wait here," she muttered and left Rianna standing at the door. The man stood rooted—no one was entering the house without him saying so.

At last movement behind the giant made him step aside, revealing the owner of the house. The past ten days had taken a toll on Maria Willems. She shuffled closer, hollow-shouldered, holding to the doorframe for support.

Mother and girlfriend's eyes met; at first hesitant—then locked. Both remained silent, hesitant. The older woman reached out first; she pushed Sarah's friend, Johan Conradie, out of the way and opened her arms for Rianna. "*Kom hier my kind.*" Come here my child.

Rianna stumbled into her arms with an "*Ag, Antie,*" before surrendering to the tears. The brown woman and the fair-skinned girl embraced, reluctant at first, then tightened their grips. They remained like this for a considerable time. It was clear they gained strength from one another's closeness.

Sarah soon choked it out, "*Mom!* No need to advertise to the entire neighbourhood the prodigal daughter has returned."

Maria shuddered and pulled the gaunt girl inside. "Come, child." Maria closed the front door and rolled her eyes at her daughter as she led their visitor through to the kitchen, like in the old days. She turned to her daughter. "Sarah, why don't you boil us some water? I know Rianna would love some *rooibos* tea." She pushed Rianna down into the first chair at the Formica table with a gentle shove, before instructing Conradie, "Johan, four cups please."

Only once everyone had found a seat around the table, steaming cups of brewed tea in hand, did Maria Willems turn to her guest. "Do you want to tell us what happened?"

Rianna omitted the details about the five hours that she and Hendrik had spent in each other's company, in each other's arms, eventually making love. She began her account from the moment the small sitting room's door was kicked open by the three intruders, pantyhose pulled over their faces. How Hendrik and she were assaulted and bound, and about the terror-filled hours that followed. Rianna required two refills of *rooibos* to finish her story. Only when she reached her account of the altercation with Nurse Edwards that same morning, did Rianna break down, once more in tears.

She sniffled loud, grasping Maria's hands across the table. "They wouldn't even let me see his . . . his body, *Antie* Maria!" Sobs shook the redhead's frame, making her host pat her arms, coaxing her. "Hush now, child. Hush now."

It took considerable time for Rianna's whimpering to subside. She was not the only one at the kitchen table shedding tears. Once she gained control over her emotions, Rianna groped for Maria Willems's hands a second time. "Did they allow you to see him, *Antie*. His body?"

Maria shook her head. "No. They whisked him away."

"What will happen now?" The fair-skinned girl shuddered. "Will there at least be a funeral?"

"There will be a memorial service, a week from today. They will give us an urn with his ashes."

Rianna let out a mournful yelp, "*Ashes?*" She slumped down on the kitchen table, head on her arms, the slush gates opened anew—there was no holding back now. Sarah tsk-tsked and excused herself and her friend, Conradie. Maria came around the table and pulled Rianna's chair up against her own, patting the weeping girl's hair.

Rianna had trouble seeing through her puffed eyes and matted hair. "Didn't you find it odd, *Antie?* The hospital authorities wouldn't even let you, the mother, the closest next of kin, see his body, and then they only provide ashes a week later?"

"They claimed it was a precautionary measure—to prevent the infection from spreading—"

Rianna hissed out a breath. "I don't believe them."

Only once she heard the front door close behind her daughter did Maria speak. "Nothing I can do about that." She reached out and tilted the redhead's chin. It would be difficult to lie at such a close range. It became clear the Coloured woman demanded answers. "Before those hooligans entered the house, what were you and Hendrik up to?"

"*Antie?*"

"Did Hendrik kiss you?"

Rianna nodded, mucous running from her nose. She sniffled loud and wiped her nose with the back of a hand.

"Did Hendrik . . . did he make love to you?"

Rianna averted her eyes, tumid and red as they were. Her face turned a deeper crimson.

"I take that as a yes?"

Rianna shivered and gripped the older woman's hands, peering into her dark pupils. "I *loved* him, *Antie*. I loved your son, Hendrik." She let out a protracted breath. "We were considering moving to Walvis Bay next year to get married . . . ."

Maria groaned as she held Rianna's hands to her lips and kissed each finger. "I know, he told me some of his plans," she murmured. "I expected as much, sweet girl."

Rianna allowed Maria Willems to make her a makeshift bed in the small sitting room to the side of the house. She had allowed Rianna to use her telephone to inform Miss Clark that she'd spend the night at the house on Cambridge Street.

The entire room had been scrubbed. Of the bloodbath of ten days earlier, there was no sign.

Rianna ignored the disapproving glares from Sarah and her friend, Conradie.

She felt no horror lying there, only a reassuring presence of her friend, Hendrik, watching over her. She pulled her blanket and pillow down from the couch and took it to the Persian carpet, stroking its velvet surface, imagining lying next to her Hendrik. She inhaled deeply, imagining she could smell Hendrik's glowing body. She kept her eyes trained on the humble calendar picture of her beloved Table Mountain. She had little trouble hearing the waves crash in the bay, breathing the salt spray. A lonesome gull was screeching overhead when the sleep stole her away.

⁂

It took Rianna two entire days of playing private investigator to track down her childhood friend, Lukas Ferreira. Then a further twenty-four hours to convince him to accompany her, without his father knowing, not with the life-long ban placed on her interacting with his son. She was glad to witness Lukas's willingness to escape his father's patriarchal hold.

It was one thing to attend a funeral service without a body to bury, but a different matter attending it alone, without a person to rub shoulders with, perhaps share a handkerchief with.

Rianna and Lukas sat in the pew behind Aunt Maria, Sarah, and Conradie, much to Rianna's relief and Sarah's discomfort.

Lukas had stretched since the time he had hiked up the mountain with her, a little over two years ago. He was as tall as Rianna now. Lean. Strong. He had seen so much sun, for a moment he reminded Rianna of her Hendrik. It was only months before Lukas's fifteenth birthday. Dressed in his suit, he had turned into a young man—gone was the gawky boy struggling with his puberty, burdened with wandering eyes.

When she was certain no one looked, she snuck her hand between them on the church bench and clasped Lukas's. She only let go when they had to stand to sing a hymn.

Afterwards, after the refreshments, following the service, Rianna allowed Lukas one kiss— on the lips. A proper kiss—the kiss he had longed for on the mountain years ago. Lukas wasn't Hendrik, but what was she to do? She allowed him to crush her to his chest for a minute before she broke the heated embrace, pushing him gently away, both their faces flushed.

"How soon before I can see you again?" he asked, catching his breath.

Twenty-Eight

ARCHIVES AND GHOSTS OF THE PAST. 1996

"*R*ain, rain, go away," Rianna chanted as she scurried for the door of her rental car. *Why did I decide on three inch heels—for flying?* In her haste to escape the deluge, she had twisted an ankle lifting her bigger case into the trunk, while raindrops plopped around her and wind gusts tore at her clothes, as if trying to make her indecent. She yanked open the door, jumped in, and slammed it shut. Overhead, menacing clouds had turned the heavens midnight blue.

Just as she glanced over her shoulder at the Hottentots Holland Mountains, a bolt of lightning crackled and snapped, ripping the somber skies apart with a crooked sliver of illumination. She shuddered. *The cable car will have to wait—not in this miserable weather. The hotel, a quick shower, then the library.*

She had to pay extra to get a room with a balcony, ocean-facing. It was worth it, she thought, as she peered across Table Bay to where the sun had slipped behind a pewter sea. She rubbed her arms, unable to stop the shivering. But it was comforting to smell the drifting rain and the city and the wet ground fifty feet below, even if it was only the tarred city streets. Thank God the water was farther away—she was spared the reek of the harbour, what with its aroma of rotting fish and decay and spilt crude oil. She hugged her shoulders; and yet, this was home.

It had stopped raining, but the wind still howled around the buildings, plucking at her tan-coloured garment, wrapping it around her knees. Rianna tucked her jacket's collar higher, glanced at the ashen skies, and took the wide steps two at a time. The Central Library looked different in daylight, cleansed from a night of rain. She had decided against going the previous evening, what with the thunderstorm and lightning strikes, the lurking jet lag.

The middle-aged man who had just entered the wide-open communal space would not have merited a second look had it not been for the librarian's crisp voice calling after him from the check-out counter. "Excuse me, sir. Professor Marais?"

At this the man turned to face the speaker—and Rianna, who had just reached the opposite end of the counter. "Yes, Miss Partridge?"

"Your special order has arrived—only yesterday afternoon."

Rianna quickened her steps, then paused at a respectable distance. It was not her habit to gawk at people, strangers in particular. Not after being immersed in British culture for so many years now. It felt an out of place thing to do. Staring and eavesdropping; improper even. *That voice. The name. Special order. Hugo Marais?* Her sole supplier of banned books thirty years ago. She took a step backward and waited for the two to conclude their business.

The sallow-faced man thanked the librarian and headed toward the computer stations at the back of the cavernous space. Rianna had to stretch her legs to catch up. "*Hugo*, is that you?" The man slowed down but didn't stop or look at her.

Only when she repeated his name did he stop and turn. "*Rianna?*"

The suit and tie failed to hide his lusterless complexion. Recognition brightened his eyes. He still suffered from too little sun, being indoors too much, she was certain. His cropped dark hair showed silver streaks over the temples. Rianna grinned widely, sped across the remaining distance between herself and the startled man, pulled him closer for a crushing hug, and then held the slim-built man at arm's length. "Rianna Vermeulen, at your service, sir!" She looked him up and down. "Hugo Marais—you haven't changed." She chuckled as she let go, then leaned back in to brush his arm. "Except for the lambs' wool suit." She whistled.

Pink-faced, Hugo pushed his glasses higher up his nose and squinted at her. "The suit's ten years old," he grinned. "The *glasses* are new."

Rianna pointed at the librarian's counter behind them. "*Special order*? I thought the bans on books and people had been lifted years ago?"

He laughed and shook his head. "Nah, it's new research I'm getting help with." He shrugged. "Ever since a certain knowledge-obsessed Westerford pupil grew up, moved away, and got important, it's been hard to find good help."

After a quick scan of the room to make certain they were not the center of attention, Rianna tapped him on the shoulder and stuck out her tongue.

Hugo glanced at his wristwatch, then grasped both her hands and pulled her closer again. "I have urgent business to attend to, but I can meet you in an hour from now." Colour rose to his face, mottling his sallow complexion, as he let go of her hands and stepped back. "Please, we *have* to talk. Catch up. I would love that." He brushed a hand through his short hair. "I'll meet you downstairs at the cafeteria. We can have brunch or a coffee or whatever you would like."

Rianna raised her hand in a small salute. "I would like that, Hugo."

Precisely one hour later, Rianna glanced over the rim of her paper cup at the bespectacled Hugo. She met his now-alert eyes. "*Professor* Marais. How impressive. Who knew? The scruffy young man, living off flat Coke, who never slept, who was always rummaging in the archives, covered in cobwebs and trading in banned books—I'm so proud of you." Her eyes laughed at her long-lost friend. "Tell me everything."

He shrugged and played with the rim of his waxed cup. "I'm not the only one who's found their calling, Rianna. I believe you've made quite a name for yourself on British soil, haven't you?"

Rianna raised her cup, rewarding him with a warm smile. "You flatter me. But that's for another day. Please, tell me *everything*."

After a short silence he told her about what had happened since after she had last met him at the Central Library in April 1966, how he had received banning orders from the police and had to report to a police station. Then, in June of 1968, the day after Rianna was summoned to Miss Clark's office and confronted by Jessica and the policeman about the banned book found in her bedroom, Hugo was placed under house arrest for three months for being the middleman in the banned-book business. House arrest was one step closer becoming a man with a price on his head. He had become "a person of interest" to the Secret Police.

Rianna's eyes brimmed as she reached for his hand. "Why did you never tell me about this?"

He squeezed her hand. "I dared not scare you. You had enough trouble of your own. Our friendship meant too much to me."

She brought Hugo's hand to her lips and kissed the tips. "You knew about Hendrik?"

"I think from the beginning."

"The *beginning*?"

Hugo laughed. "You talked a lot. I knew about him the Monday after you started working at the Table Mountain Café."

"He wasn't anyone special at that point."

"That wasn't my impression." Hugo's eyes teased her. "Whenever you talked about him, your face lit up."

Rianna let go of his hands and bit her lip. "I liked him from the day we met. He was different. Nothing to do with his skin colour. He was brave. Smart. Strong. The love came later." She blinked and wiped her eyes, breaking eye contact.

Hugo patted her hands. "While I was doing research for my dissertation, I came across the man who was instrumental in Sarah Willems's reclassification from Coloured to White woman."

"Johan Conradie?"

"Yes, the man who worked in Bantu Affairs."

"See, you know everybody! Where are you a professor these days?"

"As of last year, I'm head of the Department of Political Science here at UCT."

Rianna leaned across and placed a kiss smack on his cheek. "Are you bragging?"

His face turned pink again. "You asked. But enough about me, *Doctor* Vermeulen. You did not disappoint, my friend. How many books is it now?"

"Three . . . number four is due out the end of the year. How could I not? You taught me so much about research. My way of giving back."

The two friends sat in comfortable silence, enjoying each other's new-found presence.

Then Rianna's brow knotted. "But what about Jessica Taylor and James Martin and Andries Steenkamp?"

"You really want to know? After all these years?"

"I never understood why she hated me so much."

"Three reasons."

Rianna scoffed at her friend. "*Three?*"

"One, you're inherently more curious and far smarter than she is. She was no fool. She knew that. Two, you're brave and fascinating. You were determined to read banned books despite knowing the penalty, and you dated a Coloured boy. Three, you had real breasts." Crimson crept up Hugo's face. "Correction, you still have."

Rianna beamed as she leaned across the table and slapped his shoulder. "You have an interesting way of complimenting a lady. Are you *flirting* with me, sir?"

He tried to invert his paper cup. "I'm settled. I have a partner."

"Are you happy?"

"Fulfilled." Hugo grinned. "We haven't yet considered bashing in one another's skulls."

Taking her friend's hands again in hers, she searched his eyes, "And then that fateful night in November 1968."

Hugo stroked her fingers. "It must have changed everything."

Eyes brimming again, Rianna nodded, "She was evil—*Jessica*. She tried to maim Hendrik, kill him. In the end I guess, she succeeded." She sniffled loud. "And she had two helpers from hell."

"They were all filled with hate. Hate always destroys."

"And I've tried not to let it destroy me. But . . . well. What happened to them in the end?"

"They got off the hook with little trouble. They only did those five nights in the police cells after the arrest. I believe it was Andries Steenkamp's father who had the connections higher up. Nothing came of it. Daddy took care of everything. Pretty sure Taylor and Martin got married and moved to Australia in ninety-three, the year before the election. Steenkamp followed later."

Rianna's voice rose. "The bastards. So fitting. Three hypocrites." A shuddering sigh escaped her lips. "Hendrik Willems was only a Coloured boy. His life didn't matter."

It was Hugo's turn to squeeze her hands. He kissed her fingertips. "Hush now, my friend. You know that's not true."

Rianna freed her hands and sat back, dabbing at her eyes. "I won't give the devils the satisfaction." She plucked another Kleenex from her purse and blew her nose. Then she fixed her hair with her fingers and retouched her lips with *bésame red*, squinting into her miniature lipstick mirror. She pulled her shoulders back, cleared her throat and faced Hugo. "I've made up my mind. I want you to help me—I need to visit Demetrio Tsafendas."

Hugo raised his brow, unruffled. His complexion had returned to its regular sallow tone. Even after almost thirty years, he was prepared for anything from the redhead. Little she said would surprise him. He turned his palms heavenwards. "*If* he's still alive."

"He *is*—I've checked. Research, remember?"

"*Tsafendas*. What on earth for?"

"Why do you think I left the country the day I obtained my teacher's diploma?" Rianna's eyes were on fire. "I couldn't stay. Not after what had happened to Hendrik and me. Especially the way everything was handled by the authorities—from the hospital to the police and the government. I got work in England, went back to school, completed my doctoral studies, started publishing, and eventually worked my way into Oxford."

Hugo sighed. "I know all that, Rianna. And my heart still bleeds for you, for what you had to go through. God is my witness. But what is it with Tsafendas? How will visiting him bring any—"

"I found some articles about Tsafendas when I was doing research in the British Library's newspaper archives, written by a journalist who had really dug into his life. That's why I came back. I had to. You'll recall the essay I had to write for Mrs. Knox on Tsafendas in February 1968. When I read these articles in England a few weeks ago, it opened the old wounds and raised the old questions. The author also finds it significant that, although Tsafendas was known to suffer from schizophrenia, he was able to learn eight languages while travelling overseas. Which means, he was not a stupid man. He was not an ignorant fool, a mere madman who had stabbed the prime minister to death, in a psychotic fit, as the government of the day wanted everybody to believe. But you and I, we never thought that was a convincing story, remember?" Hugo nodded and waited for her to continue. "Even back then there was evidence that he had great concerns about his own racial classification. What I didn't know was that he had decided that he felt most comfortable with people of colour. He was confused and burdened with the problem of trying to decide where he truly fitted in."

"Confused?"

"According to this author, he had actually made statements to friends that he considered applying for reclassification to Coloured. This was *weeks* before he killed Dr. Verwoerd."

"And?"

"I wish to speak to him, Hugo."

"He's in Pretoria Central Prison."

"I know. I've told them I need to interview him for a book I'm writing, but I've got nowhere. I'm planning on flying there."

"Rianna!"

"Will you help me get the necessary permission?"

"I'm only a professor here in Cape Town. You're the Oxford scholar."

"*Bullshit*. You know people, who know people."

"Rianna . . . ."

She grasped his hands. "*Please?* Since these latest discoveries, I'm struggling all over again to accept Hendrik's death. And there's so much I still don't understand. A few nights ago in Oxford I got this overwhelming sense that speaking to Tsafendas may help me put Hendrik's shadow to rest." She shuddered, then pleaded into Hugo's face. "Help me. I can't take sleeping pills for the rest of my life."

Ten days later Rianna arrived in Pretoria, with a letter granting her permission to visit Prisoner Tsafendas. She was not entirely certain Hugo Marais would want to speak to her again after the trouble he had to go through to make the visit possible. *Bah, he's a professor now. He's a big boy. He's tough. He's an ex-banned-book supplier.* She squinted as she slipped her sunglasses in place, stepped from the rental car, and threw back her head to take in the imposing sandstone entrance of the infamous prison, towering above her, just across the street.

Back in cold rainy Oxford, with winter approaching, she had forgotten what happens in Pretoria in spring. Now she paused to glance up and down the street at the jacaranda trees that lined the sidewalks—a lilac canopy draped across the entire city. The brilliant purple-blue flowers were a constant source of pride or disdain for local residents. She inhaled the trumpet-shaped blossoms' sweet scent and then set out across the parking lot toward the prison entrance, clutching her purse and the official letter to her chest. Beautiful or not, the blue trumpets were spread like a diaphanous throw over the tarmac—a benign mine field—each one as slippery as a cake of soap in a bathtub. Thank goodness today's heels were only two inches high.

It was a strange sensation to shake the same hand that had once held the knife that took the life of the father of apartheid, Dr. Hendrik Verwoerd. Tsafendas had trouble controlling his tremors, his handcuffed hands constantly combing through his tousled white hair. *He looks a hundred.* Two armed guards hovered in the background. Rianna sat down across the table from him and explained for a second time why she had requested the meeting. The man was after all seventy-seven.

The suspicion in his eyes softened when she told him about Hendrik and Sarah and Maria. He soon *tsk-tsked* in sympathy as he nodded his head, wringing his shaking hands. *Good, I'm earning his trust.* But when she told him about Jessica and Martin and Steenkamp, he struggled to his feet, clearly upset. The guards were already at his side. Startled, Rianna raised both palms and offered the guards and their prisoner her bravest smile. After a long pause, he dropped back into his seat and began to whisper. She leaned closer—she could smell his breath. "The Immorality Act—that was the biggest bugger of all. *Vicious.* The divider. And all based on lies. It soon became my undoing . . . ."

"Excuse me, Mr. Tsafendas?"

"My *undoing*!"

"The Immorality Act of 1957?"

"Yes, my dear." The old man hunched forward, then began swaying forwards and backwards like a metronome, hands clasped to his chest. He glanced, first to the left, then to the right, to where the guards were. He lowered his voice. "You won't appreciate it today, Doctor, but having had a Greek for a father and a Mozambican for a mother, I ended up a nice chocolate—darker than a coolie. Much darker." He grinned and sighed. "My documents stated I was White. That I was not."

The man dabbed his chest. "Not in here. I never quite made peace with who I was. I was taunted as a child. Later, as soon as I could, I got away. For twenty years I travelled the world, learned many tongues. But the day I returned to the Cape, the wounds of old were ripped open afresh. I felt more comfortable with people with a darker skin colour. Whites never accepted me as one of them. I even travelled to Mozambique to try and locate my birth mother. I fell in love with a woman in the Cape who wasn't classified as White." He held up a shaking index finger, "I loved her, but Dr. Verwoerd's law declared my love illegal."

Rianna hesitated when she reached across the table with hands shaking as badly as that of the silver-haired man. She whispered, "You couldn't go underground? Leave the country?"

The elderly man pulled his shoulders upright, pierced her with his stare. "Did *you* do that? Did you leave?"

When she shook her head, he slouched forward. "I had just returned home after a journey that lasted twenty years. And immediately I had to live in fear and uncertainty again. It was immoral—the act—the implementation thereof." His eyes for the first time looked through her, beyond her, into the distant past it seemed. He shrugged. His voice trailed off. "I decided to put an end to it. The next day I took a big strong knife to work—hid it on my person. You know the rest."

⸺∞⸺

*U*pon her return to Cape Town Rianna remained undeterred—she was now, more than ever, set on uncovering what she could. She spent long days at the Central Library. She kept digging. What intrigued her was the fact that, in spite of having been certified as an unbalanced individual, suffering from mental illness, Tsafendas had been imprisoned, not sent to a mental hospital. He had whiled away his entire time since 1966 at Pretoria Central Prison. Why was that? Hugo Marais left her messages unanswered.

Her renewed research led her to read about the origins of psychiatry and its relation to state and government, about abuses that took place in the old USSR and Nazi Germany, also in the US, Canada, Australia, New Zealand, and Africa, years before. She read about how people, ordinary citizens, were placed in mental institutions when they had different political and socio-economical views, and openly criticized the government of the day.

In the nineteen-sixties, the World Health Organization and International Red Cross had made formal inquiries into a number of allegations about abuse and human rights infringements in South African mental hospitals, where the state, it was claimed, detained its political opponents. These accusations included pharmacological experimentation, black slave labour, and sexual abuse in mental institutions in South Africa. Some of the claims were substantiated, most were not. Rianna had to face the possibility that she would never be able to figure out the whole truth of the matter.

Days later, Rianna met up once again with a reluctant Hugo Marais, this time in his office on the UCT campus. "I'm still trying to understand why Tsafendas is in prison and not in a psychiatric hospital," she said. "He didn't seem that ill to me. It is possible that his diagnosis was wrong?"

Hugo scoffed. "That would be a preposterous view."

"Look, Hugo, I know I'm not a psychiatrist. But you and I both know that sometimes behaviour that the authorities label as "insane" is really an extreme outcry of the powerless. Of those without a voice. Maybe once Tsafendas made himself heard, he stopped being 'mad.'"

"And you say that based on a single visit?"

"No, Hugo. It's not just that. After the Second World War, the apartheid government was set on uplifting the 'poor white male.' Women and people of colour were shunned by psychiatric services, with the new shift of the spotlight onto 'poor white males.'" She took a deep breath. "So, higher numbers of white men, the group the government originally had set out to 'save,' ended up in mental institutions."

"Are you sure? How did you learn all this?"

"You're not the only one who knows how to do research, *Professor*. Remember?" She tapped his shoulder. "There was a stigma associated with being diagnosed with schizophrenia in a *white male*—they had to be hidden from society. But at the same time, they couldn't be allowed simply to rot in prison." She paused. "So why is Tsafendas in prison? Obviously it was simply easier for the government to declare him 'insane' than to try and explain to an anxious international world that his primary motivation stemmed from his discontent with the Immorality Act of 1957 and his ambivalence about where he fit on the colour chart. It's less obvious that his insanity, such as it was, may have been caused by that discontent in the first place. But the fact that he ended up in prison rather than an insane asylum—well. Either they realized he really wasn't mentally ill after all. Or they didn't care—because he was so dangerous that they wanted him in prison, where they could keep him under total control."

Hugo stared at his friend, not saying a word. He felt not a little proud. It seemed the student had surpassed her master. Finally, he said, "That makes a lot of sense. But maybe I can add something to your conclusions. You've been gone a long time. My research, here, has convinced me that the kind of collaborations between state, judiciary and the mental health profession you're talking about never really ceased after 1994. Governments always need to keep tabs on their people."

It was Rianna's turn to stare.

Twenty-Nine

Through breaks in the fog the lower cable station loomed closer, intimidating in its raw concrete finish, only to disappear in the next wave of twirling whiteness. The overhead whirring of the cables softened as the car slowed down. Rianna slipped from Lukas's arms, plucked off her pumps, ripped the stockings from her legs, and reached for the central console, punching buttons.

"*What* are you doing?" Lukas yelled as she lurched, barefoot, from the consoles toward the sliding door of the still-moving car that was closest to the mountainside.

"I'm getting *out.*" She pulled at the door and then gasped as she glanced through the twelve-inch gap she had created at the *fynbos* rushing past underfoot. Changing her mind, she turned on her heel, sidestepped Lukas's grasp, pushed a window wider open, and then pulled herself through it to the outside of the descending cable car. An alarm sounded from the central console followed by a robotic voice: "Warning, door opened. Warning, door opened." The metered voice, the alarm, and the flashing red light continued their synchronized cacophony as Rianna clambered outside.

"Rianna, wait!" Lukas cried after his friend as she hauled herself up the outside of the car and inched onto the roof. He hung halfway out the window himself now, his head craned. He anxiously followed with his eyes the escape route of his friend and wondered if he would be able to grab her if she slipped.

"*Lukas.* Stop looking up my dress!" Her strained laugh echoed against the cliffs.

"Dear Lord." Lukas closed his eyes as instructed, then scrambled back inside. The docking platform of the lower station was fast approaching. He returned to the open window and instructed, "Grab hold of something! We'll be docking any second!"

"Thanks for the warning, Ferreira. I see quite grand from up here." The wind stole much of her words.

Moments later clattering sounded on the roof, and a dark shadow hurled through the open window—Rianna, bursting back into the car just as it shuddered to a stop at the lower station.

Lukas steadied her, scooped her in his arms, and kissed her dirt-streaked face. "Thank God you've come to your senses—"

She shivered. "Changed my mind. It's cold up there. And too high. I should have tried it sooner, when there were fewer rocks and more vegetation. Even if my jump made it into the *fynbos*, I'd probably still kill myself."

She slipped her shoes back on, stuffed her torn stockings in her purse, and combed her fingers through her windblown-hair before clutching his hand. Her dress was a mess.

Two men in suits with sunglasses awaited them. *A welcoming party. I knew it.* The men stood, unsmiling, like a guard of honour on the docking platform. They must have cordoned off the hallway—there was no sign of tourists or cableway staff as the car came to a stop. She took a shuddering breath, tightened her grip on Lukas's hand, and stomped forward the minute the door whooshed open. "Let's face the bastards."

Hand in hand, the friends strode toward the two men. Only then did the duo in sunglasses jump into action and blocked their path.

"Excuse me, Miss, Sir?" The taller of the two reached forward. "If we could have a word, please, *Miss*?"

Rianna snapped her arm away. "Don't touch me!"

The man, unruffled by her response, dropped his hand but remained rooted. The men's hands disappeared into their jacket inner pockets and produced a badge each. It seemed the taller man was in charge. "Secret Police, ma'am." He tapped his chest, "Holmes, and my colleague goes by Schutte." He gave her an appreciating second look. "Did you just climb down from the roof of the car?"

"None of your business."

The man clicked with his tongue. "Impressive."

"What do you want from us?" Rianna glared him down before she brushed the dirt from her clothes a second time and straightened her skirt.

Holmes shrugged. "Our commanding officer needs to speak to you. Please."

Still Rianna didn't move—except to arch her brow. "Are you from Interpol?"

Schutte laughed. "Don't be silly." His high-pitched voice contrasted with his robust appearance.

Rianna took Lukas's hand and barged between the two men, heading straight for the exit. At her approach they hesitated for a second, then stepped aside just enough to let the two pass. Once past them, she stopped and spun around. "I'm a British citizen and my friend is with the United Nations." Then she leaned forward and tapped the colossal Holmes on the chest. "Do you have a warrant for our arrest?" He shook his head and she exhaled loudly. "Thought so. Then leave us the hell alone."

Holmes smirked. "My boss warned me you would be tough. He said the magic words are, 'Demetrio Tsafendas, 1996, Pretoria Central Prison.'"

Rianna sucked in her breath as she tightened her grip on Lukas's hand.

Lukas spoke for the first time, freeing his hand. "Who's your boss?"

"Colonel Vosloo."

"Means nothing to me." He glanced at his companion. "Rianna?"

"I had *official* clearance to visit Mr. Tsafendas in ninety-six. For *research*." She took Lukas's hand again. "Sorry to disappoint you, Mr. Holmes, Mr. Schutte. Please give my warmest regards to Colonel Vosloo." Once again, the two friends headed toward the exit.

Holmes was quick to call after them, "Colonel Vosloo *also* said to tell you it was Albert from Messina who had to speak to you on matters of national security."

Rianna slowed, then turned back to face the policemen. "*Bertie . . . Colonel* Vosloo?"

Holmes rubbed his hands together. "One and the same." Then he pointed a thumb in the direction of the upper station. "I'm waiting on my two colleagues to join us. You must have *almost* met them. They gave us a heads-up. We're here with two vehicles. We'll accompany you to meet the colonel." He gestured for Lukas and Rianna to proceed toward the exit. "One of our cars will go in front; then you can follow in your own, while our second car forms the rear guard."

Rianna muttered, "*Bullies.*" This time, when she took Lukas's hand, she made no attempt to lead him away from their two guides.

The uniformed man, standing motionless next to his desk, was impossible to overlook, what with his air of authority and trim physique, but what captivated Rianna's attention were the two collared cats with tufted ears, the size of six-month-old cougars, that sat at attention, motionless, their eyes trained on the colonel. It was clear, the animals awaited his command—word from their master.

Colonel Vosloo offered a hand. "Rianna Vermeulen. What a pleasant surprise."

Rianna curtsied as she shook his hand, glancing at the two *rooikats* a second time. "I see you've kept your word, O Rameses."

Colonel Vosloo bowed. "Still the class clown?"

Rianna snapped upright. "What's your story, Bertie? Or shall I say, Albert?"

"It's Colonel Vosloo."

Rianna stiffened. "In that case, you may call me *Doctor* Vermeulen."

Albert Vosloo whistled. "Touché. Fifteen all." With a gesture, he pointed her toward an empty chair.

She perched on the edge of it, tense and alert. "Holmes told me it was about matters of national security. Tsafendas has been dead five years. What do you want from me?"

"Things are not what they appear."

"Cut the crap Bertie. Why couldn't Lukas come in here with me?"

"My business is with you."

"Lukas is high up in the UN."

"I'm high up in the police."

"When did you become so pompous? I had *official* permission to meet Tsafendas in 1996."

Colonel Vosloo held up his palms. "I know that, Rianna. Settle down. *Please.*"

"Don't you *dare* tell me to settle down!" She jumped to her feet. Deep growls escaped from the cats.

Their master raised a hand at each cat. "Max, Rex, down boys." The *rooikats* immediately quieted down and lowered their heads in obedience, though their eyes never left Rianna. She had scrambled back to her chair, and now sat, hugging her shoulders.

"Sorry, Bertie."

"It's okay. These cats are trained. They'll obey me. I've trained them in hunting and guarding."

"What do you want from me?" She shivered.

"The list is long. Mostly information. You weren't satisfied with sleeping with a Coloured boy and reading banned books."

Rianna was back on her feet. The cats growled.

"That happened ages ago. Leave Hendrik Willems *out* of this."

"As you wish. You just couldn't stop digging. Tsafendas. *Really?* You bribed your friend Hugo Marais to get you permission to visit the old—"

"I did not bribe him!"

"And even that wasn't enough for you. After your visit to Pretorial Central, you had to go back and dig deeper."

Rianna shrugged.

"Why?"

"As you've said, things are not what they appear." Her eyes drilled into the uniformed man. "I'm a researcher. I've spent years learning just how governments lie to their citizens. Don't worry, it's not unique to South Africa. And in order to protect and cover the lies, governments have to silence people, intimidate them, buy their silence, or lock them away and, sometimes, even kill."

"That's a serious charge."

"Are you denying it, Bertie?"

"Please don't call me that."

"Okay then, Albert from Messina."

The Secret Service man rewarded her with a sigh.

"Seems to me the new government in ninety-four continued with the intricate secrecy games of the Apartheid operators. It's so easy to accuse the oppressors and then, once in power, do likewise."

"These are matters of national security, Rianna."

"Bullshit, Albert. Let's go back to September 1966 and the ensuing months. Let's start from the very beginning and—"

"Dr. Verwoerd's death is *history.*" His tone was threatening. The cats responded with growls. "You need to leave it in the past."

She took to her feet and snarled at the growling cats. "*Back off!*" Then she faced the stern-faced colonel once again. "*You* sent four men to kidnap me."

He smirked, just slightly. "Kidnap? *Ridiculous.* We asked you in a civilized way to join us for a meeting."

"Asked?" Rianna remained standing. "They tried very hard to intimidate me. On *your* orders. OK, I'll admit it. What happened in the cable car did scare me. Were you trying to have me killed?"

The smirk changed to a snicker. "Holmes told me you scrambled onto the roof of the moving cable car? Did you *really?*"

"You would have had my blood on your hands." She lifted her chin. "I'm not one to give up." When he said nothing, she sat down, then shuddered and sighed. "Do you know the entire Tsafendas story, Bertie?"

"You think *you* do?"

"A little. It was not merely the work of a lonely and deranged man, as Minister John Vorster had claimed him to be."

"*So?*"

"Don't you understand, *Colonel*? It was never about mental illness. It was about colour, about Black and White. And the way they treated Tsafendas after his arrest was still, always, about *colour*. People need to know the truth."

"You're so naïve. I would have thought after all the years . . . ." He rubbed his chin. "You sit safe and sound in England, huddled under your umbrella, watching the miserable skies for a ray of sunshine. Here, as for the rest of the world—including your precious *England*—it has *always* been about colour." The Secret Police man snapped his heels together as if coming to attention. His eyes burned as if on fire. "And it *always* will be."

"It's *wrong*."

"It's called reality." He scoffed. "About those banned books—"

"Contrary to what you think, the books I sought were not steamy erotica or communistic propaganda. I read books about human rights and civil rights movements and about nonviolent political change. I'm against violence. But even so, there are similarities between Tsafendas's situation and my own."

"Tsafendas committed a crime. He was a convicted murderer."

"Agreed. I don't deny that. But I am still trying to understand what happened to me and Hendrik, and learning what happened to Tsafendas—and thousands of others—helped me get closer. Why did he take the dagger to work? It was a horrendous act, but why did he go that *far*? What motivated him to do the unthinkable? And why was he punished the way he was, instead of being treated for his supposed mental illness? There's a line running through all of this."

"The Immorality Act of 1957 was there to protect the citizens—"

"Bullshit, Bertie! 'Protect the citizens.' *Nou praat jy somaar stront!*" You're a blatant liar! Rianna was back on her feet. The two cats growled and edged closer, forcing the colonel to shoo them away. Her nose and his were inches apart. "The Immorality Act was inhumane!"

"Interracial interaction causes conflict. You of all people should know that."

"Apartheid rhetoric. Why then did Hitler declare war on Britain? They were both white!"

"Our act kept the races pure."

"What is pure, Bertie?" Their eyes met. She held his glance with her own unwavering eyes, and she dared to touch his arm. "The only things that need to be pure are the air we breathe, the water we drink, and above all, our hearts." She removed her hand with a slight flourish. "And perhaps our handkerchiefs."

Bertie's rigid shoulders softened. The corners of his tight lips curled upward. For a brief moment he allowed her to see the tall boy who had once stood at the door to her compartment on the train to Cape Town, kicking at a joint in the floor. "And Tsafendas?"

Rianna shared her discovery of the new articles she had come across in ninety-six, which had led her back to South Africa, to Hugo Marais in Cape Town, and eventually to Demetrio Tsafendas in Pretoria. She told him about the inner turmoil the man had lived with in the months before he killed the prime minister.

"Tsafendas claimed he looked and felt like a person of colour. That's how he saw himself. That's how he accepted himself. But he was classified as White. Then he fell in love with a woman of colour but it was against the law to love her. In spite of being of mixed blood he was classified as White, because of his dad. He felt trapped. He wanted out."

"That was the law."

"You refuse to see the inhumanity of it all." Rianna ignored the cats and approached the wide picture window, her back turned on the colonel and his growling felines. "The government declared him mad, suffering from schizophrenia, yet locked him away for thirty years in a maximum-security *prison*, not a mental hospital. Why?"

"He was a murderer."

"I know, but this is the glaring inconsistency of the apartheid governments' policies of limiting psychiatric services to blacks and women during the fifties and sixties and seventies. The government claimed to fight for the poor white men in the country. Ironically, in the end, poor white men, like Mr. Tsafendas, were locked away, out of the public eye, because they were a shame to society."

"Hearsay."

"Believe what you wish." Rianna turned away from the window, her arms across her chest. "Why did they allow Sarah Willems, Hendrik's sister, to re-classify as White?"

"She was Hendrik's half-sister. She had a White dad. She must have looked White to have passed the test."

Rianna whistled. "I always had my doubts. See? Not only an inhumane act, but unfair."

He shrugged.

"How was Sarah's situation different from mine and Hendrik?"

"Hendrik wasn't white enough."

"Hypocrites. The whole bloody lot. He was a *brown* man with a *red* heart—just like yours."

"I never met him."

"A pity . . . . When will you see past black and white?"

"It's impossible. Not if you live in this country."

Rianna sighed. "What happened to him in the ICU?"

"He died from sepsis."

"I'm not convinced. It was murder."

"It was unfortunate circumstances."

"Unfortunate circumstances? I was *there*." Rianna scoffed. "Why was the trio never prosecuted and convicted?"

"Insubstantial evidence."

"Hogwash, and you know it."

The colonel's jaw tightened. His back stiffened.

"I believe it was Andries Steenkamps's father who had the connections higher up and bailed them out," Rianna said.

"Possibly. This was long before my time."

"Do you understand why I've been delving in the archives? I'm trying to discover what happened to Hendrik, to Tsafendas, to the trio, to us—"

"Perhaps it's time to stop. You have to bring closure. Put it behind you. It happened decades ago. I can't allow you to keep snooping—"

Rianna stepped closer and stopped in front of the colonel. "I'm not snooping. I need answers. I want the truth."

"Hah! What is truth?"

"It's simple. When there are no lies."

"The truth is rarely simple."

"You still haven't learned compassion, *Colonel*. Not even after thirty years?"

The colonel held his hands a yard apart. "Truth and compassion are often separated by miles. Okay . . . there may have been instances where the law caused some hurt . . . I guess."

"You *guess*?" Rianna surprised them both when she leaned forward, resting a hand on his arm and gave him a peck on the cheek. She blinked away tears.

The man touched his cheek as a soft rose crept up his neck. "And *that*?"

"You're not as tough as you—"

A cough behind them made both spin on their heels. They never heard the door open. A woman in uniform, cheeks matching her rouge-painted lips, flung the door wider open and marched closer.

"I didn't hear you knock." Colonel Vosloo had stepped away from Rianna.

The female officer ignored him and halted in front of Rianna, clicking her heels together. "Did you just *kiss* my husband?"

Rianna scuttled back, her palms raised; it was impossible not to inhale the woman's scent. Recognition flickered in her eyes. "Yes. On his *cheek*."

The colonel took his spouse by the arm. "Cut it *out*, Olga." He forced a laugh. "You didn't knock and you misinterpret what you—"

"I'm many things but I'm not blind." Her glance darted between her husband and his visitor. "Both your faces are *flushed*."

Bertie stepped between the women, forcing his spouse to step back. He hissed under his breath, "I said *stop*." He again took her by the arm. "Allow me to introduce Doctor Rianna Vermeulen from the University of Oxford. Rianna, meet my wife, Major Olga Nichols, who—"

"Rianna *Vermeulen*," the major whispered. She then grasped the colonel by the upper arms, pulled him closer and claimed his lips. Just as suddenly, she pushed him back, twirled around and leaned against his chest. "The Missy from the train has grown up." She gave Rianna a glaring once-over.

Rianna snapped her shoulders back. "Seems only *one* of us has grown up."

Olga Nichols threw her head back and laughed shrill. "Britain has made you brave, has it—"

"*Enough.*" Colonel Vosloo led the major by the elbow to the door, then steered the cussing woman through it ahead of him, slamming it shut behind them. Rianna was left alone with the two cats.

"Back off!" She swung her purse on its strap like a slingshot at the growling *rooikats*, which immediately inched closer. She launched herself onto the desk, snatched up the colonel's two metal letter openers, and crouched there, one in each hand, facing the felines.

The door burst open. The cats noticed their master and instantly froze. The colonel hesitated for a split second, absorbing the tableau. Then he guffawed and waved both arms at the cats. "Max! Rex! Down! Step down!" Then he bowed and held a hand at his red-faced guest, still crouched on his desk, the letter openers clasped like daggers in her hands, her eyes trained on the cats. Only once the cats were back on their allocated spots did she jump down, ignoring the offered hand.

The colonel seemed exhausted. "Sorry . . . about the out-burst," said, pointing at the door to the hallway, "and for leaving you here with these maniacs."

Rianna forced a smile, clattered the openers onto the desk, and then clutched her purse to her chest. "It seems not much has changed with lady Nichols."

It was time to leave. She stretched out a hand to greet the colonel. "Married to her. *Really*, Bertie?"

Bertie laughed, but he accepted the hand she had extended. "Love works in mysterious ways. We did the honourable thing. We've been married for close to twenty years now." He released her hand and stepped aside, leaving her a clear pathway to the door. "As you've seen, she's a major. She joined the force much later than I did. She doesn't look sixty-three, don't you think? No surgery or Botox—only rigorous exercise, diet, and discipline. The only outlandish thing she does is colour her hair."

"Why is she still Nichols?"

"She preferred it this way."

"Makes perfect sense." Rianna's eyes narrowed thoughtfully. "You're a kind man, Bertie." Then she slanted her head. "Am I free to leave?"

"I'll let you go. I shouldn't have pounded on you at the mountain café with those overzealous field operatives. My apologies. Also, for leaving you with the cats—"

"I would have killed at least *one*."

Bertie snickered. "I have no doubt." He waved at the cats. "Can we agree to another meeting? Of course, at a date of your convenience, *Doctor* Vermeulen?"

Rianna's eyes narrowed as she inched toward the door. "Certainly, O Rameses." She curtsied.

"The meeting applies to you only." The colonel stepped behind his desk and pointed at the door. "Without your side-kick." He gestured the two cats to approach, bent forward and scratched their heads, then held them by their collars.

With her hand on the doorknob she gave him a time and a date, then stuck out her tongue at him before slipping out.

Thirty

GHOSTS FROM THE PAST. DECEMBER 2004

"*R*ianna *Vermeulen*, we meet again." The affected voice preceded the outstretched hand of the lady who sailed through Colonel Vosloo's office door. Of Bertie and his two *rooikats* there were no sign. It seemed Olga Nichols now owned the office.

Rianna rose and shook the manicured hand offered to her. Gone was the uniform. But the iron grip that locked around her hand belied the feminine attire. Rianna held the older woman's penetrating glance, responding with an equally firm grip. "*Major* Nichols."

"Colonel Vosloo has been delayed. He asked me to step in."

Bertie didn't exaggerate—the appearance of his partner and spouse belied her sixty-three years. The two-piece business suit hugged her trim figure; her bosom, in its low-cut blouse, was radiant and pert, much as it had been all those many years ago. Her bright lips matched the revealing suit.

Rianna's eyes narrowed. "Why are you not in uniform?"

Major Nichols crossed her arms. "With seniority comes certain perks. In our line of business, in the Secret Service," she purred, "civilian attire often has advantages. Makes one blend with the general population; makes one invisible, so to speak."

Rianna coughed to hide her irritation. She imagined the arduous task such a provocative figure would have, blending with her surroundings. Major Nichols didn't blend. She was as unobtrusive as a lighthouse on a rocky peninsula, piercing the darkness with a strobing light.

The major gestured for Rianna to retake her seat. "What's your relationship with Professor Hugo Marais?"

"He's a friend."

"I had a look at your file. *He* supplied you with the banned books."

"My *file?*" Rianna's shoulders slumped. "That's decades ago. Colonel Vosloo knows all this."

"Why did you manipulate Hugo Marais to obtain permission to visit Tsafendas?"

"I did nothing of the kind. It was a civil request. Colonel Vosloo has already asked me this."

"Answer my questions."

"Early in ninety-six I came across several new articles about Tsafendas as part of my *research*. It reminded me of questions from decades before. Questions to which I still had no answers.

Tsafendas was elderly. My need to speak to the old man was real, and it was urgent."

"It was inappropriate."

"The only thing inappropriate is the way you're treating me, Major."

"No reason to be snotty with me, *Doctor*."

"I have no quarrel with you. I visited Tsafendas to learn about the past, firsthand. I was also digging in the archives to find out more about Jessica Taylor, James Martin, and Andries Steenkamp—the trio that had assaulted me and Hendrik."

The major sucked in her breath. "Hendrik Willems." She jumped to her feet, sneering at Rianna. "How could you? He was *Coloured*."

Rianna straightened her shoulders, meeting the flashing gaze. "His heart was good."

"His skin was brown."

"How do you know about Hendrik?"

"I'm in the Secret Police."

"Doesn't explain it. It was too long before you joined the force. Hendrik was murdered in *sixty-eight*."

"He died from sepsis in the ICU."

"He died following a *brutal assault*."

"He wouldn't have been attacked if you didn't cross the colour barrier."

"I *loved* him."

"He was Coloured."

"He didn't choose his parents. Neither did you and I."

"It was the law, for heaven's sake!"

"An *inhumane* law."

"It protected you—"

"*Bah*! That's bullshit! What's it with you people? It's not about black and white—it's about *light* and *darkness*." Rianna pounded her chest. "About what's in here. Can't you understand? We all bleed *red*."

"They're uncivilized brutes."

"Major, it's two thousand and four, not the bloody Middle Ages."

"You can dress them up as you like."

"Hendrik Willems had more kindness and integrity in his pinkie finger than—"

The major held up her hands and pointed at the chair for Rianna to sit down.

"Okay, I get it. But that's decades ago. Let it be."

"Let it be?' Rianna cried, jumping to her feet. "Why did Taylor, Martin, and Steenkamp leave the country in ninety-three?"

"How would I know? They had a change of heart. Good riddance?"

"I'm not convinced. Did you ever meet them?"

The major waved her hand, her lips tight. "Only in passing. The woman, before they emigrated."

"Why don't I believe you?" Rianna asked.

The older women smirked.

"It is highly unlikely that you would know about Hendrik unless Jessica Taylor told you."

"And your point is?"

Rianna shuddered, hugging her shoulders. "Jess was my friend—well, in the beginning. But then she changed."

"We've all changed."

Rianna swallowed. "Yes . . . certainly. Jessica, however, became evil."

"Evil's a harsh word."

"You prefer an euphemism? The three of them were responsible for my friend's death. She was the ringleader . . . ."

"Speculation."

"I was there."

"I keep forgetting . . . ."

Both women fell silent.

"Why do you despise me?"

The major gave a shrill laugh. "It's your imagination."

Rianna rose, her jaw clenched. "*Nothing* has changed. When will Bertie be here?"

The major also rose. "It's Colonel Vosloo to you."

"Major Nichols, and it is Doctor Vermeulen to you. I am no longer the uncertain fourteen-year-old on a train steaming toward Cape Town, intimidated by a lecherous woman who had seduced her attractive male pupil and bullied everyone else."

"How *dare* you?"

Rianna crossed her arms, belying the rose that crept up her neck. "When we met on the train from Pietersburg, had you at that time already slept with Bertie?"

The major marched behind the colonel's desk and then slammed a rouge-tipped hand onto it. "Oxford has definitely given you airs. A stilted arrogance. Pathetic, really. I don't have to answer to you."

"So, it's true. Bertie also denied it."

"We're married now. What's your problem?"

"Do you even love him?"

The major inhaled sharply. "Keep your hands off my husband!"

"He was my friend once. But you—" and Rianna pointed at the major. "It was inappropriate then and it's inappropriate now. He was sixteen and you twenty-five."

"He was already a man. A young man."

"You stole his youth."

The major smacked her lips. "I made him taste *life*."

"You want to own him, use him. You don't love him."

"He's mine."

Rianna exhaled with a hiss, swooped her purse from the chair and made for the door.

"Where do you think you're going, *Doctor*?"

Rianna paused in the doorway. "I'm a British citizen. Perhaps you should treat me accordingly, with a little respect, *Major* Nichols."

"Your British citizenship doesn't give you the—"

Both women took several steps back as the growls of the two *rooikats* washed over them, announcing the colonel's arrival.

"*Ladies!*" Bertie Vosloo swept into the room, directing the two cats to their respective spots next to his desk, gave his wife a peck on the cheek, and shook hands with Rianna. "I overheard your lively exchange!"

He rocked on the balls of his feet, rubbing his hands together. "Olga, do you owe our guest an apology?"

"She crossed the line."

Rianna took an audible breath.

"What's wrong, Rianna?"

Her laugh was feeble. "Oh, we got carried away . . . we've reminisced about the good old days."

The colonel cocked his brow. "Olga?"

"I was a bit hard on her. I should leave the two—"

"Don't leave." Bertie Vosloo gestured for the women to take their seats. "Did you bring the files on Taylor, Martin, and Steenkamp?"

The major jumped to her feet, her cheeks crimson. "Sorry, Hon, it slipped my mind. They're in my office."

As Olga Nichols left the room, Bertie locked eyes with Rianna. "The trio's whereabouts is one of the reasons I brought your visit forward to today. Jessica Taylor and Andries Steenkamp were detected by my people as they entered the country from Mozambique a day ago. They chartered a small plane to Nelspruit, from Maputo. Snuck in an hour before sunrise, touched down on an out-of-service runway and skipped the airport building and customs. I thought you should know."

Colour drained from Rianna's face. "And James Martin?"

"No sign. Only Taylor and Steenkamp. Martin was last seen a month ago in Melbourne. He had some run-ins with the law in the past."

"Why do you tell me this? Why would they want to harm me?" She rubbed her arms, covered in goosebumps and shivered. "Do you think . . . but it's more than thirty years ago!"

"You reappeared on the radar screens in ninety-six. You started digging. Then you visited Pretoria Central prison. You asked many questions. And not all of them were about Verwoerd and Tsafendas."

Rianna was on her feet. "What are you *not* telling me, Bertie? The three never worked for the special forces or the police, did they?"

The best the major managed was a shrug.

"They weren't informants?"

The colonel laughed. "No, *we* had to keep an eye on *them*. They always seemed to have access to vast amounts of money. Many of their business transactions bordered on illegal. Import and export. Shady deals. Their contacts stretched over the entire social spectrum. They were seen from time to time with unsavoury characters. They knew people inside and outside of penitentiaries. Perhaps the prison guards couldn't stop talking about your—"

"You're joking—"

"How often do you think Tsafendas received visitors? Not after being in prison for thirty years. Then, next thing, in walks this gorgeous researcher, a lady, all dressed up in a business suit. You think no one noticed? No one asked questions?" He scoffed. "And these past five weeks you've gone out of your way with all your searches and inquiries and renewed digging."

"Preposterous. It's professional research. It's what I do."

"Perhaps not."

Rianna paced between the chairs. "How did you know about their arrival in Nelspruit?"

"We have eyes and ears in strange places." He laughed. "Money makes people talk. It's my job to know these things."

"Why now? It's eleven years since they left the country."

"That's where I've just been. I've sent communications to my counterparts in Australia and Mozambique. Requested information."

"Why via Mozambique?"

"That's what I wanted to know from Australia." He shrugged. "It was an easier entrance port."

"Where are the two now?"

Bertie coughed. "They disappeared after being spotted in Witbank, on the way to Johannesburg, it seemed. My men are working on it . . . ."

Rianna gathered her purse as if to leave.

"Sorry, Rianna, *one* more thing. I've tasked Holmes and Schutte to shadow you. At any given time, one of them—"

"Don't be ridiculous."

"I'm not asking your permission. It's for your safety. You won't see the men." Bertie coughed. "Yes, I know. They'll do their best to be more discreet."

"Do you *really* think . . . ?"

"I do."

———✸———

"What's your relationship with Colonel Vosloo?"

Rianna dropped the towel she was drying her hair with, glancing at her friend. "Lukas?"

Lukas paced Rianna's hotel suite's living room, pausing at her open bedroom door. "That Nichols lady phoned while you were in the shower."

"She's no lady."

"She sounded upset. Said she saw you kissing her husband—"

"How could she know I'm in this hotel?"

"Isn't she Secret Service?"

"Then she must have had me followed."

"Come on, Rianna."

"How else?" Rianna's laugh didn't reach her eyes. "There's no *relationship*. I told you . . . . He's an old friend from my schooldays . . . . He tried to bully me with his attitude and his wild red cats, then, the moment he softened up, I kissed him on the cheek. That's when she chose to barge into his office—"

Lukas scowled. "It wasn't an innocent kiss according to the major."

"Lukas? Not you too. It was on his cheek. She's a bitch! Pardon the word. She seduced him when he was a schoolboy. She's nine years his senior. It's ridiculous. She's a control-freak and a bully. And she hates my guts."

"Did you also see your library friend this time? What's his name, Hugo Marais?"

"I always visit him. He's a professor now."

"Your professor friend shouldn't be a bother to them."

"They must think he corrupted me."

"Did he?"

"He broadened my horizons."

"Is that why you've always refused to settle down with me?"

Rianna spun around and took her companion's face in her hands, stood on her tiptoes and kissed him. "You know I love you. Between my teaching and research and your commitments with the UN—"

"Excuses."

"Lukas, you live more out of a suitcase than I do!"

He held up his palms. "Touché."

"You've never asked me to marry you."

"Not in so many words, no."

"Lukas . . . ."

He yanked open the balcony door and stepped outside, his shoulders stiff. After a moment she joined him, following his gaze across the harbour. She let out a shuddering breath when their hands brushed on the railing. He slipped his arm behind her shoulders, pulling her close. She leaned into him when he kissed her hair.

The moment was shattered by the sudden sound of screeching tires and a blaring horn. Rianna broke free, rubbing her arms. "I'm scared." She repeated the warning Colonel Vosloo had given her about Jessica Taylor and Andries Steenkamp.

"You don't know for certain what they're up to. It probably has nothing to do with you."

Rianna nestled closer again. "It can't be good. Not with them sneaking in during the night, skipping customs, slipping in through the back door."

"They must be involved in an illegal transaction. Perhaps finalizing a black-market business arrangement."

"The major had implied as much."

"See? *You* have nothing to worry about."

"No, Lukas. I can feel it." She thumped her chest. "There's a reason he warned me."

"What didn't he tell you?"

"I'm not sure. It has something to do with Jessica. She's on an urgent mission—and I'm part of it." She faced him. "I'm certain that's why the colonel has also dispatched one of his men to shadow me."

"To do *what?*"

"Offer me protection." She nodded, biting her lip. "I refused the service. He just laughed and said I didn't have an option."

Lukas frowned, then stood on tiptoes, leaned over the balcony, and peered below. "I see nobody with a hat and coat lurking in the shadows down there."

Rianna elbowed him. "It's not a joke."

He laughed and held her tight. "I'm sorry." She shuddered as she allowed him to embrace her. In silence they rested in each other's arms, watching the city reluctantly winding down.

"*Witbank.*" Lukas broke the silence. "It's still on the other side of the country. More than seventeen hundred kilometers from here. If Taylor and Steenkamp don't want to be seen they won't make use of public transportation."

"They'll rent a car."

"The police can track rentals."

"Then their contacts will provide them with a stolen vehicle."

Lukas laughed. "*Really?*"

"There's two of them. If they take turns, they can be in Cape Town within fourteen hours. Or sooner." She glanced at her watch and then slipped from his arms to step to the far corner of the balcony, eyes fixed on the dark ocean. A foghorn sounded from the harbour. From the streets below wafted voices, car horns, engines gearing down, and the faint aroma of tarmac and gasoline, mixed with the sour smell from the harbour.

Thirty-One

Catching up. December 2004

"Jess, how do you know Major Nichols?" Andries Steenkamp settled into the driver's seat, clipped the safety belt into place, then drummed his fingers on the steering wheel. They had just switched places.

"I met her in ninety-three when we left. What's it with all the stupid questions? We have to get going. We're already two hours behind, what with you stopping at every Ultra City." Jessica Taylor fastened her safety belt and passed Andries his sandwich.

"I had to fill up the tank. And I had to pee."

"You're getting old. It's your prostate."

"At least I'm not afflicted with hot flushes."

"Don't make it sound like a disease. I never complain. Did you wash your hands?"

Andries snorted, took a big bite and smacked his lips. "It's *Olga* Nichols, isn't it?" He picked up a sliver of cheese that landed on his thigh and shoved it into his mouth. "I need answers, Jess. Why did we have to sneak in through Maputo in Mozambique? And in the middle of the bloody night? And on such short notice?"

"Watch your mouth."

"Don't lecture me and don't leave me in the dark."

"You have to trust me."

"My God, Jessica. *Trust.* Don't make me weep. You wouldn't know faithfulness if it bit you in the ass."

"I told you to watch your tongue."

"Stop treating me like a child. I'm a middle-aged man with an enlarged prostate, according to Dr. Jessica Taylor."

She smiled at that. "Too many details will make you lose sleep at night. That's *my* job."

"You insult me. I'm only good enough to act as your bodyguard and keep your bed warm."

"You're good at it." She leaned across the middle console and scooped a streak of mustard off Andries's cheek.

"Thanks." He dabbed his mouth with a napkin. "I'm serious. You have to take me into your confidence. I have a brain, I'm not senile. I'm always saddled with doing the dirty jobs. It's bad enough about James."

"I *need* you." Jessica leaned across, turned his chin and kissed Andries on the lips. "James became a liability."

"He was my friend."

Jessica gave a bitter laugh. "You forgot that when you slept with his wife."

"You forced yourself on me."

"You didn't object too much." Andries took another bite and smacked his lips, facing his companion.

She met his gaze coolly. "James stopped taking care of himself. He became careless. He talked too much. Drank too much. I could forgive the gambling but I drew a line at the other women."

"He was discreet," Andries mumbled, chewing.

"He became a low-life. He risked blowing our cover." Jessica pushed her sunglasses back onto her forehead. "You never actually told me. Did you get rid of James?"

"I took care of him." Andries stuffed another bite in his mouth.

"You were tasked to kill him."

"See? The dirty work. He was still my friend. So, I silenced him."

"Killed him?"

"I silenced him in the Outback. He'd never get out alive from where I put him."

"Andries—"

"Cut the crap. Did this major-woman phone *you*?"

"It's not important. Let's *go*."

"I'm almost done with my sandwich."

"It's still seven hundred eighty kilometers to Cape Town."

"Come on, we're at Colesberg. We're halfway."

"We're two hours behind schedule."

"Whose schedule?"

"You're an idiot."

"That's not what you tell me when you have your big O."

"Andries, *please*." Jessica's indigo-tipped fingers played with her companion's short cropped hair, slipped to his neck and caressed his solid shoulders.

Andries Steenkamp swallowed the last piece, turned the key and barreled down the merging lane to join the traffic on the N1, heading south.

THEY SWITCHED places at the Ultra City outside Beaufort West, two hours later.

"We can't stick to a hundred and sixty the entire way. I don't want to get caught in a speed trap. No need to broadcast our arrival to the authorities." Jessica readjusted the rearview mirror.

Andries laughed. "We're now only an hour behind on your precious schedule, thanks to my driving skills. We're in the middle of the bloody Karoo. There's *nobody* here. Only windmills, merino sheep, and *tolbossies*."

"The cops have radar."

"You give them five hundred Rand and they'll let you go."

"They're not all corrupt."

Andries kicked off his shoes, and placed his feet on the passenger's side of the dashboard. He pushed his cap lower over his face. "Thirty-five years." He whistled. "It's a lifetime, Jess. Why *now?*"

"Thirty-four years."

"*Okay*. Why now? Let her go."

"I can't. I did so once. Then in ninety-six my contacts alerted me. She started asking about us. About Hendrik. She started digging in the archives. She's not stupid. She knows her way around. She's been in the country about five weeks this time and already is up to her old shit. Seems many classified documents are still available to the public eye if you know where to look. And she had that fucker at the Central Library who smuggled all the banned books and trained her all those years ago. She may just stumble—"

Andries frowned "Your language, Jess."

"Sorry—your bad influence. I'm just glad I stayed in touch with the major."

"What is *her* interest in the Vermeulen girl?"

"Vermeulen *girl*? Rianna's a fifty-three-year-old *woman* like myself."

"You look forty."

"Thanks, partner. Forty with hot flushes. *Shit*." She ruffled his hair. "I'll remember that tonight. The major's interest is more personal."

"What does Rianna know about Hendrik?"

"Only that he died in the ICU."

"Did they ever let her see the body?"

Jessica shivered as she shoulder-checked and switched lanes. "What do you think?" She fiddled with the radio. "Rianna attended Hendrik's memorial service. I'm certain she bought the story. What choice did she have? What choice did Hendrik's sister and mother have?" She gave a pained laugh. "It was for the best— that he died."

The two continued in silence. The reception of any radio station was poor at best. The wind plucked at the car, dust devils driving *tolbossies* across the browned plains. Swallows clung, determined, to telephone lines, like pegs on a washing line, swaying with the gusts.

"According to the major-lady there's apparently *new* information about Hendrik," Jessica said.

"What does it matter? He's dead."

She pursed her lips. "That may be so, but the major insisted we fly over and meet with her. She still has to brief me."

"*You?*"

"Us."

"I never really understood. Rianna and you were roommates. Best friends. What went wrong?"

"I told you you're an idiot."

"You're not sleeping in my bed tonight."

"I was jealous of her."

"You beat her at running."

"Only because she let me. She was smarter. More beautiful. Well-read. All the teachers except Mrs. Knox adored her. I guess I couldn't forgive her for the banned books . . . breaking the law. She was so brave. I hated her nerve. The ultimate betrayal was when we caught her having sex with Hendrik. I always suspected she was in love with him, hoping we were wrong." She shook her head. "When I saw him deep inside her, I lost it. And yet, they were both so beautiful. But it's wrong. Sex with a Coloured man."

"He had quite a body on him."

"He was a *brown* man."

"They were in love, I'm sure."

"Are you going soft on me, Dries?"

"You've ever been in love?"

"Hah! What's love? I always preferred a quick and wild roll in the hay. Still do. I did what was necessary. It was about principles. About what was proper. What she did was against the law. It was and still is about racial *purity*."

"Okay, okay. I get it." He took his legs down, turned on his side and tried to snuggle in a comfortable position against the door. "All of this is emotionally draining." He smiled at her. Soon his snores mixed with the soft grumbling of the six cylinders.

⁂

*A*ndries woke when the car turned off the highway and the suspension danced across the poorly maintained gravel road. He stretched in the confined space, stifling a yawn. "Wrong turn?"

"No, I'm meeting with our contact."

"Contact?"

"I told you you're ignorant. What do you think? *Firearms.*"

"Are you starting a war?"

"How else will I get rid of Vermeulen?"

"Well . . . what then? A sniper gun? It's ages since you've practiced with any—"

"You underestimate me, Steenkamp."

"Rocket launchers?" Andries laughed.

"Handguns, idiot."

"You're serious? *Kill* her?"

"Absolutely."

"Why not just scare her?"

"She doesn't scare easily."

"Jess . . . ."

"Are you turning on me, Steenkamp?"

Andries shook his head. "And she's unarmed?"

"The major had her suite searched."

"What about her purse?"

"Security-checked and patted down when she went to see the colonel."

"Did you check her car?"

"Negative."

"She's your friend."

"She's *not* my friend. I need to settle the score. Close the case down. Complete the purge. This will never end for as long as both of us are alive. Just imagine what she's teaching in fancy bloody Oxford—lofty English and bloody history and the mixing of races. God forbid!"

"Olga, can you come to my office?"

Bertie was sitting in the leather-upholstered armchair at the window, looking out into the private garden. Olga paused for a moment in the doorway. The head of Max, the bigger one of *rooikats*, rested on the colonel's lap, its eyes closed in enjoyment as Bertie scratched him between the ears. Both cats snapped to attention when the woman entered, their ears pulling down, tails lashing at the carpet. "What's up, Bertie?"

"Have you had any recent contact with Jessica Taylor and Andries Steenkamp?"

"Tell your animals to *behave*."

Albert Vosloo laughed, waving her toward the second chair at the window. "Did you have *any* contact with them?"

Olga Nichols gave a forced laugh. "Yes, in the months prior to their departure in ninety-three."

"What about last year when you visited Melbourne?"

"Negative."

"Why are your cheeks flushed?"

"I had to run here."

"How about making contact with Taylor last week?"

Olga jumped to her feet and walked over to the window. She pressed her noise against the glass for a moment, as if trying to see what he had been looking at. Then she looked at him over her shoulder. "Are you implying I'm lying?"

The colonel shrugged. "Something strange is going on. We picked them up in Nelspruit, lost their trail in Witbank last night, and two hours ago they were spotted in Colesberg."

"*So?*"

"Why are they in the country all of a sudden?"

The major looked down her nose, straightening her back. "You know they're involved in shady import and export deals." She averted her eyes befored his penetrating glare. "It's their usual routine."

"Why did you have Rianna's hotel room checked?"

"Precaution."

"I didn't mandate such a search."

"I *am* a major."

"I'm in charge."

"On paper."

"Don't overplay your hand, Olga."

"Are you threatening me?"

The cats inched closer to Bertie, both now growling at the major. She edged away from the window and shrank back into her chair, the desk between her and the animals. Her hand rested on her service pistol. "Bertie, control your animals."

"Don't you dare do anything to my cats."

"You're not controlling them well. They are foul-tempered and poorly trained. More to the point: why do they hate me? They did so from the very beginning."

"They sense your aggression."

"Now I'm aggressive. You're the one cross-examining me!"

"You're not being truthful."

"So, I'm lying?"

"Are you?" He rubbed his hands. "They sense when you're upset. They sense hostility. You have to earn the cats' trust."

Her laugh was shrill. "*Trust.*"

"Why did you phone Rianna the moment she left here? You spoke to her friend, this Ferreira guy who's tied up with the United Nations."

"How dare you?" Major Nichols was on her feet. "You've tapped my lines!"

"What did you tell him? What did you ask him?"

"Bastard." The major turned her back on her husband and strode toward the door. "Why do you ask if you already know?"

"Checking. Whatever you're up to, be *careful* Olga. Consider this a warning."

The major reached the door and pulled it open. "Then don't let me catch you doing as little as touching Vermeulen's arm— or looking at her the way you did yesterday!" The large window rattled as the door slammed closed behind the major.

Thirty-Two

"Do you have any other daypacks smaller than twenty-five liters?" Rianna raised the bag for the shop assistant to see. The assistant of the Table Mountain Curios shop, nestled behind the upper cable station, stepped closer. "But one with more pouches, *with* zips?" Rianna thumbed the bag she held in her hand.

Alert eyes shifted between Rianna and the bag. "I'll have a look in the back." The assistant smiled. "Madam realizes that, as one goes toward the twenty-liter size the zippable outside bags decrease in number."

"Will you still have a look?" Rianna called after her, pacing toward the entrance and back, peering through the French windows, as if she was hoping to see snippets of the ocean, far below. Try as she might, she had been unable to spot either Holmes or

Schutte, who were supposed to look after her. Bertie must have given them a pep talk to sharpen up their stealth.

"Perhaps *I* can help?"

Rianna turned toward the new voice and audibly inhaled, her hand flying to her mouth.

The younger woman held her hand in greeting. "Sorry if I startled you. I am Geraldine Williams, owner of the shop." She laughed as she let go of Rianna's hand. "I was just leaving my office in the back, on my way out, when I overheard you and Melanie."

Rianna stammered, "T-t-thank you, Miss Williams. I'm sorry. You reminded me of someone . . . ." She ran her hand through her hair and tightened her grip on her purse. "It was a pleasant surprise to find this small assortment of hiking paraphernalia," and she lowered her voice as she waved an arm to include the one corner of the shop, "instead of all the useless curios and arts and crafts and mementos."

The proprietor laughed as she shook her dark mane, which caught the midday sun that reached them through the tall windows. "Someone had to take the plunge. I've become a hiking addict myself. Best thing Dad ever taught me. *Excuse me*. Let's see what's keeping Melanie." She called over her shoulder. "I'm certain I have something you'll like. I cater for serious day-hikers."

Minutes later, while Rianna paid for her newly found daypack and handful of other hiking odds and ends, Geraldine Williams reappeared at her side, glancing at her purchases as the assistant bagged them.

Rianna smiled at her. "I'm impressed with the wide range of choices you have available. I'm a seasoned hiker, but my gear was a bit run-down. You know the hiker's mind and you stock quality; it was impossible to resist."

"My pleasure. Do you know the mountain?"

Clutching the shopping bag to her front, Rianna peered out across the ocean before answering. A soft rose had crept up her neck. "My love affair with the mountain started the day I arrived by train from Pietersburg as a fourteen-year-old. She bit her lip. Something in the younger woman's eyes made her continue. "I've been away for many years . . . I was glad when I discovered five weeks ago that the love had not diminished."

"What a remarkable story!" For a moment the younger woman's hand rested on Rianna's arm. When she took a step back she maintained eye contact. "Forgive me . . . I have a half-hour meeting with the people at the front. I'd love to hear more over a cup of coffee after that if you're not too pressed for time."

Rianna hesitated. She was supposed to meet with Hugo and she had not yet responded to Lukas's latest text message.

The younger woman's sleek olive-skinned hand rested a second time on Rianna's arm, then squeezed. "*Please.*"

Rianna smiled, then nodded.

Andries Steenkamp whistled when Jessica pulled off to the side of the two-track road and opened the tote bag with their latest acquisitions.

"Glocks. *Nice.*" Andries took the gun he was handed.

"The under-arm holster's for you." She handed him the next piece. "*My* gun will remain in my purse."

"Magazines?"

"Two each. Each carrying seventeen rounds."

"What else?" Andries pulled on the bag but Jessica snapped it away.

"Here's a bulletproof vest. One each."

"Body armour? *Really*?"

"We're not using air guns."

"Grenades?"

Jessica snorted. "I thought you didn't want bloodshed."

"You're damn right I don't want any. I still say we only startle lady Vermeulen. *Frighten* her."

"Don't undermine me, Steenkamp."

Andries filled the magazines with rounds and laid the pieces down on the floor mat at his feet. He opened his door. "She was always a nice girl."

Jessica clasped his forearm. "Wake up, soldier. That's a long time ago. The time for games is over." She slipped her loaded magazine in place and, in one quick move, pulled the slide back and aimed it outside her window. Just as suddenly, she turned back, unclipped the magazine, let it drop in her lap, and retracted the slide twice, in rapid succession. The ejected round landed in Andries's lap.

"Show-off." He handed her the round.

"So, are you with me? It's her life or ours. Simple."

"It's never simple." He covered her hands in his. "What exactly are you afraid of? Rianna can't harm us. There's no need for any of this with us in Australia and her in the UK—"

Jessica pulled her hands free. "You're wrong. If she keeps digging she may find enough to reopen the case."

"She *may* find?"

"*Will* find."

He shook his head. "No way. It's been thirty-four years."

"*Steenkamp*. Stop this cross-examination!" She stared down the dirt road. "There's more."

"More? What are you not telling me?"

"It's complicated. More people are involved. Recent developments. That's why we're here. The major notified me. You and I will put a stop to this. I'm not going to jail."

She spun back and grasped his shoulder, the knuckles blanched white. "I will tell you more when it's time. Please trust me." Then shook him. "Are you with me?"

"Yeah, okay . . . I'm in." He grimaced as he removed her clasping fingers, unfolded himself from the sedan, and stepped into the tall grass next to the twisting dirt track. "I need a pee."

"I'm setting up an appointment with a urologist when we get home."

Andries's laugh washed over the veld, bounced off the few Cape holly, stone pine and firs, the scattered rocks, and the dirt-covered car they had been traveling with.

"I'm glad you could stay for coffee."

Rianna smiled at the owner of the gift shop over the rim of her cup. They sat to the side, as close as possible to the low stone wall. The breeze, swooping up the mountainside, tucked at both women's hair.

"Who did I remind you of?"

"Oh . . . a friend from long ago. It was so unexpected. For a moment—"

"Excuse me, *Geraldine*. Sorry to interrupt, ladies."

An older couple had appeared at Geraldine's shoulder, and Rianna had to shield her eyes against the late morning sun, despite her sunglasses.

Geraldine cried out, scraped her chair backward, and shook hands with the stout man and hugged his petite companion. "*Rupert*! *Gloria*! Let me introduce you to my new friend . . . Doctor Rianna Vermeulen."

Rupert Read pushed his sunglasses up his head and squinted at Rianna, as he took her hands in both of his. His weathered face was quiet before it broke into a wide smile. "Vermeulen! *Klipspringer*. *Oreotrachus oreotrachus*." He pulled her closer for a firm hug, then held her at arm's length. "You've grown into a remarkable woman."

"*Meneer*!" Rianna squealed in embarrassment, hugged him a second time, then drew a hand over her eyes. "You don't look too bad yourself." She touched his solid arm. "Seems just as fit."

The man with the silver temples laughed. "I try hard."

Rianna turned, then, and grasped the hands of Gloria, who had clicked with her tongue when Rianna gave her companion that second hug. "Hello, Gloria," she said, and pulled her closer for a careful hug. "It's not Whitehead anymore? I hope it's *Read*?"

Gloria elbowed her companion. "I succumbed to his charm after a courtship of fifteen years."

Rianna glanced at her old gym teacher. "*Meneer*? Really. Fifteen?"

"'Tis true." Rupert cocked his brows. "I thought *you* were hard-headed, Rianna. I was wrong."

Gloria elbowed him harder. "It was mutual."

Rianna remembered her guest and reached for her hand once they all found seats. "Sorry, Geraldine. You must have guessed— I've met this couple before." She laughed at her long-lost friends. "We were good friends—many, many years ago." Her eyes brimmed and she grabbed the napkin from the coffee tray and dabbed her eyes, turning away.

Her companions shared glances, then smiled and refrained from talking, enjoying the plateau and the wind.

Taking several deep breaths, Rianna turned her attention to her old teachers. "How did you and Geraldine become friends?" She sniffled in the napkin. "Like me? Looking for a fancy daypack?"

Gloria and Geraldine answered almost simultaneously. "We share a love for the mountain." They laughed. "We met during a hike up the berg."

Rupert leaned forward. "If you think you were obsessed with the mountain, Rianna, *she* has it bad," and he pointed at their shop owner friend. "Incurable. It will not surprise me if she throws out *all* the curios and only stocks hiking and mountaineering equipment."

"I *have* considered it. The parks board wouldn't allow me," Geraldine groaned.

Rupert turned back to face Rianna. "*Doctor.* I like that. Does Mrs. Knox know you got your PhD?"

Rianna blew her nose, shaking her head. "She wouldn't care. She's probably still researching the latest findings on *The Great Trek.*"

Geraldine laughed. "Your beloved history teacher?"

Rianna shrugged. "Without ever intending to, I challenged her about everything she taught us. I just always wanted more, you know?"

When the server approached them, Rianna jumped to her feet. She gave Geraldine's arm a gentle squeeze. "I *have* to go." She handed her a card. "Here's my number. I wrote the hotel's number on the back. I would love to meet with you again before I return to the UK."

Then, turning to her old friends, Rianna handed Rupert two cards. "I am so sorry, *Meneer*. I simply have to go. Why don't you write your cell number on the extra card? Any time after six tonight—" she felt Gloria's eyes on her, "or any other time or day will work for me. I'm here for another week. If it's okay with *both* of you?"

With Rupert's number still in her hand, Rianna waved at her friends as she jogged down the stone steps toward the upper cable station. Outside the building she scanned the area, pretending to study the mounted visitor's map. Nothing out of the ordinary. She smiled. Holmes and Schutte were good.

Thirty-Three

"Why do we need two separate rooms?"

"Not *now*, Andries," Jessica muttered and handed her credit card to the lady behind the hotel's reception desk.

"Now is a good time."

"Why don't you think a little, Steenkamp?"

"That's what I've been doing."

"It's not working. All that stupid boxing. It's more *inconspicuous*. Two rooms."

"You mean as *in good taste*?"

"*Exactly.*"

"But still . . . ."

"We're not married."

"As good as," Andries countered.

"Why don't you be a nice boy and bring our bags from the car? *Please*, honey?"

"I'm only 'honey' when you need me."

"Andries, I said 'please.'"

When he turned away to retrieve their luggage, she laid a hand on his arm. She could feel his hesitation. She was strong. She pulled him closer and lowered her voice, brushing his ear with her lips. "There's an interconnecting door between the two rooms."

He shrugged as he pulled away. "In that case you can come to *me*, Your Highness. I'm done crawling in your direction."

"Ｗhat brought you back to South Africa?"

Rianna took a sip from her drink before she answered Rupert Read. He sat across from her and Lukas, next to his wife, Gloria, who had agreed it was acceptable to meet again on the same day, even on such short notice.

"Friends." She winked at Gloria. "And, I was hoping I would run into *you*."

They all laughed when Gloria kicked her under the table.

Gloria turned to Lukas, pointing at Rupert and Rianna. "She was his teacher's pet the day she declared her love for hiking and running."

"Teacher's *pet*?" Rianna choked on her drink. "That's an untruth." She shrugged. "I had to earn his respect. He was merciless. He had no favourites. And yes, soon enough, I couldn't get enough of running or the mountain."

Gloria laughed. "That's the least of it. You and the other young ladies constantly flirted with him. Even lusted after him. The running was an excuse. As was the hiking."

"He was cool and sexy . . . and you're the one who refused to join our running group."

"She's turning red!" Gloria threw her arms in the air, clapping her hands.

"*Nonsense.*" Rianna bit her lip.

Lukas faced her. "Why are you blushing?"

As Rianna shook her head, Rupert leaned forward and rested a hand on Lukas's arm. "Why don't you tell us what exactly you do for the UN?"

"Classified information."

"The UN is no secret organization!"

Once the laughter subsided, Lukas told them about his missions and postings and how he was based in Manhattan. At the moment he was mixing work with vacation. He turned to Rianna and ran an index finger the length of her arm. Their eyes locked and she kissed his cheek. Rupert and Gloria cheered. By the time their meal arrived, Lukas was as much part of the team as if he had shared all the hikes and trips with the other three.

Gloria insisted on coffee and a cheese platter for dessert.

An espresso cradled in her hands, Rianna beamed at Rupert. "You're retired now, *Meneer*? How do you stay out of trouble?"

He combed his receding hair with his fingers. "It's difficult with this feisty lady." He dodged his companion's jabbing elbow.

"I'm still a voracious reader and participate in masters cross-fit events."

"I can see that." Rianna smiled. "Any wins?"

"I usually place among the first five competitors."

Gloria grabbed his upper arm and pulled him closer. "He *lies*. He usually wins."

"Hats off, *Meneer*! When last did you hike? Ever walked the Wild Coast again?"

Rupert gave his spouse's shoulder a gentle bump. "She forbade me—petrified we could run into the German nudists again!"

Gloria cried out and jumped to her feet to ruffle his hair. "You're such a charlatan!" She pursed her lips. "That woman had the figure of a goddess . . . Aphrodite personified." She clasped her arms around Rupert, hugging hard. "I had my eyes on *this* guy. Couldn't afford to lose him to some *Lorelei*." The table erupted in laughter once again.

As soon as they caught their breaths, Rianna insisted. "What else, *Meneer*?"

"Tell her about your guns." Gloria elbowed him.

"Guns?" Lukas and Rianna both asked.

Rupert gave a little shrug. "Rifles. I collect rifles."

"Understatement. He hunts."

"At least twice a year I go to Namibia or Botswana to hunt." He brushed Gloria's shoulder. "She accompanies me—too afraid some female hunter will lure me away."

"One never knows when Lara Croft will decide to go on safari."

"How many rifles?" Lukas asked.

"Ten."

Rianna whistled. "All for hunting?"

Rupert shook his head. "Some are collector's pieces." The smile was gone. "Some for self-defense. The country is changing. We're ten years into the new dispensation and things are not looking up." His fingers drummed on the table. "I have handguns too. I have one with me now—under my clothes."

Rianna narrowed her stare at the couple across the table.

Gloria nodded, her lips pursed, her voice lowered. "'Tis true."

"Have you considered Australia?" Lukas asked.

Rupert scoffed. "Been there. Loved the surfing and the motorcycling. But you can only do it for so long. Hated the crocodiles. Didn't last two years. *This* is my land." He wiped over his eyes. "I love this city; the mountain and the two oceans." He sighed. "And yes, its *people*."

Thirty-Four

A SHOOTING IN CAPE TOWN. DECEMBER 2004

"Why didn't you knock first?"

"The door was unlocked." Andries closed the interconnecting door behind him. He sniffed the air. Then shook his head.

"*What?*"

"You told me it was a phase. That it was over. So, *this* was the reason for separate rooms."

"You're such a drama queen. It was the only way she would part with her information—"

"The major?"

"Everyone has their price."

"Did you *enjoy* it?"

"Get out."

"Suit yourself. I'm going golfing."

"You can't do that."

"I can. I asked you to trust me. Confide in me. But, *no*. You wouldn't." He paused, eyes fixed on her hands. "Did she give you that?"

Jessica shrugged. "We'll need the two-way radios."

"I didn't know *she* was part of our clandestine operation."

"She's not."

"Suit yourself. *I'm* leaving. *Ciao*." Andries yanked the inter-connecting door open again.

Jessica darted after him, grabbing his arm and pulling him back into the room. "I'm *sorry*, Andries. It was the only way. I now have my plan together."

"To take Rianna out?"

"Among other things."

"Then why didn't you get a sniper's rifle?"

"My contact's asking price was too high. And it won't work for what I have in mind." Jessica's eyes rested on her companion's scowl.

"Perhaps it's time you tell me exactly what you *do* have in mind."

When she said nothing, he turned to leave. "You don't really need me, outside of driving and in the bedroom. Well . . . that was *before* the major. I'm off to rent a set of golf clubs."

"I'll tell you."

Andries's hand paused on the door handle.

"If you sit down, I'll tell you."

*R*ianna surprised herself when she didn't cry out at the sight of her friend, slumped forward and motionless on his desk in his office. Blood had made a dark pool under Hugo Marais's head, slumped to the side. Strange, his glasses were still in place. It was impossible to miss the gaping hole in the back of his head. *I must be the first person to find him. Dear Lord, on the university campus. And I thought they were coming for me.*

Paler than her professor friend's whiteboard, she gripped the side of his desk, shaking. She struggled to regain control over her breathing. When she was able, hesitant steps took her to beside his chair. She touched his shoulder. "Hugo?" Eyes now brimming, she felt his neck for a pulse. Nothing. His skin was cool.

She hugged her shoulders as she slumped into the chair across from his. Took a deep breath. Dialed Bertie's number. *My God, where is Holmes? He should have prevented this. And Bertie?* His phone went directly to the answering machine. Hands shaking again, she sent him a text message. Next, she tried Lukas's number. *Lukas, please answer. Dear Lord, what have I done? Poor Hugo. Oh, Lukas!* His phone went to voicemail. Sobbing now, she left an incoherent message.

Rupert Read answered on the fourth ring. "Take a deep breath, Rianna. Okay . . . now tell me again." She repeated what had transpired.

A second call came through on her cell phone. It was Bertie.

"Rupert, I have to go . . . I have Colonel Vosloo from the Secret Police on the other line." She gave Rupert the address of Hugo's office.

Bertie listened without interrupting. "Have you phoned the emergency number, the 10-111?"

She was now in better control of herself. "No. No . . . I phoned you and Lukas and—"

"Don't phone them. Not yet. I'm sending in Holmes. There's a coffee shop across the street from the building you're in now, in the student center. Wait for me there."

"Bertie, *who* would do such a thing?"

"That's what we're going to find out. Wait for me at the coffee shop."

"Bertie . . . ."

"Rianna, don't leave Hugo Marais's office until Holmes reaches you. Then go with him and *wait* for me at the students' coffee shop."

It felt like forever before Holmes arrived and released her from the ghastly scene. When she crossed the street to the coffee shop, with Holmes at her side, Lukas's call came through.

<hr>

Once inside, Holmes pointed out a table she should sit at. He himself took a table toward the back, near the door to the kitchen, from where he could keep an eye on the vast establishment. She sat down, still speaking to Lukas, and grabbed a paper napkin from the dispenser. She kept having to pause to dab her eyes with it, until it turned into a soggy ball. She managed to get out the important question. "Are you coming here?"

"I'm in a meeting . . . listen. Rianna, sweet—*listen.* I'm cancelling everything. Yes . . . I'm coming. I agree . . . . These people can wait."

She gave him the address.

A minute after she hung up, Rupert's square figure appeared in the entrance. He was scanning the room, so Rianna waved him closer. She rose when he got to her table, and he hugged her long and hard. When she stepped back from his hug at last and dropped her arms, her hands brushed over two hard objects at his waist, behind his back, hidden by a pale bush jacket.

When they sat down, she grasped his hands and asked in a low voice, "You came armed?"

"To the teeth." His piercing glare was unwavering. "There are more in the truck. Rifles. It's no longer a game."

While they waited on Colonel Vosloo and Lukas to join them, Rianna recounted the night Hendrik and she were assaulted by the three assailants, her visit to Tsafendas in 1996, as well as the events of the past several weeks and the role Hugo Marais had played in all of it.

"*Meneer*, how Jess could turn this dark is still beyond my understanding."

"We don't know for certain it was Jessica Taylor."

"Who else?"

"That's for the police—"

"Then what are you doing here, armed like a *Recce*?"

He puffed up, beaming at her. "To help you—"

But he was interrupted by the sudden appearance at their table of Lukas, who swooped her up and enveloped her in his arms. This immediately reopened the floodgates for Rianna. Behind them, Colonel Vosloo cleared his throat. They had not noticed him entering, either. He was accompanied by Schutte and two other men in sunglasses; the trio remaining at a discreet distance. Wiping her eyes, Rianna did the introductions.

Bertie insisted on speaking to her alone, but Rianna clung to Lukas's arm and shook her head. So Rupert rose and offered Bertie his seat, nodded at the Secret Service men, and moved to an empty table on the opposite side of the coffee shop. His eyes did not leave Rianna's table for a moment.

"Whoever killed Hugo Marais knew what they were doing," Bertie told Rianna and Lukas, once the three of them had sat down. "The place was wiped down. No empty shell casing—"

"Any leads as to who—"

He shook his head. "It's a police investigation now." He reached for her hands. "I'm sorry about Professor Marais. I understand he was a close friend?"

Rianna sniffled, nodded, and blew her nose with the handkerchief Lukas handed her. "Since the very beginning . . . ."

"Something else . . . ." Bertie's lower lip seemed to tremble for a moment, then he pulled himself erect in his seat and squared his shoulders. He met Rianna's eyes. "Rex and Max were shot this morning in my office . . . ." He swallowed several times. "I'm still trying to connect the dots . . . Olga, Major Nichols, left me a note—s-s-she's leaving me. Flying to Sydney . . . later this morning. Apparently."

"She *hated* the cats. Do you think—"

"I can't believe she would go *that* far." Bertie, always the gentleman.

"Oh, *Bertie*." Rianna reached for his hand. "They meant so much to you . . . ."

They sat silent for several moments.

Colonel Vosloo was the first to shake free from the gloom surrounding them. "All right. So, *this* is what we know so far—"

Schutte had stepped closer and now touched the colonel's shoulder, handing him a slip of paper. When he read it the colonel leaped to his feet. After a hushed and hurried conversation with Schutte he beckoned Holmes to join them. More urgent whispering followed.

When the colonel sat down once more, his face was flushed. His glance shifted between Rianna and Lukas. "A new development." He cleared his throat. "A gunman, a woman apparently, has taken a hostage. The Table Mountain curios shop owner. She's holding her at gunpoint."

Rianna gasped. "Geraldine *Williams*?"

The colonel frowned. "You know her?"

"I met her a few days ago . . . where are they?"

"The two of them are holed up at the upper cable station. The hostage taker had everybody vacate the premises. She wounded two tourists first, shot them in the legs. Sent everyone in a panic down the cable cars and fleeing down the mountain."

"What is she demanding?"

Albert Vosloo hesitated, then got to his feet. He avoided eye contact. "I've already said too much. I have to get to the lower cable station and orchestrate my men." He gestured at the window. "She couldn't have chosen a worst day. The weather is horrible. You can cut the fog at the top of the mountain with a chainsaw."

He strode toward the door, accompanied by Schutte and Holmes, but Rianna pulled away from Lukas and caught hold of Bertie's arm. "What is she demanding?"

"She insists that her captive's father, Herman Williams, join them at the top."

"*Why?*"

"She didn't give a reason."

"How soon?"

"He has one hour before she shoots Geraldine."

"She's not asking for money?" Lukas asked.

"None. No other demands."

"Can you guys use police helicopters and approach from the back of the mountain?" Lukas persisted.

The colonel grinned as he stepped back and held up his hands. "Enough questions. Please excuse me." He glanced at Lukas as he turned away. "It depends on whether the fog will allow us."

Rianna was quick and clutched Bertie's arm again, shaking it. "*Herman Williams.* Who is he?"

"Rianna, I *have* to go. Herman Williams is Geraldine's father."

"I know that." Then she sucked in her breath. "Who *exactly* is Herman Williams, Bertie?" In spite of the coffee shop's dim lighting, it was impossible not to notice the sudden pallor of Rianna's face, as she clasped Bertie's arm—to demand an answer, but also for support. "How about the *truth?*"

"Rianna, please."

"*Bertie.*" It was impossible to miss the pain and the plea in her voice as she clung to him.

"Herman Williams used to be known as *Hendrik Willems* in a previous life."

Lukas and Bertie lurched forward to catch Rianna's limp body.

Thirty-Five

PIECES OF THE PUZZLE

"How will we get past security with our firearms?"

"*Really*, Andries? Just *come*." Jessica swung her small backpack into place, her gaze darting between the creeping fog up the side of the mountain and her companion. They had parked the vehicle on the side of the road, halfway up the paved vehicle road to the lower cable station. "I'll spell it out. We're hiking up the *berg*. We're not taking the cable car."

"The fog is setting in."

"You *know* the *berg*."

"You've always hated hiking."

"I hate racial inbreeding more."

"Shit Jessica. It happened thirty-four years ago!"

She slapped him across the face. "Do you want to go to jail?"

He rubbed his cheek. "How *dare* you hit me?"

"Because you're an asshole!"

"You've crossed a line."

"It's either Rianna or us."

"I deserve some respect."

She spun around. "I'm sorry, but you can't be so ass-headed. Don't you get it? We have to *hurry*."

"It's eleven years since we've been up this—"

"*Sissy*." Jessica stretched her legs and disappeared between two sugar bushes.

He sprinted after her. "How will kidnapping Geraldine get you to Rianna?"

"Use her as bait. I want Daddy to come to us first."

"And Rianna?"

"She'll come running as soon as she hears we have her Hendrik at gunpoint."

"I thought Hendrik was dead?"

"He was. Until my friend the major discovered that Herman Williams, Geraldine's father, is the same person as Hendrik Willems."

"*What?*"

"Yes, sir. The government made some kind of plea bargain with him and his mother and sister—decades ago. I don't know all the details. They made him die on paper, then brought him back with a new name and identity." She paused. "Something to do with his sister going all White. Point is, Hendrik Willems is not really dead." She called over her shoulder, starting off with a jog. "We have to move faster, before the fog catches us."

"How do you know Geraldine will be in her shop?"

Jessica threw her arms in the air and groaned in exasperation. "Because I've *phoned*, Andries. I made an *appointment,* pretending to be a supplier of a new type of daypack." She chuckled. "The major was a great help."

———

"*W*hy would Hendrik Willems have *lied* to me all these years?" Outside the lower cable station, Rianna, still pale, held on to Lukas's arm. Rupert Read stood next to them.

"You don't know the particulars of what he—" Lukas said.

"Bullshit!"

"*Rianna?*"

"We were in love—"

"Many things can happen during thirty-five years . . . ."

"You don't understand our relation—"

"*Ladies and gentlemen*, stand back, please. Everybody move back!" Two police officers busied themselves with cordoning off the entrance area with yellow police tape, while three others made the few onlookers step back.

Rianna and Lukas and Rupert were of the first of the public and journalists to get there, following on the heels of the Secret Police and the flying squad. Police radios crackled with instructions to cordon off the road to the cableway car at the foot of the mountain. More spectators would not be helpful.

But the three of them had no intentions of leaving. As the two old friends pondered their next move, Read tapped Rianna on the shoulder. "I'll see you guys in a little while."

Rianna spun around and caught his arm. "You're not planning on going up there, *Meneer!*"

Read shrugged, laughing. "Don't be silly."

"*Meneer*, I can see it in your eyes . . . ." She grabbed hold of him again. "What about the fog?"

"I *know* the mountain." He freed Rianna's hands still clinging to him. "I can't leave Geraldine and Hendrik in that unstable woman's claws . . . ."

"Do the police know you'll be there?"

"I have my 375 with telescopic sights. It's only necessary that I see *them*."

The next moment he was gone.

"Lukas, I'm *scared*." Lukas enveloped her in his arms, her shivering shaking them both.

Lazy tongues of mist had reached even the lower station, now snaking between their legs. It was impossible to see further than a hundred yards up the mountain. Vehicles crunched to a standstill behind them. A sedan with tinted windows, a police riot vehicle, and three ambulances pulled up.

"Stand back please!" Police officers surrounded the car.

A man in a striped suit emerging from the back of the unmarked, dark sedan, not fifteen feet away. He was immediately flanked by two police officers. Rianna had Lukas's hand in a death-grip as she stared.

She locked eyes with the stranger. He paused and stared back. The colour left his face, despite his olive skin. She recognized Geraldine in his features. Herman Williams. It was her Hendrik. Hendrik Willems, now with silver in his dark temples. Just as sturdy and solid as the night she had stayed over with him in the house on Cambridge Street in District Six. There was no question. "*Hendrik?*"

"My God . . . how? . . . *Rianna?*"

At that moment, as if from nowhere, Colonel Vosloo appeared beside the baffled man. "Excuse us, Doctor Vermeulen," he called. "Perhaps later. Mr. Williams, if you can come with me please? We need to get you closer." He glanced at his wrist, clearly intent on whisking Hendrik away. Rianna strained to hear what he was saying. "We have *seventeen* minutes to negotiate a deal with the kidnapper. I'm not taking any more chances. She's just sent her accomplice down, half-dead, in the last cable car. Bullet through his neck."

At that moment, paramedics raced past them with a stretcher. Rianna shrieked. "*Steenkamp?*"

Vosloo gave her a curt nod and then turned away, all business. He tightened his grip on the man called Herman Williams and steered him up the stairs toward the lower cable station. Try as he might, Williams—*Hendrik*—was unable to hide his slight limp. "I want you to listen closely, Mr. Williams. My men have been deployed. A team has been dropped off on the mountain, at the back of the plateau, far enough away that she wouldn't have heard the rotors, and one team is climbing from below. *This* is what we're going to do . . . ."

Rianna and Lukas followed, staying a few feet behind the men.

*T*he police radio crackled with static. Jessica's voice, however, was clear. "Colonel, you have sixteen minutes. *Where* is Hendrik Willems?"

"You mean *Herman Williams*?" Colonel Vosloo, together with Holmes and Schutte, stood next to Hendrik, around the corner from the cable car docking port, watching impassively as the paramedics fought to stabilize the shooting victim, Andries Steenkamp.

"Cut the crap, Colonel. *Willems. Williams.* Whatever. It's now down to fifteen minutes. Do you think neutralizing Hugo Marais was a joke? You must have taken reception of Steenkamp." She gave a chuckle. "He kept questioning my methods. My authority." Loud breathing. "The *purge* has begun."

"I have Mr. Williams here."

"Put him on the radio."

Rianna tugged Lukas's arm. "How can she have the police radio frequency?"

Lukas gave a small shrug. "Major Nichols, perhaps?"

Herman Williams stepped closer and took the handpiece from the colonel. "Um . . . hello, Herman Williams here."

"Mr. Williams, if you so prefer. I prefer Willems. Do you want to see your daughter alive?"

"What kind of question—"

"*Do* you want your daughter to live?"

"Absolutely, *yes!*"

"Then why are you not up here?"

"The-the-the colonel said—"

"You have *thirteen* minutes."

"Miss Taylor, listen please," Vosloo interjected. "If you send down Miss Geraldine Williams, I will personally—"

"Are you that daft, colonel? *You* are the one not listening." A shot ricocheted over the radio and a woman cried out.

"Miss Taylor!"

"She's now missing a finger, colonel. You are trying my patience. Every minute I will fire a shot. Next one is though her foot, then her knee, then her abdomen . . . ."

"Miss Taylor, *listen* to reason!"

Over the radio they could hear Geraldine whimpering. "Daddy, she's serious . . . ."

"Tick-tock, Colonel—six minutes from now it'll be through her head."

"How do you think you'll get away with this?"

Jessica Taylor laughed shrilly. "The fog for once is my friend. I hate the mountain and I hate the fog. Nature is benevolent today. You'll *never* find me—I'll disappear in the white nebulas. Mr. *Williams,* can you hear me?"

"Quite clearly, Miss Taylor."

A cry followed, as Jessica yanked her captive closer. "*Daddy!*" "*Geraldine!*"

"Mr. Williams, I told you to get your *ass* up here!"

A second shot sounded, followed by shrieks and louder sobbing.

"That was her *foot,* Colonel."

"Taylor, you've lost your *mind!*"

"Calling me names will get you nowhere, Colonel. Mr. *Williams,* if I were you I'd get in that bloody cable car and come straight up the mountain."

"We're sending him right up, Miss Taylor!"

"I'd hurry if I were you. Colonel, you have ten minutes. *Tick-tock.*"

COLONEL Vosloo faced Holmes and Schutte. "How far are the two Tango teams up there?"

"Last communication said they were making good progress."

"Shit, guys. There's no time for *making* progress. They need to make things *happen*!"

Vosloo yanked the handpiece of a second radio from one of the officers. "Tango one, this is Charlie Victor, *over*."

The radio crackled to life. "Charlie Victor, this is Tango one. We have established visual contact of the cafeteria and curio shop. Over."

"Tango one, this is Charlie Victor. Proceed with caution. I believe suspect is in the upper station building. She has shot her victim twice. Victim is still alive. We're sending the victim's father up in the cable car. Use caution. Over."

Colonel Vosloo had Herman Williams by the arm. "Let's get you on board the car. I was hoping we could talk some sense into that woman."

When Herman Williams stepped onto the docking platform for the waiting cable car, Rianna broke free from Lukas's embrace and dashed forward, getting hold of Herman's sleeve. "*Hendrik*, please be careful!"

Jessica's laugh boomed over the radio. "Rianna, sweet child, is that you?"

"Y-y-yes, Jess, it's me."

Another shrill laugh. "Don't *Jess* me. Those days are over. The purging has begun. *Colonel*."

"What do you want now, Taylor?"

"Why don't you put both our lovebirds in the cage and send them up?"

"Don't be ridiculous! That was not our agreement. I'm sending Mr. Williams as you demanded. He's coming."

A third shot sounded over the radio and they could hear Geraldine's whimper.

"That was her *knee*, colonel."

"Stop this madness, woman!"

"My demands have changed. *Rianna*! Take Hendrik's hand and get on board!"

"Yes, Jessica . . . w-w-we're coming!"

As the colonel steered Hendrik Williams and Rianna Vermeulen into the car, he spun back toward Holmes. "*Quick*! Get two men to clip themselves in place under the car as it leaves the dock."

"Colonel?"

"Make it happen, Holmes. You've got thirty seconds. Go, go, go, guys!"

"Taylor, they're on their way! You should see the cable car leaving the dock any second now."

"I see the car." Jessica Taylor hollered over the radio. "And remember, Colonel, the ride itself takes *four* minutes. *Tick-tock*."

"I need your word, no more shooting. They're on their way!"

"Any tricks and they *all* die, Colonel."

"Got that, Miss Taylor. *No* tricks."

THE SECOND radio crackled again. "Charlie Victor! This is Tango one. Aborting plan one. One man down. Kidnapper must have an assistant on top of the mountain. Silencer was used. Over."

"Tango one, what is your visibility?"

"Zero to six meters."

"Tango one. Change of plan on our side too. Now sending a civilian man as well as a woman up in cable car. Plus two of our special ops men clipped underneath the cable car."

"Copy that, Charlie Victor. Greedy kidnapper it seems."

"Tango one. She's unstable. Improvise as you go. Make it happen! Over."

Epilogue

*R*ianna and Hendrik stood like tin soldiers, as far apart as possible inside the cable car. Due to the absence of a cable car controller, the circular floor did not follow its usual 360-degree scenic rotation. Not that it would have made any difference. Hendrik had his back turned on her, his shoulders stiff. The motor hummed as it taxied up the overhead cables. They were not fifteen meters away from the lower station and already the mist had swallowed them whole.

The heady smell of fog and *fynbos* vegetation crawled into the circular space. There would be no sighting of the city and the bay far below or of the sheer mountain cliffs above them.

"*Why*, Hendrik?"

It was impossible not to hear the aching of thirty-five years that had lain dormant, hidden in the deep recesses of a wounded heart, only to be ripped wide open, hours ago, as if with a red-hot pitchfork. His shoulders snapped forwards at each word, as if struck with a whip, much as they had done each time Jessica Taylor had shot Geraldine.

He turned to face her but remained across from her, his knuckles white on the handrail. He met her eyes only for a moment. "*Hendrik Willems* died decades ago, according to legend, from sepsis and kidney failure. He even had a funeral. I am *Herman Williams*."

She gave a little laugh as she moved a foot closer, holding onto her side of the handrail. "I was one of the many who were duped and attended your funeral, which you didn't even had the decency to attend!"

"I'm sorry for any pain—"

"You're *sorry?*" The car shuddered and the overhead cables groaned, making them both tighten their grips. "So now you're a little *sorry*, Hendrik? Did you even love me?"

Hendrik cringed. "For goodness sake, it's thirty-five years ago . . . ."

Rianna moved a foot closer along the handrail. Her eyes spit fire. "Did you *ever* love me?"

"Rianna . . . ."

"Did you *love* me? You said you wanted to take me to South West Africa and get married."

Hendrik dropped his eyes, and his shoulders slumped. But he said nothing.

"How about the *truth*?"

He grimaced at that. "I was besotted with you. I was madly in love. Then those monsters came and destroyed my life . . . our lives . . . . I was too ill. My sister did most of the negotiations with the government. With Johan Conradie's help—her fiancé. Mother also helped with the plea bargain. I was effectively out of action. As soon as we agreed to the terms, I was whisked away to a hospital in Port Elizabeth, where I stayed another six months. Lots of physiotherapy followed. Rehabilitation. I had to learn how to walk properly. I had chronic kidney failure. I had lost almost a hundred pounds—all muscle. I looked like a starved child from Biafra."

"The terms of the plea bargain?"

Hendrik sighed and wiped his eyes. "You and I broke the law. The Immorality Act."

"The Act was wrong! It was inhumane."

"I agree, but that's not the point. I should have gone to jail. But I was too ill. Sarah would not be allowed to be reclassified and Mother would have been banished—"

"Banished?"

"Yes, banished, as in exiled to a remote part of the country where I would never see her again. The government enforced these bannings."

"Hendrik . . . ."

"I did it because I loved you." He began to move toward the curved sliding doors that stood between them. "I was a very sick man. Physically broken. What choice did I have?"

"Why the fake funeral?"

He shrugged. "Wasn't my idea." He had crossed the space in front of the doors now and stood close to her, holding the railing on her side.

"You're married?" Rianna's voice was a whisper now.

"Was. Lost her last year to ovarian cancer."

"I'm so sorry." Her hand brushed his on the railing.

For a moment a window in the fog opened, and they were blessed with a glimpse of a part of the city and the ocean far beyond it, glistening in the midday sun before the white curtain wrapped itself tight around their car again.

"Don't be. We were just comfortable friends. There was little passion. But she was a good mother . . . . The cancer was swift. Only three months."

The only sound was the whirring of the cables and their breathing.

"And Geraldine?"

"We only had her. She's all that's left now. Mother passed ten years ago, and Sarah and Johan moved to Edinburgh."

Rianna covered his hand with hers. "Did you ever try and . . . *find* me?"

His eyes brimmed as he met her unwavering glance. He nodded, almost imperceptibly. "I kept in contact with Hugo Marais—"

The car jolted and Rianna cried out, clasping Hendrik around the waist. She buried her head in his shoulder, shivering. "She killed him, Hendrik."

"Hugo Marais is dead?"

She was sniffling now. "Murdered this morning."

"Jessica Taylor?"

Another nod, then a loud sniff.

For a moment they could see the mountain. The rocks seemed familiar. They were close to the upper station.

Suddenly she relaxed her grip, stood on tiptoes, and kissed him full on the lips.

"Rianna!" He clasped her upper arms and pushed himself away from her. She groaned as he staggered backward.

"This may be our last minute, Herman. She's going to kill us."

"She won't dare."

"She will. She's evil."

"She's filled with hate."

"Evil."

His expression changed and he stepped toward her again, pulled her into his chest. He buried his face in her hair and kissed the top of her head. Still holding her, he asked gently, "What about your friend, down there? Is it *Lukas*?"

"Yes. He's my friend from Zambia."

"Married?"

She stiffened. "Friends."

"*Lovers*?"

She sucked in her breath. "Good friends."

The wind had picked up, billowing the fog like giant diaphanous curtains. It was now plucking at the car, causing it to sway ever so gently from side to side. The upper station was thirty meters above them. The car jolted as the brakes slowed their progress in preparation for docking. Rianna spun around inside his arms and leaned with her back against his chest. She pulled his arms tighter around her. "Please hold me, Hendrik. What more can I ask for? I'm back on my beloved mountain. Back with the man I loved. Smell the *fynbos*. Do you smell the mountain, Hendrik?"

"Rianna . . . ."

"She's going to *kill* us. Even if she lets Geraldine go. She has no other option."

"You're *not* going to die today."

Rianna turned back, took his face in her hands and claimed his lips. Her cheeks were wet. The car shook as they came to a bumping halt at the upper station. One of the glass windows exploded behind them.

"*Down*, Rianna!" Hendrik's reaction to the shot was instant. He rolled to the floor, yanking Rianna with him, shielding her with his bigger body.

———

"*R*ianna!" The voice came from the platform. It was getting closer. "You have some nerve kissing that brown bastard! Die bitch, *die!*"

Several shots now ran out. Hendrik crawled away from the glass doors, trying to put the more solid side of the cable car between them and the shooter, with Rianna tucked under him like a chick under a mother hen. Glass fragments crunched under them.

"Shit!"

"You're *bleeding*, Hendrik!"

"Shuus . . . don't let her hear or see you." He cupped his hand over her lips. "It's only glass."

She kissed the fingers covering her lips. He groaned and shook his head, his eyes brimming. "It's *Herman*, Rianna."

Anything she might have said next was drowned out by bursts of automatic rifle fire, interspersed with single measured rifle shots, as well as several handgun shots. A second window of the cable car shattered into a thousand pieces, and two more rounds slammed into the middle console, sending sparks and smoke trailing from behind the destroyed buttons.

Above the cacophony rose a voice, a woman's. "Bastards! The *purge!*" Then it faltered. "Let me complete the purge . . . . Oh, my God . . . this hurts . . . ."

Above the woman' voice thundered a gruff baritone. "Step *down. Police. Step down!*"

Scores of booted feet ran closer.

Then silence. The wind cried with forlorn force around the jagged rocks below them. In the distance a hadeda called its mate.

Rianna dared to look when she heard someone approaching the doorway of the cable car, glass shards crunching with each step. One of them dropped to a knee next to the two bodies still crouched together on the floor. "Mr. Williams? Doctor Vermeulen? It's okay. You're safe now. Who's bleeding?" He snapped to his feet. "Medic? Where's our medic?"

$\mathcal{G}$eraldine Williams was stabilized, first by the special forces members who had reached them at the upper station, and only transferred on a stretcher, by cable car, to the lower station once the paramedics, who arrived next, were satisfied with her status.

Jessica Taylor also received treatment, but was unconscious by the time they reached the lower station, which required the paramedics to place a breathing tube down her trachea to assist her breathing. She had, after all, sustained a shot to the shoulder, a shot to the lower abdomen, and another to the side of the head, her bulletproof vest notwithstanding.

Hendrik's wound was non-life-threatening, but he was still placed in the same ambulance as his daughter.

Rianna refused to go to hospital and insisted on treatment in the third ambulance that was waiting in front of the lower cable station. It was, she insisted, only superficial scratches from glass fragments.

The body of the killed policeman was brought down next.

The police radio continued to crackle, as a mountaineering group was called in to help scale one of the deep crevasses to retrieve the body of the second assailant, a female apparently, who, when pursued by the officers closing in on the upper station, had misjudged her way in the mist. She had plunged sixty-five meters to her death.

---

*H*ours later, Rianna led Lukas by the hand around the dilapidated boom gate at the top of the narrow road that wound down to the harbour. The road had not been used in years. Weeds grew waist-high. The cranes were quiet. The dockworkers were absent. That part of the harbour was no longer in use.

"Where to?"

"I want to show you a special spot." She steered him between the shipping container, now mahogany with rust, and the old concrete barrier wall. Then she stopped and motioned with her head. "Up *there*."

The ease with which she scaled the wall surprised her as well as her companion. Once she had reached the top she reached down to give him a hand. They sat side by side and watched as a gull screeched in a steep dive toward the murky foam on the water that lapped against the pier. Far out, close to the harbour mouth, a ship sounded its horn.

They sat in comfortable silence, their thighs brushing, eyes on the horizon where a red wedge of a sun slipped behind the rim of the ocean.

"Your favourite spot during high school?"

She rested her chin on her knees and hugged her ankles. "Hmm . . . Hendrik's and mine."

Lukas moved away an inch, his back suddenly rigid. "Are you going *back* to him?"

Rianna moved closer and took his hand. "No, silly. I was in love with *Hendrik Willems*. He died all those many years ago. I even attended his funeral." She shivered as she snuggled closer, leaning in under his arm, kissing him on the lips. "I was wrong. The man I met today is *Herman Williams*. I found him to be a total stranger."

END

Appendix: Word list

Ag nee wat, niggie, hy sal nie – Afrikaans - Don't worry, cousin, he won't.

Antie – Afrikaans – Aunt, auntie, informal for lady, form of respect for a female

Bakkie – Afrikaans for pickup truck, also a small dish or bowl

Bantu – African – meaning man, person. Used by the South African government to indicate black people.

Boskaas – Afrikaans - unkempt hairdo, untidy hair

Brandfort – town name, Afrikaans – burning fort

Chichewa – Also known as Chinyanja or Nyanja, a language spoken in Zambia and Malawi

Dominee – Afrikaans – minister of religion, pastor, preacher

Dronkie – Afrikaans - Drunkard, inebriated person, euphemism for someone under the influence

Fynbos – Afrikaans - indigenous vegetation found in the Western Cape—made up of shrubs and reeds with over 9000 species of plants, including the protea species.

Groote Schuur – World-renowned hospital in Cape Town

Groot Trek – Afrikaans - Great Trek, great move. The movement that saw pioneer farmers in 1836 move inland, away from the Cape colony, in an attempt to escape British colonial rule.

Helkat – Afrikaans – often an angry outcry at a feisty female – (hell kitten)

Holland - Dutch. Means, "hollow land."

Hotnot – Cape Dutch – derogatory term for people of mixed race found in the Cape region

Hottentot - Name of indigenous group encountered in the Cape region by the early settlers in the 17th century

Idonki – Xhosa – donkey, ass

Isiphukuphuku – Xhosa – idiot, unwise person

Kaffer – Afrikaans – as in (kaffir), derogatory term for person of colour, meaning similar as Negro or "n*gger."

Kaffer boetie – Afrikaans – Derogatory term for someone who sympathizes with black people (i.e., "n*ggerlover")

Katete – Mission station in Eastern Zambia

Kha vha sale zwavhudi – Venda language – Goodbye

Klipbok – Afrikaans - similar to klipspringer, meaning, rock antelope

Klipspringer – Afrikaans - a small antelope found in southern and eastern Africa, meaning "rock" "leaper."

Kloof – Afrikaans - valley

Koppie – Afrikaans - small hill, small mountainous outcrop

Krans – Afrikaans - cliff, rock ledge

Kroonstad – town name, Afrikaans – The crowned city

Lap hoedjie – Afrikaans - diminutive for a "cloth hat"

Ma, wat was dit? – Afrikaans – Mom, what was that?

Meneer – Afrikaans – Sir, a gentleman, male teacher

Messina – Most northern town in SA, on the Limpopo River, which forms the border with Zimbabwe.

Ndi matseloni – Venda language – good morning

Nou praat jy somaar stront – Afrikaans – crude way of saying, You're talking rubbish

Paishuko – region and small village in eastern Zambia

Pasop – Afrikaans - beware, watch out! Be careful!

Pietersburg – Town in northern Transvaal in South Africa

Platteland – Afrikaans – rural, rural community

Riempie – Afrikaans – Chair seat made with lattice work of thin leather thongs, thin riempies

Robben Island – a small island in Table Bay, South Africa. Dutch for *seal island*. Famously known for housing political prisoners

Rooikat – Afrikaans – Red cat, Caracal, Gazelle cat, Persian lynx

Sepedi – Northern Sotho—another one of the nine indigenous languages of SA, spoken more by people originally from the central region of the Transvaal

Southwestern – "Suidwester" in Afrikaans –a strong wind, coming from the southwest, famous in the Cape Town region.

Standard six – Equivalent to grade eight. In South Africa, the school system used grades 1 & 2, and then instead of grade three, started with standard one. Standard ten then was the same as grade twelve and so forth.

Stoep – Afrikaans – veranda, porch

Teef/tefie – Afrikaans - bitch, nasty woman, female acting in a mean fashion

Ukuba elikhulu – Xhosa – you are loud, you make a lot of noise

Unjani – Xhosa – How are you?

Usuku olumnwandi – Xhosa – Good day

Venda – one of the nine indigenous languages in South Africa, not counting Afrikaans or English—spoken by people in the northern part of the Transvaal or Northern province

Voorhuis – Afrikaans – entrance hall, portal, foyer

Welkom – town name, Afrikaans – Welcome

Wie's dit, Ma? – Afrikaans – Who's that, Mom?

Winburg – name of town in the Free State, Afrikaans – fort of
victory

Windpompe – Afrikaans - windmills, wind pumps: used to pump
underground water.

Acknowledgments

For a book to see the light of day, a team effort is required. Granted, the research and writing parts are solo-endeavours, but the first (beta) readers' feedback is crucial. Then there's the necessary copy editing, the internal formatting, and graphic design for the cover, as well as a publishing and printing house.

Thank you to my beta readers. A special thank you to Lesley Peterson for going far and beyond copy editing the manuscript. Thank you to my launch team—without you, the book cannot fly.

Thank you to the ever-patient Isabella, for understanding that writing helps keep me sane and content.

I am indebted to the authors of the following books, which shed significant light on my path during this novel's writing. They impacted how I approached and eventually pictured elements of the story: *Psychiatry, Mental Institutions, and the Mad in Apartheid South Africa* by Tiffany Fawn Jones (Taylor & Francis, 2012); *Stride Toward Freedom: The Montgomery Story* by Martin Luther King Jr. (first edition 1958); *Born a Crime: Stories from a South African Childhood* by Trevor Noah (Doubleday Canada, 2016); *Cry, the Beloved Country* by Alan Paton (first edition 1948); *Sharpeville: An Apartheid Massacre and Its Consequences* by Tom Lodge (Oxford University Press, 2011).

My research has led me to numerous online resources, which are not listed here but are available upon request.

A big thank you also to you, the reader. Thank you for reading. Thank you for your support. Thank you for sharing.

ALSO BY DANIE BOTHA

Be Silent
Be Good
Maxime
Young Maxime
An Unfamiliar Kindness
Two Bowls of Joy

You can visit me at https://daniebotha.com